SABBATHMAN

GRAHAM HURLEY

SABBATHMAN

MACMILLAN

First published 1995 by Macmillan

an imprint of Macmillan General Books
Cavaye Place London SW10 9PG
and Basingstoke

Associated companies throughout the world

ISBN 0 333 60994 8

1 3 5 7 9 8 6 4 2

A CIP catalogue record for this book is available from
the British Library

Typeset by CentraCet Limited, Cambridge
Printed and bound in Great Britain by
Mackays of Chatham plc, Chatham, Kent

for Bill Scott-Kerr
with gratitude, love, and lots of laughter

The English, the English, the English are best
I wouldn't give tuppence for all of the rest . . .

Traditional

PHASE ONE

CABINET OFFICE

70 WHITEHALL, LONDON SWIA 2AS

Mr Hugh Cousins
The Security Office,
PO Box 500, London

17 September 1993

Subject: "Sabbathman"

The Prime Minister has asked me to thank you for your note
of 15 September regarding the above. The Security Service
brief on the precedence issue was, of course, discussed fully
at JIC on Tuesday but he found your comments extremely
timely. Co-ordination remains in the hands of the
Metropolitan Police Commissioner but the issue is clearly
fluid and remains under review.

PRELUDE

They were making love for the second time when she heard the door open. At first, she made nothing of it: a small, domestic noise, the cat perhaps, or the last of the gale that had kept her awake most of the night.

She looked up at Max, expecting a reaction, but his eyes were closed, his face contorted, the usual half-grimace, an expression that always reminded her of a child wrestling with a particularly difficult sum. She lay back, fitting herself more closely to him, letting her own eyes close.

The noise again. Someone in the room. Definitely. She opened one eye. A man stood by the bed. He was slight, not tall. He was wearing jeans and a white cotton shirt. The eyes behind the ribbed black balaclava were watching her, the palest blue she'd ever seen. He had leather gloves on. He held a gun.

She gasped, and tried to scream. Max, getting it wrong, began to climax. She stared up at the man, numb with shock, trying to interpret the movement he was making with the gun, the tiny sideways gesture. Then she understood. He was telling her to move over, to get out of the way. He'd come to kill Max. That was why he was standing there. That's why he'd brought the gun.

She began to squirm, trying to wriggle free, but Max was on the edge now, pressing down on her, panting and panting. She dug her nails into his back, a voiceless warning, feeling his body stiffen, and all the time her eyes never left the man by the bed, the way he held the gun, quite still.

When the noise came, it was infinitely soft, a gentle phut, Max's long body collapsing limply onto hers, the pillow beside her face

7

suddenly wet with blood, and tissue, and fragments of bone. The gunman fired again, Max's body jerking with the impact, and she lay still a moment, not believing any of it, the strength in her arms quite gone. Then she began to ease the deadweight of Max's body, trying to lever him sideways. Finally she managed it, struggling upright on the bed, cupping his shattered skull in her lap, looking desperately for the man with the gun, not finding him.

ONE

Kingdom stood in the tiny lavatory, ridding himself of the remains of lunch. He'd been drinking in the Eagle at the top of the road, the first time he'd been up there since he'd moved back home, and he'd almost forgotten how dour and gloomy English pubs could be. Belfast had its compensations. And one of them was laughter.

The phone began to ring downstairs. He listened for a moment or two, curious to know whether his father would answer it. When he didn't, Kingdom backed out of the lavatory and went down to the phone himself. The phone was in the lounge. Overhead, in his father's bedroom, he could hear the old man pacing up and down again, three steps one way, two the next, patrolling the oblong of threadbare carpet. From time to time he'd pause and there'd be a low mumble of conversation, one voice only, his father addressing a succession of personal demons. He'd been like this all week, rarely pausing to eat or drink, a prisoner of his own shadowy fears. Banged-up, Kingdom thought grimly. In what little remained of his head.

He picked up the phone, stiffening when he recognised the voice at the other end, Mickey Allder, the Commander in charge of the Anti-Terrorist Squad, authority blunted by the ugly Kentish vowels.

'Kingdom?'

'Sir?'

'My apologies.'

'Sir?'

'It's Sunday. And I understand you're still on leave.'

There was a pause. Kingdom could hear the kids at the other

end, and then an abrupt silence as Allder told them to be quiet. He waited for Allder to return, wondering why he'd phoned. In theory, he didn't start the new job for a week, though already he could guess where the conversation might lead.

Allder came back on the phone, his mouth half-full. 'You know where Thorpe Park is? The theme place?'

'Yes. Off the M25. Heathrow way.'

'That's right. There's a complex beside the Thunder River water slide. Cafes and bars and so on. I'll be at the one that does teas and snacks. I think it's called the Oasis.' He paused. 'Half-four too tight for you?'

Kingdom looked around him. The place was a mess. In the pub, he'd told himself he'd spend an hour or two trying to sort it out. Then there were the kids down in Bexleyheath. He'd promised to drop in for tea. Wendy had said she'd bake a cake.

'Is it important, sir? Only—'

'You have a problem?'

Something in Allder's voice told Kingdom that now wasn't the time for a conversation about the small print of his domestic life.

'No, sir. Should be OK.' He paused, glancing at his watch. 'But why Thorpe Park? Why not the Yard? I could be there for half-three. Easy.'

There was a silence at the other end of the phone. Then Allder again. 'My youngest's birthday,' he said briskly. 'Family treat.'

Kingdom stood in the open doorway of his father's bedroom, peering in. The thin curtains were pulled tight again, partly shutting out the daylight, but he could see the old man folded into the armchair beside the bed, his hands clasped around his knees, the thin, bony ankles protruding from the bottoms of his pyjamas, the big, ravaged face tilted back, the eyes watching the door. The salad Kingdom had prepared earlier was, as far as he could judge, untouched. Beside it, on the floor, was a briefcase.

'Not hungry? Only I've got to go out.'

'Eh?'

'Out, Dad. Back later.'

He began to explain, a call from his boss, a meet on the other side of London, but his father's attention had wandered already, his hand reaching down for the radio beside the armchair, the thick calloused fingers running up and down through the stations. At length, he returned to *Gardeners' Question Time*, a lively exchange about organic composts. Then his hand strayed towards the briefcase and he picked it up, putting it on his lap, nursing it with both hands. Kingdom crossed the room. The car keys were on the dressing table. He held them in front of his father's face.

'OK?'

His father looked at the keys, frowning, and Kingdom wondered whether he really knew what they were. The entire week had been like this, each new day with its fresh quota of surprises, its sad tableaux, a man he'd loved and thought he knew dissolving into a total stranger. At first, after the shock, it had depressed him, the pathos of the situation, his father's wild mood swings, moments of lucidity followed by tantrums and then hours of brooding silence. Now, for reasons he didn't fully understand, the feeling was closer to anger. He pocketed the keys and picked up the tray.

'I'm off on a job,' he repeated. 'I may drop in to see the kids afterwards.'

His father didn't say a word. He was staring at the pocket of Kingdom's jeans, the outline of the keys under the worn denim. Kingdom bent low towards him, still holding the tray. His father stank of onions. He ate them day and night.

'Kids?' Kingdom said, 'Remember kids, Dad?'

'Eh?'

His father looked up, blank-faced, unshaven, the eyes huge, the mouth slightly open, the jaw slack.

'Kids?' Kingdom said again. 'Matthew? David?' He paused. 'Fathers? Sons?' He stepped back, towards the door, voicing what – deep down – he'd been wanting to say all week. 'Me?'

Leytonstone, where Kingdom's father lived, is in north-east London. The drive down to Thorpe Park took nearly an hour and a half, and Kingdom spent most of the time wondering whether he'd made a mistake applying for the job in the Anti-Terrorist Squad. After graduation from Hendon Police College, he'd served almost his entire career in the Met Special Branch. Latterly, the last five years, he'd been attached to a department called SO12, pulling together and analysing bits and pieces of intelligence about the IRA. The first part of the attachment had been mainland-based, chiefly London, but the last couple of years he'd been on liaison and surveillance duties in Belfast, working at the coal face, sharing a tiny two-man office at RUC headquarters at Knock.

Operationally, he'd enjoyed himself. There'd still been mountains of paperwork but he'd got on well with the RUC boys and they'd taken him along on a number of outings. The two years in Belfast had certainly made him an asset back home, and when Allder's admin officer had invited him to apply for the latest A–T Squad vacancy, he'd jumped at the chance. The Belfast secondment, in any case, was nearly over. Far better to stay at the sharp end, he'd told himself, than return to the daily tussle with the SO12 computers. Now, though, he wasn't so sure. Time was suddenly precious and his new boss had made it brutally clear just who had first claim.

Kingdom found the Oasis cafe with ten minutes to spare. He could see Allder sitting at one of the tables with his wife and daughter. A bodyguard was there too, a young lad from the Close Protection Squad whom Allder occasionally thought prudent to invite along, family outings mainly, times when he felt especially exposed. Kingdom had known the bodyguard vaguely before he'd gone to Belfast and he watched him now, sitting at the next table, nursing a portable telephone. Now and again he reached forward to scratch his ankle, and when his jacket hung open Kingdom could see the dull metal butt of the Browning Hi-Power tucked into his shoulder holster. Kingdom had one too, though just now it was locked inside the glove box of his father's car.

Kingdom glanced at his watch and hung back a moment longer while Allder demolished an enormous hamburger. Until the interview, he'd known Allder only by sight and by reputation. At the Yard, he'd always been given a certain grudging respect as someone who'd taken life on the nose. Physically, he was unforgettable with his pug face, and his tiny frame, but a lifelong urge to punch above his weight had taken him to the rank of commander. One of his nicknames was 'Dinky' but the description carried a certain ironic salute. Despite his size six shoes, and cherubic haircut, Allder set a brutal pace. He was also ferociously loyal, a loyalty that began and ended with the Metropolitan Police. For the rest of the world, apart from his family, Allder had nothing but contempt.

Kingdom finally stepped towards the cafe and Allder looked up as he approached, wiping his mouth with a paper napkin, waving the bodyguard back into his seat, and introducing his wife and daughter. His daughter, busy hosing artificial cream onto a thick slice of apple pie, stared up at Kingdom, wide-eyed, while Allder rapped the table with his knuckles and told her not to be so rude. The child blushed, hiding her face, and Kingdom wondered again about tidying himself up for a return to mainland duties. Shoulder-length hair and a single gold earring had been perfect for West Belfast but real life might call for a different disguise.

Allder licked the last of his ketchup from his fingers and nodded at the empty seat beside him.

'Glad you could make it,' he said. 'Something's come up.'

Allder paused, glancing at his wife, and she picked up her shoulder bag at once, taking her daughter by the hand and leading her across the plaza towards the queue for the Thunder River ride. Allder watched them both for a moment, then reached for the untouched apple pie and began to help himself.

'Little incident down on the south coast,' he said through a mouthful of cream. 'You probably heard on the news.'

Kingdom shook his head. 'No, sir.'

'Local MP got slotted. This morning. His name's Carpenter, Max Carpenter. Rob's patch, as it happens.' Allder looked up. 'Ever meet Rob?'

Kingdom nodded. Rob Scarman headed the Hampshire Special Branch. Kingdom had met him three years back when Scarman had been an up-and-coming DCI on secondment to SO12. From there, he'd moved on to the A–T Squad, which is where he'd presumably made his number with Allder. Allder drained the last of his daughter's Coke before starting on the pie again.

'Rob thinks it could be tricky,' he said. 'He's got the Ops ACC breathing down his neck, and press everywhere. Evidently our friend was over the side.'

'Carpenter? The MP bloke?'

'Yes.'

Kingdom nodded. 'Over the side' was canteen-speak for what you did when family life got dull. It happened a great deal in the police force and also, Kingdom had always assumed, at Westminster.

'Is that big news?' he queried. 'Bloke having a mistress?'

'When he gets shot, it is.'

'Why?'

'She was there. The only witness.'

'Where?'

'In bed. Tucked up with Mr Clean.'

'Shit.'

'Exactly.'

Kingdom began to laugh, but stopped when Allder glanced across at him, crumpling his daughter's paper cup in his small, neat hands. Then he unzipped the pocket on his shell suit, and produced a creased brown manila envelope. Kingdom watched him flattening the envelope on the table, saying nothing. The shell suit was a mistake, he thought, probably a present from his wife, lovingly bought, loyally worn. But the colours were awful – bright green and white – and the fit was at least a size too big, making Allder look even more suburban than he undoubtedly was.

Kingdom smiled and looked away, remembering a story one of the boys from the Photographic Branch had told him. Commissioned to produce an updated official portrait of the Anti-Terrorist Squad's commander, he'd pulled every trick he knew to bring depth and interest to the tiny pudding-face. The results, predictably, were awful but Allder had ordered a dozen supplementary copies, distributing them to his huge array of relatives. Back on the Isle of Sheppey, what mattered was gold braid. The rest of it was vanity.

Now, Allder was looking for his daughter. She was sitting in a rubber boat, waiting for the ride to start. She looked terrified.

'What happened?' Kingdom said.

Allder lifted an arm and began to wave.

'Quick in and out. Two bullets from a handgun. Both through the head. They've got a description from the woman but nothing useful.' Allder glanced across at Kingdom. 'Class job.'

'Face?'

'Covered. He was wearing a balaclava.'

'Voice?'

'Never said a word.'

'Nothing?'

'Not a dickey.'

'So why us?' Kingdom frowned. 'Why me, sir?'

Allder's eyes were back on his daughter. The boat tumbled down a chute and disappeared behind a curtain of water.

'Rob's been on all afternoon. He tells me the Chief's under siege down there. The press want an angle, a hook, something for the morning papers. Apparently our MP friend was asking for it. Arrogant, careless, and none too popular. You know the sort.'

'Tory?'

'Of course.'

'High profile?'

'Very.'

Kingdom nodded. 'So are we talking Belfast? Is that why you phoned?'

'No.'

'No, Belfast? Or no, why you phoned?' Kingdom paused. 'Sir?'

Allder didn't answer for a moment. Fifty yards away, his daughter had emerged from the ride, steadied by her mother's hand. She was soaking wet, and still convulsed with laughter. The pair of them began to walk towards the cafe tables, then Allder's wife looked up and caught her husband's eye. Allder shook his head, showing her the remains of the apple pie, and his wife paused, bending to her daughter, lifting her up, changing course, heading for a take-away advertising a million kinds of pizza.

Allder smiled, watching them disappear inside. 'How's your dad?' he said.

Kingdom stared at him, astonished. 'Nuts,' he said finally, ''round the bend.'

'Are you serious?'

'Yes. I wish I wasn't, but . . .' Kingdom shrugged. '. . . that's the way it looks to me.'

'You've talked to anyone about it?'

'Not so far. Only the GP.'

'He any help?'

'She.' Kingdom shook his head. 'Not really. She says it's probably a phase. Like adolescence. I told her she had to be joking . . .' He frowned. 'I think she's very busy. You know, stretched . . .'

Allder nodded, toying with the envelope. 'Sounds like Alzheimer's,' he said. 'Have you thought of that?'

'That's what my sister thinks.'

'Can't she look after him? Help at all?'

'No. Not really her style.'

'You serious?'

'Yes.' Kingdom looked across at him. 'She lives in Woodford Green now. Other side of the tracks. Plus she has a family of her own to look after.'

'So you're the one? Moves in? Takes over?'

'Yes . . .' Kingdom hesitated, uncomfortable now. 'I have to, for his sake.'

'And yours?'

'I'm not with you, sir.'

'No?' Allder studied him for a moment. 'You're divorced, right?'

'Yes, sir.'

'Two kids? Heavy maintenance? Nowhere to live? After Belfast?'

Kingdom nodded, saying nothing, wondering how many more questions Allder needed to ask, and why.

Allder was still looking at him. 'So who looks after your Dad? After you're back in harness?'

'God knows. I'm working on it. There'll be a way. Neighbours. The welfare people. I'm, ah . . .' he smiled thinly, '. . . making inquiries.'

'And what if I asked you back early?'

'Like when?' Kingdom blinked. 'Sir?'

'Like next week.' Allder paused. 'Like tomorrow.'

Kingdom smiled, recognising the feeling inside himself, an instant lift of the spirits, the old call to arms, every other responsibility instantly deferred.

'No problem,' he said, 'I'll find a way.'

Allder looked at him for a long time, a coldness in his eyes. Then he reached for the envelope on the table and got up. 'There's another side to this,' he said. 'Someone else we ought to talk about?'

'Oh?'

'Yes.' Allder nodded, putting the envelope back in his pocket, 'Annie Meredith.'

They began to walk around the Thunder River ride, the bodyguard several paces behind. Annie Meredith worked for MI5, one of the young highfliers in 'T' Branch, the new arm of the service responsible for terrorist activities. It was an open secret amongst certain sections of the Metropolitan Special Branch that she and Kingdom had enjoyed what Allder now termed 'a close relationship' Allder was standing by a line of palm trees, peering at an artificial swamp.

'None of my business,' he said, 'But fair comment?'

'Yes.'

'Northern Ireland?'

'There and other places,' Kingdom nodded, 'yes.'

Allder glanced across at him. 'And still friends?'

'We still meet. She's a busy woman, as you can probably imagine.'

'But do you trust her? Are you still close?'

Kingdom frowned, not answering, uneasy again about the drift of Allder's questions. Annie Meredith was small, tough-minded, vivacious, and resolutely cheerful. She made no secret of her career ambitions, and he'd never met anyone so ruthless, but the times they'd shared in Belfast were the warmest Kingdom could remember. Loyalty wasn't a word that Annie had much time for, but just now, under these circumstances, it was as good as any other.

Allder was still waiting for an answer. 'Well?' he said.

Kingdom looked down at him. 'It's an odd question,' he said. 'Do I trust her how?'

'Does she ever lie to you?'

'Not that I've noticed.'

'Not even to spare your feelings?'

'Never. Quite the reverse.'

'So is she frank? With you?'

'Very. Like I just said.'

'But does she tell you everything?'

Kingdom stared at him, at last beginning to understand. 'You mean the job? Gower Street? All that?'

Allder returned Kingdom's stare, not bothering with an answer, and for the first time that day Kingdom laughed, shaking his head, turning away. 'Christ, no,' he said. 'Why should she want to? And why should I ask?'

Kingdom left Thorpe Park half an hour later, joining the queue of homebound families, the contents of Allder's envelope still a mystery. He and Allder had returned to the cafe, Kingdom parrying more questions about Annie – where she lived, how often they saw each other, whether they ever went away together – irritated by the advantage the older man was taking of his rank. Kingdom had done his best to terminate the conversation, to indicate that there were certain limits, but Allder simply ignored the signals. When it came to the light touch, the deftly placed question, the need to play the sympathetic boss, the man had all the tact of a pneumatic drill.

Back at the cafe, Allder had sent his wife and child for yet another ride on the Thunder River and pursued the interrogation with renewed vigour.

'So when are you seeing her next?'

'I don't know.'

'Soon?'

'Maybe.'

'Don't you really know? Is it that casual?'

'No, not at all . . .' Kingdom had paused here, seeing no point in not stating the obvious. 'You want me to give her a message? Ask her to ring you? Fix a meet, or something? Only it might . . .' he shrugged, '. . . be easier if you told me just what you wanted. Then I could oblige.'

'Or not.'

'Yeah,' Kingdom nodded, 'or not.'

Allder had left the conversation there, no explanation, no more questions, just a tug on the sleeve of his shell suit, a quick look at his watch, and a gruff reminder about the traffic.

'Best be off,' he said, 'before it gets sticky.'

Now, Kingdom inched forward. The traffic was backed up for at least a mile, nose to tail. Two teenage girls in the back of the estate car in front were giggling at him, pulling faces. One of them was chewing bubble gum, the stuff ballooning from her scarlet lips. Kingdom stared at them, unseeing, still thinking about Allder, still wondering about the bluntness of his interest in Annie. Internal politics, he thought. Has to be. It wasn't Annie he was after, not the little blond ruffian he'd got so fond of, but the people she worked with, the people in Gower Street, the ones who were suddenly making life so hard for the likes of Allder.

The relationship between Scotland Yard and MI5 had never been simple, but Kingdom knew that the last few years had been especially tricky. The end of the Cold War had left the spycatchers with very little to do, and MI5 had lobbied hard for a change of role. They'd insisted that what they were best at – gathering intelligence – applied as readily to terrorists as it did to foreign agents, and one result of this had been a hefty push onto Special Branch turf. The Yard had fought the incursions tooth and nail, arguing the toss through countless Whitehall committees, but the battle had finally been lost and a recent Home Office announcement had confirmed what many had long suspected inevitable: that MI5 now took the lead in the intelligence war against Provo terrorism on the UK mainland.

Quite how this would work in practice was still anybody's guess, but Kingdom knew the prospects were far from rosy. The top men at the Yard – good thief-takers, shrewd detectives, natural leaders – had no intention of simply providing 'backup' to the faceless *apparatchiks* of MI5. On the contrary, they saw themselves as society's rightful shield against the madness of the Provos. Guys who used Semtex in public, who risked spilling kids' blood for some half-baked Republican ideal, were little more than lunatics. To call them enemies of the state, to accord them warrior status, cut little ice with the Mickey Allders of this world.

Kingdom lit a cigarette, feeling the car juddering as he crawled forward on the clutch. While the mainland battle for primacy was recent news, Belfast was a different story. There, the real war had always been between the local police – the RUC – and the various intelligence arms of the British Army, but even so, there'd still been room for a series of other skirmishes, lower down the pecking order, and in these the winner had, without doubt, been MI5. In the seventies, they'd seen off MI6. In the eighties, under the eyes of the locals, they'd carved out a handful of well-protected foxholes, sheltering behind the authority of the Director of Intelligence at Stormont, running agents on both sides of the water, monitoring Army and RUC activity, quietly thickening their computer files, looking all the time for fresh advantage, more juicy windfalls to put in front of the mandarins in Whitehall.

And the strategy had worked. No question. Indeed, Kingdom's own posting, the two-year spell in Belfast, was itself evidence that MI5 were firmly in the driving seat. On paper, the job specification had talked of 'target evaluation' and 'intelligence co-ordination' but face to face the commander in charge of Special Branch operations at the Yard had left him in no doubt about the real priorities. 'Keep an eye on Five,' he'd said. 'Don't let the bastards grab it all.' Kingdom hadn't. And Annie was the living evidence. But that, too, was a different story.

At last the traffic began to move, and Kingdom eased the big old car up through the gear box, hearing the familiar whine as the worn-out syncromesh engaged. Back on the motorway now, he settled in the centre lane, a steady 60 mph, lighting a cigarette and pulling out the little silver ashtray recessed into the dashboard. The car was his father's prized possession, a 1964 Wolseley, immaculate bodywork, polished walnut interior trim, unmarked dense-pile carpet, deep-stitched leather seats front and back. The old man never drove any more, but the very thought of the Wolseley, parked in the lock-up across the road, still appeared to be some comfort to him. It had somehow represented everything he'd ever worked for, his reward for all those years in the market, all those pre-dawn starts, driving his ancient van to Covent Garden, collecting the hessian sacks of fruit and veg, dressing the stall on Leytonstone High Road, bagging the stuff out, the parsnips, the spuds, the ice-cold mountains of Brussels sprouts. As a kid, on Saturdays, Kingdom had helped out, responsible for his own corner of the stall, warmed by his father's enormous popularity. Then, they'd called him Ernie's boy, Little Ernie, and somewhere he still kept the filthy pair of fingerless gloves he'd worn on the colder winter days. Wendy had once tried to throw them out but he'd rescued them from the dustbin, ignoring her gibes. What would she know about the wonders of being Ernie's boy? What would anyone?

The drive back took an age, an endless series of traffic snarl-ups. Dropping in from the M25, two miles short of Leytonstone, Kingdom glanced at his watch. Twenty to eight, the pubs well and truly open, a chance for a pint or two before another long evening in the gloomy silence of the tiny terrace house. He turned into the car park of the first pub he found. Inside, the lounge bar was empty except for a couple of lads locked in conversation over pints of lager. In one corner, away from the bar, a television stood high up on a shelf, and Kingdom recognised the face on the screen, an ex-Minister, one of the many who'd sealed their careers with a 600-page memoir and one of the lucky few to cap it with a series of well-funded TV documentaries.

Kingdom ordered a Guinness and sat down. The ex-Minister was talking about loyalty and the final days of Margaret Thatcher. His own conscience was clear, he was saying. He'd supported her to the hilt, and he was appalled at the way the party had closed ranks against her. Kingdom sipped at the Guinness, recognising the rhetoric for what it was: a bid to get the story straight before the historians reached for their pens, and demolished the fantasy.

Kingdom settled back against the red velvet banquette. Early in his Special Branch career, after the driving school, and the comms classes, and the firearms course at Lippitt's Hill, he'd spent nearly three years in the Close Protection Squad, as bodyguard to a succession of public figures. One or two he'd liked, minor members of the Royal Family especially, decent people with a ready sense of humour and seemingly limitless patience. But the politicians, by and large, had been a different proposition: men and women trapped in a web of their own making, caged by their civil servants, rushing pell-mell from meeting to meeting, progressively more detached from the punters they were supposed to represent.

The ones he'd known best – the ones he'd guarded, advised, shopped-for, discreetly shepherded up and down the country – had simply been overwhelmed by the job: by the paperwork, by the never-ending phone calls, and by the growing realisation that little they did would ever make any difference. The latter was the real killer. That was when their grip began to slacken. That's when the exhaustion, and the alcohol, finally took over.

Kingdom took a long pull at the Guinness, still half-watching the screen. Towards the end, he'd noticed, you could see it in their eyes. They lost focus, especially on the rougher days. And then that first drink of the day, the one that got you back to normal, would produce an instant sheen, a filminess that slowed them down, and returned a smile to their ravaged faces, steadying the nerves enough to dish out more of the usual nonsense. Kingdom smiled. The ex-Minister was talking now about enterprise. The people, he said, had been set free. The dead hand of government had been lifted. Only now, with the blessings of real choice, could Britain truly prosper. Kingdom looked round the empty pub, the young lads gone, the landlord half-asleep, the unfed fruit machine winking in the corner, the lunchtime pasties still curling in the hot cabinet. Enterprise? Prosperity? Choice? He smiled, reaching for his glass again.

Kingdom left the pub an hour and a half later. He'd found a copy of the *Observer* and read it front to back. Beside the lavatories, on the way out, he spotted a pay phone. He fumbled for change, piling coins on the window-sill, and then dialled his ex-wife's number. She and the two boys still lived in the modest semi on the edges of Bexleyheath. For thirteen years, he'd called the place home. The number answered, his ex-wife's voice.

'Wendy? Alan. If the boys are still up I'd like to—'

'You said you'd come round.'

'I know. I got held up.'

'They were expecting you, Alan. You said you'd come.'

'I know, I know, I told you, I—'

'Have you any idea how much they want to see you? Have you any idea what that means to them? Do I have to spell it out again?'

'No, love, it's just—'

'Don't "love" me, Alan. That's a word I don't want to hear. If you loved any of us, you'd have come. You'd have been here. Instead of . . .'

She broke off, the usual mixture of anger and grief.

Kingdom frowned. 'Instead of what?' he said.

Wendy blew her nose. Then she came back on the phone, her voice unsteady. 'You're in the pub again, aren't you?' she said. 'Alan, don't bugger me about, I can almost smell it.'

There was a click as she put the phone down and then the line went dead. Kingdom hesitated a moment in the darkened lobby. Then he retrieved his coins from the window-sill and pushed through the door.

Out in the car park, he unlocked the Wolseley and slid in behind the wheel. The smell – partly leather, partly the sweetish scent of the little pink deodorising balls his father used to hang from the driving mirror – engulfed him again, and for a minute or two he simply sat there, immobile. Leaving his kids had been the hardest thing he'd ever had to do. He'd thought at the time that nothing in life could ever be more painful. Now, though, he wasn't so sure. The old man in the house up the road wasn't his father at all but someone else, and the shame of it was that he'd never had a chance to say what he'd wanted to say. Simple things. Things like goodbye, God Bless, and thanks. Now, the phrases would be meaningless, more fragments in the gibberish that passed for conversation, but once they would have meant everything. His father would have earned them. And, being the man he was, they would have brought tears to his eyes.

Kingdom frowned, fumbling for the keys he'd dropped on the floor, surprised and a little alarmed by the force of his own feelings. Checking the mirror, he stirred the old engine into life, and swung out of the car park onto the main road. His father's house was a few minutes away, an easy drive in light traffic, and Kingdom relaxed his long frame, one hand on the wheel, the other reaching for the radio. The radio was tuned to Classic FM, an evening concert, a piece of Dvorak, suitably wistful. He reached out, adjusting the mirror, recognising the shape of a Ford Escort perhaps ten yards behind. The Escort was black with low-slung suspension and rally lights. There were two men inside. One appeared to be talking into a handset.

Kingdom frowned. A well-developed instinct for danger had served him well over the years. It was something that had surprised a succession of guv'nors. They'd always said he looked too sleepy, too detached, too laid-back, but it was there nonetheless. Indeed, in Northern Ireland, it had twice saved his life. He had a natural eye for detail, for the smallest print of any scene, and now he knew that something was wrong. At the next intersection he turned left, no warning, hauling the big old car round the corner, and changing down a couple of gears to urge it up a shallow climb. He was in a quiet suburban road now, bay-fronted semis behind neatly trimmed hedges. He checked the mirror again. The road behind was empty, the junction at the foot of the hill receding into the dusk. Then, unmistakably, the lights of the Escort reappeared, and he heard a squeal of tyres as the driver floored the throttle.

Kingdom closed his eyes a moment, cursing himself for the Guinness. Two pints would have been adequate, three pints a treat. But four? Given the likely outcome of the next few minutes, four pints was madness. If he'd read the threat properly, if the guys in the Escort were who he thought they were, he was in imminent danger of making the late news. He knew the way they'd do it, up alongside him, the passenger window wound down, the ski masks on, the guy on the sharp end taking his time, levelling the automatic, those specially drilled rounds they liked to use to guarantee a decent hole. In Belfast they called the guns 'shorts', and Kingdom remembered the word now, cursing again as he did so.

How had they traced him? How long had they been watching? Had they found the house? His father's place? Had they shadowed him all the way to Thorpe Park? Had Allder's bodyguard put them off? Was that the way it had been?

Kingdom turned left again, another street, narrower, quieter realising too late that he'd driven into a cul-de-sac. He accelerated towards the end, slewing the car sideways on the handbrake, reaching for the glove compartment, relieved to find the big automatic still there. He pushed the door open, rolling onto the cold asphalt on the blind side of the car, hearing the howl of gears as the Escort changed down. On his knees now, the gun readied, he peered into the gathering darkness. The Escort swung into view at the mouth of the cul-de-sac, and Kingdom began to raise the heavy Browning, his hand steady, his eyes narrowed against the glare of the headlights, a perfect head-on shot. Then he paused. Something else was wrong, something else that made no sense. On top of the car, blinking, was a blue police light, the portable kind you stick on for emergencies. Kingdom stared at it. A trick? Something new in the repertoire?

The Escort braked sharply, and stopped no more than ten yards from the Wolseley. The headlights stayed on, and one of the doors opened. Kingdom was still crouching behind the Wolseley's boot. Someone got out and began to walk towards Kingdom. Only when he was very close did Kingdom let him see the gun.

'Stop there,' Kingdom said, 'Put your hands on your head.'

The man did what he was told. Against the headlights, his face was a mask of darkness.

'What's this about then?'

Kingdom peered at him, saying nothing. It wasn't the voice he'd expected. It wasn't a voice from the Falls, or the Ardoyne, but a London voice, youngish, flat, slightly muffled by a heavy cold.

'Well?' the man said. 'You gonna tell me or what?'

Kingdom, still crouching, shifted his bodyweight. In the Escort, the driver had the radio tuned to the police control frequency. Even at ten yards, Kingdom could hear enough to know it was authentic, though it might still have been a ruse, a cassette tape recorded earlier, or one of the cheap scanners available everywhere.

'Police?' Kingdom said warily.

The figure in front of him nodded. 'Yeah . . .' He paused. 'CID.'

'Prove it. Tell your mate to call in.'

The man in front glanced over his shoulder at the driver in the car.

Kingdom heard the driver start mumbling into the handset. 'Speak up,' he shouted, 'I can't hear.'

'Juliet Three,' the driver said, 'corner of Blackstone Road and Park View. I/C One. Thirty. Thirty-five. Tall. Thin. Estimate six-one, six-two. Black hair, long. Jeans. Leather jacket. Bloke's armed.' He paused, 'Urgent assistance.'

Kingdom looked hard at the man in front of him. 'Urgent assistance' was a call for the cavalry, the balloon you sent up when you were facing a thousand drunks, or a tooled-up drug dealer. Under different circumstances, it might have been funny. Now, it was anything but.

The driver signed off. There was a silence.

Kingdom stood up. 'Shit,' he said. 'My mistake.'

The man in front stepped forward and extended a hand. Kingdom shook it.

'The gun, you clown. Give me the fucking gun.'

Kingdom stared at him a moment, then did what he was told. The detective briefly examined the gun. Then he tucked it into his waistband and told Kingdom to turn round and put his hands flat on the car roof.

'Why?'

'I'm going to search you.'

'Why?'

The detective didn't bother answering. After the search was over, he patted the butt of the gun.

'What's with this, then? What've we spoiled?'

Kingdom felt in his jacket and found his ID. 'SB,' he said briefly, 'The name's Alan Kingdom.'

The driver from the Escort joined the detective beside King-dom. They both examined the ID in the glare of the headlights, then the driver took it back to the car. Kingdom could hear him on the radio, checking the details. The man beside him was very close.

'Been on the hit and miss, have we?' he muttered. 'Life getting a bit dull?'

'Listen . . .' Kingdom began.

'No, clown, you listen—'

The detective pulled Kingdom round, the top of Kingdom's shirt bunched in his fist, the gun in his other hand, an inch from Kingdom's ear. Kingdom looked at him, wondering whether he hadn't been right all along, two hit-men, hired locally, with a personal message from the folk across the water. Clever, he thought, eyeing the Escort. Fucking clever. The driver left the car and joined his colleague.

'What they say?'

'Kosher.'

'Oh . . .'

The detective let Kingdom go, pushing him away, disappointment sopping up the last of the adrenalin. Kingdom brushed the sleeve of his jacket, the night air suddenly cold on his face.

'So why the pull?' he said after a while. 'Why the aggro? Why all this?'

The two detectives exchanged glances.

Then one of them patted the Wolseley. 'Nice motor,' he said. 'We've got it down as nicked.'

TWO

THE HOME OFFICE
50 QUEEN ANNE'S GATE, LONDON SW1H 9AT

The Prime Minister
10 Downing Street
London SW1

20 September 1993

Subject: "Sabbathman"

A note to confirm our telephone conversation of yesterday afternoon. Max Carpenter's death certainly gives the current series of killings a new and troubling dimension and I have, this morning, ordered the formation of a committee charged with co-ordinating all information from the three current police inquiries.

While not meeting in the Cabinet Office Briefing Room, the new committee will be similar to COBRA in function and importance and I have, accordingly, named it PYTHON.

The committee will convene on a twice-weekly basis for as long as necessary and will, as you suggest, be under the direct control of my Permanent Secretary. I have, as agreed, resisted demands from both the Metropolitan Commissioner and the Director-General, MI5, for a resolution of the precedence issue. I have also passed on your insistence that both agencies collaborate to the maximum practical extent.

Charlie Truman was reading a copy of the *Daily Telegraph* when Kingdom finally made it to the office. Kingdom sat in front of his desk, his trench-coat dripping rain onto the worn square of Afghan rug. He'd come across to Ilford by bus, a journey of eight miles that had taken just under an hour. Charlie looked up, one finger still anchored in the middle of the front page. Upside down, Kingdom could read the headline. 'MP SHOT DEAD,' it went, 'HUGE POLICE HUNT.'

'Well, well,' Charlie said, 'I was beginning to worry.'

Kingdom muttered an apology, explaining about the bus. Truman studied him, the newspaper abandoned.

'They took your licence? Last night?'

'Yes.'

'And they definitely charged you? You're sure about that?'

Kingdom pulled a chair across the room and sat down. The rain had penetrated the trench-coat, and his trousers were streaked with damp stains.

'Do me a favour, Charlie,' he said, 'I'm a policeman.'

'Just.'

'Very funny.'

Charlie reached for a switch on the intercom and asked for two coffees, and Kingdom watched him as he turned to a small trolley beside the desk, piled high with paperwork. At school, Charlie Truman had been small, pugnacious, loyal, and famously brave. Quite why he should have ended up as a solicitor, Kingdom had never understood, but the passing years had changed him very little. The same tight cap of curly black hair. The same crooked teeth. The same ready grin. The same habit of moving his body from the waist up, bending into the conversation, enjoying it.

'We never see you at the reunions,' he said, still working his way through the files. 'Abandoned us, or just shy?'

'Neither. I've been away a lot. Most of the time, in fact.'

'The job, still? Is that it?'

'Yeah.'

'Abroad? Somewhere nice? Somewhere glitzy? Miami? Las Vegas? Bogota?'

Kingdom pulled a face. 'Belfast, mostly,' he said, 'if you call that glitzy.'

'Yuk.'

Charlie found the file he wanted, and put it on the desk. Kingdom noticed that he was trying to grow his nails.

'I don't suppose I made much sense on the phone,' he began, 'but I expect you caught the drift.'

Charlie nodded. 'I got the authorised version this morning,' he said. 'I gave the station a ring and spoke to the duty sergeant. According to him it was pretty straightforward. You were pissed and you'd been driving a stolen vehicle. They arrested you. They took you in. They stuck you with the breathalyser. And then they charged you.' He paused. 'Sub-plot?' he said. 'Something I missed?'

Kingdom shrugged. 'Not really,' he said.

'You *were* pissed?'

'Yes.'

'And the car *had* been reported stolen?'

'Yes,' Kingdom nodded, 'I'm afraid so.'

Kingdom put his head back so it rested on the top of the chair, his long body sprawled towards the desk. All his conversations with Charlie Truman seemed to develop this way, Kingdom on the defensive, semi-apologetic, stuck for words. Charlie was a success: solid marriage, good business, lovely kids. His life was the best possible evidence that you could – with a little luck and a lot of effort – get it right. But Kingdom had never got it right, not Charlie's kind of right, and as time passed he'd begun to realise that he didn't much want to. The hole you ended up in, as his dad used to say, was the hole you probably wanted to dig.

Charlie was still looking at him.

'So what about the car?' he said. 'How do you explain that?'

Kingdom closed his eyes a moment. The office was warm, the central heating on full blast, and he could feel his coat beginning to stiffen around him.

'You remember my dad, Charlie?'

'Ernie? Of course I do.'

'You remember the kind of bloke he was? Sharp? Funny? Give you the clothes off his back?'

'Yes. Lovely man.' Charlie was leaning forward now, genuine concern. 'Why? What's happened?'

Kingdom opened one eye, shifting his weight in the chair, hearing the secretary juggling cups in the corridor outside.

'It was his car,' he said, 'Ernie's car. The Wolseley.'

'The grey one?'

'Yeah. He thought I'd nicked it, and he reported it stolen.'

'Why did he do that?'

Kingdom gazed at him a moment, wondering quite how to phrase it, not wanting to spoil Charlie's memories of his father. Then he shook his head, seeing no point in dressing up the truth.

'He's gone mad, Charlie,' he said. 'It's the saddest thing you ever saw.'

Over coffee, Kingdom explained the situation, where the last two years had taken him, his lack of money, what he'd found at home when he'd returned from Northern Ireland. For the time being, he said, he was looking after his dad, but soon he knew he'd have to make other arrangements. The legal position, he suspected, was dodgy. In Kingdom's opinion, his dad was no longer sane enough to cope.

'Meaning?'

'He'll have to go into some kind of home. Local authority. Private. God knows.'

'And who pays?'

'That's the problem. That's really why I'm here, Charlie. Sod the drunk-in-charge. I need advice about Ernie.'

'But does he have money? Apart from his pension? Does he have any savings at all? Investments?'

Kingdom laughed. 'Ernie? Investments?'

Charlie shrugged. 'No? You're saying no?'

'I'm saying I doubt it.'

'Then ask him.'

'I can't. He won't tell me. He won't tell me anything about money, the house, savings, whatever he's got stashed away. He keeps it all secret, locked away, literally. Fucking great briefcase. Carts it around the house with him, everywhere he goes.' Kingdom paused. 'You know? Room to room? In his tatty old dressing gown? With a briefcase?'

Charlie nodded, not looking at Kingdom, rolling his pen up and down the blotter on his desk. 'My aunt got like that,' he said, 'Barking.'

'Mad?'

'No, that's where she lived. Barking.' He looked up. 'Drove my Uncle Frank round the bend.' Charlie sighed and stood up, his hands thrust deep in his pockets, staring out of the window. Charlie's premises were a couple of streets back from the High Road, typically modest, typically sensible.

'So what do I do?' Kingdom asked. 'What do you suggest?'

'You need Power of Attorney,' Charlie said at last. 'He should agree to let you decide his affairs. There's a form. It's very straightforward.'

'He'll never do it.'

'How do you know?'

'Because he won't, Charlie. He barely knows me. Last night, after all the nonsense, I came in. I wasn't raving. I wasn't even angry. I just wanted to know how come he'd phoned the police in the first place. They had the call logged. They showed me. Five past three in the afternoon. He must have been onto them the moment I laid hands on the car. That's how long it took him to forget who I was. I'm telling you, Charlie, he's lost it. His memory lasts five seconds. By the time he gets out of the armchair, he's forgotten where he's going. He's shot. Cream crackered. All he's good for now is carrying that bloody briefcase around . . .'

'And keeping an ear for the car?'

'Yeah,' Kingdom nodded, 'and that. I'm telling you, he's on patrol. All day. Every day. He doesn't trust anyone. Not me. Not the milkman. Nobody. We're all out to get him. He doesn't need a house. He needs a bloody trench.'

Charlie nodded, sympathetic, tilting the blotter towards him, catching the pen as it dropped off.

'The house,' he began, 'could be a problem.'

'How come?'

'If he goes into a home, he'll have to pay for it. Unless he's down to his last few quid.'

'How much is that?'

'Eight grand. They total up your assets.' He frowned. 'He owns the house?'

'I expect so.'

'Same place you used to live? Mafeking Street?'

'Yeah.'

'Is there a mortgage on it?'

'Dunno. Maybe. Maybe two.'

'What's it worth?'

'You tell me.'

'Seventy grand? Give or take? Top whack?'

Kingdom shrugged.

'OK, seventy grand. Plus whatever else. All that goes to the nursing home. At three hundred quid a week, minimum . . .' he paused again, reaching for a calculator, 'that's fifteen grand a year, at least.'

Kingdom frowned, doing the sums. Charlie was right. Whichever way you looked at it, the house would have to pay for the rest of his father's life, leaving Kingdom with nowhere to live.

Kingdom looked up. 'What if he gives me the house?' he said. 'Transfers it into my name? So it's no longer his?'

'And he still goes into a home?'

'Yeah.'

'Doesn't work. There has to be a six-month gap. Otherwise it's a fiddle.'

Kingdom nodded, another door shut in his face. He looked up again. 'But what if I get him certified? What does that take?'

'Two independent psychiatrists.'

'Shrinks?'

'Yes. And they both have to agree.'

'OK,' Kingdom nodded, 'so they both look him over and agree he's a fruitcake. Clinically insane. Then what happens?'

'There's something called the Court of Protection. They appoint a Receiver. That could be you. But it doesn't solve the problem.'

'Why not?'

'Because one, the shrinks might not see it your way. And two, you'd still have to sell the house. Whatever happens, if he's got more than eight grand he's down to pay.'

Kingdom was leaning forward now, his elbows on Charlie's desk. The rain had made the ends of his hair go curly.

'Not see it my way?' he repeated. 'The shrinks?'

'That's right.'

'Meaning they'd think he was normal? Going on like he does? Sane one minute? Nuts the next? All the stuff in his room? All the things I haven't told you about?' He paused. 'You know how many locks he's put on his door?'

'No.'

'Four. Four locks. Two bolts. Two padlocks. Locks himself away. Literally. If the place catches fire, he won't have a prayer. I tell you, Charlie, it's a mess. Him. Me. Every fucking thing.'

Charlie nodded, ever-patient, saying nothing. The last time Kingdom had asked him for advice had been over his divorce. Then, Charlie had told him to be tough, to hang out for half of everything and ignore the voices in his head, but Kingdom had dismissed the advice, telling him that conscience meant more to him than cash. Charlie had laughed at the phrase, telling him he was talking nonsense. No father with a conscience left his kids. That wasn't the way it worked. You want to stay in the marriage, he'd said, you stay. You want to play the field, then take half the money and run. The conversation had ended when Kingdom pushed back the chair and stormed from the office, but now – two years later – Kingdom knew that Charlie had been right. Whatever you do, do it properly. Even if it meant betraying more or less everyone who'd ever loved you.

Kingdom shook his head, lost for words. The copy of the

Telegraph still lay on the desk, neatly folded, the top half of a photograph clearly visible. Kingdom reached for the paper, spreading it flat. The photograph showed a man in his early forties, a studio pose, narrow face, purposeful expression. Underneath, the caption read 'Max Carpenter, slain MP'.

'So what do I do?' he said. 'Poor old sod.'

'You or him?'

'Him, Charlie, him. My dad. Ernie. What happens next?'

'You've tried the doctor?'

'Hopeless. Rushed off her feet. Too busy.'

'Social services?' Kingdom shook his head. 'Try them. You'll need a reference from the GP. They draw up something called a Care Plan. It's an obligation. They have to do it.'

'And where will that get us?'

'Back here, probably. But it's a start.'

Kingdom hunched deeper into his trenchcoat, then glanced at his watch. Nearly twelve. Time for a pint. He got up and extended a hand. Standing in front of the desk, he could see the photo Charlie kept by the phone, three kids arranged in a formal pose like notes in a descending scale, each of them perfect replicas of their father: eager, bright-eyed, hungry for life. Charlie was leaning back in his chair, his hands clasped behind his head.

Kingdom began to button his coat. 'Pint?' he said.

Charlie shook his head. 'No, thanks.'

'Later?'

'Maybe.'

The two men looked at each other, knowing full well that the invitation would never be taken up. Not on Kingdom's terms. Not on Charlie's. Then, abruptly, the phone began to ring. Charlie reached for it.

'No calls?' he said briskly. 'Didn't I say no calls?'

Kingdom could hear the receptionist downstairs making her apologies. Then another voice, older, male. Charlie's frown had gone. He was nodding now, following the drift of the other man's conversation. Finally, he glanced up at Kingdom.

'Of course,' he said, 'I'll pass it on.' He put the phone down. 'Your dad,' he said.

'Ernie?'

'Yes. Says your boss has been on. Says it's urgent. Says you ought to call him.' He paused, then indicated the phone. 'Sounded OK to me.'

Kingdom took the tube to St James' Park, and walked the few hundred yards to New Scotland Yard. Allder's office was on the nineteenth floor. It always felt bigger than the rest of the offices on the corridor, partly because it occupied a corner of the building, and partly because Allder himself was so small.

Kingdom knocked twice and went in. Allder was sitting behind a desk by the reinforced, blast-proof windows. He was wearing the dark three-piece suit he favoured for television interviews and press lunches, and there was a small white carnation in his buttonhole. His face looked newly pinked, as if someone had just given him a good scrub.

Kingdom hesitated by the door for a moment, then Allder waved him into one of the chairs arranged in a loose semi-circle in front of the desk. Kingdom wondered whether anyone else was coming, and who they might be, but Allder was already on his feet, crossing the office, making sure the door was shut. Back at the desk, he produced a driving licence from the tray at his elbow. He put it between the two telephones where Kingdom could see it.

'Yours,' he said, 'with my compliments.'

Kingdom reached to pick it up but Allder beat him to it, covering the licence with his hand. Briefly their eyes met. It was Kingdom who looked away.

'Sir . . .' he began.

Allder leaned forward, across the desk. He'd been drinking at lunchtime. Kingdom could smell it.

'Not interested,' he said softly, 'not fucking interested. What-ever happened, whatever you were up to, nothing to do with me. Understood?'

'Yes, sir.'

'Good. Now then . . .' Allder relaxed slightly, leaning back in the big leather chair, making a bridge with his pudgy fingers. 'Read the papers this morning?'

'Only the *Telegraph*.'

'Read this one, then.' Allder produced a copy of *The Citizen*, pushing it across the desk. Kingdom glanced down. The Carpenter murder filled the front page. 'BLOODBATH AT SEASIDE LOVE-NEST,' ran the headline, 'MISTRESS TELLS ALL.' Kingdom turned over the page, aware of Allder watching him.

'Down the bottom,' Allder said. 'Page two.'

Kingdom found the block of text Allder had already ringed. Three brief paragraphs recalled two earlier murders, both very recent, both still unsolved. The first had taken place in the Channel Isles, two weeks back, 5 September. The chairman of a big clearing bank had been shot on the terrace of his Jersey home. A single bullet from a high-powered rifle had hit him in the throat. An exhaustive search of the garden and the neighbourhood had revealed nothing. No footprints, no disturbance, no sightings by potential witnesses. Nothing.

Kingdom looked up. 'Sir Peter Blanche,' he said, 'I remember the reports on TV.'

Allder nodded. 'And the other one?'

Kingdom returned to the paper. The second incident had happened a week later, this time in the north of England. A civil servant, Derek Bairstow, had been killed at a Premier League football match at St James' Park. The game had been a sell-out, and Bairstow had been standing on a terrace packed solid with supporters. He'd been knifed in the back, and it had been several minutes before anyone realised he was dead. *The Citizen*, the following day, had headlined the story 'THIRTY THOUSAND WITNESSES – AND NO ONE SAW A THING', though the rest of the media had been a little more restrained.

Kingdom looked up again, recognising the brown manila envelope from yesterday. Allder passed it across.

'Open it.'

Kingdom did so. Inside, he found a single sheet of photocopier paper. On it was a typed message. No indication of where it might have come from. No addressee. *'Welcome to the Kay Zee,'* it ran. *'A minute or so before Blanche died, his wife brought him a second mug of tea. If you don't believe me, ask her. The mug came from Euro-Disney,*

*by the way, which says more about my choice of optics than his taste.
Blanche got no more than he deserved. Ditto the rest of the cull. Next
time, I'll be getting a little closer. Yours, at extreme range,*
SABBATHMAN.'

Kingdom read the message again. 'Kay Zee?' he queried.

'Killing Zone.' He frowned. 'I assume.'

'And Sabbathman?'

'Work it out. Look at the dates.'

Kingdom returned to the newspaper. Kelly had been killed on
the 12th, exactly a week after Blanche.

'You think this bloke, whoever he is, killed them both?'

'The dates,' Allder said again. 'Look at the dates.'

'I just did.'

'And yesterday's date?'

Kingdom looked at his watch. Today was the 2oth. Yesterday
was the 19th. He glanced across at Allder.

'Sundays,' he said, 'they're all Sundays. Including yesterday.'

'Quite.' Allder nodded. 'Thus Sabbathman.'

'You're saying Carpenter as well?'

'More than likely.'

'You're serious? Same bloke?'

Allder shrugged, holding out his hand for the typed message.

Kingdom didn't move. 'But does it tally?' he said. 'This stuff
about Blanche? The cup?'

'Mug.'

'The mug? Euro-Disney? All that? Anyone been onto the Jersey
boys? Checked it out?'

'Of course.'

'And it fits?'

'According to the wife,' Allder nodded, 'yes. To the last detail.'
He paused. 'Which I imagine was the point of the note. No one
could have written that. Unless they were there.'

'And Bairstow? Was there another note?'

'Probably.'

'Why probably?'

Allder didn't reply for a moment. Then he swivelled the chair
behind the desk until he had a good view of the rooftops, receding

towards the river. Watching him, Kingdom had the impression it was something he did regularly, practising until he was inch-perfect.

'Where would you say the Jersey note went to,' he asked, 'in the first place?'

'Haven't a clue.'

'Think, Kingdom. You're killing people. You want profile. You need an audience. For whatever reason, you don't want to keep it to yourself. So,' he glanced over his shoulder, 'who do you go to?'

Kingdom blinked. A conversation with Allder was like being at school. 'Telly?'

'Too risky. They're not geared for it. Not for something like this . . .' Allder's eyes drifted down towards the desk, his lips beginning to frame another question.

Kingdom beat him to it, picking the message up. 'The press?' he said. 'The tabloids?'

'Yes, of course.'

'*The Citizen*?'

'Yes.'

'This went to them? Is that how you got it?'

'Yes.'

'And they've got another one? About Bairstow?'

'So I understand.'

Kingdom nodded, taking it in, quickly sorting through the implications.

'And they haven't used it?' he said. 'A story like that?'

'We haven't let them,' Allder said smoothly. 'They sent across the first note, the way they should do, and we managed to persuade them to hold off.' He smiled. 'A mixture of flattery and mild threats. You know the line. National interest. Impending privacy legislation. Favours in the bank. All that. They weren't happy, but they played along.'

'And now?'

'Now?' Allder pursed his lips. 'Now they're taking a different line. They're still holding onto whatever they've got on Bairstow, and since yesterday there's Carpenter, too. Carpenter's a hot story. And I gather matey's been in touch again . . .'

He waved his hand towards the message, back on the desk, and it moved slightly, disturbed by the draught. Kingdom was still gazing at it.

'What did he say this time? And what did he say about Bairstow?'

'They won't tell us.'

'They have to.'

Allder offered a bleak smile. 'The law's created by politicians,' he said, 'and after the last twelve months, they're careful who they upset. *The Citizen* claims four million readers. That's a lot of votes.' He paused. 'The word is to go easy.'

'Are you serious?'

'Yes.'

'So what do we do? If you're sure these notes exist? Bairstow? Carpenter?'

'We wait. Until Wednesday morning. Like everyone else in the country.'

'They're going to run the story?'

'Yes.'

'So why wait until Wednesday morning? Why not go with it now?'

'They're trailing it in the paper tomorrow. And on TV tomorrow night. They're putting on half a million extra copies.' He shrugged. 'When it comes to the crunch, they'll claim the last two messages were late arrivals. Bound to.'

'Shit.'

'Exactly.'

Allder got up and went across to the cabinet beside the door. He produced a bottle of whisky and two glasses, returning to the desk. He put the whisky on the desk. Kingdom looked at it. It was Jamieson's. Nice touch. Allder had the top off the bottle. He glanced at Kingdom.

'Yes?'

'Of course, sir,' Kingdom nodded.

Allder poured two generous doubles, apologising for the lack of ice. Kingdom barely heard him, still thinking about the three Sunday killings. MO was CID shorthand for *modus operandi*, the tell-tale characteristics that linked assorted crimes to a single operator. In this case, at first glance, the MO links looked pretty solid: cold, professional killings executed with some style. No panic. No clues. No silly mistakes. Not a single useful eyewitness, unless you counted 30,000 football fans and a traumatised mistress. And all that to sell half a million extra newspapers. Kingdom smiled. Some serial, he thought. Some killer.

Kingdom frowned. 'These blokes he's offed,' he began, 'what's the link?'

'There isn't one,' Allder said, 'apart from our friend.'

'*Nothing?*'

'Not that we can find. None of them seemed to have known each other. They all moved in different worlds.'

'Pure chance, then? Names from the phone directory?'

Allder shrugged, capping the bottle. 'You tell me.'

Kingdom nodded, examining the message afresh. Killing zone. Cull. Sabbathman. Phrases to ice your blood.

'So who's next?' he said aloud. 'And where does it stop?'

'Quite.' Allder offered a smile of his own. 'My thoughts exactly.'

Allder was back in the chair now, nursing his drink. Kingdom studied him for a moment, not knowing quite what to say next.

'So why me?' he asked at last. 'Where am I in all this?'

Allder looked at him for a while. Then he began to swill his whisky round the glass. 'So far,' he said, 'we've managed to keep it pretty tight. The editor came to us first, thank Christ. That meant the top floor and me. Half a dozen people at the most. But then the Commissioner told Downing Street, and that's when the wheels came off.'

'What happened?'

'What do you think happened?'

'They roped in Five.'

'Of course they bloody did.'

'And what did they make of it?' Kingdom paused, then answered his own question. 'Are they saying Belfast? An away team operation? Our Baltic Exchange friends?'

Allder nodded. 'Of course they are. They have to. It makes the case for them. It makes it theirs for the asking. It gives them carte blanche . . .' He shook his head. 'If they can hang this on the Provos, they've won the bloody contest. We'll end up making the

47

sandwiches. I'm serious, Kingdom. I'm telling you. We let them get away with this, it's all over. Game, set and match.'

'And you? What do you think?'

Allder shrugged. 'Me? I'm like you, Alan. I'm a copper. Coppers deal in facts. No parlour games. No fannying around. No fancy tricks. Just good old-fashioned spadework. The kind they teach at Hendon.' He paused. 'You with me?'

'Yes, sir. Of course.'

Kingdom looked hard at his drink a moment, trying to mask a smile. Allder was as political an animal as any of the MI5 drones in Gower Street. The only difference was that just now he was losing. Badly.

'So,' Kingdom looked up, trying to phrase the question anew, 'what can I do?'

'You know Belfast. Better than most of us.'

'Of course.'

'You know the current state of play. You've worked with some of these guys before. You're no fool. You won't have the wool pulled. So . . .' He shrugged. 'I'm putting you into play. All three killings. You'll have temporary DI rank, effective immediately, and I'll smooth the path wherever you have to go. You're answerable to me and me alone. Anyone makes it hard for you, they'll be dealing with me. Understood?'

Kingdom blinked, his heart sinking. 'You want me to go back to Belfast?'

'Only if it's necessary.'

'Where, then?'

'Hampshire first. Talk to Rob Scarman. And the DCS in charge. Have a poke around. Then Jersey. And Newcastle. And wherever else. Get yourself briefed. Find out what they've got. Use your loaf. And for God's sake keep an open mind.' He paused. 'Who knows, it may well turn out to be Belfast. If it is, too bad. But equally, it might be something totally different. A loner. A nutcase. Some other conspiracy.' He leaned forward, his glass empty now. 'I'm serious, Kingdom. The truth never hurt anyone. There are names at the end of all this, and I want you to find them. That make sense?'

'Yes, sir.' Kingdom nodded. 'It does.'

Kingdom lifted his glass to his lips, feeling the whisky scorching the back of his throat. He swallowed most of it in a single gulp, eager to end the conversation. The list of things he had to do was endless. Alcohol, for once, wouldn't help. He drained the last of the Jamieson's and stood up.

Allder was watching him carefully. 'There's one complication,' he said, 'Not my idea. Someone much higher up.'

'Oh?'

'Yes.' Allder unscrewed the bottle and tipped it towards his glass. 'Five are in the frame, like I said. In fact they've already set up a special desk. Generous staffing. Extra monies from the secret vote. Lots of support from Downing Street. You know how easily politicians scare.'

Kingdom nodded. 'So?'

'So we've had to agree an extra measure of collaboration.' He poured the whisky until the glass was a third full. 'Downing Street want an insurance policy. They're nervous about the pair of us getting in each other's way. Five have nominated a liaison officer. Someone they trust implicitly. I'm doing the same. The two of you have to stay in close touch. Five's phrase, not mine. Otherwise we're all in the shit.'

'Of course, sir.' Kingdom reached inside his jacket for a pen. 'So who is it? And where do I find him?'

'Her,' he said softly, 'find her.'

'Her?'

Allder smiled and raised his glass again. 'Annie Meredith . . . on the usual number.' He paused, savouring a mouthful of Jamieson's. 'How's your dad, by the way?'

By the time Kingdom got to his sister's house, it was nearly eight o'clock. Ginette lived at the expensive end of Woodford Green, a leafy suburb on the edge of Epping Forest. Kingdom had always thought the house grotesque: a sprawling, ranch-style hacienda set in nearly an acre of garden. Security floods bathed the front of the property in a harsh, white light, and there was a yellow mechanical digger parked on the sweep of gravel drive. Between the digger and the gate was one of the family's two Mercedes. It belonged to Steve, Ginette's second husband, and the numberplate had been a recent present to mark his fortieth birthday. HUNK, it read, 21.

Kingdom pushed in through the gate and squeezed between the Mercedes and the digger. As ever, he hadn't warned Ginette he'd be coming. Passing one of the wide picture windows at the front of the house, he glanced in. By the look of the table in the dining room, she was expecting guests.

Ginette came to the front door. Steve had recently bought her an Alsatian, and now it stood by her side, sniffing the night air. Kingdom was still wearing the trench-coat, the collar turned up against an earlier shower. He could tell by the expression on his sister's face that she hadn't a clue who he was.

'It's me,' he said, 'Alan.'

Ginette blinked, turning on the porch light, not quite believing him.

'What have you been up to?' she said. 'What have you done to your hair?'

'Nothing. It's coming off soon.'

Kingdom stepped inside, edging carefully round the Alsatian. Through an open door, across the tiled hall, he could see Steve standing behind a tiny bar. He had a bottle of tequila in one hand and a small cheroot in the other. Like Ginette, he was very tanned.

Steve looked up. He recognised Kingdom at once. He had a deep, slightly gravelly voice that suited the Cockney accent.

'Al,' he said, 'long time, no see.'

Kingdom grunted. Steve sold cars from a huge compound on the A12 out towards Romford. He was a stocky, thickset, powerful man, beginning to run to fat. He'd always been dotty about Ginette, and constantly showered her with presents of his own. The house, years back, had been one of them, and Kingdom suspected that the digger outside had something to do with another. He bent to pat the Alsatian, aware of Ginette waiting for an explanation for his visit. They'd never got along as kids, and now the gap was wider than ever.

Kingdom glanced up at her, still fondling the dog's ears. 'What do you call it?'

'Gary.'

'You serious?'

'Yes. Anything wrong with Gary?'

Kingdom smiled, shaking his head, saying nothing. Steve

appeared with a bottle of Pils. Kingdom took it and followed Ginette into the kitchen. At thirty-three, she was a couple of years younger than Kingdom, and Steve's money – carefully spent – had made her look younger still. She had Kingdom's build – tall, angular, bony – and she'd learned to highlight the hollow spaces of her face to maximum effect. The tan suited her and the jewellery, for once, was nicely understated: simple gold earrings, a thin gold necklace, and a tiny row of diamonds set in a slender gold ring.

Ginette shut the kitchen door behind Kingdom, and looked pointedly at the bowls of canapes carefully arranged on matching silver trays. The message was obvious. People were coming. Time was short. Kingdom ignored the hint.

'Been somewhere nice?'

'Agadir.'

'Where's that?'

'Morocco,' she said heavily. 'You?'

'Belfast.' Kingdom reached for a Twiglet. 'It rained a lot.'

They looked at each other for a moment, the usual declaration of war, mute, unforgiving, rooted deep in their respective child-hoods. Ginette had slunk through adolescence with a long list of grievances and a mild dose of anorexia. Nothing had ever been good enough for her and the blame had always been Ernie's. He'd had the wrong job. The wrong friends. The wrong tastes. He'd sent her to the wrong school, and he'd never begun to understand the kind of person she'd really wanted to be. Even their mother's early death, from breast cancer, had somehow been Ernie's fault. Quite what Ernie had made of all this, Kingdom had never quite fathomed, but he'd certainly done his best to cope, raising a second mortgage on the house when Ginette abruptly announced she was getting married. The loan – £2000 – had let Ernie push the boat out at the reception, though Kingdom had known at first glance that the marriage would never last. At thirty-three, Ginette's first husband had been twice her age, an art college lecturer with a history of student conquests.

Now, Kingdom buttoned his trench-coat. 'Seen Dad recently?' he said.

'No.'

'Not phoned at all?'

Ginette shook her head. 'We've been away. I told you.'

'Oh.' Kingdom nodded. 'Well, he's got worse.'

'Really?'

Ginette reached for a drying-up cloth and opened the eye-level oven. Inside, Kingdom could see a small mountain of couscous in an earthenware dish. Ginette took the lid off a casserole on a lower shelf and sniffed it.

'So what's happened now?' she asked, frowning.

Kingdom explained about the way his father had been, the way he couldn't cope any more, the tricks his memory played, the fact that he wouldn't even eat properly. Ginette was busy with the plates, six of them, rimmed in gold.

'So what are you saying? You want Dad to come here?'

'It's a thought. Unless you fancy Leytonstone.'

Ginette shot him a look. She'd always hated Mafeking Street. Wrong address. Wrong area. Wrong vibes.

'Are you serious?' she said.

'About Leytonstone?'

'No.' She shook her head. 'About here. Dad coming here.'

Kingdom shrugged. To his certain knowledge, Ginette had six bedrooms. Even with two kids, that still left a couple spare. 'Yes,' he said, 'I am. Just for now. While I find something longer term.'

'But I thought you'd got nowhere to live? That's what you told me on the phone.'

'It's true. I haven't.'

'So why don't you move in with Dad? Kill two birds with one stone?'

'I would. Will. Except I'm never there.'

'Why not?'

She turned and looked at him. In certain lights, Kingdom could still see the stroppy child in her face, the slightly tilted jaw, the unspoken accusations.

'Because I have to work for a living. Like everyone else.'

'Give it up, then. If it's that important.'

'Oh, yeah?'

Kingdom felt the blood beginning to pump, his temper quickening. Ginette always did this to him. Always. She knew exactly where to place the knife, exactly how hard to press. Now she was turning away, affecting indifference, reaching for a pile of dessert bowls.

'Yes,' she said, 'if Dad matters that much, I'd have thought he was more important than any job.'

'And what about the kids? David? Matthew? Where does the money come from for them?'

'You never see them. You're always somewhere else.'

'That wasn't the question. We're talking money, Ginette. Maintenance. Hard cash.'

Ginette shrugged. 'God knows,' she said. 'That's your problem.'

She counted the dessert bowls and put them on the side. Then Steve's hands appeared through the hatch, a glass in one, a bottle of Pils in the other. By the look of it, Ginette was drinking Campari and soda. She passed the bottle to Kingdom without a word. Kingdom put it on one side.

'So you're saying no,' he said, 'is that it?'

'I'm saying it wouldn't work. It's not fair on the kids, either. Not at their age.'

'Not having their grandfather around?'

'It's not that. He gets funny. You know he does. You know what it's like. Dribbling and farting. And all those onions he's been eating recently . . .'

Ginette looked up, realising instantly what she'd said. Kingdom looked at her. There was a long silence.

'So when did you really see him?' he said at last.

'A week ago. Just after we got back. While you were still in Belfast.'

'He never mentioned it.'

'Well, he wouldn't, would he? He can't remember anything. Just like you say.'

'So what was he like? When you saw him?'

Ginette shook her head, biting her lips, refusing to answer.

Kingdom caught her by the arm. 'Tell me,' he said, 'tell me what happened.'

'Not much. Enough.'

'Enough what? Enough for you to know? Enough for you to know he's off his rocker? Our Dad? Ginette?'

She pulled away from him, and he let her go. She was wearing perfume, something expensive, and she left the scent of lemons in the air. She stood by the sink, defensive, rubbing her arm.

'There's nothing I can do,' she muttered. 'The state of him. It's disgusting.'

The front door chimes began to ring. The Alsatian loped out of the kitchen and Kingdom heard Steve's footsteps in the hall. Ginette was crying now, her head in her hands. Kingdom found another drying-up cloth and tossed it across to her. It fell on the tiles by her feet, but she made no effort to pick it up. Kingdom looked at it a moment, then shrugged and turned away. In the hall, Steve was kissing a woman in a red dress. The man behind her was holding a magnum of champagne. Kingdom brushed past, heading for the door. Outside, it had begun to rain again. He was nearly at the gate when Steve caught up with him. He had an envelope in one hand. He gave it to Kingdom. He was slightly out of breath.

Kingdom took the envelope. 'What's this?' he said.

'A cheque. It may help.'

Kingdom looked at the envelope, then opened it. Ginette was standing at the front door. She peered out, shielding her eyes against the floodlights, then she disappeared inside, pulling the door shut behind her. Kingdom extracted the cheque and examined it under the floodlights. It was drawn on Steve's company and made out to E. Kingdom in the sum of one thousand pounds. Steve, for once, was looking awkward.

'Call it a downpayment,' he said. 'I couldn't help listening.'

Kingdom studied him for a moment, then nodded at the digger. 'What's that for?' he said.

'Swimming pool. Out the back.'

'Present for the kids?'

'Ginnie.'

'Ah . . .'

Kingdom glanced at the cheque again, then gave it back to Steve.

Steve stared at him. 'You don't want it?'

'No, it's not that.'

'What then?'

Kingdom tapped the cheque. 'It's the name,' he said. 'You should make it out to me, not Ernie.'

'Why?'

'Because . . .' he hesitated, then shrugged. 'Ernie's a goner, mate. He's off his head. You should know that. Being part of the family.' He looked at Steve a moment longer, then patted him on the arm. 'Bon appetit,' he said, turning away, back towards the road.

THREE

FROM: Assistant Deputy Commander, "C" Branch

TO: Commissioner, Metropolitan Police

DATE: 21 September 1993

Subject: "Sabbathman"

Thank you for your note of 20th September. I have this morning ordered Level Three enhancement to protective arrangements for all ministers, senior service personnel, and VIPs covered under the 1984 protocol. You should shortly receive an assessment of the manpower and budgetary implications under separate cover. Bodyguard details will be doubled and, where appropriate, trebled.

Next morning, Tuesday 21 September, Kingdom spent nearly an hour on the phone to the local Social Services Department. Half a dozen calls took him from office to office as he explained his father's situation, until finally he secured the promise of a visit from a social worker. Meeting Ernie face to face, the social worker would be able to assess his needs and start work on a Care Plan. In the meantime, with a confirmation from Steve that another £1000 cheque was on the way, Kingdom phoned an agency and bought the services of a contract nurse. For £7.25 an hour, she'd call round three times daily and make sure Ernie was watered and fed. Her name, the agency manager said, was Angeline. She'd worked in nursing homes all over the country, and she was especially fond of what the manager delicately called 'characters'.

Kingdom gave Ernie the good news and told him to open the front door when Angeline knocked. The old man did his best with the name, muttering it to himself as he shuffled across the hall to see Kingdom out. The last Kingdom saw of him, waving goodbye, was a bemused smile as the old boy stood blinking in the pale autumn sunshine. He had a chopping board in one hand and the briefcase in the other, and there were dribbles of soup down the front of his dressing gown.

From Waterloo, Kingdom took the train to Winchester. He'd still had no time for a haircut and the young uniformed WPC who met him at the station asked him for ID before escorting him out to the car park. Kingdom sat beside her for the brief five-minute drive to police headquarters.

'Is it that bad?' he said, not expecting an answer.

61

She glanced across at him, unsmiling. 'We like to check, sir,' she said, 'especially these days.'

Rob Scarman occupied an office near the top of the tall, slab-sided block that housed the headquarters staff of the Hampshire police force. He was a thin, lanky man with a taste for homespun jumpers and worn tweed suits. When he'd been at the Yard on attachment, he'd deliberately fostered the image of the slow, provincial copper but Kingdom hadn't been fooled. Behind the soft country burr and the schoolmasterly stoop, Scarman was very sharp indeed.

The two men shook hands. Sunshine flooded the office, gleaming on the polished emptiness of Scarman's desk. Scarman, Kingdom remembered, had a hatred of paperwork, preferring to keep as much information as he could in his head. Now, he waved Kingdom into a chair and briefed him on progress in the Carpenter case.

The murder had taken place in a private house off the sea-front on Hayling Island, a retirement and holiday area east of Portsmouth. An incident room had been established at the police station in Havant, on the mainland, but the investigation had taken the usual twenty-four hours to bed down. The publicity, Scarman said wryly, had been a blessing, and neither manpower nor overtime were proving a problem. The Detective Chief Superintendent in charge had budget coming out of his ears, and was deploying three teams on the ground. One of them, mainly uniformed men, was still combing the immediate area. Another was doing house-to-house inquiries in a slowly widening circle. A third, Scarman's own boys, was tramping through the small print of Carpenter's public and private lives, trying to put together a detailed profile of the man: his financial interests, his political debts, his sexual preferences. The key word, as ever, was elimination, chucking every particle of evidence into the sieve in the hope that something, sooner or later, would slip through the mesh and offer a decent lead.

Kingdom nodded, recognising the textbook approach. 'And?' he said.

Scarman pulled a face. 'Nothing,' he said, 'so far.'

'Nothing as in nothing? Or nothing wonderful?'

'Nothing wonderful. Plenty of rubbish, bits and pieces, but nothing worth killing for. Not in my judgment.'

'What about the lady he was in bed with? Where does she fit?'

Scarman opened a drawer and took out a sheaf of photographs. The one he gave Kingdom showed a woman in her late forties: well-preserved, fetching dimples, steady eyes and a fringe of artfully-cut blonde hair. The photo had recently come from a frame of some kind. Kingdom could feel the indentations on the edges. Scarman reached for the photograph, glancing at it before putting it back with the others.

'Clare Baxter,' he said, 'correspondence secretary in the constituency party. Widowed back in the eighties. Not short of a bob or two.'

'Big fan of Carpenter's?'

'Seems so, according to the letters we found. They'd been at it for a good year and a half. Sunday mornings, mostly. He'd pop down to . . . ah . . . discuss the week's post.'

'Did the wife know?'

'She says not.'

'Do you believe her?'

Scarman said nothing for a moment. Finally he shrugged. 'Hard to say. Carpenter was a devious bastard. Did his best to keep the compartments watertight . . .' He paused. 'The two women certainly knew each other, but that proves nothing.'

'So what about the wife? How's she taken it?'

'Badly. She's staying with relatives at the moment. Her mother and her step-father. She's a nice woman. Bright. Cheerful. It's a real blow.'

'Any kids?'

'Three.'

Scarman delved in the drawer again and tossed Kingdom an election pamphlet. On the front, under a big black and white photo, it said 'Max Carpenter – the Voice of South-east Hampshire'. Kingdom studied the photo. Carpenter looked young, sharp, and pleased with himself, a prosperous estate agent after a particularly good day at the office. His wife, beside him, was sheltering behind a quiet smile. The kids looked uncomfortable. Kingdom opened the pamphlet. The first paragraph was a sermon on family values. The rest was a promise to cut taxes, raise standards, and return the country to greatness.

Kingdom looked up. 'So what's his background?' he said. 'Where does he come from?'

Scarman sat back in the chair and began to polish his glasses with the fat end of his tie, a habit Kingdom remembered from their days together at the Yard.

'Forty-four years old,' Scarman began, 'cut his teeth on Richmond Council. Big following in Central Office, adopted by the locals in '86, won the seat in '87. Right-wing, pro-Thatcher, bit of a favourite. Missed her terribly, people tell me. Trained as a chartered accountant. Still retained a couple of consultancies, both listed in the Commons register. One's a construction company. Motorways, dams, that kind of thing. The other's a big hotel group, London-based. Carpenter did a lot of travelling. Got himself onto various fact-finding delegations. Bit of an eager beaver. Very keen to make a name for himself.'

'Any promotions?'

'No. He was tipped for PPS last time round, one of the DTI ministers, but it never happened.'

'Any idea why?'

'No.' He shrugged. 'He wasn't a popular man.'

'Any serious enemies?'

'Not that we've found so far. The odd constituency letter. A lot of fuss about one or two local issues. But nothing to justify this . . .'

Scarman reached for another of the photos and slid it across the desk. It showed Carpenter's naked body laid out on a mortuary slab. His face was half-turned towards the camera. There was a gaping hole where his right eye had once been, the flesh torn, the eyeball pulped, a thin trickle of cerebral fluid still glistening in the flashlight from the camera. Kingdom looked at the election pamphlet again, wondering about the journey the MP had made in six short years.

'Just the two shots?' he said.

'Yeah, here.' Scarman nodded, fingering the soft tissue behind his left ear. 'Point-blank range. Powder burns. Real mess, as you can see.'

Kingdom nodded. 'And the SOCO found the bullets?'

'Yes. The report's due back this afternoon but they gave me the gist on the phone, Monday lunchtime.'

'And?'

'Two softnose 9mm. Nothing exciting.'

Kingdom nodded. The Scenes of Crime Office would have been at the house since Sunday, working slowly outwards from the bed, looking for every last particle of evidence: blood, bone, hair, semen, palm and fingerprints. The bullets, Kingdom assumed, would have lodged in the mattress beneath the pillow. Tweezered out and stored in clear polythene bags, they'd have been taken to the Home Office Forensic Laboratories at Aldermaston. Reports back normally took three days or so, depending on the length of the queue. In this case, they'd obviously pulled their fingers out.

Kingdom leaned back in his chair, the sunshine through the window warm on his face. 'Anything else?' he said. 'Anything obvious?'

'Not really. Look for yourself.'

Scarman got up and went to the corner of his office. A computer terminal stood on a wooden trolley beside the bookcase. Scarman turned the monitor on and tapped an instruction through the keyboard. The screen came to life and he began to punch through a series of displays. Kingdom joined him, peering over his shoulder, recognising the distinctive layouts. The computer software had been developed specially for storing and cross-indexing the flood of information generated by any murder inquiry, and the programme was known as HOLMES, a laboured acronym for Home Office Large Murder Enquiry System. It had already saved thousands of man-hours in hundreds of inquiries, and had been adopted nationwide.

Now, Scarman paused on the Special Inquiry file. Each of the house-to-house calls generated a separate pro forma. Anything requiring further investigation was handed to teams of CID officers. So far, by the look of it, the Special Inquiry teams had been less than busy. Scarman glanced over his shoulder, closing down the system again. Both he and Kingdom knew that the lack of leads was a bad sign. Murder inquiries tended to be solved early – the first couple of days – or not at all.

The two men went back to the desk. In his pocket, Kingdom had a photocopy of the first of what Allder was now calling the Sabbathman communiqués. As far as he knew, the Commissioner at the Yard had now been onto the three respective police forces at Chief Constable level, pointing out the possible links, leaving further action to their own discretion. Given the contents of tomorrow's *Citizen* exclusive, he could hardly do otherwise, but Kingdom was uncertain exactly how far down the system the news had filtered. He looked at Scarman a moment, wondering whether or not to tell him. Scarman beat him to it.

'I take it you've heard,' he said.

'About?'

'Our Fleet Street friend. This Sabbathman.'

Kingdom nodded, feeling slightly foolish. 'Yes,' he said, 'I was about to mention it.' He produced the photocopy and passed it across.

Scarman studied it. 'Is this kosher? The real thing?'

'It's a photocopy.' He nodded. 'But that's what it looks like in the flesh, yes.'

Scarman read it again, then put it carefully to one side. 'Do you believe it?' he said, looking up.

Kingdom shrugged. 'I believe he was there in Jersey, yes. Whether he pulled the trigger, God knows. But he was definitely there.'

'And Newcastle?' he gestured vaguely out of the window. 'Hayling?'

'I haven't seen the messages, whatever it is the guy wrote. But if it's as specific as Jersey, then . . .' he shrugged again, '. . . yes.'

Scarman gazed at his desk a moment. 'Fits,' he said at last. 'Fits with the MO. Beautiful job. Thorough recce. Own key. Gloves. Balaclava. No other witnesses. Nice and discreet. In and out . . .?'

Kingdom nodded. 'Class act,' he agreed.

Scarman laughed. 'That's what Five said.'

'They're here?'

'Yesterday. They've got an outpost in Portsmouth. Couple of blokes in an office near the docks. They liaise a lot with the Immigration people, and the Navy boys.

'And they've taken a line? Already?'

'Of course, but you know the way they work. Conclusions first, evidence second—'

'—glory third.'

'Exactly,' Scarman laughed, 'plenty of that.'

'And they're saying Northern Ireland? They think the Provos would pull this sort of stunt?'

'That's the drift.'

'But why no call? No code-word? Why aren't they letting the world know how clever they are?'

Scarman shrugged. 'I don't know,' he said. 'I didn't believe it either but when Chief called me up last night and read me the text . . .' he tapped the photocopy, '. . . all this guff, I must say I began to wonder.' He paused, looking Kingdom in the eye. 'They're pulling our peckers, aren't they? Planting something as obvious as "KZ"? Making it look like some crazed ex-squaddie.' He paused. 'What would you say, Al? Scale of ten? Gut feeling?'

Kingdom shook his head, refusing to be tempted. Special Branch and MI5 were meshing closer every month, an uncomfortable shotgun marriage, and although he trusted Scarman he wasn't keen on gossip trickling back through the system. Allder, after all, had been specific. He was to concentrate on the facts. He was to collate the real evidence. And contact with MI5 was to begin and end with Annie Meredith.

'Couldn't manage a car, could you?' Kingdom said, changing the subject, 'just for a couple of days?'

'With a driver? Could be a problem.'

'No,' Kingdom shook his head, 'just me.'

Scarman gazed at him a moment, not answering. 'Congratulations,' he said at last, 'I understand you've made D1.'

'That's right,' Kingdom grinned, 'as of yesterday.'

'Promotion on deposit?' Scarman said heavily. 'Or something you've actually done?'

'God knows.'

Kingdom buried the inquiry with an extravagant yawn, apologised, and then stood up. The view from the window, in the limpid autumn air, was sensational: the maze of city centre streets, the jumble of rooflines, the squat grey bulk of the cathedral, and much further away, on the edge of the city, a huge chalk scar in the flank of a distant hill. Kingdom stepped across to the window, narrowing his eyes against the glare of the sun. He could see tiny yellow machines, criss-crossing the chalk, and a milky cloud of dust, hanging over the hill. At the foot of the hill, half-concealed behind a line of trees, was a long queue of traffic, lorries mostly, tiny points of light where the sun lanced off their windscreens.

Scarman joined him by the window, following his pointing finger.

'Twyford Down,' he said, 'our claim to fame.'

Kingdom glanced across at him. The name was familiar, the ancient hill that lay in the path of the M3's missing link. Plans to carve the hill in half had become a national issue, a symbol of the juggernaut eighties. Kingdom remembered the news reports, the ragged army of young protestors standing in front of the first bulldozers. They'd talked of Mother Earth, and Iron Age burial sites, and when the security men threw them off they'd simply regrouped and started all over again. Watching, Kingdom had rather admired them. Terrible odds. Real beliefs. And guts, too.

'Those kids,' Kingdom murmured, 'they had a name.'

'Dongas.'

'Yeah, Dongas . . .' He looked at Scarman, hearing a new note in his voice, raising an eyebrow. 'So what's with them?'

'Nothing.' Scarman frowned. 'Except . . .'

'What?'

'Carpenter.' Scarman turned away. 'He'd taken a view as well.'

'Theirs?'

'Hardly.'

'What, then?'

Scarman was back behind the desk. He was scribbling something on a notepad. He passed it across to Kingdom.

Kingdom looked at it. 'Who's Jo Hubbard?'

'Junior Registrar at the A and E centre. The Queen Alexandra Hospital. Down at Portsmouth.'

'What's she got to do with the Dongas?'

Scarman didn't answer for a moment. Then he folded Kingdom's photocopy and passed it back across the desk. 'She was on duty when they brought Carpenter in, and she's got a lot to get off her chest.' He smiled, his eyes back on the view from the window. 'About Twyford Down.'

Kingdom left police headquarters at twenty-five past three, driving a red unmarked Astra on a couple of days' loan. Before he'd left, Scarman had given him a three-page digest, the fruits of the first Special Branch trawl through Max Carpenter's public and private lives. He'd also phoned ahead to the Incident Room at Havant Police Station, warning the DCS in charge of the investigation that Kingdom was on his way. Kingdom could tell from the tone of the conversation that Allder had already been in touch from London. It wouldn't have been Allder's style to bother with the finer points of interforce protocol, and Kingdom was uncertain how welcome he was going to be. He'd never met Arthur Sperring, the Detective Chief Superintendent in charge of the Carpenter inquiry, but the man hadn't become Hampshire's top detective for nothing, and even Rob Scarman chose his words with care.

'King Arthur?' he'd said, shepherding Kingdom out of the office. 'Real museum piece.'

'Past it?'

'Christ, no. Anything but.' Scarman had paused by the lift, punching the down button. 'Just don't mention Sheehy.'

Kingdom arrived at Havant forty minutes later. The police station occupied a corner of a spacious civic development behind the railway station. It was an unexciting sixties building, flat-roofed, enclosing a small courtyard. Two Volvo estates, parked outside, carried the logo of the local TV station. Max Carpenter, it seemed, was still making the news.

Kingdom showed his ID at the desk and waited to be escorted through. The Carpenter inquiry was being co-ordinated from a suite of rooms on the top floor. The main office lay at the end of the corridor that ran the length of the building. The door was shut and there were two pieces of paper sellotaped beneath the small square window. One of them had been laser-printed. In bold, black capital letters, it said 'WELCOME TO CAMELOT'. The other was hand-scribbled in red Pentel. 'SILENCE.' it read, 'FILMING IN PROGRESS.'

Kingdom peered in through the window. The room was oblong. There were blinds on the windows, and a dozen or so small desks arranged around three walls. On each of the desks was a computer terminal, and most of the terminals were manned, the operators bent over thick sheaves of inquiry reports, cross-checking names and addresses, entering details. In the middle of the room, a large, bulky man sat on the edge of a conference table. He was wearing a silver grey suit and a dark red tie. His grey hair was cropped short and his eyes were narrowed as he squinted into the TV lights. A young reporter stood beside a TV camera. She had a clipboard pressed to her chest and she was using her free hand a great deal, the way people do when they're nervous.

Kingdom watched the performance for a moment or two, the man in the suit totally impassive, following the question with the merest nod of his head, a suggestion of amusement in his face when he began to answer. The face went with the body: the big square head, the skin pouched under the eyes, the heavy jowls, the folds of flesh beneath his chin.

Kingdom glanced at the uniformed constable who'd escorted him upstairs. 'Arthur Sperring?' he asked.

The constable nodded, showing Kingdom into an adjacent office. 'You'd better wait here, sir,' he said, 'I'll fetch some tea.'

Sperring emerged from the interview five minutes later. Kingdom could hear the TV crew collapsing the light stands as he stepped into the office and shut the door. Kingdom was sitting behind the desk. He stood up, extending a hand. 'DI Kingdom, sir. A-T Squad. My guv'nor sends his regards.'

'Micky Allder?'

'Yes, sir.'

'He was on this morning.' He paused. 'How is he?'

'Fine, sir. Thriving.'

'Thank fuck someone is.' Sperring gestured over his shoulder, an assumption that Kingdom had been briefed about the TV interview. 'You know the angle those clowns are missing?'

Kingdom shook his head. The reporter was standing outside in the corridor. Face-on, she was very pretty.

'Haven't a clue, sir.'

Sperring waved Kingdom out of his way and sank into the chair behind the desk. Like many big men, he wore an air of almost permanent irritation. He growled something Kingdom didn't catch, and then he rubbed his face. His flesh tones were awful, more grey than white, with blotches of colour where the veins had broken on both cheeks. He fumbled for a cigarette and pushed the packet of Kingdom.

'Carpenter,' he said briskly, 'was an arsehole.'

'Yeah?'

'Yeah. He's been trying to shaft us for years. Him and his fat friend.'

Sperring didn't wait for a response but began to rummage through a wire tray at his elbow. Towards the bottom, he found a Police Federation leaflet. On the front, in heavy black capitals, it said SHEEHY: THE TRUTH. Kingdom took it, beginning to understand. Patrick Sheehy was an industrialist who'd made his name heading the British-American Tobacco Company and the government had asked him to run his management slide-rule over the police. His report, recently published, had argued that the police were over-paid and under-motivated, and one of his prime targets had been officers in the senior ranks. The service, according to Sheehy, was top-heavy. There should be no more guarantees, no more jobs for life. The buzzwords now were 'performance' and 'value for money', and old-style coppers like Sperring were still in shock.

Kingdom looked up. 'You feel that strongly?'

'Dead fucking right. As I understand it, Carpenter's the pillock who suggested Sheehy in the first place. They needed someone to set the dogs on us and Carpenter obliged. He's the one who put his name forward. Some bloke who'd been flogging cigarettes all his life. What would he know about coppering, eh?' Sperring nodded at the packet of cigarettes, still lying on the desk. 'Spends his entire career poisoning us with these fucking things, then has the nerve to pass judgment on what we do. What does he think we are? Box of filter tips?'

'And Carpenter?'

'Deserved everything he got. Live by the axe. Die by the fucking axe.'

'You said that?' Kingdom nodded towards the reporter, still standing in the corridor outside. 'On the record?'

'Christ, no.'

'But you're serious? You mean it?'

'Of course I do. Don't you? Doesn't everyone?' He narrowed his eyes, the way he'd done in front of the camera. 'I'm telling you, son, anyone looking for a motive for Carpenter should start here, with me, with my boys. I can think of a hundred blokes who'd have taken a pop at him. Good fucking riddance, I say . . .' He let the sentence expire in a thin stream of blue smoke. Then he laughed, a gravelly noise deep in his throat, and shook his head. 'No,' he said, 'of course I don't mean it. But it just goes to show, doesn't it?'

'Show what?'

'Divine retribution.' He laughed again, 'Bless Him.' Sperring tipped his head back, drawing down the next lungful of smoke, another tiny victory for Mr Sheehy. Then his eyes settled on Kingdom again. 'So what do you want, son?' he said, 'How can I help you?'

Kingdom framed a careful answer, knowing now that Allder had already been in touch. When he mentioned Sabbathman, Sperring looked interested.

'What do you make of that, then?'

Kingdom shrugged. 'Dunno, sir,' he said, 'yet.'

'But you think it might be a runner?'

'Definitely.'

'Single bloke? Nutter? Appears every Sunday? Has a pop?'

'Maybe.' Kingdom paused. 'Have you talked to Jersey at all?'

'Yeah.' Sperring nodded. 'They're definitely interested but then they would be, wouldn't they? So far they've got fuck all. Just Blanche in the fridge. You ever been to Jersey? The place runs on imported money. They need a name, any name, something to get them off the hook. Sabbathman, whatever he's called, does just fine. Just fine. Perfect. A real gift.'

'And here?'

Sperring took another lungful of Silk Cut and leaned forward, tapping ash into Kingdom's empty cup.

'You should go out to Hayling and take a look,' he said. 'My

blokes next door will tell you how to find the place. It's a nice
house, hundred grand easy, nice neighbourhood too. They stick
together, those kind of people. Hayling's a village, especially down
their end. It's not easy, getting in and out, shooting a guy. Not
easy at all.'

'Was the door locked? That morning?'

'Yes, she swears it was. He was very particular, our Max. Hated
interruptions.'

'And no sign of forced entry?'

'Nothing. Not a dicky bird. Not a single mark. Matey had a
key. Assuming he exists . . .'

'Meaning?'

Sperring spread his hands wide. 'It could have been her. Fuck
knows, of course it could. He's married. He won't leave his wife,
his kids. He's told her that. He's made no bones about it. OK, he'll
turn up when it suits him. He'll do the business, tell her she's
wonderful, tell her she's the most important woman in his life. But
what's that when you're on short rations? Eh? Couple of hours a
week?' He paused. 'People have killed for much less. As we all
fucking know.'

'Was she that keen?'

'Yes, according to the letters.'

'Whose letters?'

'His. We've got about a dozen. They go back a fair way, about
a year and a half. He doesn't actually spell it out, but you can tell.
She's dying for it. When he can be bothered.'

'And what's her version?'

'She hasn't said much but she obviously loved the bloke, crazy
about him, no question. Terrible taste, but we can't do her for
that.'

'And the weapon?'

'Fuck knows. Definitely a hand-gun, probably an automatic,
but it's a goner. If it was her, she could have done anything with
it. You can make a lot of plans in eighteen months.'

'Forensic? Anything on her hands?'

'Nothing.'

'And nothing in the house? No traces of gun oil? Some place
she might have hidden a weapon? Nothing like that?'

'No.' He paused. 'Not yet.'

'You're still looking?'

'Of course we fucking are. We want a result, don't we?'

There was a long silence and Kingdom remembered Allder, how confident he'd been, Carpenter cut down by the lone assassin, the mysterious Sabbathman.

'You really think she might have done it?' he said at last.

'I don't think anything. All I know is nobody saw anyone come or go. Now that's pretty extraordinary, son, whichever way you look at it.'

'So why haven't you pulled her in?'

'Clare Baxter? With her connections? On the evidence we've got? Are you serious, son?'

Kingdom didn't answer for a moment, eyeing the ash floating in the remains of his tea.

'How about Carpenter's wife?' he said at last. 'She'd have plenty of motive. If she knew.'

'She says she didn't.'

'You believe her?'

Sperring frowned. Like most detectives, black and white answers weren't really his style. 'Yes,' he said at last, 'I do.'

'Why?'

'She's an honest woman. She's naive, too. She trusted him.'

'But where was she? When it happened?'

Sperring glanced up. For the first time, he was smiling. 'Half-past ten?' he said. 'Sunday morning?'

'Yes.'

'Church. With the kids.' The smile widened. 'Not too many witnesses. But enough.'

'A hit-man, then? A contract? Someone she paid to do it?'

Sperring looked briefly pained. Then he got up and brushed the ash from his trousers.

'You London blokes are all the same,' he said, yawning. 'You think life's one long fucking movie.'

Before he left the police station, Kingdom returned to the Incident Room. Sperring put him in the hands of a young detective sergeant and the DS took him across the room to a big street map pinned to a board. The map showed the whole of Hayling Island. The island itself was about five miles by three, a wedge of land, wider at the coastal end, cut off to the north by a tidal creek. Access to the mainland was by a single road bridge. Immediately to the west, across the mouth of Langstone Harbour, lay the city of Portsmouth. To the east, across another harbour mouth, was the long curve of sand and shingle that led to Selsey Bill.

Kingdom studied the map a moment. There were coloured pins dotted round a grid of roads on the south-west corner of the island. A black pin marked the murder site. The name of the road was Sinah Lane. The house, according to photos displayed on the wall beside the board, was called 'Little Douglas'. Kingdom looked at the pins, recognising the pattern of house-to-house calls, an ever-widening circle that would expand and expand until Arthur Sperring chose to call a halt. To the west of Sinah Lane, about a quarter of a mile away, was a holiday camp. Kingdom nodded at it.

'Nothing there?'

'We're still checking. They've got individual units, chalet places. You rent them for a week or a fortnight, depending. We're going through the bookings at the moment.'

'How far back?'

'*Two years.*'

'*Two years*'

'Yes. It's not as bad as it sounds. We've got contact phone numbers for most of them through the booking people, and we're leaning on other forces for the follow-ups. Otherwise . . .' he shrugged, '. . . it would take forever.'

'But two years . . .?'

Kingdom shook his head. For a man who'd evidently done his best to butcher the police force, Carpenter was certainly getting star treatment. Kingdom returned to the map. Beyond the holiday camp, the island narrowed into a little curl of land that reached north into Langstone Harbour. From here, a ferry crossed to Portsmouth.

Kingdom looked at the DS. 'How quickly did the woman get on the phone? After matey was shot?'

'Pretty quickly. Her own phone was dead so she used a neighbour's. But we're talking minutes. No more.'

'So you closed the island down?'

Kingdom indicated the bridge to the north, the single road to the mainland. The DS nodded.

'Yes. The log's over there.' He pointed to a loose-leaf binder on a shelf beneath the photos of the house. 'We put a traffic car on the bridge first, couple of our motorway guys. Then armed back-up half an hour later.'

'And here?' Kingdom's finger found the ferry.

The DS nodded again. 'Three blokes. Two on the beach, on the seaward side. One on the landing stage.'

'When?'

'Within the hour.'

'An hour? That long?'

'We phoned the harbourmaster first off. He's got an office down by the ferry. He cancelled all sailings for the rest of the morning. Until our lads arrived.'

'And?'

'He saw nothing.'

'No cars abandoned? Motor bikes?'

'Nothing.'

Kingdom frowned, trying to picture the scene, trying to match the time frame to the distances involved, trying to calculate the odds on getting off the island before the police and the harbour-master between them sealed it off. Getting to the mainland over the bridge was at least a ten-minute drive, probably longer. Using the ferry, on foot from the house, would have meant walking into the arms of the harbourmaster. Whichever way you looked at it, Hayling Island was a lousy place to plan a murder.

Kingdom glanced at the DS again, following his eyes to a line of winking telephones on the other side of the room. He still had questions to ask, things to get straight in his mind, but now clearly wasn't the time. In any case, Sperring was right. He ought to get down there himself. He ought to put a little flesh on the bones of the map on the board. He touched the DS lightly on the arm.

'This house,' he said, nodding at the black pin on the board, 'who's got the key?'

'No one.' The DS frowned. 'Why?'

'I want to get in. Have a nose around.'

'Then knock, sir.' He smiled. 'I'm sure the lady will oblige.'

It was late afternoon by the time Kingdom found the house on Hayling Island. He'd driven round the area for half an hour or so, trying to get a feel for the place. By mid-September, the holiday-makers had long gone, and a grey chill had settled on the streets of endless bungalows. On the seafront there was a tiny funfair. A neon sign still winked on the roller coaster but tarpaulins shrouded the line of empty cars, and the turnstile entrance was padlocked shut. Across the road, in a bus shelter, three schoolgirls picked moodily at bags of chips. Kingdom watched them for a moment, depressed by the bleakness of it all, then turned right on the sea-front, heading west towards the area where Sperring had so far based his inquiries.

Carpenter himself had lived along the coast, a two-acre prop-erty on the edge of a village called Bosham, and Kingdom tried to visualise him making this same drive, two or three Sundays a month, establishing the pattern with his wife, dressing up adultery as some kind of weekly chore, the need to stay abreast of constitu-ency affairs. In this respect, Carpenter's choice of mistress had been ideal: Clare Baxter, the woman who handled all the constituency correspondence, the woman who, above all others, would know exactly what was going on. Back at the police station, Kingdom had read the statement Carpenter's wife had made. In it, she said that Carpenter had called Clare Baxter his 'early warning system'. She was good at spotting problems. She had a real nose for trouble. She was, in another of Carpenter's phrases, 'a treasure'.

'Little Douglas' lay half a mile back from the sea-front in a quiet, tree-lined avenue already thick with fallen leaves. The area was visibly more prosperous than the rest of the island. 'K' reg BMWs. Expensive house alarm systems. Glimpses of tennis courts and the odd swimming pool behind the dense, well-trimmed hedges. There were flattened scabs of horse dung on the road, and when Kingdom parked and got out he found a sign on a tree threatening a £20 fine for leaving his car on the grass verge.

Kingdom ignored it, turning to look at the property across the road, recognising the place from the photos in the Incident Room. It was an ample, handsome, thirties house with leaded windows and warm red brick. Virginia creeper enveloped one corner, the leaves already scorched with autumn. To Kingdom's surprise, there was no sign of any police vehicles.

Kingdom crossed the road. Fifteen yards of gravel drive led to the mock-Tudor front door, and the garden had recently been tidied for the winter. Kingdom paused a moment, sniffing the air. From somewhere round the back came a curl of woodsmoke. Kingdom rang the bell and the door opened at once. A woman in her late forties stood in the pale afternoon light. She was small and trim, and Kingdom could smell the woodsmoke in her clothes. She was wearing jeans and a brightly-patterned roll-neck sweater. Her hair was tied back with a carefully knotted headscarf, and there was a tiny smear of wood ash high on the side of her face. Kingdom recognised her at once from Scarman's photo.

'Mrs Baxter?' he said. 'My name's Kingdom.'

He showed her his ID and stepped inside, aware immediately that he wasn't welcome.

'I'm sorry to bother you,' he said, 'you must be sick of us by now.'

'It's not that,' she said, 'it's just one has a life to lead.'

'Have the others gone?'

'Half an hour ago. But I expect they'll be back.'

She gave him an icy smile and led the way through to the kitchen. The kettle was beginning to boil but she turned her back on the waiting teapot, and answered his questions in a brisk, even voice, much as one might deal with an unwanted questionnaire on a busy street. Yes, she'd seen the man who'd killed Max Carpenter. Yes, he was slight, well under six feet, jeans, white shirt, blue eyes. Yes, he'd been wearing a balaclava and leather gloves. Yes, he'd never said a word. No voice. No accent. Not a single useful clue. She made the experience sound almost second-hand, someone else's nightmare, and when Kingdom finally knew there was no point going any further, she voiced his thoughts exactly.

'You'll think me hard,' she said, unknotting the headscarf and shaking out her hair, 'but there've been so many questions. Your colleagues, the press, the television people, my own friends. I know you all mean well. I know you've got jobs to do. But . . .' She shrugged. 'I'm sure you understand.'

Kingdom nodded. 'Of course,' he said, 'It must have been a trial.'

'Yes. It has.'

'Best forgotten.'

'Best solved.' She began to twist the headscarf between her fingers. 'If he's done it once, he can do it again. That's why I'm . . .' she frowned, '. . . prepared to go through all this. If it helps, I'll answer any number of questions. Of course I will. No one's saying it's been a pleasure but, heavens, I could be in Sarajevo. We all could. No?'

'Yes,' Kingdom blinked, 'of course.'

'So . . .' She looked at him, unsmiling. 'Was there anything else?'

'Yes. How did he get in?'

'Key. Must have been. I heard nothing . . .' She broke off, frowning again. 'Actually, that's not quite true. I heard just a little noise, you know, wind getting into the house, things disturbed, just for a moment. That's when he must have opened the front door. But nothing else. No footsteps. Nothing like that. Next I knew, there he was . . .' Her eyes closed for a moment, and then she turned away, and for the first time Kingdom sensed the darkness beyond the clipped answers and the icy self-control.

'You were in bed,' he said, 'with Carpenter?'

'Yes.' She nodded, looking at him again, her eyes steady, total candour. 'We were making love.'

'And he never heard a thing?'

'No.'

'Never saw anything?'

'No.'

'Nice way to go then. Under the circumstances.'

She looked up at him for a long moment. Then she reached out and picked a long black hair from the collar of his trench-coat.

'You're the first man who's had the guts to say that,' she said quietly. 'The rest of them have thought it. I've seen it in their faces. They probably had a laugh about it, too, out in the car, the way men do . . .' She broke off, not knowing how to continue the thought, not wanting to go any further.

'The key,' Kingdom said gently, 'you were telling me about the key.'

'Yes.' She nodded. 'He must have had a key. It's a good lock. Big mortice thing. Cost the earth.'

'So how? How did he get hold of a key?'

'God knows.'

'Did Carpenter have a key?'

'No. I offered once but he said he'd only lose it, or leave it around for his wife to find.'

'Did she know? About . . .?' Kingdom shrugged. 'You and her husband?'

'No.'

'Are you sure?'

'Absolutely . . .' She paused, studying Kingdom carefully.

'Why?' Kingdom asked. 'Why are you so sure?'

'Because Max told me.'

'And you believed him?'

'Yes.' She paused again, her arms folded across her chest. 'Max was a child, you ought to know that. He lied all the time, of course, but he lied like children do. His lies were transparent. If you knew him well, you could see through them. That's why he never lied to me. I knew him better than anyone.'

'Better than his wife? Didn't she see through him?'

'I don't think so. I don't know but I don't think so. They weren't close. Not . . . you know . . .' she shrugged, '. . . like that.'

'Like what?'

'Like us, Mr Kingdom.'

Kingdom nodded. The kettle had switched itself off now but he was no nearer getting the tea.

'You loved him?' he said.

She smiled for the first time, and Kingdom realised that she was flattered by the question.

'Yes,' she said, 'I loved his enthusiasm and his energy. And I loved the way he could get lost so easily. The child again. The puppy. So easily distracted. So wonderfully irresponsible.'

'Hence not having the key?'

'Exactly.'

'So how did he get in?'

'I used to leave the key out for him.'

'On Saturday night?'

'Yes.' She nodded. 'I sometimes slept in on Sunday mornings. Once or twice he even had to wake me. Shameful, isn't it?'

Kingdom ignored the gibe. 'So where did you leave this key? As a matter of interest?'

'Under a stone. We had a secret place. Amongst the shrubs.'

'Always the same place? Same stone?'

'Always.' She smiled again. 'Politicians aren't very practical. You get to learn these things. It doesn't do to stretch them. Especially at weekends.'

'No,' Kingdom agreed. 'I imagine that might be a problem.'

She looked at him sharply, her expression changing, and Kingdom sensed at once the limits to the conversation. In her cool, brisk way she'd mapped out for him the shape of the relationship. She'd mothered her MP in bed, as she'd doubtless mothered him in the constituency. She'd made a nest for him when he'd needed it, and she'd put up with having to take her turn with his wife, and his kids, and his career, and the countless other demands on his time.

'Did you think there was ever a future in it?' Kingdom asked. 'You and Carpenter? Was that something you ever discussed?'

She shook her head, a small, neat, emphatic disavowal. 'Max and I? God, no. He'd drive me mad. And me him. He'd find some other widow, some other bed to leap into. Why would I ever want that? When I had the best of him already? Don't misunderstand me, Mr Kingdom. I loved the man very much, and I enjoyed him too. We were very good together. We made it work. But I never mistook any of it for real life, not once. Believe me, I know my limits.' She looked down at her hands. 'And his.' She glanced at her watch, then up at Kingdom. 'You're a clever man, Mr Kingdom. I applaud you. You've got more out of me in ten minutes than anyone else in the last twenty-four hours. But then I suppose it's the questions, isn't it? And the way you listen to the answers?'

Without waiting for a reply, she began to shepherd Kingdom

back towards the hall. Kingdom went without protest, aware of her own role in the conversation, how cleverly she'd played it, how neatly she'd planted her own version of the relationship. Whether it was entirely true or not, Kingdom didn't know, but he'd certainly seen enough of Clare Baxter to know that Sperring had been wrong. This wasn't a woman who'd bother murdering Max Carpenter. He simply hadn't mattered enough.

By the front door, Kingdom paused. On a small occasional table, beside a delicate spray of orchids, was a photograph in a silver frame. It showed a middle-aged man in an army uniform. He had a strong, broad face, and a look of quiet determination. Kingdom studied it for a moment. It could have been a shot from the forties, a face from another age.

'My husband,' Clare Baxter said. 'He was killed in '86. Car crash. Don't have much luck, do I?'

'Did Carpenter know him?'

'No, they never met. Just as well, really.'

'Oh?' Kingdom looked up. 'Why?'

Clare shook her head. She was still looking at the photograph. Finally she reached for the door, opening it.

'Chalk and cheese,' she said quietly. 'I'm afraid men like my husband don't exist any more.'

Kingdom drove back along the sea-front, re-running the conversation in his mind, more certain than ever that Clare Baxter was telling the truth. Regardless of any links to the Jersey murder, and the knifing on the terraces at St James' Park, his instincts told him that Carpenter had been shot by the man Clare Baxter had described. The temptation, of course, was to disbelieve her. A woman less strong-minded, less self-possessed, might already have fallen victim to Arthur Sperring's impatience for a 'result'. God knows, a chance set of fingerprints, a misjudged statement or two, a revealing phrase in a letter, might well have seen her facing a murder charge. But Clare Baxter? Kingdom shook his head, turning off the sea-front road, parking beside a cafe, knowing that they had to look much further. Given that the man in the balaclava existed, the key issue was motive. Why shoot Carpenter? Why come to Hayling? And why, if the links were solid, notch up two other killings en route?

Kingdom was still letting the questions revolve in his head when a red light began to wink on the dashboard radio console. The light indicated a message from Force HQ. Kingdom picked up the handset and called in, recognising Scarman's voice at once.

'Al?' Scarman said. 'Your Guv'nor's been on.'

'Oh?'

'Wants you to give him a bell. After nine tonight. Says it's urgent.'

Kingdom wrote down the number, then smiled when Scarman asked what progress Arthur Sperring had made. He'd been trying to make contact himself but for some reason the DCS had vanished.

'So what news?' he said, 'From Camelot?'

Kingdom grinned. 'Sheehy did it,' he said, 'and he's on a nicking.'

Scarman was still laughing when Kingdom hung up. He switched off the radio and got out of the car, buttoning his trench-coat. Dusk was falling now, and he could just make out a lone figure in a long coat on the shingle beach, ghosting away towards the waterline. Kingdom watched for a moment, wondering whether to take a walk himself, then decided against it, turning on his heel and making for the cafe.

The cafe was at the back of an amusement arcade. At the counter, Kingdom ordered a coffee, drinking it at one of the yellow formica tables, gazing out at the beach through a wall of salt-smeared glass. Motive, he thought again. It's all about motive. Somewhere in Carpenter's life there had to be someone who'd been angry enough, or hurt enough, or desperate enough to kill. He pursued the thought a little further, remembering Rob Scarman's line about Twyford Down. Leaving Winchester, earlier in the afternoon, Kingdom had taken a look at the construction site. Close to, the scale of the excavations had been awesome, a huge white cutting that simply brushed geography aside. Enormous bulldozers ground to and fro, dwarfing the passing traffic, and the outlines of the first bridge had begun to appear, the grey concrete already spray-painted with protest slogans. '*Save the Planet,*' went one. '*What on Earth Are We Doing?*' asked another. Kingdom could see the point, the remains of an ancient landscape thundering past in the backs of the towering spoil trucks. But was that enough to kill for? And if it was, would Carpenter have been the right target? And if so, why begin by killing a Jersey banker? And then some civil servant at a football match?

Kingdom shook his head, not knowing the answer, making a mental note to talk to the medic Rob Scarman had mentioned. He had her name in his pocket. Jo Hubbard. Registrar in the local accident and emergency department. He ought to give his dad a ring, too. What had the old boy made of Angeline? And, even more important, what had she made of him?

Kingdom returned his empty cup to the counter and made his way back through the amusement arcade. By the door was a version of Streetfighter 2, his favourite game. The last few weeks in Belfast, he'd developed a passion for it. He'd even posted the month's winning score, a mind-blowing 34,867. Now, he felt in his pockets for a twenty-pence piece and settled again in front of the console, his fingers riding lightly on the punch and kick buttons as he tried to flatten the first of his opponents, an alarming figure in a green jump suit called Guile. Guile was still on his feet when someone pushed in through the door, and Kingdom felt the damp kiss of the incoming air. The door closed again and Kingdom launched his streetfighter into a spectacular flying kick, barely missing his opponent's throat. On the screen, just, he could see a reflection, a face, someone standing behind him. Guile advanced, jabbing at the empty air, and Kingdom's fingers slipped for once, letting him come too close, the game ending in a blur of green.

Kingdom heard a soft laugh behind him, then the rustle of coins as someone looked for small change. Kingdom frowned, leaning back from the console, feeling a hand settle on his shoulder.

At the same time, a voice he knew, an inch from his left ear, rich, mischievous, amused: 'Beaten? Already?'

Kingdom turned round. The woman behind him was holding out a twenty-pence coin. The long scarlet coat was open, and he recognised the black woollen one-piece underneath. Last time he'd seen it was a fortnight ago, draped carefully over the back of a chair. Belfast again. One of the nights he wasn't playing Street-fighter 2. Kingdom grinned, for once caught off-balance.

'You,' he said.

Annie Meredith kissed him lightly on the cheek, then leaned forward, easing the coin into the slot. 'My turn,' she said, reaching for the buttons.

FOUR

TIMES NEWSPAPER GROUP

INTERNAL MEMO

TO:
FROM:
DATE:
CC:

23 Sept. '93

Dear Hugh,

I raised the turf issue with the features editor again this morning but he still feels we need a more distinctive hook for a half-decent piece. The Sabbathman extravaganza is ideal, of course, but he thinks we've already lost the high ground to the tabloids. In his own phrase, the whole thing's become "opera bouffe" - largely because the wretched man's still writing his own script. What we need is a breakthrough, a mistake on his part. Then I think we can let the nation in on the real story: how the Mets getting stuffed by you guys..

yours aye,

Robert Devereaux

'Your fault,' she giggled, 'not my idea.'

Kingdom sat in front of the mirror in the hotel bedroom, a towel draped over his naked shoulders, examining the worst of the damage. Fourteen months' growth of hair littered the carpet around his ankles, and she was still cutting. He reached for one of the glasses they'd looted from the bathroom. The first bottle of Rioja lay upended in the wastepaper bin, the second was nearly empty, and a third was still in the plastic carrier bag by the bed.

'What's the time?' Kingdom said.

Annie glanced at her watch. As usual, it was the one item she hadn't taken off. 'Twenty-past eight,' she said. 'Am I keeping you?'

Kingdom grunted, turning his head left and right, trying to find an angle that softened the brutality of what she'd done. She'd been at it now for nearly half an hour, hacking away. She cut hair like she tackled more or less everything else in her life, with cheerful optimism and a ruthless self-belief. No prisoners. No apologies. Not a single moment wasted on wondering whether she really knew what she was doing.

Kingdom swallowed another mouthful of the wine. It didn't change the image in the mirror, but it helped.

'So why aren't you telling me it looks great?' he said. 'Isn't it all about psychology? Keeping the customer happy?'

'It looks bloody awful.'

'So why don't you stop?'

'How can I? You'll get arrested looking like this.'

She stepped back a minute and Kingdom watched her in the mirror as she pondered the next cut. He'd always thought she had a lovely body: small, neat breasts, flat belly, silky, muscled legs still pinked from the bath they'd shared earlier. Coming to the hotel had been her idea. She had a room booked for the night and saw no point wasting it.

Now she looked up, scissors raised. She had tiny, delicate hands, beautifully shaped nails, and she always started the day with a fresh coat of varnish. The varnish was the colour of arterial blood, a bold scarlet, and it suited her personality exactly. She had a tattoo, as well, a tiny rose between her breasts, blue and red, very delicate, and the tattoo was equally characteristic, wholly in keeping with the person she was determined to be: independent, unconventional, in tune with no one's music but her own. Kingdom had often asked her about the tattoo, why she'd had it done, what it meant, but so far she'd never told him. Their whole relationship, as Kingdom had realised early on, had been conducted this way, Annie in charge of the map, deciding which bits were safe, deciding exactly where to put the No Trespassing signs.

Kingdom offered to top up her glass.

She shook her head. 'Maybe I'll just take the lot off,' she said. 'Do you ever wear hats at all?'

'Never.'

'Pity.'

The scissors descended on a tuft above his left ear, and Kingdom abandoned the bottle and reached up, catching her wrist. She was much stronger than she looked and she resisted for a moment or two before sliding onto his lap. He whispered in her ear, watching her face in the mirror as she grinned and nodded, anticipating his next suggestion. As ever, she was ahead of the game.

'Why not?' she said. 'It's the least I owe you.'

She led him to the bed, removed the towel, and made him lie face down on the rumpled sheets. She retrieved the bottles of body oil she always kept in her travelling bag and laid them carefully in a line across the pillow beside his face.

'You choose,' she said. 'Your treat.'

Kingdom's eyes remained shut. 'Coconut,' he murmured.

She picked up one of the bottles and began to dribble the oil down his back. Kingdom could smell the heavy fragrance and the memories stirred him. Other rooms. Other cities. Nearly a year of the best lovemaking he could ever remember.

Annie capped the bottle and then got on the bed, straddling Kingdom's long body, her head towards his feet. She began to work along the bottom of his spine, her weight on her flattened hands, pushing outwards from the knobbly line of bones, kneading the muscle between each rib with her thumbs, and Kingdom felt himself drifting away, rafting slowly down some delicious river, the taste of the wine, the smell of the oil, the taunt of Annie's fingertips as they brushed across his buttocks and danced between his open thighs.

He turned over, smiling, reaching up for her, pulling her back towards him, turning her round until she was sitting on his face, settling herself to the shape of his mouth, his tongue lapping and lapping, his eyes open now, looking up at the tilt of her breasts as she began to gyrate. When she was ready, she eased herself free and kissed him on the lips, sliding herself back down his body, fitting him into her, supporting her weight in a low squat, lifting herself up and down, slowly, slowly, tiny movements, taunting him, taking him to the very edge, then tipping him over as she sank onto him, her mouth sucking his nipples, one after the other, her body still pumping and pumping, emptying him of everything.

She was still asleep, half an hour later, when Kingdom's hand found the phone. He dialled Allder's private number, reaching for a pen from Annie's bag. Allder answered almost at once, gruff as ever. The missing Sabbathman communiqués, he said, had been delivered to the Yard two hours earlier. They'd be public knowledge by breakfast time but it would be nice if Kingdom got a head start. He began to read them at dictation speed, while Kingdom scribbled across the back of a room service menu. When he'd finished, Allder described the scene at the Yard. One of *The Citizen*'s senior executives had brought the material over personally. He'd been boasting about the impending media storm, and predicted an upward leap in the parent group's share price. He'd also, said Allder in disgust, been pissed.

'Not driving, I hope, sir,' Kingdom murmured, still trying to decipher his own writing.

Allder grunted. 'Seen your friend yet?'

'Yes, sir.'

'Productive?'

'Yes, sir. Very.'

'Good,' he grunted again, 'just don't get us screwed too, OK?'

Allder hung up and Kingdom permitted himself a small, private smile. Annie was awake now, her body curled around Kingdom's, her skin still flecked with small black hairs. She looked up at him, sleepy, content, the one moment in their relationship when she always seemed – to Kingdom – to be truly relaxed.

'My Guv'nor,' Kingdom said, nodding at the phone. 'He thinks we've been at it.'

Annie ran a finger round the line of his mouth. 'Outrageous,' she whispered. 'What else did he say?'

She got up on one elbow and peered at Kingdom's scribble. 'Are you going to tell me?' she said. 'Or do I wait for tomorrow's paper?'

Kingdom studied her a moment. So far, they'd barely talked about the Carpenter killing but it was inconceivable that Annie hadn't been fully briefed. She'd know as much as he did. Probably more.

'You serious?' he said. 'You don't know about this guy?'

'Mr Sabbathman?' She shook her head. 'Not the latest.'

'I don't believe you.'

'OK.' She shrugged, and her hands went upwards, exploring his ravaged scalp. 'Ever thought of the Foreign Legion?'

Kingdom said nothing, leaning back against the bedhead, reaching for a cigarette. MI5 were the biggest players in the information game, always had been. On the back of a couple of hundred Home Office warrants a year, they were routinely installing tens of thousands of telephone taps. Mail intercepts, surveillance, and a small army of freelance agents brought them the other bits of the jigsaw. Once Downing Street had sounded the alarm about Sabbathman, *The Citizen* would have become a priority target. They'd be monitoring the mail flows in and out of the building. They'd have identified and bugged the key telephones. They'd have their fingers on the pulse of the place, they'd know exactly what was going on. And Annie would be part of it all. Had to be. Kingdom glanced down at her now, her cheek nestled against his chest. She looked sweetly innocent.

'Well?' she said, fingering the room service menu, 'You going to tell me or what?'

Kingdom shrugged. If it was a game she wanted, so be it. 'Which one first?'

'Bairstow, please.'

'OK.' Kingdom peered again at the back of the menu, picking his way through the lines of hasty scribble. '*Bairstow had dandruff and a skin problem,*' he read, '*you could see it on the back of his neck. Probably acne in adolescence, poor bastard. But what's a guy like him doing with a season ticket to Zurich? Wasn't Andy Cole enough for him? All that excitement at St James' Park?*'

Annie yawned and stretched, her hands beginning to wander again. 'Andy Cole?'

'Newcastle number nine,' Kingdom said, 'find of the season.'

'And Zurich?'

'Haven't a clue.' He glanced down at her. 'I thought you might know.'

'No.' Annie shook her head. 'What about the other one? Our MP friend?'

Kingdom was watching her, his eyes back on the tattoo, her souvenir from some previous life, and she touched him again, walking her fingertips up and down, moistening her lips with her tongue.

'You're sure about this?' Kingdom said.

'Yes.'

'You definitely want me to carry on?'

'Yes' – she ducked beneath the sheet and planted a line of kisses down Kingdom's belly – 'please.'

'OK.' He shrugged. 'Here we go. *Adieu Max Carpenter. Off to the big party meeting in the sky. No more freebies in Abu Dhabi. No more nonsense about omelettes and eggs. Guy got what he deserved. Like Blanche. And our friend on the terraces. His tart wears Chanel, by the way. And the sheets were blue. When will they ever learn, these guys? How many Sundays can I spare?*'

Kingdom put the menu down, amused by the final phrase, its

air of faint exasperation. Aside from the carefully placed bona fides
– the perfume, the colour of the sheets – he loved the way the man
wrote, how direct he was, the lightness of his touch. Nothing could
be further from the dour two-line statements the Provos put out.
There was nothing here about 'the armed struggle' or 'final victory'.
On the contrary, Sabbathman appeared to be enjoying himself,
choosing his targets with some care, spicing their deaths with
cheerful comments about football and trips abroad. The key, once
again, was motive. Why choose these men? Why go to the trouble
of killing them? Where on earth was the connection? What was the
point of spilling so much blood?

Kingdom let the menu fall to the floor, aroused again. He
could see Annie's head bobbing slowly up and down beneath the
duvet. Finally he reached down for her, pulling her back up the
bed.

'Listen,' he said, 'we ought to talk about this.'

'Why?'

'That's what you said earlier.'

'I know.' She picked a hair from the end of her tongue. 'But
what is there to talk about?'

'We're supposed to be liaising.'

'We are.'

'Seriously.' Kingdom frowned. 'You think this is some kind of
joke?'

Annie was back up on her elbow again, gazing at his haircut,
trying not to laugh. 'Well?' she said, 'Isn't it?'

Kingdom shook his head, feeling himself being backed up the
usual cul-de-sac. Despite the physical closeness of their relationship,
its warmth, its humour, there were certain kinds of intimacy Annie
refused to share. She hated sentimentality. She loathed cosiness
and she'd always refused point blank to discuss anything to do with
their respective jobs. Partly, Kingdom suspected, because she was
a great deal more senior than she'd want him to know. The older
woman. With the bigger desk.

'It matters,' Kingdom said slowly, 'that we talk.'

'I don't want to talk. I want to screw again.'

'I know. But we ought to get one or two things straight.'

'My thought entirely.' Annie disappeared beneath the duvet.

'Listen to me. Behave yourself.'

'No.'

'Please.'

'No. How about . . .?'

Kingdom missed the rest of the sentence, her voice lost amongst the bedclothes. He reached down for the second time, easing her head away from his crotch, peeling back the sheet, exposing her body. She lay quite still for a moment, her eyes closed, then she sat up in the bed. There were parts of her that no amount of sex, no amount of wine, could ever reach. In certain moods, she could be truly frightening. It was one of the many reasons Kingdom thought he loved her. Unlike most of the women he'd met, she could never be entirely his.

'We're supposed to be swopping notes,' he said, 'we're supposed to have formal meetings, keep minutes, report back, all that. It's in the job description. I've read the script.'

'I know.'

'So when do we make a start?'

Annie was out of bed now. Kingdom could hear her in the bathroom, running the shower, maximum boost. When she reappeared, her hair was plastered against her skull, a tight blonde cap. She began to towel herself dry, twisting sideways, examining her back in the mirror.

'Bloody hair,' she said, 'everywhere.'

'We going to talk?'

'Of course, if that's what you really want. I just didn't realise that's what this was about.' She glanced round, nodding at the bed. 'Sorry, my mistake, won't happen again.'

She reached for her clothes and began to put them on. Kingdom watched her without comment. The wine was giving him a headache. Bad sign. He pulled back the blanket and patted the sheet beside him.

'Come here,' he said.

'I just did.'

'No . . .' He found himself frowning again. 'Please.'

Annie wriggled into the black one-piece and did up the buttons at the top. Then she ran a comb through her hair, opened the window, and settled in the armchair beside the television. She had a small, thin mouth and when she was angry it puckered slightly at one corner.

'You're pissed off,' Kingdom said.

'No. Just paying attention. The way you like it.'

'Have I ever said that?'

'No. That's why I'm surprised. I thought' – she shrugged – 'we'd got things pretty well organised, that's all. We've had some nice times. Why spoil them?'

'Had?' Kingdom blinked.

'Yeah. Had.' She nodded, hooking her bag towards her with her foot. 'So where do you want to start? Carpenter? Bairstow? The other guy? Do we have a plan here? Some kind of agenda? Only that matters . . .' she smiled thinly, eyeing the semi-circle of hair on the carpet in front of the mirror, '. . . to us working girls.'

Kingdom closed his eyes a moment. Then he swung out of bed and went into the bathroom. The remains of his cigarette made a small, sizzling noise as he dropped it in the lavatory. For a second or two he examined himself in the mirror. He looked half-crazy, a lost soul from the asylum, some demented fool who'd given the nurses the slip and made it over the wire. He fingered the worst of the damage, semi-bald spots patterned randomly over his scalp, and he thought suddenly of his father, poor Ernie, sitting in the darkness, nursing his precious briefcase. Then he shook his head, and doused his face in cold water. What mattered, what really mattered, was Annie. This thing they had between them, raw and strange and lop-sided though it undoubtedly was, had kept him sane for the best part of a year. It had come from nowhere, a frank exchange of glances in one of the interminable RUC liaison meetings, and it had taken hold of both their lives, an insatiable urge for each other, a physical journey without end. In the space between two busy lives, they'd created a small pocket of warmth, a refuge, that he knew he didn't want to lose. Not now. Not ever.

Kingdom squeezed the flannel dry and laid it carefully over the side of the basin. Then he returned to the bedroom. Annie was lighting one of his cigarettes, the first time he'd ever seen her smoke, and it shook him because it was so obviously something she did often, in some other life. He sat on the edge of the bed, a towel around his waist. He held out a hand. She didn't respond.

'Listen,' he said, 'I'm sorry. This isn't as serious as it sounds.'

She looked at him a moment, then ducked her head behind a cloud of smoke. 'Isn't there someone else they could have found?' she said bitterly. 'Isn't it a bit obvious sending you along?'

Kingdom awoke in total darkness. The digital clock on the bedside table read 04.37. He could feel a presence beside him, someone bending over him, and for a second he didn't know who it was.

'You awake?' Annie whispered.

Kingdom grunted, rolling over. Their interdepartmental meeting had lasted all of five minutes. Despite the third bottle of wine, the rest of the evening had been a disaster.

'Here,' Annie said now, 'drink this.'

She found his hand in the darkness and gave him a glass. It was water.

'Thanks,' he said.

'I've been thinking.'

'Oh?'

'Yes.' Kingdom could see her teeth in the darkness. It meant that she was smiling. 'You could back off. It's not too late. You could tell them you don't want the job.'

'This job? Allder? Tell him I can't cope?'

'Yes.'

'Why?'

'Because then we wouldn't have all this . . . you know . . . we could just get on with it. Like before.'

'You in your job?'

'Yes.'

'Me making the tea?'

'Don't be silly. You'd just go back to ordinary duties. They'd understand.'

Kingdom laughed. 'You're joking,' he said tersely. 'In any case, I need the fucking money. What with Dad and everything.'

'I thought you said your brother-in-law had chipped in?'

'He has.'

'So what's the problem?'

Kingdom peered up at her in the darkness. 'You know how long a grand lasts?' he said, 'at agency rates?'

'No.'

'About a month. Just over.'

'So what happens then? Come November?'

'You tell me.' Kingdom sipped at the water again. 'But what I don't need is Allder on my back. With that guy, you either hack it or you're out. Ordinary duties isn't a phrase he understands.'

Annie didn't say anything. Kingdom could hear her swallowing the last of the water.

'What about you?' he said at last. 'Why don't you back off? Make a little room for us?'

There was another silence, then a soft laugh and a clunk as she returned the empty glass to the bedside cabinet.

'Is that some kind of joke,' she said, 'or are you serious?'

Three hours later, waking again, Kingdom heard the soft thud of the newspaper he'd ordered being dropped outside the door. He was still retrieving *The Citizen* when Annie emerged from the bathroom. She was wearing a stylish two-piece, cut low around the neck, and she was having trouble with one of her earrings. Kingdom returned to bed. The glass of water in the middle of the night had done nothing for his headache, and he felt slightly sick. He began to unfold the paper, taking in the enormous headline. SABBATHMAN, it ran, WORLD EXCLUSIVE.

Annie knelt on the bed beside him. She offered him the earring, one of a pair Kingdom had given her in Belfast, a delicate silver circle with the shape of a dove suspended inside.

'Please?' she said.

Kingdom laid the paper on the wreckage of the bed. Beneath a blow-up of the latest Sabbathman communiqué, there was a line of three photographs: Blanche, Bairstow, and now Carpenter.

Kingdom began to ease the silver hook into Annie's earlobe. Trying to focus on the tiny hole made his head ache even more. Annie had finished with the front page, turning over. On page two, another photo. This time it showed the executive from *The Citizen* whom Allder had mentioned delivering a large envelope to a uniformed policeman outside New Scotland Yard. Below, in a signed article, the paper's editor explained just how responsibly *The Citizen* had behaved. The headline, this time, warned: WHY THEY MUST BE CAUGHT!

Kingdom finished with the earring. He was frowning. 'They?' he said. 'Why they?'

Annie was looking at the paper. She pointed to another piece on the facing page. The paper's Northern Ireland correspondent was warning that the Provisionals had 'mobilised'. There were rumours out of Belfast that 'terrorist chiefs' had ordered 'the big push'. The link with the mysterious Sabbathman was evidently explicit. 'Are these the perfect killings?' the final paragraph began. 'A lethal weekly message from the Provos – aimed at the heart of the British establishment?'

Kingdom looked up. Annie was standing by the door. She had her suitcase in one hand and her car keys in the other.

'Off already?' Kingdom asked.

Annie nodded, doing her best to smile. For the first time, Kingdom realised that she'd been crying.

'I'd suggest breakfast,' she said bleakly, 'but I don't want you upsetting the waitresses.'

The hotel was on the edges of Havant. By nine o'clock, Kingdom was sitting in a barber shop in the town centre, listening to a youth with a nose stud explaining why a Grade One crew cut was his only sensible option.

'What happened, man?' he kept muttering. 'Traffic accident?'

Kingdom ignored the jibe. High on the back wall of the shop was a television. It was tuned to one of the morning magazine shows, and Kingdom could watch it in the mirror. Already, back in the hotel, he'd seen a little of the news coverage. The BBC, it seemed, had established some kind of presence outside Clare Baxter's house, and the presenter in the London studio was firing questions to a succession of interviewees about the progress of the investigation. Hampshire's Deputy Chief Constable was promising 'a nationwide hunt' while a pundit from some think tank or other had speculated darkly about 'the threat to legitimate government'.

There was no such thing, he seemed to be saying, as 'absolute security'. Anyone with support, and determination, and the relevant skills could blow a large hole in the most carefully laid plans, and for this proposition the Sabbathman killings appeared to be ample proof. Pressed to explain the word 'support', the pundit acknowledged at once that no one on his own could have pulled off all three murders. Somewhere along the line he had to have backing, which meant that the nation was confronting not a solo killer, a lone assassin, but some kind of conspiracy. This latter thought was put to the last of the interviewees, and Kingdom had returned from the shower, towelling himself dry, to find Arthur Sperring's face on screen, pondering the question. 'Someone's been killed,' he growled at last. 'If you're talking about facts, that's all we know.'

Now, in the barber's chair, Kingdom's eyes left the television and watched the last of his hair disappearing under the busy clippers. The face that was emerging beneath the bristle was the face of a stranger: pensive, hollow-cheeked, the eyes deeply sunk, the beak of a nose somehow longer and thinner than ever. The image was mildly shocking, not the person he thought he knew, and looking at himself, Kingdom was reminded of the faces he'd first seen at school, the afternoon the history teacher had shown the 'O' level year a film about the Nazi holocaust. The sequence that had stuck in his mind had nothing to do with gas chambers or burial pits. Instead, it showed men jumping into the snow from a line of railway cattle wagons. Stumbling upright, some of them had looked straight into the waiting camera lens, and they were mirror images of what Kingdom now saw before him. They looked suspicious. They looked bewildered. They'd come a long way in great discomfort for no good purpose. And now, deep down, they knew there was worse to come.

Kingdom frowned, surprised and disturbed by the way his mind was working. His eyes returned to the television. On the magazine show they were still discussing the Carpenter killing but the focus had changed from the earlier news shows. Now, in the studio, the wife of a backbench Tory MP was confirming that the pressures of contemporary politics were intolerable. Parliamentary hours were absurd. The facilities were mediaeval. Family life was a joke. Small wonder the weaker brethren went to the wall. The show's presenter, heavily pregnant, eased into the obvious question: was Carpenter the exception or the rule? How could any political marriage survive?

The MP's wife squirmed on the sofa, laughing nervously. 'My husband's never been shot,' she said, 'if that's what you're getting at.'

Back at the police station, Kingdom found Arthur Sperring in his office. His morning appearance on nationwide television seemed to have cheered him up. Expecting a dig or two about the haircut, Kingdom was relieved when the DCS nodded gleefully at the telephone.

'You know what they've given me now?' he said. 'Now that the penny's dropped? All this coverage? Radio? Telly? The press boys?' he grinned. 'Three hundred men. Three hundred blokes. Can you imagine the catering problems? Getting them all down there? Transport? Can you imagine how thrilled my clerks are? Getting all those door-to-doors into the system?' He shook his head. 'If it wasn't happening, I'd never believe it. Someone upstairs must be shitting bricks. Three hundred blokes. Jesus . . .' He pushed his chair back from the desk, reaching for an ashtray on the windowsill, and for a moment Kingdom thought of Clare Baxter, waking up to find the street full of white Ford Transits, and men from the BBC with anoraks and fancy clipboards. Sharing a little of Max Carpenter's life had, in the end, carried a certain price.

Kingdom leaned forward, refusing a cigarette. 'I was looking at the timings,' he said, 'that chronology your lads put together. If I've got it right, our friend never had time to get off the island, not by road.'

'That's right.'

'And you've kept the road block on? Ever since?'

'Yeah. Twenty-four hours a day. Priority from HQ. The Guv'nor insisted.'

Kingdom nodded, unsurprised. The Chief Constable would have got the word about Sabbathman as early as Monday, presumably from the Commissioner at the Yard. Given the likely headlines, maintaining a checkpoint on the island's only bridge would pre-empt the obvious criticisms. Nothing made the guys upstairs dive for cover quicker than the threat of publicity.

'So matey's either still there,' Kingdom mused, 'or he's come out some other way. By sea? Boat of some kind?'

'Could be.' Sperring nodded. 'We're still checking, but yes.'

'Marinas? Jetties? Moorings?'

'One marina on Hayling. Up in the north-east.' Sperring frowned. 'Then there's a new one over the water, on the Portsmouth side. Plus moorings on the harbour, as you say.'

'And?'

'I told you. We're still checking.'

'But supposing there's nothing? No trace? What then?'

'Then we carry on with the door-to-doors.'

'The whole island?'

'Of course.' Sperring yawned. 'What else do I do with three hundred blokes?'

Kingdom found an empty corner in the Incident Room. Handwritten reports were already piling up from the newly extended search area and there were operators at all the computer terminals, their fingers blurring over the input keys. Kingdom reached for the telephone and dialled his father's number. The voice, when it answered, was unfamiliar, a deep, rich baritone.

'Angeline?' Kingdom queried.

'Barry. Angeline's not here.'

'Ah . . . so where's Angeline? The nurse I hired? My name's Alan Kingdom. Ernie's son.'

'She's sick, sir. I'm Angeline. For the time being.' Barry laughed. 'You want to talk to your father, sir? I'll get him.'

'No. Wait. How is he?'

'Fine. OK. Nice man.'

'Is he eating? Does he talk to you?'

'All the time. Talk, talk, talk. Lovely man. Hey, you wait a moment—'

'What?'

Kingdom stared at the phone, hearing a door slam at the other end. Last time he'd spent an evening with his father, nothing could make him talk. Now, it seemed, he couldn't stop. Barry came back on the phone. In the background, he could hear his father singing. He hadn't done that, either. Not for years.

'Barry?'

'Sir?'

'Can I talk to my father?'

There were more noises, then Kingdom recognised his father's voice. He sounded a little out of breath, but undeniably cheerful.

'Dad?' Kingdom said blankly.

'Who's that?'

'Alan.' Kingdom paused. 'Alan?'

'Who?'

'Me, Dad. Your son. Alan.'

'Ah . . . yes. Alan. He'll be back soon, I expect. Sunday.'

'What?'

The phone changed hands again, Barry back in charge. Kingdom turned towards the window, embarrassed, trying to protect the conversation from listening ears. Barry said something about the people at the agency. They needed a deposit. He said it was urgent.

'How much?' Kingdom asked.

'A week, sir. A week's attendance. It's standard terms. Part of the contract.'

'How much is that, then?'

'Ah . . .' Barry paused, but Kingdom could tell he'd already worked it out. 'Say £400, sir. Maybe more.'

'Four hundred quid?' Kingdom stared hard at the window.

'Yes, sir. Seven hours a day. Plus travelling.'

'Seven hours?'

'Yes, sir. That's the way we've worked it out.'

'Who's we?'

'Me and your dad, sir. Mr Ernie.'

Kingdom paused a moment, wondering whether to press the nurse any harder on the phone or leave it until later. Seven hours a day sounded like a lot of meals. Maybe Ernie was making up for lost time. Or maybe they were simply getting ripped off.

Kingdom bent to the phone again, remembering Steve's promise to send a replacement cheque.

'Barry?'

'Yes, sir?'

'Is there any mail for me? Envelope with a Woodford postmark? Or maybe Romford?'

Kingdom heard Barry on the move. At length he found the letter.

'OK,' Kingdom said, 'tell the agency they'll be getting a cheque, and tell Dad to behave himself. I'll be back tonight. See you later.'

Kingdom hung up, staring at the phone for a second or two, trying to get his thoughts in order. At this rate, Steve's money would last even less than a month. After that, Barry would have to go. So how long would it take the Social Services to come up with an alternative? And what was he supposed to do if they didn't?'

Kingdom shook his head, knowing there was no simple answer to any of the questions. Two desks away, one of the WPCs had pushed her chair back and was putting on her jacket. Kingdom went across and introduced himself. When he asked to borrow the terminal, she agreed at once. She was due for a coffee. She'd be back in ten minutes.

Kingdom thanked her and settled down behind the terminal. Before he switched the machine on, he caught sight of his own reflection in the screen, the narrow, bony outline that framed his new face. He moved slightly, a little profile, left and right. In the depthless grey of the monitor screen he looked OK, different, but OK. Maybe he could live with it. Maybe it wasn't quite as bad as he'd thought. He shrugged, mildly embarrassed by his own vanity, then reached for the power switch. The screen came to life and he keyed in the standard code to access the menu. The menu scrolled up from the bottom of the screen and Kingdom studied it a moment before entering another access code of his own, a seven-digit number and a password to get into the big Special Branch computer at New Scotland Yard. The computer was heavily shielded from electronic prowlers and sometimes it could take literally hours to negotiate entry. Today, though, Kingdom was lucky. The screen cleared and he recognised the distinctive Special Branch directory. Towards the bottom, it offered an update on the latest surveillance data filed by MI5's 'A' Branch, the Gower Street specialists who kept physical track of selected targets.

Kingdom began to scroll through the entries for the past twenty-four hours. In the main, they were routine surveillance reports on specific Provisional terrorists, known players with a place on what Northern Command still called 'The England Team'. Each contact was coded with a number. The numbers were changed every week but Allder kept an up-to-date list and Kingdom consulted it now, matching each of the names on Allder's list to numbers that tallied on the screen.

Amongst the trace reports were seven specific targets, all filed under the same batch code. The batch code indicated that the targets all formed part of the same inquiry, and Kingdom studied their names with interest. He knew them all. He'd spent two busy years in Belfast amongst the small print of their private lives, a paper chase through endless RUC files, supplemented with stills and video surveillance. He'd never met any of these men or women in the flesh but they were like old friends. He knew about their families, who they lived with, whether or not they'd had kids. He knew what they liked to wear, the kind of meals they went for when they ate out, whether or not they were drinkers. He knew how they behaved under arrest, whether they'd ever shown signs of buckling under the heavier sessions at the RUC interrogation centre. And he knew, too, that none of them carried the suffix (X), indicating a possibility that they might be turned. No. These guys were the real thing, the hard cases, the biz. They belonged to the top cadre of sharp-end operators.

Kingdom frowned, easing back from the screen a moment, recognising the logic behind this sudden outburst of surveillance activity. Given three high profile killings, it obviously made sense to check out the Premier League Provos, the men and women who – conceivably – might have lent a hand. In every case, as far as he could see, they were in the clear but that, too, was significant. It meant, as Kingdom was already beginning to suspect, that Sabbathman had nothing to do with the Republicans. It meant that the contents of this huge computer were largely irrelevant. It meant that they had to start all over again.

Kingdom called up the next page of the file, the one reserved for trace requests logged in the last hour. Here, there was just one entry: 56734. He cross-checked the number against Allder's list, finding a name he didn't recognise. Sean McTiernan. Kingdom gazed at the name, searching back through his memory. He'd heard of a McTiernan early on, in the first months at RUC headquarters, but he was sure the first name had been Michael. He reached for a pad and scribbled down the number. Then he glanced at his watch: 10.42. He hesitated a moment before picking up the phone. Allder's secretary answered on the first ring. The Commander was about to leave. There was a car outside. Couldn't it wait?

'No,' Kingdom said.

The secretary grunted, and then Allder came on. Kingdom read him the number.

'I've got a Sean McTiernan on Five's trace list,' he said. 'I'm not sure that's kosher.'

There was a silence. Then he heard Allder chuckling. More than anything else in the world, he loved being ahead of the game.

'He's changed his name.' he said, 'I thought you'd have known.'

'No,' Kingdom said. 'So what was he before?'

'Eddie McCreadie.'

'Fat Eddie?'

'Yes.' Allder sounded suddenly impatient. 'Anything else?'

'No, sir.'

Allder rang off and Kingdom wrote the new name on the pad beside the number, sitting back again in the chair, his pencil between his teeth. Fat Eddie had been an active republican in Belfast, a quartermaster, a man near the centre of the Provisionals' Northern Command. The violence that he'd witnessed over the years had finally sickened him, and towards the end of his days in Belfast he'd provided enough hard intelligence to save dozens of lives. The operations he'd compromised had always carried the risk of civilian casualties, and to Kingdom's certain knowledge he'd never asked for a penny in payment. As such, Fat Eddie had left his Army handlers in a state of some bewilderment: why did he do it? What was his real motivation? How could they hope to bind him hand and foot, the way they did the rest of the touts?'

In the end, Fat Eddie had left Belfast, preferring his own version of retirement to a violent death in the bottom of some ditch in South Armagh. He'd moved his wife and family to a housing estate on the edge of Birmingham, and he'd at last accepted Army help in the shape of a job at a local engineering works. Kingdom had inherited him as a 'dry source', someone to go to for background – history, really – and over the course of several conversations he'd taken a real liking to the man. He was generous and funny, one of life's survivors. He doted on his family, and the last time they'd met, in the upstairs restaurant at Birmingham Airport, Kingdom had ended the evening with the purchase of five plastic footballs, one for each of Eddie's kids. Like Eddie, the kids were soccer-mad, and Kingdom remembered the scene now, Eddie juggling the footballs on the down escalator, returning to the car park, trying to wave goodbye. Away from Belfast, the man was reborn. He had a new life. He could sleep at night without worrying about knocks at the door, or petrol through the letterbox, or neat little parcels of Semtex taped to the underside of his car. So what was he doing back in the frame? Why had he changed his name? And why had he so suddenly appeared on the MI5 trace list?

Kingdom pondered the questions, aware of the WPC standing behind him. Back from the canteen, she was studying the screen with interest. MI5 display files were evidently a rare sight in provincial police stations.

'Can you make any sense of that?' she said, nodding at Fat Eddie's trace code.

Kingdom glanced up. 'No,' he said truthfully, 'I can't.'

FIVE

22 Sept. 1993

Dear Rob,

Thanks for yours of yesterday. "Surrendering the high ground to the tabloids" sounds like a contradiction in terms, but no hard feelings. Journalists, like our friend in the black balaclava, move in mysterious ways. As for our brothers in blue getting stuffed, what can I possibly say? Shame to intrude into private grief....

Yours ever
Hugh

Portsmouth's main hospital, the Queen Alexandra, lies on the lower slopes of Portsdown Hill, the steep fold of half-quarried chalk which looks down on the city from the north. Kingdom had phoned the Accident and Emergency Department from the Incident Room and had arranged to meet the Junior Registrar at eleven. With luck, she said, she'd be free for coffee. They could talk in the staff room.

Now, Kingdom stirred sugar into his coffee and waited while the young doctor dealt with yet another inquiry on the internal phone. Jo Hubbard was in her late twenties, stocky, solidly-built, with broad shoulders and a pleasant open face under a startling haircut. The hair, tinted a rich auburn, was scissored in a straight line level with her ears. At the back and sides, beneath the line, it was shaved to a close nap. The overall effect was two-fold. At first, meeting her, Kingdom had thought it was ugly. Now, on closer inspection, it said something else. In this, and probably every other respect, Jo Hubbard was very definitely her own person.

She put the phone down at last and apologised for the interruption with a grin. She grinned a lot. Outside, while he'd waited in the casualty department, Kingdom had watched her stepping from cubicle to cubicle, bending to examine an ankle or a knee, reassuring the younger kids with a squeeze on the shoulder or a tickle under the chin. She had natural warmth, and she seemed to leave little parcels of it behind her wherever she went.

Now, she poured herself another coffee and sat down. Rob

Scarman, it turned out, was a distant relative. She'd talked to him on the phone about Carpenter, more out of curiosity than anything else, but she hadn't made any kind of formal statement. She sipped at her coffee. Carpenter's medical notes lay beside her on the low occasional table.

'He was a mess,' she said. 'Strictly speaking, he was still alive but that had more to do with the ambulance boys than anything else. They were brilliant.'

Kingdom looked at the notes. An outline of Carpenter's head was bisected by a careful line of pencilled dots. Kingdom frowned. In his experience, two bullets in the head led straight to a drawer in the mortuary.

'Alive?' he queried.

'Yes.' Joe Hubbard picked up the notes. She extracted a sheet of blue scribble and peered at it. 'They'd worked on him in the ambulance. His BP was way down and his breathing was pretty shallow and once I got the dressing off it was obvious he wasn't going to make it, but . . .' she looked up, the grin again, '. . . he was still with us, just.'

'What did he say?'

'*Say?* You think he was still conscious? Wound like that?' She laughed. 'Afraid not.'

'So what did you do?'

'I got some fluid in him and tried to do something about his breathing but in the end I had to put him on the respirator. Machine that did his breathing for him.'

'Knowing he wouldn't make it?'

'Yes.'

'Why?'

She hesitated a moment, thinking about the question. There was a copy of *The Citizen* lying on the table. Someone had put their coffee on the photo of Max Carpenter and he peered up through a wet, brown circle.

'I was the only one who knew who he was,' she said at last. 'We had no ID at the time, nothing from the para-medics, but I'd seen him before.'

Kingdom nodded at the table. 'In the papers?' he said. 'On telly?'

'No. In the flesh.'

'And that's why you put him on the machine? Kept him alive? Because he was who he was?'

'Yes.' She nodded. 'I suppose so. God knows why. It wouldn't have made any difference. Switch off the machine, and he'd have died anyway.'

'Which is what happened? In the end?'

'Yes, more or less.' She consulted the notes again. 'I got the neuro-bods over. Better they took the decision than me. They agreed it was hopeless. He came off the machine at' – she picked up the notes – 'ten past one. Went into cardiac arrest about a minute later.' She glanced up. 'And that was that.'

'He died?'

'Yes.'

'You didn't try . . .' he shrugged, '. . . anything else?'

'No.' Jo shook her head. 'No point.'

Kingdom nodded, making a note on his pad. Then he looked up. Jo was studying the newspaper and for the first time Kingdom wondered whether she'd seen it before.

'This new to you?' he said. 'All this stuff? Sabbathman?'

'Yes.'

'No one out there talking about it?' He nodded at the door. 'You didn't hear the news this morning? Watch TV?'

'No.' She shook her head. 'Have I missed something?'

Kingdom smiled. His question exactly. 'I don't know,' he began. 'There's a theory that says Carpenter was down to a serial killer. Someone's writing to the press. Claiming responsibility. Carpenter and two others.'

'Why? Why should they want to do that?'

'I've no idea.'

Jo was looking at the paper again, her eyes returning to the blotchy photograph of the dead MP.

'You say you knew him?' Kingdom said at last.

'I met him. Once.'

'Where?'

'At Twyford Down.' She hesitated. 'You know about Twyford Down?'

Kingdom nodded, remembering the huge white scar in the hill

overlooking Winchester, the big yellow diggers clawing at the chalk.

'Yes,' he said, 'more or less.'

'Well . . .' Jo toyed with her coffee. 'He'd gone along there to be interviewed. There was a big demo that day and everyone knew something would happen. There were security men there, hundreds of them, and police too. There was bound to be violence. It was bound to happen. He must have known it.'

'Who?'

'Carpenter. He turned up with a TV crew. I was there when he was being interviewed. He just milked it, the demo, the scuffles, everything. It was . . .' She looked away, shaking her head. 'Doing this job, it's hard sometimes not to get involved. You shouldn't but you do. You see the way people get themselves injured. Most of it's carelessness. Domestic accidents. RTAs. People driving too fast, not paying attention, coming to grief. You get horrible injuries, truly horrible, and that's bad enough. You get violence as well, fights, the drunks on Friday nights, knife wounds, people beaten up, even us sometimes if we're unlucky, and that's pretty awful, too. But Twyford Down . . .' Her eyes were back on the paper. 'That was worse, much worse, the way I see it.'

'Why?'

'Because it was deliberate. They did it in cold blood. And that man didn't give a damn.'

Kingdom was watching her carefully now, recognising a new tone in her voice, real anger and something close to disgust.

'They?' he said. 'Who's they?'

'The security men. The goons they hire to protect the site.' She looked up. 'Isn't that a joke? Protecting something they're busy destroying? Signing on all those psychopaths? Two pounds an hour plus all the violence they can handle?' She shook her head. 'I'd never have believed it if I hadn't been there. If you'd have told me that kind of thing could happen here, in England, I'd have laughed at you. Truly . . .' She nodded, emphasising the point, telling Kingdom how naive she'd been, and how out of touch. She should have known better, she said. She should have taken the hint.

'Hint?'

She nodded again. 'We'd had a young girl in here about a month earlier. She'd been living up on the Down with the rest of them, one of the Dongas. There'd been some kind of scuffle about a Land Rover and she said she'd been beaten up. By the security guys.'

'What was the matter with her?'

'She was bruised around here . . .' Jo tilted her head back, showing Kingdom her throat and the underside of her chin. 'She said it hurt whenever she swallowed and she was obviously shocked. She said one of the security guys had put a choke hold on her but . . .' She shrugged. 'She was young and hysterical and you get to hear lots of stories like that.'

'You didn't believe her?'

'I didn't know. I gave her the benefit of the doubt but I didn't know. She certainly had oedema – bruising – and there was a little bit of swelling round her larynx but . . . who can say?'

'What about the police? Why didn't she contact them?'

'She said there was no point. The security guys were on their own property. I suppose, technically, she was trespassing. Anyway, she didn't trust them. In fact the state she was in, she didn't trust anyone. And I didn't blame her.'

Kingdom nodded. 'Is that why you went up there yourself? Later?'

'Partly, yes. If you're doing our job, it's obviously better to be there. But I'm against it, too, what they're doing with the road. I think it's absurd, really stupid. I suppose you could say I was demonstrating.'

'And what happened? When you went?'

'We got nowhere. Absolutely nowhere. There were hundreds of us, maybe thousands. We weren't lefties. We weren't revolutionaries. We weren't trying to bring down the state. We were just trying to make a simple point. We were just trying to say no. But there was no dialogue, no exchange of views. Just one lot of people shouting, and another lot of people itching to beat them up. It was the first time, truly. The first time.'

'The first time what?'

'The first time I realised you can't do anything. The way the system works, it's hopeless. The system is the system. It's there, and that's it. There's lots of stuff they tell you about consultation, and the democratic process, and all that, but it's a joke. The decisions are made already. Whatever we did, whatever we said, the road would go through. It didn't matter how strong our case was. It didn't matter about the facts, the evidence, the way we all felt. None of that counted for anything. There could have been ten thousand of us up there that day, twenty thousand, and it wouldn't have changed anything.' She paused a moment, her eyes back on the newspaper. 'And do you know what he said? During that interview he did? Carpenter?'

'No.'

'He said you can't make omelettes without breaking eggs. That's all. Just that. Just dismissed the—'

Kingdom was leaning forward.

'He said what?'

'He said . . .' She frowned, trying to think of another way of putting it. 'He meant . . .'

'No, no. What did you say just then?'

'When?'

'Just now? About omelettes and eggs?'

She stared at him, uncomprehending, and Kingdom reached for the newspaper. The quote was on the front page. '*No more nonsense about omelettes and eggs,*' Sabbathman had written. Kingdom pointed it out and Jo read it, colouring slightly, aware of Kingdom watching her. Eventually she looked up.

'That's what he said,' she repeated. 'He said you can't make omelettes without breaking eggs.'

'When did he say it? When did this happen?'

'Oh . . .' She looked at the ceiling. 'October last year. No, later, maybe November. I can check, if you think it's important.'

Kingdom noted the date. 'And what did he mean, do you think?'

'Mean?' She blinked, the colour flooding into her face now. 'It meant he just dismissed us, just dismissed the whole thing. You want change, you want decent roads, you want five minutes off the journey to Southampton, then you just move the landscape round a bit. Easy as that. That's the implication. That's what he meant. That's how simple it all was. To him . . .' She paused, her hands

120

around the cup. 'And it was the way he said it, too. He said it with a smile on his face. That nasty little smile they've all got. Mr Smug. From the Smug party. Yuk.'

'You sound angry.'

'Anyone would. Working here. In the NHS. The things they're up to . . . But I was, yes, you're right, I was angry, very angry.'

'And you're still angry? About what they're doing? Up on the hill?'

'I suppose so.' She nodded. 'Yes, I am. But what do you do about it? Where do you start?'

Kingdom said nothing. They were both looking at the newspaper again. The ring on Carpenter's face was beginning to dry.

'It was on television,' Jo said at last, 'about the omelettes and the eggs. I don't know whether you're interested but it was on the local news, that bit. I remember seeing it in the evening. It made me even madder. I felt like putting something through the set. Funny, isn't it?'

'Which channel?'

'What?'

'Which channel was it on? This interview? Which station?'

'I don't know.' She frowned. 'The one that's on at nine-thirty. Before the weather forecast. BBC South. Try them.'

'And do you have a date?'

'I told you. October, November time.'

'An exact date?'

'No.' She shook her head, startled by his sudden interest. 'Should I? Is it important?'

Kingdom looked at her, not saying anything, then made a note on his pad. When he glanced up again, she was still watching him.

'They took pictures of Carpenter after he died,' she said quietly. 'Have you seen them?'

'Yes.'

'You saw his face? What was left of it?'

'Yes.'

She nodded, saying nothing for a moment. Then she sat back in the plastic armchair, her eyes glazing, and for the first time

Kingdom realised what it was that made her so attractive. She was totally honest. Whatever she thought, whatever she felt, whatever she believed, she let you see it. See it and share it.

'That man was a real mess,' she said. 'Alive, he was pretty awful. But dead, he was much worse. No one deserves that. Not even him.'

She looked down at the coffee a moment, then tipped the cup to her lips. Kingdom nodded, remaining silent, knowing the conversation had touched an important nerve. She swallowed the last of the coffee and put the cup down.

'There are answers,' she said with a smile, 'but you have to go a bloody long way to find them.'

'Yeah?'

'Yes.' She nodded. 'I was up in Scotland, the start of the summer. I spent ten days on an adventure course. It's the kind of thing I do occasionally, the kind of thing I love. And it was incredible, really tough. You had to be out of your mind to even think about doing some of the things we did. Crazy things. Things that made me shudder, just remembering them. But you know something? It worked. It really did. And there was a moment at the end of it all when none of this other stuff mattered. It was just you, and the mountains, and the silence. Amazing. Quite amazing. Made up for everything.'

'Even the rain?'

'Yeah.' She stood up, the grin returning at last. 'Even that.' She held out her hand. 'I have to go, I'm afraid. Was there anything else?'

Kingdom stood up, pocketing his note-pad. A jam-jar by the door held donations for a sponsored ambulance pull.

'Not really,' he said, 'not yet.'

'Yet?'

'Yes.' he smiled. 'I might be back.' Kingdom paused by the door, dropping a pound in the jam-jar. A trolley rattled past in the corridor outside. 'Scotland sounds wonderful,' he said. 'I could do with some of that.'

Jo smiled, pulling her white coat around her, one hand feeling for the stethoscope in the pocket. 'Me, too,' she said, 'the way this place is going.'

*

Back outside, in the hospital lobby, there were two public telephones. Kingdom rang Arthur Sperring and told him about the omelettes and the eggs. Carpenter had apparently used the phrase on television. If the report had only been transmitted locally, the field would begin to narrow.

Sperring listened without comment. He was too good a detective not to recognise a useful lead, or betray the slightest enthusiasm when one appeared.

'When was this, then?'

'November, last year, give or take.'

'OK, leave it to me.' Sperring paused. 'Anything else?'

Kingdom thought about Fat Eddie for a moment, then shook his head. 'No,' he said. 'You?'

'Yeah.' Sperring began to laugh. 'Your guv'nor is coming down. Amazing what the telly does to some people.

Kingdom was back on Hayling Island by midday. A checkpoint on the bridge from the mainland was monitoring a long queue of northbound traffic, and for the first time Kingdom spotted armed police. There were two of them, on opposite sides of the road. They were wearing bullet-proof vests over black jump suits, and both men carried identical sub-machine guns, the stubby Ingrams BPK. At the bottom of the island, close to the sea-front, there was a line of white Transit vans parked by the side of the road. Uniformed men were piling out onto the pavement, each with a clipboard and a flat zip-up briefcase. Kingdom drove slowly past, recognising the scene for what it was, an extravagant display of police resources, a public flexing of muscles, more pictures for the evening news.

Kingdom drove west, along the sea-front. At the head of Sinah Lane, a traffic car was parked diagonally across the road, limiting access to the width of a single vehicle. Two uniformed officers stood on the grass verge. One of them was muttering into a radio, while the other was looking hard at Kingdom. Kingdom wound down the window as the policeman approached. He gave him his ID.

'Where do I find the ferry?' he said.

The officer nodded west, down the coast road, still examining Kingdom's ID. When he gave it back, he lingered a moment by the open window.

'A-T Squad?' he said.

Kingdom nodded. 'Yeah.'

'Your guv'nor's here' – a thumb jerked in the direction of a line of parked vans – 'if you're interested.'

'Allder? Small guy? So high?'

'Yeah,' the officer permitted himself a thin smile. 'Big car, though.'

The ferry lay at the end of the coast road. Kingdom parked beside a pub and walked down the pebbles to the water's edge. The last of the flood tide was pouring in through the harbour mouth, tugging at the buoys that marked the deep water channel to the open sea. Fifty yards upstream, protected by a spit of land, a ferry was moored to a landing stage. Beyond the landing stage, as far as the eye could see, was the flat grey expanse of Langstone Harbour.

Kingdom walked back up the pebbles and wandered across to the landing stage. According to the timetable, the ferry sailed at weekends every half hour. The fare was £1.60 and bicycles were extra. Kingdom gazed out across the water. The harbour mouth was narrow, no more than a couple of hundred yards, but the last thing you'd do in a hurry was depend on the ferry. No, if you wanted to get off the island by sea you'd use a boat of your own or have someone waiting. That way, you could be over in Portsmouth or heading out to sea in minutes. Especially if the tide was right.

Kingdom disentangled Arthur Sperring's chronology from his inside pocket and shook it open. The tide on the morning of Carpenter's murder had been high, no movement in or out, ideal – Sperring had noted – for getting across to Portsmouth. Yet no one, once again, had seen anything worth reporting. Not the Harbourmaster, who'd been alerted in minutes. Nor any of the handful of locals who'd been fishing from the shingle on both sides of the harbour mouth. Nor the husband and wife team who operated the ferry. No, whoever it had been in the balaclava must have taken a different route. Either that, or he was still on the island.

Kingdom trudged back to the car. A thin rain was drifting in from the north-west and it had got appreciably colder. Kingdom sat in the car with the engine running, tuning the radio. In the spare half-minute before the weather forecast, at five to one, the announcer was promising a special report on the murder of Max Carpenter. The report, she was saying, would come live from Hayling Island, and would include latest developments in the hunt for the MP's killer. Kingdom smiled, slipping the car into gear, understanding now why Allder had appeared so suddenly on the scene. The man had an obsession with publicity. It fuelled him the way money or sex fuelled other men. In the three years since he'd headed the Anti-Terrorist Squad, his name had rarely been out of the papers. What he lacked in height, as the acid young man in the New Scotland Yard press office had recently put it, Allder certainly made up for in column inches.

Kingdom drove back to Sinah Lane. The two policemen at the head of the road waved him through, and he joined the convoy of parked vehicles outside Clare Baxter's house. Two of the bigger vans belonged to BBC television. Thick black cables snaked across the road, and Kingdom counted three cameras mounted on tripods on the other side, their long zoom lenses shrouded against the falling rain. Behind the last van was an estate car from BBC Radio Solent, and Kingdom could see Allder inside, the back of his head leaning against the rear window.

Kingdom turned the car radio on again, in time to catch the opening headlines on the one o'clock news. The Carpenter murder, and the Sabbathman revelations in *The Citizen* were the lead story, and when a reporter in the studio began to run through the morning's developments, Kingdom could see Allder readying himself for the inevitable interview. Since the morning news shows, the editorial line seemed to have hardened – the country definitely appeared to be facing another outbreak of terrorism – and when Allder came on, he did nothing to suggest any other motive. On the contrary, he confirmed at once that his very presence at the scene of the crime suggested yet another battle with the Provos. They'd been at it for years, he said. They'd developed formidable expertise. They were clever, and they were ruthless, and it took a very specialised kind of police work to track them down. In one sense, he said, they were like the AIDS virus. Whatever you did, whichever way you played it, they always came up with something new.

The latter thought was a gift for the reporter, and while he carefully framed the obvious question – wasn't that the counsel of despair? – Kingdom caught sight of Allder's face. He'd been attracted by something on the other side of the road. He'd half-turned in the car, and he was looking out through the side window, still holding a microphone to his lips. Kingdom watched him, recognising the coldness in his eyes, and the way he remained wholly expressionless, a face devoid of anything but a pasty indifference. When the reporter finished putting his question, Allder told him there was no such thing as despair. Laws get broken. Arrests are made. Justice triumphs. The last phrase, for once, brought a smile to his lips and he was still nodding to himself when the reporter finally asked about the next move in the inquiry. Allder looked briefly pensive.

'Work,' he said at last on Kingdom's car radio. 'Days of it. Months of it. Until we get a result.'

'And you will? You're sure of that?'

'Of course,' Allder snapped, 'that's what we're here for.'

The reporter thanked him for his time and turned his attention elsewhere. The door of the radio car opened and Allder stepped out. He ignored the proferred handshake from inside, buttoned his coat against the rain, and began to walk away. Kingdom caught him up beside a hamburger van. Allder was eyeing the hot dogs.

'Double onion,' he was saying to the girl behind the counter, 'and lots of ketchup.'

Allder glanced at Kingdom, acknowledging him with a grunt. 'What happened to your hair?'

'Had it cut, sir.'

'Just as well.'

Allder reached up for the hot dog and licked ketchup and mustard from one side.

'I've got ten minutes before the next one,' he said. 'You hear any of that?' Allder nodded back towards the radio car.

Kingdom said he'd heard the whole thing.

'OK, was it?'

'Yes, sir.'

'Sound OK, I mean? Make sense? Do us justice?'

'Yes, sir.'

Allder looked at him a moment, wanting him to go further, wanting Kingdom to spice his performance with a dollop or two of praise.

'We could go back to my car, sir,' he said instead, 'out of the rain.'

'No, son, we'll use mine.' Allder peered at the hot dog. 'It's bigger.'

Allder and Kingdom sat in the back of Allder's car. Allder had told the driver to keep an eye open for the BBC producer in charge of the lunchtime television interviews, and now he stood outside in the rain, talking to one of the cameramen.

'It's war,' Allder announced, gazing out at the scene, 'and if you ask me, we're winning.'

'Sir?'

Kingdom glanced across at him. Twice he'd tried to raise the subject of Twyford Down, what it might mean, why it might suggest an alternative to yet another IRA plot, but now he realised it was hopeless. Allder was working from a different script, a different agenda. What mattered now was the battle with MI5, and what mattered even more was getting the media to sit up and take notice.

So far, in seven busy hours, he'd been pushing the Anti-Terrorist Squad to more than a dozen assorted reporters. Doubtless, some of the dickheads would get hold of the wrong end of the stick. Doubtless he'd be misrepresented, quoted out of context. But slowly, very slowly, he was getting the message across. When it came to terrorism, Scotland Yard were in charge. They were the ones who knew about evidence. They were the ones who'd have to bring the buggers to court. They were the ones who'd have to secure convictions, lock these tossers up, protect society. What did Five know about any of that? What did they care about evidence? Building a case? Following the whole thing through? How could they when officially they barely even existed? Had to appear in court behind specially erected screens? Calling themselves Mr A or Mr B?

Allder snorted with contempt, wiping his mouth with the soggy remains of the paper napkin. His breath reminded Kingdom of Ernie.

'You know why it's so important, don't you?' He poked one greasy finger in Kingdom's face. 'Because it's the thin end of the wedge, that's why. They're not just after our little piece of the cake, those bastards. Christ no, they want it all. They want the whole lot, fraud, drugs, organised crime, everything that's intelligence-based. That's what they're up to. That's what they're after. That's why they're bending ears all over the bloody shop. You think I'm kidding? Look around you. Whitehall, Westminster, Central Office, you name it, they're in there. Reform Club, the Carlton, they never miss a trick. You want to know who really runs this country? Talk to Five. You think the masons have anything to answer for? Forget it. I'm telling you, son. This is war.'

Kingdom could see the driver coming across to the car. He bent to the window and tapped his watch. There was a raindrop on the end of his nose. Kingdom opened the door and Allder wriggled out, brushing the crumbs from his coat. A man from the BBC was signalling from across the road. He looked frantic. Time was evidently tight.

Allder reached out, struck by a sudden thought. 'That TV interview you mentioned,' he said. 'The one Carpenter did. We've got a pile of stuff on Twyford Down. Talk to Alice.'

Kingdom was back in London by late afternoon, the borrowed car returned to Winchester. He took the tube from Waterloo to the Yard, and found Alice at her desk behind a door marked 'Special Branch Records', one floor below Allder's office.

Alice had been in charge of the filing system since Kingdom could remember. She was a pale, thin, watchful woman who had always had an extraordinary knack of identifying the rising stars in the department. On these men and women she lavished special favours – out of hours retrieval, limitless photocopies – and as a direct consequence she'd survived being swept away by countless administrative new brooms. Quite why she'd got so fond of Kingdom, no one could explain, least of all Kingdom himself, but she greeted him now with a warm smile and the offer of a little treat with his cup of tea.

'Twyford Down,' Kingdom mumbled through a mouthful of doughnut. 'Guv'nor says we're loaded.'

Alice put a saucer on her teacup and disappeared into the warren of racks that held current intelligence. The best of this material was home-grown, intelligence gathered by Special Branch detectives, uncontaminated by non-SB sources. The other bits, less reliable, were leftovers from other people's plates. When Alice returned, she was carrying three large files. Two were Special Branch. The other one belonged to MI5.

Kingdom went across to a table near the window, licking sugar off his fingers. He settled back in the plastic chair and opened the fatter of the Special Branch files. The index began with a brief resumé of the Twyford Down affair, and Kingdom scanned it quickly, committing the important dates to memory, trying to understand exactly what it was that had aroused so much anger.

In essence, it seemed that successive governments had wanted to fill the one remaining gap in the London–Southampton motorway. Twyford Down, and the adjoining St Catherine's Hill, stood in the way of this three-mile stretch. One route lay across water meadows between the downland and the city of Winchester. Another would mean a long detour around the other side of the hill. A third, the most direct, went straight through. The locals had protested vigorously, fighting their case through three public inquiries. In the end, the issue had come down to a straightforward choice between a cutting through the hill, and a tunnel underneath. The tunnel would have preserved the hill. The cutting was cheaper. To the fury of the locals, the cutting won.

Kingdom turned to the back of the file. According to Alice's collection of press clippings, the locals were accusing various arms of government of lying, cheating, and bullying their way through the democratic process. They'd slanted the evidence, cooked the books, and finally sidestepped an EEC directive to halt construction by a secret, backstairs political fix. One result of all this had been an extraordinary alliance of protestors, from disillusioned local Tories to various factions on the extreme left. The membership of this rag-bag army was the meat of the Special Branch file and was carefully analysed in an accompanying report. The report included an A4 envelope of photographs, and Kingdom emptied the envelope onto the desk, sifting through the black and white prints.

Most of the shots, according to a stamp on the back, had come from a private detective agency in Southampton. Hired by the Ministry of Transport, they'd attended all the major demonstrations. The photographers involved had been using powerful telephoto lenses, and the anger and frustration was evident in shot after shot. Kingdom bent over the desk, fascinated. These were faces from middle England – people in Barbour jackets, corduroy trousers, stout boots – yet here they were, shouldering their placards, marching uphill, taking on the State they'd once believed to be their own.

Towards the end of the pile, Kingdom found a face he recognised. She was wearing jeans and a heavy polo-necked sweater. She was kneeling over somebody in the short tufty grass, an open rucksack by her side. There was a roll of crêpe bandage in one hand and a pair of scissors in the other, and her head was up, her face clearly visible. To the left, perhaps ten yards away, was a group of men. One of them had a camera on his shoulder. Another carried a microphone on a long pole. Others, in anoraks, formed a protective phalanx around the interviewee.

Kingdom borrowed a magnifier from Alice and returned to the desk, peering at the face of the man in front of the camera, recognising the blond curly hair, the shape of the chin, the contemptuous half-smile. In his buttonhole, clearly visible, there was a poppy, and Kingdom made a note on the pad at his elbow. 'Carpenter/Twyford Down/Armistice Day?' he wrote. He returned to the girl in the foreground. Someone had ringed her face in white chinagraph and there was an index reference scribbled inside it. He found the reference in the accompanying file. 'Jo Hubbard,' it said, '16 Tokar Road, Eastney, Portsmouth.' There was a note of her telephone number and the (E) suffix that indicated a non-warranted tap. Telephone taps without a Home Office warrant were strictly illegal. Special Branch rarely used them. Others weren't so fussy.

Kingdom frowned, looking up. Alice was watching him across the room.

'Problem?' she said.

Kingdom nodded. 'Who's got the logs,' he said, 'for these taps?'

'Which taps?'

'Twyford Down. November. Last year.'

'Ah . . .' Alice got up and stepped across, adjusting her glasses as she peered over Kingdom's shoulder. 'Anyone in particular?'

'Yes.' Kingdom found the photograph, 'Her.'

Alice studied first the photograph, then the file. 'Pretty girl,' she said at last. 'I'd ask Five if I were you.'

Kingdom phoned Annie from his office. There was no answer. Alice had made him a copy of the photo of Jo Hubbard and he propped it against the telephone. On the reverse side he'd pencilled her address and phone number. He looked at it now, wondering whether it was a flat, what it looked like inside, whether or not she lived alone, and then he turned the photograph over again. The way she was bent over the figure in the grass had stirred him, and now he felt it again. It wasn't as straightforward as physical attraction. She was good-looking, and open, and he'd enjoyed talking to her, but it wasn't that. It was something else entirely, something infinitely more difficult to define.

The photo looked like a scene from a battlefield. There was smoke drifting in the background. People were advancing pell-mell uphill, their faces down, their bodies bent, as if they were confronting bullets or a particularly vicious wind. And there, in the middle of it all, was this sturdy young doctor with her funny haircut and her muddy jeans, her eyes on the men round the camera, as angry and as guileless as the rest of them. He looked at the photo a moment longer, wondering why on earth anyone would have bothered with a phone tap, knowing that he needed to find out, then he slipped the photo into his briefcase and glanced at his watch. Six o'clock. Rush hour. Time for a pint.

Kingdom was back in Leytonstone by half-past eight, mellowed by the beer. He walked slowly back from the tube station, avoiding the cratered paving stones, and the chip wrappers, and the flattened smears of dog turd. There were no trees here, nothing to indicate the passage of the seasons, just a succession of ever-earlier dusks and the ceaseless thunder of traffic grinding north, towards the outer suburbs.

Kingdom turned off the High Road, into the maze of streets that led down towards the cemetery. A thin drizzle was still falling, gauzy under the street lamps, shrouding the line of parked cars. In his youth, Kingdom remembered few cars. The streets had been largely empty, a safe playground for the kids. Now, though, there were cars everywhere, ancient Datsuns, dented Capris, big old Bedford vans, builders' ladders roped to the rusting roof racks.

His father's house lay at the end of the street. Outside was a car Kingdom didn't recognise. He paused for a moment, fumbling for the key to the front door. The car was an Escort, newer than the rest, 'B' reg. A sticker on the back window read 'Keep a Smile for the Lord'.

Kingdom let himself into the house. At once, he could hear voices, laughter. A long narrow hall led to the kitchen at the back. To the left was the living room. Kingdom closed the front door very softly and tiptoed down the hall, enveloped at once by the sour, musty smell of his father's new life. By the door to the living room, he paused, listening. He could hear his father chuckling. He was describing how things used to be in the summer, thirty years back, when Kingdom and his sister were kids.

Auntie Peg, he was saying, used to have a bungalow out on the coast, at Clacton. For a fortnight in August, he and the missus would lock up the house, and march the family down to Stratford Broadway, and take the Grey Green coach to the seaside. Mid-morning, halfway there, the coach would stop at a pub for a drink. He'd have a couple of pints. The kids had crisps and lemonade. The missus drank tea. Kingdom smiled, hearing him talk about it now, totally coherent, back in his mind outside the pub, enjoying the sunshine, chatting with the driver, taking the mickey out of mum for putting too much fish paste in the sandwiches she always packed.

Kingdom leaned back against the wall. He'd loved those holidays, the fun they'd had, the four of them. He'd loved the feel of being away from home, the days they'd spent at the little beach hut they'd rented, the taste of salt on his drying skin. Clacton was where he'd first learned to swim, first been served in a cafe by a proper waitress, first seen summer fireworks, first kissed a girl. He remembered it all, and so did Ernie, his recall absolutely perfect.

Kingdom went back to the front door, opened it and then pulled it shut with a bang as if he'd just arrived. In the living room, his father looked up from the chair beside the record player as he came in. He was wearing a clean shirt and a pair of trousers Kingdom hadn't seen for years. There was colour in his face, and a glass in his hand, and the only evidence of madness was a day's growth of stubble on his chin.

Kingdom grinned at him. 'Dad?' he said, 'Alright, then?'

Ernie blinked up at his son, and for a moment Kingdom thought they were back at square one, mutual strangers. Then he remembered the haircut, and his hand went to his shorn scalp.

'Bit of an accident, Dad,' he muttered. 'Never argue with a barber.'

Ernie nodded, his eyes returning to the figure sitting opposite. 'My boy,' he said, 'Alan.'

Kingdom grinned again, extending a hand. 'Barry?'

'That's right. Good to meet you.'

Barry was a small, plump West Indian. He stood up, taking Kingdom's hand. He was wearing a yellow and blue hooped pullover and black jeans. He looked about fifty, and had the warmest smile Kingdom had ever seen.

'Still no Angeline?' he said.

'I'm afraid not. Like I said on the phone, she's sick.'

'And you've had to stand in?'

'A pleasure, sir. A real pleasure.'

He gestured at Ernie. Ernie beamed up, then reached for another of the cans of Guinness on the table beside him. Barry was already on his way to the kitchen, looking for a glass.

'Son?' Ernie said, offering the can.

Kingdom hesitated for a moment, unbuttoning his coat. Then he sank into the other armchair.

'Why not?' he said.

*

Barry stayed the rest of the evening, while father and son worked their way slowly through the rest of the Guinness. Kingdom hadn't a clue where the cans had come from, and didn't care. The neatly stacked plates on the draining board in the kitchen, and the remains of a sizable salad in the fridge told their own story. Barry had taken over. Barry was in charge. Somehow, this round-faced, cheerful little soul had stirred the embers in Ernie's fire and brought him back to life. When it came to the here and now – wheezing upstairs to the toilet, trying to remember where he'd left his Rizlas – the old man was still clueless, but that didn't matter because Barry had returned to him the bits of his life that were still crystal clear. And when Ernie began to talk about these episodes – especially the courtship that the war had turned so suddenly into a marriage – Kingdom could hear again the voice that had shaped so much of his own childhood. The father he remembered, the dad who'd never left without a chuckle and a hug, was back in the armchair, whole again. Quite how Barry had worked the miracle, Kingdom didn't know but when the little West Indian finally got up and looked at his watch, Ernie looked heartbroken.

'Off?' he said, 'Already?'

'Quarter past ten, Ernie. My wife will kill me. I told you. She's a monster.' He stooped to pick up the empty tins. 'Back tomorrow, eh?'

'Yeah?' Ernie was beaming up at him. 'What time?'

Barry glanced at Kingdom.

Kingdom took the cue. 'Early, Dad,' he said. 'I'll sort it out with Barry.'

'You sure, son?'

'Of course.'

Kingdom followed Barry into the hall. The empties were already in the kitchen bin. Kingdom held out a hand.

'You've been brilliant,' he said. 'I'm amazed. Honestly. Amazed.'

Barry gazed up at him. 'No problem,' he said, 'we've a lot in common. Your dad, he was in the markets. Mine, too.'

'Here? In London?'

'Kingston. Back home. My dad's family all worked on the plantations. My dad used to sell some of the stuff.'

'So did Ernie's dad.'

'I know. He told me. So I guess we were similar kids, me and your dad. The things we got up to, you know, the way you do . . .'

'Damn sight better, eh?'

'Better than what?'

'Better than now.'

Barry frowned. 'You mean your dad?'

'No, just . . .' Kingdom shrugged. 'Everything. I used to work the markets, too, as a kid, helping Dad. It was different, that life.'

He smiled bleakly, wondering how far to pursue the thought, but Barry was already at the front door. He paused, looking back down the hall at Kingdom.

'You OK?' he said.

'Fine, I'm fine. Just worried about Dad, you know.'

'You sure?'

'Yes.'

Barry was still looking at him. He had a pair of car keys in his hand. 'You believe in God, Mr Kingdom?'

Kingdom shook his head. 'No.'

'Ever thought about any of that stuff?'

'No, not really.'

'Think you should? Think it might help?'

'With Dad, you mean?'

'No. With you.'

Kingdom laughed, shaking his head again, reaching for the door handle. Outside, the rain had stopped.

'The money's no problem,' he said, changing the subject. 'That envelope I asked you to find. It's . . .' He shrugged, '. . . all there.'

Barry was getting into his car. Kingdom could see Ernie in the front window, staring out, one thin hand raised.

'You back tomorrow?' Kingdom said. 'Only I should give you a key.'

Barry wound down the car window and smiled. 'I've already got one,' he said, nodding at Ernie and lifting a hand in response to the old man's wave.

*

135

Next morning, Kingdom was at the bank by half-past nine. He gave Steve's replacement cheque to the woman at the counter and told her he needed the money transferred as quickly as possible. She told him there was a fee for express clearance, but even so, it would still take a couple of days. Kingdom frowned, looking at the cheque.

'Couple of days?' he said. 'But it's drawn on the same bank.'

'Makes no difference.'

'So what are you saying?'

'I'm saying it makes no difference.' The woman paused, then shrugged and slid off her stool. 'I'll just check,' she said. 'Maybe we could do something.'

She disappeared behind a partition. The ribbed glass blurred the outline of her body but Kingdom could see her bent over a computer screen. He watched her, thinking of Ernie again. He'd been up and dressed before Kingdom was properly awake. He'd even made them both a pot of tea. Barry was coming. Maybe they'd take a drive out towards Ongar, stop at a pub, have a pint or two. The woman returned. She was still holding the cheque. She gave it back to Kingdom.

Kingdom frowned. 'What's the problem?' he said.

The woman looked at him a moment, then nodded at the cheque. 'That account's empty,' she said.

'Meaning?'

'Your cheque just bounced.'

PHASE TWO

CONSERVATIVE CENTRAL OFFICE

32 SMITH SQUARE, LONDON SWIP 3HH

TELEPHONE: 071 222 9000

<u>BY FAX</u>

27 September 1993

My dear Hugh,

I write in connection with our Sabbathman friend. Today's
departure of <u>The Citizen</u> from the orthodox editorial line is,
to put it mildly, unhelpful. Whilst in no ways seeking to
compromise the newspaper's independence, might it not be
productive to interest Mr Grant in an alternative approach?

Andrew Hennessey
Controller, Special Projects

PRELUDE

The first time she saw him, she thought nothing of it. Another bird-watcher. Someone else with a flask of coffee, and sensible camou-flage, and a pair of powerful binoculars. Someone else dug in for the day, making the most of the glorious September weather.

An hour later, he was still there, tucked into a hollow amongst the saltmarsh, a small khaki rucksack by his side. This time, she took a closer look. He was wearing jeans and some kind of smock. The smock was olive green, but she only saw the back of it because he was looking out to sea, away from the estuary and the teeming flocks of waders that were feeding on the exposed mudbanks. She thought this a little odd, and she tried to follow his eyeline with her own binoculars, wondering what she'd missed. Maybe the greenshanks and godwits were arriving early. Or maybe he was simply looking for something else.

She adjusted the focus on her binoculars, and a distant blur resolved itself into a motor cruiser. The boat had just entered the buoyed channel that dog-legged into the river mouth. It was modest in size, sturdily built, with an open cockpit at the back and a rubber dinghy bobbing in the wake. She knew virtually nothing about boats, and this one looked much like the others she'd seen already, butting upriver on the flooding tide.

She went back to the figure in the saltmarsh again, still curious. He was kneeling over the rucksack. He'd taken something out, something small and square and black. Funny colour, she thought, for a sandwich box.

A cormorant passed her, flying low, hugging the shoreline, and she followed it with her glasses for a full minute, forgetting about the sandwich box and the man in the saltmarsh, fascinated as always by the flight of the bird, how sure it was, how certain, suddenly climbing for height, scanning the water below, then plunging down for a fish or a sand-eel. She fiddled with the focus again, waiting for the cormorant to surface, distracted by a gaggle of oystercatchers pecking at the nearby mussel beds.

She could hear the motor cruiser now, the solid thump-thump of a diesel engine. She looked round. It was nearly abreast of her, no more than a quarter of a mile away across the marram grass. Here, the channel was narrowed by a series of exposed mudbanks. On the Exmouth side of the channel, the beach was dotted with people. Bodies sprawled in deckchairs. Kids playing football. Even the odd swimmer.

She trained her glasses on the little motor cruiser. There was a man in the cockpit. He was wearing a white pullover with a deep 'V' neck and he had a little red hat on the back of his head. He was standing up, one hand on the wheel, the other nursing a mug of something or other. Idly, she began to wonder where he was heading, where he'd come from, how long he'd been at sea, when the image abruptly disappeared. In its place, a monstrous blossom of flame, growing and growing, and a second or two of silence before the roar of the explosion rolled over her, and the ground shook beneath her feet and the air was suddenly full of the flap-flap of beating wings.

She gasped, finding herself flat on her face, her mouth full of sand, a ringing in her ears. Slowly, with great care, she raised her head above the lip of the hide. Where the motor cruiser had been there was nothing but wreckage and a glassy pool of spreading oil. On the beach beyond, through the billowing smoke, she could hear someone screaming. She blinked, not quite able to believe it, wondering about the man in the saltmarsh, whether he was alright.

She reached for the binoculars again, trying to find him,. but when she finally managed to steady her shaking hands, the hollow in the saltmarsh was empty and the man had gone.

SIX

Two days after the Exmouth explosion, Tuesday 28 September, Annie Meredith was sitting in a small French restaurant in North London. Across the table, his back to the wall, was a man in his late thirties. He was slightly built, with a pale, freckled face and carefully parted sandy hair. His name was Willoughby Grant, and he was the founder and editor of *The Citizen*.

Grant broke open his second bread roll and smeared the inside with butter. For a thin man, he seemed to have a ravenous appetite.

'But didn't you see the pictures?' he said, 'on TV?'

'Of course I did. Everyone did. The whole country did.'

'And you think we're in business to ignore all that? You think we'd lead with anything else? Given the . . .' he looked up, licking the butter off his fingers, '. . . inside track?'

'No, that's not my point. It's just . . .' Annie frowned, leaning back from the table to let the waiter take her plate, '. . . the way you're starting to handle it, the way . . .'

She looked at the man across the table, annoyed with herself, trying to think of a better phrase. The brief, after all, had been explicit. Get hold of Willoughby Grant. Invite him to lunch. Befriend him. Flatter him. Seed the conversation with the odd hint, the odd whisper. Make him feel trusted. Make him feel part of the operation. Get him *onside*, for God's sake.

Annie reached for the bottle of Chablis. Most journalists she'd ever met liked a drink, though in Grant's case she'd seen little sign of it. In fact he'd barely finished his first glass.

'More?'

Grant shook his head, covering his glass with his hand.

The choice of restaurant, La Petite Marmite, had been his. It was off the beaten track, out in the wilds of Highgate. Evidently he used the place a good deal.

'I'm still none the wiser,' he said, 'about why you asked me out. We're quite happy dealing with your people through the usual channels. Anyone else, for that matter. Police. CID. Special Branch. So,' he smiled, 'why the invite?'

'I told you. I thought we might talk.'

'About what?'

'About this morning's paper.' Annie reached for her calfskin briefcase and slid out a copy of that morning's *Citizen*, laying it carefully on the table between them. Two days after the explosion, Grant was still milking the incident for all it was worth. On Sunday, his stringer in Exeter had bought up the world rights to video footage shot by a weekend tripper on the beach. The footage, highly graphic, had shown the first rescue helicopters dipping over the wreckage minutes after the explosion. Grant had sold the pictures to TV outlets all over the world, but had saved the best sequence for his own paper the next day. The picture had nearly filled Monday's front page, a grainy close-up of divers manhandling a pathetic bundle of flesh and rags, all that was left of the boat's owner. Over the picture, the headline had read: HOW DARE THEY?

The picture on the front page of the paper on the table, a day later, was equally stark. It showed a middle-aged woman in a state of near collapse. Her name was Nicola Lister and she'd been waiting for her husband on a quayside four miles upriver from the scene of the explosion. The woman's face was contorted with grief. She'd just been told about her husband's death and she was plainly in shock. In its own way, the picture was as horrible as Monday's front page, but the tone of the headline had changed completely. Instead of the ritual outcry at yet another terrorist killing, it had pointed the finger at someone totally new. MR ANGRY, it asked, ARE YOU WATCHING?

Grant bent forward across the table. He looked, if anything, proud of himself.

'Well?' he said, 'Anything the matter with that?'

'Not really. Except it's wrong.'

'You read our piece inside? Page two?'

'Of course.'

'And you still think we're wrong?'

'Yes.' Annie nodded. 'That's what I keep telling you. That's why I'm here.'

Grant smiled benignly, shaking his head, leaning back in his chair, and Annie studied him a moment, wondering yet again about the paper he so obviously babied from edition to edition. *The Citizen* had been on the news-stands for less than a year, but already it was a legend in the industry. No one in his right mind launched new titles any more, not in the middle of a recession, yet somehow this pale, freckled, slightly stooped figure had pulled it off. The Registry personal file that Annie had read had been less than helpful, a terse recitation of the facts. Willoughby Grant had a background in television. He'd cut his teeth on current affairs documentaries. Then he'd edited a highly successful morning show, building a reputation for bold new formats. He'd taken some of them to the States and made a great deal of money. Yet everywhere he'd been, all those places he'd worked, he'd left very little behind him, no fund of stories, no scandal, no fervour, no hatred, no adulation. Just mountainous viewing figures, a healthy balance sheet, and a couple of phone numbers in case anyone came up with a great new idea.

Annie glanced down at the paper again. *The Citizen*, Grant's latest brainchild, was brash, tasteless and thick-skinned. It never pulled back and it never apologised. Media buffs and sundry lawyers predicted disaster every week, yet every rule it broke, every finger it poked in society's eye, attracted more readers. In some strange way, it seemed to have caught the public mood. The country was stuffed. The gloves were off. It was time, courtesy of *The Citizen*, for some straight talking. Nice idea.

'You really think it's some loony?' Annie said. 'This Sabbathman?'

Grant smiled again. 'Yes,' he said.

'Then why have you been pushing the Northern Ireland line? Until now?'

'Because we didn't think hard enough. Because we were running with the pack.'

'And this psychiatrist person you've found, the one you feature on page two, he's changed all that?'

'Yes.' Grant reached for another roll. 'Are you sure you've read it?'

Annie nodded, ignoring his invitation to take a second look. The drift of the piece was infantile, some provincial shrink invited to cobble together a description of the would-be killer. The profile he'd handed to the paper talked of 'The Rambo complex', and 'Hungerford-by-instalments', and predicted the probability of more bloodshed to come. The man was dangerous. The man was outraged. Killing meant nothing to him. One of the subs had evidently dubbed this invention 'Mr Angry', and Willoughby Grant had promptly put him on the front page. Now, ten hours later, his enthusiasm was undimmed.

'A bottle of Krug says I've got it right, OK?' Grant tapped the morning's headline. 'Bloke gets fed up, like we all do. Writes to the papers, phones his MP, gets nowhere.'

'What's he fed up about?'

'Doesn't matter. I can think of a million things. So can you. So can anyone. Politicians. Taxes. The weather. The point is, he's fed up. Period.'

'Mr Angry?'

'Exactly.'

'So he starts killing? Murdering people? In cold blood?' She gazed at him, 'Is that the way it goes?'

'Yes.'

Annie began to laugh. A passing waiter glanced down at her and Annie nodded at the wine list.

'A bottle of Krug,' she said, 'on Mr Grant.'

The waiter looked inquiringly at Grant.

Grant shook his head. 'You can do better?' he said.

'Yes. As it happens.'

'Go on, then.'

'Off the record?'

Grant conceded the condition with a shrug. 'If you like.'

Annie leaned forward, recognising the chance at last to plant her precious seeds. Not too much, the Controller had said, and not too many. But enough to stuff the genie back in the bottle and get the bloody politicians off the hook.

'OK,' Annie said, 'this is for background only. Things are

happening in Northern Ireland. There's a genuine move towards peace. It hasn't surfaced yet but it's there.' She paused. 'The IRA people have been talking to us.'

'Us?' Grant frowned. 'You mean Whitehall? Talking to the Provies?'

Annie nodded, glad that at least a little of the current affairs journalist had survived in Willoughby Grant.

'Yes,' she said, 'believe it or not, yes.'

'Why? What's in it for us? Who'd ever do it? Why take the risk?'

'Money. The bombs in the City really hurt us. The figures you've seen are underestimates. We're talking billions.'

Grant reached for his wine glass, touching it speculatively, like a man suddenly confronted by a long-forgotten friend.

'Am I supposed to believe this?' he said slowly. 'The Brits forced to the table?'

'Yes. But that's not the point. The Provos are split. The peace faction want to make history. The hardliners still want to make war. It's become a way of life for them. They'd be lost without it.' She paused. 'So the bad guys are looking for opportunities, mischief, anything, any alliance, to strangle the peace talks at birth.'

'And you're saying Sabbathman . . .?'

'I'm saying nothing. Because right now we don't know. Not for sure. And that's being totally honest. But we're finding out.' She paused again. 'That's all I can say. Apart from the obvious, of course.'

'Obvious?'

'What happened on Sunday. A planted charge. Detonated by radio signal.' She smiled. 'Ring any bells?'

Grant looked briefly hurt, then smothered a yawn. 'You mean Mountbatten?'

'Yes.'

Grant nodded. Monday's papers, in the immediate aftermath of the Exmouth explosion, had been full of reminders about the way the Provisionals had disposed of the Queen's cousin, fourteen years ago, blowing up his fishing boat off the coast of Western Ireland. The technique had been identical and the Monday broadsheets had run weighty articles analysing the various parallels. In parts of Whitehall, including Gower Street, there'd even been talk of 'the missing piece of the jigsaw' and 'conclusive proof'.

Annie fingered the wine list. Krug was on page three.

'Well?' she said. 'You can't just dismiss it.'

'We didn't. We mentioned it yesterday.'

'I know. Three lines. I counted them.'

Grant ignored the dig, sipping his Chablis, deep in thought. Finally, he shook his head. 'No one's interested in Ireland any more,' he said. 'I think I'll stick with Mr Angry.'

The main course arrived. Grant was having Dover Sole but he only played with it, picking at the flakes of pale flesh, building walls of mashed potato with his fork, making little ponds of melted butter, leaning back to admire the effect. Annie did her best to steer the conversation back to Northern Ireland but Grant wasn't interested. The story, he kept repeating, was Mr Angry. That was the angle they were working on now. That was the line that would put them ahead of the competition. That, and of course the communiqués, the paper's exclusive link to the mysterious Sabbathman.

'But he hasn't been in touch,' Annie said. As far as I'm aware.'

'I'm sorry?' Grant glanced up. He'd been planting sprigs of parsley in the mashed potato, trying to make them stand upright.

'The communiqués,' Annie repeated, 'those messages you've been getting. The ones we've seen. The ones you've put in the paper.'

Grant nodded. His hand reached for his own briefcase. He pulled out an envelope and passed it across.

'Sorry,' he said again, 'meant to show you earlier.'

Annie opened the envelope. Inside was a single sheet of paper. She glanced up. 'Is this the original?'

'No. That should be with Scotland Yard,' Grant glanced at his watch, 'about now.'

'So how did you get hold of it?'

'It came by post.'

'This morning?'

'Yes.' Grant looked pained. 'Terrible service from the West Country. Even first class.'

'What was the postmark?'

'Dawlish. It's just down the road from . . .' he smiled, '. . . where it happened.'

Annie looked at him a moment, wondering how much to believe. Getting the message late meant extending the story for yet another day. More headlines. Another nice idea. Grant was still watching her.

'Read it,' he said, 'then we might talk about Mr Angry again.'

Annie unfolded the sheet of paper. She recognised the typeface at once. Same machine. Same spacing. *Farewell then, Mr Lister,*' it read, '*£160,000 in share options. Thirty-eight per cent increase in salary. And all for flogging water. Obscene money, Mr Lister, which is why I decided to disconnect you. Even with your lucky hat on.*' Annie looked up. Jonathan Lister had been Chief Executive of the region's recently privatised water company. There'd been a storm of protest about the size of local bills but no one, to Annie's knowledge, had yet suggested Semtex.

Annie read the note a second time. 'May I keep this?'

'Of course.'

Annie folded the sheet of paper and laid it beside her plate. Grant was watching her.

'Well?'

'Perfect,' Annie lifted her wine glass, an ironic toast, 'fits your Mr Angry like a glove.'

'Exactly. You believe me now?'

'No.'

'Why not?'

Annie didn't answer, putting her glass down again, beginning to wonder for the first time whether this strange man and his silly paper might not, after all, have got it right. Not Willoughby Grant's little fiction, of course. Nothing as simple as Mr Angry. But maybe one man. One man with a lot of back-up. One man with nothing to do with Northern Ireland.

She looked up. 'Why the hat? What did he mean by the hat?'

'It was Lister's lucky charm. He only wore it to sea. He said it kept him safe.'

'Who knew that?'

'Most of the workforce. Apparently it had been in the company rag.' He paused. 'And his wife, of course. She knew.'

'I don't imagine she did it.'

'No,' Grant looked grave, 'wrong sex.'

'I'm sorry?'

'Mrs Angry? I hardly think so. Hasn't got quite the same ring. Lacks impact.' He spread his hands wide. 'No offence.'

Annie looked at him for a long time, trying to separate the whimsy from the hard-nosed journalist that she knew must be in there. At the Gower Street morning conference, when she'd raised the question of tactics, her controller had been impatient, almost dismissive. If Downing Street wanted Willoughby Grant pulled into line, then so be it. It wouldn't be a drama. It wouldn't even be difficult. Any journalist, he'd assured Annie, would jump at the Irish exclusive, even if it was embargoed until later. That's what they all wanted. That's what made these people tick. A little flattery. A little self-importance. A week or two in the front circle. It had worked before and it would doubtless work now. At the time, listening to the theory, Annie had simply nodded in mute agreement but now she knew the Controller had been wrong. Willoughby Grant was different. He didn't respond to any of the normal blandishments. No one could rein him in. He was well and truly off the leash.

'Tell me something,' Grant was saying, 'Why are your lot so upset by Mr Angry? Why is he such a threat?'

'He kills people,' Annie said simply.

'No, I meant our Mr Angry. The way we ran it this morning.'

'That's no threat.'

'Yes it is. That's why you're here. That's why they sent you. They're trying to warn us off. Not that we'll take any notice.'

He looked across at her, waiting for an answer. Annie, for once, refused to meet his eyes.

'Listen,' she said at last, 'the point about your Mr Angry is simple. The theory's wrong. That's all I came to say.'

Grant thought about it for a while, eyeing his plate. Then he shook his head. 'No,' he said, 'the point about Mr Angry is that he sells papers. It doesn't matter whether we're right or wrong. We're not talking right or wrong. If you're interested in all that then you go and buy some other paper.' He paused. 'Don't you?'

'I've no idea. I read the *Daily Telegraph*.'

'There you are then. You want a laugh, you read our paper. You want to get mad, have a cry, you come to us. The rest of it . . .' He shrugged. 'It's a free country.'

'Meaning?'

'Meaning we carry on building the story. I've a feeling we might be hitting a nerve. Our Mr Sabbathman. Our Mr Angry.' He smiled. 'Have you seen the figures? The copies we've put on? Since Wednesday? How can we afford to drop a campaign with figures like that?'

'*Campaign?*'

'Yes.' Grant began to laugh, summoning the waiter at last, ordering the champagne. 'Believe me, you ain't seen nothing yet.'

Annie was back in Gower Street by half-past three. 'T' Branch, the recently-formed counter-terrorist department, occupied a drab suite of offices on the fourth floor. Since her return from Belfast, Annie had been assigned a cubby hole across the corridor from the Controller's office. The place was tiny – a single desk, a telephone, a battered grey filing cabinet, a newish safe – but to have an office of your own was a sure sign of status, and Annie was glad of the privacy.

She shut the door and dialled a four-digit number on the internal network. Her controller had told her to ring as soon as she returned, and he answered the phone at once. His name was Francis Wren, a 54-year-old, unmarried, cautious, one of the few of the MI5 old guard who'd managed to survive the Thatcher administration. Annie had worked for him now for nearly two years, and rather liked him. He was honest, and painstaking, and his office nickname – 'Jenny' – did him less than justice.

Now, he sounded irritable and out of breath. He was over at Thames House, the new MI5 headquarters on Millbank. The place was still being fitted out, and he was trying to secure some last-minute changes to the 'T' Branch office layout. Negotiations were obviously going badly.

Annie described her lunch with Willoughby Grant. She said he'd no intention of abandoning Mr Angry. On the contrary, he was evidently destined for greater things.

She paused. 'But why is it so important?' she queried. 'Why does it matter?'

She heard Wren smothering one of his little coughs. It meant that the question was unwelcome, ill-advised, and Annie thought again about the conversation they'd had earlier on, prior to the lunch, when he'd briefed her on the line she should take. Even Wren himself had seemed uncomfortable with the Northern Ireland leak.

'I tried,' she said, 'I really tried. But he just wasn't interested. It's all about sales figures. Money. Circulation. The facts don't bother him either way.'

There was another silence and Annie wondered for a moment whether Wren was still there.

'I went to the briefing this morning,' he said at last, 'at the Yard. As far as I can gather, Allder's put himself in charge of more or less everything.'

'Oh?' Annie frowned. 'What did he say?'

'Not a great deal. The Devon and Cornwall people are doing what they can but there's not much to get excited about. Not so far.'

'What about the woman that came forward? The bird-watcher you mentioned?'

'She's made a statement and they've got a description of sorts. They're circulating details but no one's come forward yet. No other sightings that I'm aware of.'

'And the marina? At Torquay? Where Lister kept the boat?'

'More inquiries. Our friend obviously gained access at some point or other but no one seems to have seen anything.'

'No evidence on the boat itself?'

'Hardly.'

'I meant the wreckage. The bits and pieces they've recovered.'

'Oh, I see.' Wren hesitated. 'No, I don't think so.'

His voice faded and in the silence that followed Annie could hear the sound of men hammering.

'Anything on Lister?' she said brightly. 'Anything on the shelf?'

'Nothing. Except a great deal of money.'

'Accountable?'

'All of it. He did well out of privatisation, as you might have gathered.' He paused. 'Did Grant show you the latest? From our Sabbathman friend?'

'Yes. What did Allder make of it?'

'He said it was very interesting.'

'Is that all?'

'Yes.'

'And what do you think?'

'Me?'

There was a sigh and then he fell silent again. Annie tried hard to think of another question to ask, something that might ease whatever it was that deadened his voice. She'd never heard him so depressed.

'You're due at the Home Office at five,' he said at last. 'I gather it may go on a bit.'

Annie frowned. 'Home Office?'

'Yes.' Wren was brisk now, deliberately matter-of-fact. 'They've set up some kind of steering group. They're taking the whole business pretty seriously. It's standard procedure but I'm assured we have the inside track. Go through the master files. They're in your safe. And for God's sake don't let us down.'

Annie was still staring at the phone. 'But why me?' she said. 'Shouldn't you be there?'

Wren didn't answer for a moment. Then, for the second time, he changed the subject. 'There's a man called Cousins,' he said. 'He'll be opening the batting for us. He's young, and bright, and extremely forceful.' He paused, half a beat. 'I expect you'll like him.'

Annie spent a little over an hour with the master files. Building them up, one for each of the Sabbathman murders, had been Wren's responsibility and he'd guarded them with his usual manic dedication. On this and other operations, Wren always played the spider, crouched in the middle of the web, sensitive to the least vibration, analysing the raw data from the contact notes, weighing one piece of evidence against another, ruling out rogue factors, dismissing coincidence, looking all the time for that single chain of events that would enable him to make sense of everything else. It was a job he'd always done well but he favoured a particular style, an almost obsessive secrecy, that occasionally made him a difficult man to work for. Like many in the Service, he regarded information as power and he handed the stuff out in such tiny parcels that Annie sometimes found herself operating in a state of almost complete ignorance. Since she'd joined the department, she'd done her best to come to terms with it. To be working for 'T' Branch, the one arm of the Service that was still expanding, carried a certain cachet. But lately, since her promotion, the frustrations had started to get the better of her. She was good at taking a brief and turning it into a series of actions. She excelled at writing the subsequent report, with its annexe of 'bullet points'. But even now, when she was effectively Wren's deputy, her reports simply disappeared into nowhere. The bigger picture, hidden in the intricate lattice that was Wren's brain, remained a blur.

Annie shook her head, flicking through the master files, surprised at how thin they were. Wren, she'd begun to suspect, was on the skids, and the news that she was to represent him at the Home Office probably confirmed it. Quite what would happen to him she didn't know and in some respects she was surprised he'd survived so long. The Service was changing fast. The shock troops of the new Tory right had finally kicked the doors in and a new MI5 was emerging for the government to play with, still unaccountable, still beyond public reach, but nicely tuned in to the Downing Street line.

Wren hated it. She knew he did. She'd seen it in his eyes that very morning, the way he'd briefed her before she'd talked to Willoughby Grant, the way he'd shaken his head when she'd asked why they were going to all this trouble, the way he'd sidestepped the question again, just minutes ago when she'd tried to ask him on the phone. But men like Wren were in a time warp. To them, MI5 was still independent, still its own creature, the servant of Queen and Country, not the puppet of a government hell-bent on absolute power.

Annie smiled, closing the last of the files, wondering again what would happen to Wren. He'd be replaced, of course. Of that, she had no doubt. But in a way it was a blessing. He was an old man. He didn't belong in any of this. The world he'd known had gone. With luck, by Christmas, he'd be over the worst and planning a decent leaving party. Then he could do what they all did. Retire to Wiltshire and brood.

Annie took a cab to Queen Anne's Gate. The traffic, for once, was no problem and she found herself standing outside the Home Office with ten minutes in hand. She'd never liked the look of the building – its bulk, the big concrete overhangs, the tiny windows, the feeling that it was somehow impervious to daylight – and she crossed the pavement at once, showing her pass to the uniformed security man inside the door.

The reception area was dotted with padded benches and she was about to sit down when she noticed the man standing by the lifts. He was tall, and young, and she knew at first glance that she'd seen him before. He had a strong, square face and the kind of complexion that comes from prolonged exercise in the open air. He had short, blond, curly hair and over the check shirt and tweed jacket he wore a long, green Drizzabone raincoat, a cavalier touch amongst the neat grey suits and blank, carefully barbered faces.

He was reading a newspaper. He looked across at her and smiled. The lift arrived, and the doors opened, and he stood back, letting her in.

'Northern Ireland,' he said, as the lift purred upwards, 'last year.'

'Of course.' Annie nodded, putting her finger on it at last, Thiepval Barracks, the Army's headquarters in Lisburn. She'd seen him in the mess. Someone had pointed him out. They may have been introduced.

He was looking at her now, extending a hand. 'Hugh Cousins,' he said, 'in case you'd forgotten the name.'

The meeting took place in a conference room on the sixth floor. The room was dominated by a big octagonal table, and there was a series of ill-matched prints hanging on the walls. The windows were screened with venetian blinds and it was incredibly hot.

Annie counted the seats round the table. There were ten. Two of the seats were positioned just behind the rest and Annie sensed at once that one of them was hers. She eyed it speculatively. Cousins was talking to someone from the Ministry of Defence. The two men obviously knew each other well. A door opened at the other end of the room and a small posse of civil servants came in. An older woman in their midst went at once to the table and invited everyone to sit down. Annie felt a hand on her arm. Cousins shepherded her towards one of the spare chairs.

'Give me a dig when I get it wrong,' he murmured. 'I'll be asking you to talk about our friend.'

Annie glanced at him, thinking again about the master files. 'Sabbathman?'

'No.' Cousins smiled. 'Willoughby Grant.'

The meeting began. The woman from the Home Office introduced herself and established the ground rules. The Cabinet Office crisis committee, an organisation known as COBRA, had ordered the formation of a small sub-committee for the duration of what she termed 'the emergency'. The sub-committee, code-named PYTHON, was to exchange information and advise on various options. Her own task was to report back to her minister, who in turn would brief COBRA. The Cabinet were aware, above all, of the dangers of making a tricky situation worse. Public order and the safety of key individuals was paramount. Both, it was clear, were currently under threat.

She ended her opening remarks and introduced the representative from New Scotland Yard, Commander Michael Allder, head of the Anti-Terrorist Squad. A tiny man in an immaculate three-piece suit stood up, one hand in his trouser pocket. The spare chair, just behind his own, was still empty. He spoke from a neat pile of notes, a faint scowl on his face, and Annie listened as he briskly outlined the progress of the investigations to date. She'd never seen Allder in the flesh before and she smiled at the accuracy of Kingdom's descriptions. The way he stood, rocking back and forth on his feet. The way he used his hands, poking out one finger to emphasise a key point. The way he locked eyes with individual men and women around the table, staring them out with his slightly bulbous eyes until they finally gave in and looked away. He ended his report by acknowledging how little progress had, in fact, been made. Four separate police forces. Thousands of trained personnel. Hundreds of thousands of man hours. And not, so far, a single worthwhile lead.

When he sat down there was an audible murmur around the table and Annie watched the little policeman's face as he tried to mask a smile. He was just like Francis Wren, she thought. He'd left them exactly where he wanted. In a state of total ignorance.

The meeting came to order again and Hugh Cousins stood up. He talked easily, almost conversationally, the kind of voice you'd listen to in a crowded bar. He made a reasonably funny joke about marauding psychopaths, apologised to any ex-Paras in the room, and then took the committee smoothly through his own presentation. Unlike Allder, he invited their confidence. Unlike Allder, he asked them to share the challenge of penetrating what he called 'this curious conspiracy'. Regretfully, he said, MI5 had little hard data. As his colleague from the Yard had already established, there were no firm leads, nothing for the huge Curzon House computer to bite on.

They were, however, looking under certain stones. Some kind of Republican connection was an obvious starting point, and inquiries were under way on both sides of the Irish Sea. These inquiries, he said, were highly sensitive and the committee would forgive his reluctance to go into details, but certain developments did look promising. There were indications that certain hard-line Provisionals were trying to abort a move towards a ceasefire. There was evidence that they'd put a so-called 'lilywhite' into play, someone from the Republic, someone with no record on any UK computer, someone who might conceivably be linked to the latest wave of killings.

Cousins looked briefly down at Annie, and Annie found herself nodding in agreement. Quite why she did it, she didn't know but she sensed that this powerful, impressive young man, so different to Francis Wren, had exactly gauged the mood of the meeting. They were listening to him in a way that they hadn't listened to Allder. He'd taken them by the hand. He'd made them trust him. She glanced up at Cousins again, hearing her name. He was inviting her to report on her dealings with Willoughby Grant. She had, he said, 'coaxed him to the trough'.

161

Annie stood up. She'd never been frightened of speaking in public. On the contrary, she loved it. She loved the way it raised her pulse and quickened her wits. She loved the extra twist it gave to that spring she kept coiled inside her. Above all, she loved the knowledge that people were watching her, listening to her, the sole focus of their attention.

She described her conversation with Willoughby Grant. She kept the details brief and factual. She explained the genesis of Mr Angry and she passed on Grant's promise of more to come. For the first time, there was a question from the committee.

'What can we expect next? Can you be more specific?'

The question came from a young man sitting beside the woman who'd opened the meeting. He didn't bother with a name and neither did she. Annie looked across at him, remembering a phrase or two from Grant's file.

'I've no idea,' she said, 'and I suspect he doesn't either. He's very good at letting things develop. He has a knack of picking winners. He's nerveless, too. Doesn't panic under fire.'

'An opportunist, in other words.'

Annie nodded. In the young man's mouth, the description sounded like an insult.

'Yes,' she said.

'And he thinks Mr Angry's a winner?'

'Yes. Most definitely.'

'So we'll be seeing more of him?'

'I'm afraid so.'

The young man looked pointedly at Cousins. For someone his age, he seemed to have a great deal of authority.

'What do we have inside the building,' he inquired. 'At *The Citizen*?'

'Human sources? Or Sigint?'

'Either.'

Cousins glanced round the table, a man whose command of his brief was disturbed only by a sensible concern for discretion.

'We have both,' he said carefully. 'We have a woman on the subs' desk, plus a number of taps in place.'

'And?'

'Our source confirms what we've heard.' Cousins tilted his head towards Annie. 'This new angle's been around a couple of days and now they're all delighted with the result. They'll push it. There's no question about that.'

'Push it where? In what direction?'

'They don't know. And we can't say.' Cousins offered the committee a smile. 'Opportunism isn't an easy condition to deal with. The usual drugs don't work.'

There was a ripple of laughter. The young man was making notes. Then he whispered something in the older woman's ear, stood up, and left the room. The older woman introduced the man from the MOD and Annie sat down. Cousins turned to her as the man from the MOD began to outline contingency plans in the event of further killings. Annie thought she heard the phrase 'special forces' but she couldn't be sure.

'Drinks on me,' Cousins was whispering. 'You were brilliant.'

They walked to a pub off Buckingham Gate, a big old Victorian tavern already comfortably full. Cousins found a quiet table in the corner and Annie wriggled out of her coat while he queued at the bar for drinks. Her blood was still pumping from her moment of glory and she could feel the warmth in her face when he returned with the beers.

'You always drink pints?' he asked.

Annie nodded. 'On a good day,' she said, 'definitely.'

They talked for nearly an hour. Annie had been right about Francis Wren. He was being moved sideways, to a temporary position in 'A' Branch where he'd be compiling some kind of report on MI5's dealings with British Telecom. The phone tapping operation, Tinkerbell, had recently been attracting outside attention and it was Wren's job to find out why. It was obvious at once that the appointment was a major demotion, a hint – Annie assumed – that Wren should devote some serious thought to early retirement.

'He's a nice man,' she said for the second time, 'I like him.'

'I like him, too. But that's life. He's past his sell-by date. I'm just surprised he's hung on so long. You lose the appetite for it. And it pays to be hungry in this game.'

They exchanged glances and Cousins smiled. There was a sub-plot here, a reef beneath the conversation, and they both knew it. The lagoon's full of sharks, Cousins was saying. Weaken, and they'll have you.

'The guy on the committee,' Annie began, 'the one who asked me about Grant.'

'Andrew Hennessey. Tory Central Office.'

'A party worker?'

'Sort of. He heads something called Special Projects.'

'I see.' Annie nodded, surprised at the reach of the Tory political machine. Emergency committees like PYTHON offered a seat in the dress circle, ministers and key officials only. Riff-raff like Hennessey normally belonged at Tory headquarters in Smith Square, along with all the other party hacks. 'So why the questions?' she asked. 'How come they're all so worried about Willoughby Grant?'

Cousins didn't answer for a moment. His eyes were the lightest blue and he had the knack of holding her gaze without the slightest hint of aggression. It was a piece of body language that sat oddly with the SAS tie and Annie was fascinated by it.

'Downing Street have got the shits about all this,' he said, 'and Andy's the guy with the bucket and the mop.'

'But why Willoughby Grant? He's no threat, surely?'

'You're right. He's not. But Mr Angry . . .' Cousins shrugged. 'Who knows? Politicians are an odd bunch. You don't realise it until you meet them. They're like kids. Babies. Deeply insecure. They're in the popularity business. Forget all the stuff about tough decisions and taking the medicine, all that crap. They want to be loved. They need it. So Mr Angry makes them very nervous.'

'But he's inane.'

'Yes. But he'll be incredibly popular. Even in Downing Street they know it's all going wrong. They know they're hated. They know the country's in the shit. They call it voter-deficit. Come the next election, that'll be a posh word for losing.' Cousins balanced a beer mat on the edge of the table, and flipped it upward, catching it before it fell. 'Politicians hate losing,' he said, 'which is where we can sometimes help.'

'By trying to bribe Willoughby Grant?'

'By marking his card.'

'Same thing,' Annie smiled, 'isn't it?'

Cousins didn't say anything for a moment. Then he leaned forward across the table, lowering his voice, Mr Sincerity.

'I know what you mean, Annie, and I agree. Believe me, I do. Where I came from, no one cared less about politicians. We just did what we did. We got on with it. But this game . . .' He shook his head. 'It's different. They matter. You have to get to know them. You have to get to know the way they think, what frightens them, what turns them on.'

'Simple.' Annie grinned. 'Power. Getting it. And keeping it.'

'Sure.' Cousins nodded. 'But there's more to it than that. Think what you like, they *are* in touch. In fact they're probably *too* sensitive. Like I say, it's every little nuance. Every little breath of wind.' He paused. 'Papers like Grant's worry them a good deal. He can deliver, when he wants to. And other times, he can be a bloody pain. Which is why we want to nip Mr Angry in the bud.'

'So he is a threat?' Annie leaned forward, touching him lightly on the hand. 'Is that what you're saying?'

Cousins smiled at her, those same blue eyes, and reached for the beer mat again. 'Tell me about Flavius,' he said, changing the subject. 'Tell me what you made of us all.'

'How did you know about Flavius?'

'I read your file. This morning. Plus . . .' He fingered his tie. 'You made a bit of an impact. The blokes aren't blind. Far from it.'

Annie looked away a moment, warmed by the remark. Her first job for MI5 had been down in Spain, liaising between the SAS and the local intelligence people in Malaga. The Spaniards had mounted long term surveillance on three Provo terrorists planning a bomb attack on nearby Gibraltar. In the end, the operation code-named Flavius had been botched, three killings in broad daylight that had made headlines around the world, but the preceding months of patient preparation – laying out the bait, closing the trap – had been Annie's first taste of undercover work. She'd been amazed at the reach of MI5, the corners it could cut, the strokes it could pull, the rules it could ignore. Being part of all that, even as a lowly liaison officer, had given her a feeling of immense power.

'I loved it,' she said to Cousins. 'I truly loved it.'

'You were very good. From what I hear.'

'Well . . .' She shrugged. 'Whatever. But I thought it was amazing.'

'Better than real life?'

'Much.'

Cousins went back to the bar for some crisps and when he returned, Annie found herself telling him the rest of the story, starting way back, leaving school with 'A' level distinctions in French and German and a hunger to work abroad. She'd signed on with a big travel company, working for a pittance as a rep in Lloret de Mar. She'd been good at it – tireless, good-humoured, happy to cope with whatever came her way – and she'd soon found herself supervising other reps, first in Lloret, then throughout the Costa Brava. After Spain, she'd returned to London, hopping from company to company, learning the business from the inside. She'd ended up with the market leaders. They'd given her a car, and an office, and finally a brochure of her own, and by her twenty-ninth birthday she was one executive promotion away from a seat in the company's boardroom. At this point, typically, she'd resigned.

'Why?' Cousins asked.

'I got another offer. Big German firm.'

'More money?'

'A little. But lots of scope. Lots of responsibility. Starting a whole new operation from the ground up. Blank sheet of paper. Fantastic.'

She beamed at him, remembering it, reaching for her drink. Cousins smiled back.

'And then we came along?'

'Yes. A year or so later.'

'And wrecked it?'

Annie shook her head, returning the glass to the table. The approach from Gower Street had come out of the blue. She'd been at a travel fair in Frankfurt. They must have had an eye on her for a while. They'd taken her to the restaurant in the Sheraton-Century Hotel, two of them, a man and a woman from an executive recruitment outfit in London. They seemed to have known every last detail about her life: where she'd come from, the stops she'd made, the long list of battle honours on her professional CV.

Wherever she'd paused for breath – a new desk, a new company – they'd taken more soundings, and by the end of that long, long meal they'd made it plain that a job with MI5 was hers for the asking.

For reasons she'd never properly understood, Annie had found the offer immensely flattering, but she'd begun negotiating at once, leaving them with a series of stipulations. If they were serious about her talents – her languages, her drive, her track record, her singlemindedness – then it would have to be the fast lane. She didn't want to be moored to some desk or other, endlessly reviewing files. She didn't want to be snared by office politics, or any stone age ideas about the role of women. She wanted to be out there, doing it. She wanted to listen, and to learn, and in due course – take over.

Cousins blinked. 'Take over what?'

'The Service. The top job.'

'Are you serious?'

'Yes.'

'Still?'

'Of course. The D-G's a woman. Why not me?' Annie drained the rest of her pint. 'Not now, not yet, but one day . . .' She nodded. 'Sure, why not?'

They talked about Belfast, Annie more cautious now, sensing a new element in the conversation, a nerve in Cousins that her naked ambition seemed to have touched. The smile was a little less benign, a little less patronising, and when she brought the story up to date – nine months running agents of her own in Belfast – it vanished altogether.

'You've really seen my file?' she was asking.

'Yes.'

'And what did you think?'

'Impressive.' He nodded. 'Very.'

'What does that mean?'

Cousins shook his head, raising his glass, refusing her the satisfaction of an answer. Soon afterwards, the pub noisy now, he semaphored that he had to go. Annie nodded as he stood up, shaking her head at the offer of another drink, mouthing goodbye. She watched him as he picked his way through the crowd, wondering if she'd already said a little too much for her own good. Cousins, after all, might be the new 'T' Branch Controller. It would be a wildly imaginative appointment, not at all Five's style, but she knew they were after fresh young blood, and she doubted whether blood came fresher than Cousins'.

She was still deep in thought when she felt someone nudge her chair. She looked up quickly. Alan Kingdom was standing behind her. He had two pint glasses, one in each hand. He put them carefully on the table, one in front of Annie, and sank into the other chair.

'So who was that?' He nodded towards the door. 'Friend or foe?'

SEVEN

SECURITY OFFICE

PO BOX 500, LONDON

Andrew Hennessey
Conservative Central Office
Smith Square
London SW1

29 September 1993

Dear Andy,

As you'll know from the PYTHON meeting, we did our best with Mr Grant but I suspect he puts readership before everything else. Indeed internal sources at <u>The Citizen</u> have now confirmed that he has no intention of changing the editorial line.

There are, of course, other ways of applying pressure but I'd need formal guidance from an appropriate political source before I could sanction further measures.

Best regards,
Yours sincerely,

Hugh Cousins

Kingdom was drunk before he admitted that he'd followed her to the pub from the Home Office. Annie studied him carefully over the remains of her Chicken Masala. They were in an Indian restaurant off the Fulham Road. The place was nearly empty.

'How come?' she said. 'How did you know I'd be there?'

'I didn't. I was supposed to be at the meeting. With the Guv'nor. I got there late.' He looked at her. 'An hour late.'

Annie nodded, remembering the empty seat behind Allder. 'I'm not sure you missed much.' She tidied the rice on her plate. 'So where were you?'

'At the bank,' Kingdom said thickly, 'with my bank manager. Discussing Dad.'

'On the firm's time.'

'Yeah.'

'Why?'

Kingdom lifted a weary hand, trying to attract the waiter's attention, signalling for more lager. So far, including the pub, Annie had counted seven pints. When the waiter came over, she let him take her empty glass.

'Your dad?' she said to Kingdom.

'Yeah?'

'You were talking to the bank manager?'

'Yeah.'

'Why?'

Kingdom studied the tablecloth for a while. Where his plate had been, there was a neat circle of yellow stains.

'I was relying on some money,' he said at last. 'It didn't happen. It's not going to happen. It's gone.'

'Steve? Your brother-in-law?'

'Yeah. He's in the shit. Like everyone else. Business problems. He's down to his last swimming pool. Sad.' Kingdom shook his head. 'Fucking sad.'

'And your dad?'

'My old dad? He needs looking after. I've found the guy. Mr Right. No question about it. Barry. Believe me, Barry is the biz. What he's done for Dad . . .' he shook his head again, looking up. 'You wouldn't begin to understand.'

'No?'

'No.'

'Not going to try me?'

'No.' Kingdom tried to flick a grain of rice off the tablecloth. 'No fucking way.'

Annie shrugged, easing her chair back, stretching her legs. She'd been this way with Kingdom before, occasional evenings in Belfast when huge doses of alcohol had unlocked a door inside him. In these moods, it always seemed to her that he viewed himself as spoiled goods, damaged in transit, one of life's casualties. It wasn't as simple, or pathetic, as self-pity. She wouldn't have tolerated that for a moment. No, it was something else, a sense of deep bewilderment, a conviction that he could have played things a little more cleverly, that he could have done better.

'Were you after a loan?' she said. 'At the bank?'

Kingdom was trying to find money to pay the bill. In the end, he gave the waiter a credit card. Then he reached for the lager the man had brought. He sipped it carefully, as if he hadn't seen a drink all evening, thinking about the question.

'Yes,' he said at last, 'I was. Eight thousand quid. Secured on yours truly. My salary . . .' He looked up, wiping his mouth. 'And my prospects.'

'And what did he say?'

'He asked me what for, what I needed the money for. I told him it was for Barry and Dad. I explained it all. Everything. Everything that little man means to him.'

'And what did the bank manager say?'

Kingdom adjusted his chair, leaning back against the flock wallpaper. The candlelight deepened the hollows of his face, giving him a strangely vulnerable look, haunted and slightly manic.

'He said it was a lousy investment. Not in so many words. Not that phrase exactly. But that's what it boiled down to. That's what he meant.' He nodded. 'My dad. His sanity. A lousy investment.'

'So how long would eight thousand pounds last?'

'A year. Barry and I had sorted it out. Eight thousand for cash. Nothing on top for the agency. He said he'd have left the agency, and he would, too. He meant it. He'd have given Dad a year of his life.' Kingdom's fingers crabbed back towards the grain of rice. 'He's got a family, this man, you know that? Kids of his own to feed. Responsibilities. Yet he'd still have done it. A whole year. Eight grand. Guy's a real Christian.'

'And the bank manager?'

'Turned me down. Gutless bastard.'

Annie reached out, touching Kingdom's face. 'It's a fortune, my love,' she said softly. 'He has bosses of his own to answer to. That's the way it works now. I'm not surprised he turned you down.'

Kingdom stared at her, motionless. 'His words exactly.' He nodded. 'The bit about the bosses.'

They drove west, out through Hammersmith, Annie at the wheel of her new Escort Cabriolet. Kingdom had phoned his father from the restaurant and Barry had answered. He and Ernie had been to the dogs, over at the Walthamstow track, and Ernie had even won a quid or two. When Kingdom said he was tied up, back late, Barry had said not to worry. Ernie would be fine. If necessary, he'd even stay the night.

Now, Kingdom sat hunched in the passenger seat, his collar turned up, his face pale under the passing street lights.

'I was watching you in the pub,' he said. 'I was there all the time. Funny, isn't it? I couldn't help myself.'

'What does that mean?'

'I dunno.' He didn't look at her. 'So who was he?'

'A friend,' she said, 'I think.'

'Known him long?'

Annie shrugged. 'About an hour and a half.'

Kingdom nodded, saying nothing. It was early, not yet ten, and the traffic was still heavy, heading out of London. At Chiswick, Annie turned left, crossing the river. She had a top floor flat in a quiet cul-de-sac near Kew Gardens. Kingdom had stayed there before.

'Funny,' he said at last, breaking the silence, 'I felt quite jealous.'

'When?'

'In the pub. Watching you two together.'

'You shouldn't.' She glanced across at him. 'There's no one else, I promise. Not as far as I'm concerned.'

'You mean apart from you?'

Annie said nothing, ignoring the taunt. Kingdom leaned forward, reaching for the radio. There was a cassette already loaded in the player, Puccini, *La Bohème*, and he listened to it for several minutes before turning it off again.

'His name's Hugh Cousins,' he said quietly, 'and you want to be fucking careful.'

'How did you know that?'

'I phoned Allder from the pub. I'm not stupid.' He looked at her a moment. 'This liaison thing's a joke. We all know that. Me, Allder, you, but there are lots of other things happening, my love, and Cousins is one of them. He'll be your boss by tomorrow. Did you know that?'

Annie was trying to overtake a lorry. When a bus appeared in the road ahead, she pulled back in.

'Sort of,' she said, eyeing the mirror, letting the bus sweep past, then trying again.

Back at the flat, Annie made coffee. When she brought the mugs through to the living room, Kingdom's long body was sprawled across the carpet, his eyes closed, his head pillowed on his arms. She found mats for the mugs and then knelt down and loosened his shoes. The room was cold and she lit the gas fire, kneeling beside it, warming her hands.

'Who's peddling the line about Northern Ireland?' Kingdom said softly. 'Is it a career move? Is it you?'

'No.'

'Who, then?' Kingdom opened one eye.

Annie shook her head, refusing to answer. 'Your coffee,' she said. 'It's getting cold.'

'Is it Cousins?'

'I can't say.'

'You're a fool, then.' Kingdom got up on one elbow. 'And you'll regret it.'

Annie nodded at the coffee. Kingdom was about to say something else. 'Don't,' she said.

'Don't what?'

'Don't talk about it. It's irrelevant. You do your job, I'll . . .' she shrugged, '. . . do mine. I'm perfectly capable of looking after myself. I've done it most of my life. If there's a real problem . . .' She smiled at him, reaching out. 'You'll be the first to know.'

Kingdom got up, still holding the coffee mug, and disappeared into the kitchen. Annie heard the clunk of the fridge door and the slurp of milk. When he returned, Kingdom had both hands round the mug. Annie made room by the fire.

'Cold?'

'Freezing.'

'Come here.'

Kingdom shook his head, sitting down on the sofa. Then he produced a piece of paper and gave it to her. Annie looked at it. It was a gas bill. On the back, in Kingdom's scrawl, was a telephone number.

'Zero seven zero five?' she said, looking up.

'Portsmouth. Subscriber by the name of Hubbard. I want you to do me a favour.'

'Alan—'

'No, listen, please. The number was wired last year, around November time. I don't know for how long. It may still be on. I think it was an A1A job.'

Annie looked at the number again. A1A was a section of 'A' Branch. They specialised in breaking and entering. They were the people you went to if you wanted a tap installed.

Kingdom sipped at the coffee. 'You'll have logs. There may be transcripts.'

'So what do you want?'

'Both.' He looked at her. 'Please.' He paused. 'I've put a request in through the usual channels but fuck all's happened.'

'Why's that?'

'You tell me.'

Annie frowned, eyeing the gas bill again. She gestured at the number. 'So who is this again?'

'Her name's Jo. Jo Hubbard. She's a young doctor.' He looked at his coffee. 'That's all you need to know.'

'And is she the subscriber?'

'As far as I know.'

'Have you met her?'

'Yes.'

Annie was still studying the number. 'And?'

Kingdom didn't reply but drained the rest of his coffee and joined her by the fire, warming his hands against the line of dancing flames.

'My Guv'nor says you've been lunching with the intelligentsia.'

Annie smiled. 'Willoughby Grant? He's weird. Not what I expected at all. I thought they all wore green eye-shades and threw things. This guy's still in the nursery.'

'Sharp, though.'

'Oh, yes, no question, very.'

'And right?'

'I doubt it.'

'You don't go along with Mr Angry?'

'No.'

'Why not?'

'Because . . .' She glanced across at him, still reluctant to pursue the conversation. 'He's a fiction. He's in the paper to get the punters going. Grant admits it.'

'And the rest of your mob? What do they think?' Annie didn't answer. Kingdom was still staring at the fire. 'You going to tell me?' he said at last.

'No.'

'Anything at all?'

'No.'

'Does that mean you buy the Irish line? Is that what you're saying?'

Annie folded the gas bill and gave it back to Kingdom. Then she stood up and yawned, loosening the belt on her dress. 'I'm going to bed,' she said.

Past midnight, Annie crept back into the living room. The lights were off and the curtains were pulled back but the gas fire was still on and she could see Kingdom's body curled on the hearth-rug. He was still fully clothed. His knees were tucked up to his chin and he'd thrust both hands between his thighs. She watched him for a full minute. Then she knelt beside him and began to cover his body with the spare duvet. She felt him twitch and then wake, one bloodshot eye staring up at her.

'If you really don't want to,' she said, 'at least keep warm.'

Kingdom grunted, pulling the duvet around him, closing his eyes again, not saying a word.

Next morning, Annie awoke with a start. The clock on the bedside table said 07.06. She could hear rain at the window and the rumble of the morning rush hour traffic down Sandycombe Road. She sat up in bed, peering into the living room through the open door. The curtains were closed again and the room was in near darkness but she could see no sign of Kingdom.

She got up and slipped into a dressing gown. Next door, the gas fire was off but still warm. She hesitated a moment, wondering how long Kingdom had been gone, then she went into the kitchen. The cereal packets were undisturbed and the kettle was stone cold. She filled it and plugged it in and she was still scissoring the top off the last carton of milk when she saw the gas bill. It was lying on the side, an egg cup on each corner. No message. No goodbye. Just the number: 0705 932851. She looked at it, remembering the name, Jo Hubbard, then she heard the rattle of the letter box down the hall. She glanced at the clock on the cooker, wondering why the postman had been so early, but when she got to the front door she found a folded newspaper waiting for her on the mat. She looked down at it, frowning. She never had the papers delivered. She always called at the newsagent at the bottom of the road.

She retrieved the paper and returned to the kitchen. It was a copy of *The Citizen*, the front page dominated by a grid of photographs. There were five in all. The first four contained head and shoulders shots of the known Sabbathman victims: the Jersey banker, the Newcastle civil servant, the south coast MP, and now Jonathan Lister. The fifth box was blank, just a silhouette head and shoulders. Inside the head was a huge question mark. Stripped across the top of the front page was the morning's headline, Willoughby Grant's wake-up call to the nation. *COME ON MR ANGRY*, it ran, *GIVE US A CLUE*.

Annie looked at it a moment, hearing Willoughby's voice in the restaurant, how gleeful he'd been, his beloved Mr Angry leading four million readers in a wild conga, away from the facts, away from the complications, away from the real world, back to the never-never land where *The Citizen* and its backers could make serious money. She began to laugh at Grant's chutzpah, and she realised again exactly what it was that had so unnerved the politicians. This man was beyond control. He simply didn't care.

The phone began to ring in the living room. When Annie answered it, she recognised the voice at once. Hugh Cousins.

'We need to talk,' he said crisply, 'this morning.'

'I know. I've just seen it.'

'Seen what?'

'Grant's rag.'

'Oh?'

Annie fetched the paper from the kitchen and began to describe the front page. When it occurred to her that Cousins wasn't interested, she stopped.

'There's something else?' she said.

'Yes. I'm camping at Euston Tower at the moment. Seventeenth floor. Room 1710. Meet me there at twelve.'

Annie took the tube to Gower Street and was at her desk by a quarter past nine. She tried Francis Wren's extension three times but it was nearly ten before he was there to pick up the phone. He sounded faint, as if the line was bad, and a night's sleep had done nothing for his morale. When Annie asked for ten minutes of his time, he sounded surprised.

'Of course,' he said. 'Now would be convenient.'

All the controllers occupied spacious offices on the Gower Street side of the building and one perk that came with promotion was the right to choose a colour scheme. Wren had settled for chocolate and cream, a combination that gave his office the feel of a 1930s railway waiting room, an exercise in nostalgia that somehow fitted the man to perfection.

Annie knocked and went in, taking a seat in front of the desk and waiting for Wren to finish reading his morning mail. On the way to work, strap-hanging on the tube, she'd wondered quite how to play it. The news of Wren's demotion was by no means official but it was clear to both of them what had happened.

'I'm sorry,' she said at last. 'It must be horrible.'

Wren reached for another letter with a barely perceptible shrug. Regardless of the hard truth about his sell-by date, Annie knew he was a proud man. He looked up at her. The hinge on his glasses was secured with sellotape.

'Not horrible,' he said, 'but not altogether pleasant, either.'

Annie smiled at the phrase. Typical understatement. Typical Wren. 'I'm sure,' she said again, 'and I'm truly sorry.'

'Thank you.' He offered her a bleak smile. 'How can I help?'

Annie opened the file she'd brought over. She'd transferred Kingdom's precious phone number and she quoted it now. Wren reached automatically for a piece of paper and wrote it down.

'And?' he said blankly.

Annie explained about the tap. There would surely be a log. There may even be transcripts. Might there be a chance of acquiring either? Or even both? Wren peered at her a moment over his glasses, still the boss, still the man who guarded the departmental purse. Laying hands on a phone transcript wasn't easy. All tapped calls were routed to BT's Gresham Street headquarters. Voice-activated tape recorders in the basement captured all outgoing and incoming calls on targeted numbers. Specially vetted transcribers spent their working lives typing transcripts. Because the system had proved so expensive, transcripts were only produced to order and every request had to be carefully justified.

Wren was looking at the number again. 'Should I ask why?' he said. 'Would that be a sensible question?'

'No.'

'I see.' He paused. 'What makes you think I have the inclination? Or, indeed, the opportunity?'

'I didn't mean . . .' Annie hesitated. 'I just thought . . . this new job of yours . . .'

She sealed the sentence with a grin. Wren liked her. She knew that. He liked her enthusiasm, and her energy, and her cheek. Once, at the Pig and Whistle, MI5's bar over at Curzon House, he'd even told her she'd make someone a nice daughter-in-law.

Now, he folded the number and slipped it into his pocket. For the first time, Annie saw the packing cases, stacked neatly beside the larger of his three filing cabinets. It meant that the navvies from Admin would be round soon, boxing twenty years of Wren's life and carting it away. If he had any sense, he'd take a holiday and let them get on with it. Florence, or perhaps Vienna. Somewhere with a bit of class.

Wren had inched his chair sideways and was gazing out of the window. Raindrops blurred the shape of a 747 breaking through the clouds, probing the flightpath into Heathrow.

'Seen the paper this morning?' he mused. 'Our friend Mr Angry?'

Annie nodded. 'First thing,' she said. 'It made me laugh.'

Wren glanced round. It was the first time she'd seen him smile for weeks.

'Me, too,' he said.

There was a silence between them. Then Annie stood up. She told him again how sorry she was to see him go and this time the awkwardness in her voice gave the phrase a real warmth. Wren smiled and waved his hand rather vaguely at the paperwork on the desk, a gesture – Annie thought – of stoicism, even relief. His time in the sun was over. The world had moved on. By the door, he called her back.

'How did you know I was going to Tinkerbell?' he said. 'That's supposed to be confidential.'

Annie tried to make light of it. 'In this building?' she said. 'Confidential?'

'I'm serious. Who told you?'

Annie looked at him a moment. The least she owed him, under the circumstances, was the truth. 'Hugh Cousins,' she said. 'He told me yesterday.'

'Ah . . .' Wren nodded, turning away again, gazing out at the rain. 'Our Mr Cousins.'

There was a long silence.

Then Annie stepped back into the room. 'That brief you gave me yesterday.'

'For our journalist friend?'

'Yes.' Annie nodded. 'Where did it come from?'

'Me.'

'But before that, before you? Who authorised the line about Whitehall talking to the IRA? Who's idea was that?'

Wren sighed, rearranging the pile of letters on his desk, and Annie knew she'd overstepped the mark. Nothing would soften Wren's reluctance to part with information. Not even now, when he was about to be put out to grass, joining the rest of the old guard in the paddock.

'Tell me about Cousins,' he said at last. 'Did you like him? Did you get on?'

'Yes.'

'And do you trust him?'

'I don't know,' Annie said truthfully, 'I suppose we wait and see.'

Wren sighed again. 'But nobody waits any more,' he said softly, 'and nobody sees.'

Annie got to Euston Tower prompt at noon. Room 1710 turned out to be two offices, and she sat with the secretary for five minutes before the inner door opened. She recognised Andrew Hennessey at once, the young man from Tory Central Office. She got to her feet, calling him by his Christian name, extending a hand. Hennessey had changed suits since the PYTHON meeting. Today he favoured a rather tweedy look which made his face seem even paler than yesterday's charcoal stripe had.

Annie nodded at the folded newspaper under his arm. Willoughby Grant's jaunty headline was clearly visible.

'My commiserations,' she said, 'but I did warn you.'

Hennessey pulled a face. 'Don't,' he said, stepping past her and sweeping out into the corridor.

Annie turned to find Cousins standing in the open doorway. He was wearing a pair of beautifully cut twill trousers and a light blue shirt. With his jacket off, he belonged in the pages of a men's fashion magazine, *GQ* perhaps, or *Esquire*. His face was pinked with colour and he looked newly washed, as if he'd just stepped out of the shower. He asked Annie into the office and shut the door behind her. He had a briskness she hadn't seen the previous evening and she wondered exactly what had passed between the two men before she'd arrived.

Cousins sat down behind the desk. He selected a file from a neat stack at his elbow and passed it across to her. She looked at it, recognising the name in the box on the front. Derek Bairstow, the civil servant knifed to death on the terraces at St James' Park.

'A little bit of give at last,' Cousins said, 'a little bit of movement.'

'I'm sorry?'

'Bairstow worked for the PSA. He was in charge of the department supervising the tender process. A great deal of money went through his hands.' He smiled. 'And a great deal didn't.'

Annie nodded, opening the file. The PSA was the Property Services Agency. They were part of the Department of the Environment and looked after hundreds of government buildings. Because they commissioned so much work from the private sector, the scope for corruption was immense.

Annie glanced quickly through the file while Cousins made a phone call. The northern outpost of the PSA was in Newcastle-upon-Tyne, and the bulk of the file had evidently come from the local Fraud Squad. They'd been conducting a covert investigation into corruption allegations for nearly a year, and Bairstow had been only days away from being arrested when he'd been killed.

In an annexe at the back of the file, Annie found a list of PSA contractors. There were more than ninety in all, ranging from a big civil engineering company in Croydon to a Hartlepool plumber bidding for the contract to lag pipes in a Young Offenders Institution. Someone had already been through the list with a green hi-lighter, and Annie looked up as Cousins replaced the phone and made a note on the pad at his elbow.

'O'Keefe?' she queried.

Cousins glanced down at the file on her knee. Then he nodded. 'Irish company. They make office furniture. Desks, chairs, storage cabinets, wooden stuff mainly. They've got a factory in Longford. That's in the Republic, of course.'

'But why the interest?'

'We're not absolutely certain,' Cousins pushed his chair back from the desk, and swivelled it slightly, 'but it looks like Bairstow had been ripping them off. When he called in tenders, he always asked for a sweetener. He called it a deposit. We know that for sure. He did it with everyone. Normally fifty quid. Regardless.'

'Of what?'

'The size of the contract. And it was non-returnable. That's the point. If you wanted to be in on the bidding, you had to pay the entry fee. To Bairstow. In person.'

'And O'Keefe?'

'Apparently got in a muddle. Thought it was five hundred pounds, not fifty.'

'And he paid it?'

'Yes.' Cousins nodded. 'He was bidding for a big job. One of the admin branches of the DoH had relocated up to the north. Hundreds of staff. Brand new premises' – he smiled – 'and lots of office furniture. The contract was worth £350,000 to O'Keefe. That's why he didn't bother too much about the five hundred quid.'

'But did he win? Did he get the contract?'

'No. It went to a Leicester firm. Their bid went in after O'Keefe's. Ten quid cheaper.'

'Ten pounds? In three hundred and fifty thousand?'

'Yes. They obviously knew O'Keefe's bid. I imagine Bairstow told them.'

'Why? Why would he do that?'

'Because they'd pre-agreed a deal with him. Three percent of the contract price.'

Annie frowned, trying to do the maths. 'Three per cent. That's . . .'

'Ten thousand five hundred quid. To an account at the Neue Allianz Bank,' he smiled again, 'In Zurich.'

Annie returned to the file, following the logic. Zurich was the city that had cropped up in Sabbathman's second communiqué, the one that had gone to Willoughby Grant. *But what's a guy like him doing,* he'd written, *with a season ticket to Zurich?*

Annie glanced up. 'So what happened to O'Keefe's five hundred pounds?'

'Nothing. Bairstow kept it. Evidently there was another big job coming up and he told O'Keefe to put another quote in. Under the circumstances O'Keefe could hardly rock the boat.'

'And this second job? Did O'Keefe get it?'

'No. It went to the same Leicester firm.'

'On the same terms?'

'I imagine so.'

'But . . .' Annie frowned. 'Is five hundred pounds enough to kill for?'

'It wasn't just the five hundred pounds. O'Keefe believed he'd got the second contract. He thought it was in the bag. He'd put in forward orders. He'd risked a lot of his own money. He came out tens of thousands down.'

'And Sabbathman? Where's he supposed to . . .'

Cousins stood up, turning his back on Annie, staring out of the window. The rain had stopped now, and sunshine puddled the green swell of Hampstead Heath.

'Longford's a political town,' Cousins said, 'strongly republican. O'Keefe's the kind of man to carry a grudge. If you were putting together a hit list, if you were looking for names . . .' He shrugged. 'You could do worse than pencil in Derek Bairstow.' He turned round, leaning back against the window-sill. 'It's a clever campaign. Four killings so far, all of them public figures, none of them very popular. Think about it, Annie. A banker, who likes bankers? A civil servant on the take. A right-wing MP, one of the real ultras. And now a man who's making a small fortune out of water. *Water*, for God's sake. No wonder Willoughby Grant's rubbing his hands.'

'Are you serious? The Provos? Playing Robin Hood?'

'Absolutely. See it their way. They'll be mobbed in the street. No civilian casualties. No kids hurt. Just the guys you love to hate. Knocked off one by one. To order. Have you seen this?'

Cousins opened a drawer, forestalling any more questions, and slipped out a sheaf of contact notes. He glanced quickly through them, then gave them to Annie.

'The top one,' he said, 'that's all you need.'

Annie read the note. It carried yesterday's date. It had come from the agent handling the source inside *The Citizen*, the journalist on the subs desk who was passing on Willoughby Grant's latest thoughts on Mr Angry. Evidently Grant was contemplating a national competition. Readers would be invited to nominate Sabbathman's next victim. Contenders, in Grant's phrase, had to be 'fully paid-up members of the rip-off society'. The name of the winning nomination would be published, an implicit invitation for Mr Angry to do his worst.

Annie looked up. The very crassness of the idea made her smile. 'When does he plan to publish?'

'Nobody knows. I gather he's run into legal problems. There's a feeling on the Board that he may be inciting murder. Grant says they've lost their bottle and he's probably right. None of them are keen on a gaol sentence.'

'I bet.'

Annie returned the contact notes, thinking about Cousins' theory again, that Sabbathman might somehow be a proxy for the Provisionals.

'So you think someone's running Sabbathman from Belfast?' she said slowly, making no attempt to hide the scepticism.

'Yes.' Cousins nodded. 'That's exactly what I think. At the moment they're playing with us. Hints and guesses. No phone calls afterwards. No code-words. None of the usual stuff. Just good, solid professional hits.' He slipped into the chair, leaning forward towards her, a man determined to prove his point. 'Isn't that what they've always been good at? In Belfast? Good approach work? Good dickers? Good back-up? The weapon off in one car? The hit man off in another? Eh? Then there's Lister, the boat down in Devon, identical to the Mountbatten hit, *identical*.' He paused. 'These guys have a sense of humour. They're trailing their coats. To them, it's a game. Hide and seek with a difference. Believe me, they're loving it.' He leaned back in the chair, watching her carefully. 'You seriously think it could be anyone else?'

Annie had gone back to the file. 'How about the others?' she said. 'The other names in here?'

'The Fraud Squad are checking them out, but they don't stack up.'

'And O'Keefe? Are we saying he's active? Or a sympathiser? Or what?'

Cousins hesitated a moment, looking at her. 'You're very blunt, aren't you?'

'Yes. Annie nodded. 'I find it pays in the end. Especially in this building.'

'I can imagine.'

'Yes.' Annie smiled. 'I expect you can. So,' she tapped the file, 'tell me about O'Keefe.'

'He's a businessman. Longford born and bred. The town's rock solid Fianna Fail and he's one of the biggest wheels. Make of that what you will.'

The phone rang again and Cousins reached back, lifting the receiver, listening, his eyes still on Annie. Annie ignored him, thinking about Desmond O'Keefe. Fianna Fail was the party of Eamonn de Valera, the guardians of the republican flame. They'd spent most of the last decade in office and they were pledged, one day, to extending Dublin's rule to the Six Counties in the north. Deep down, they'd always hated the Brits, and getting screwed by the likes of Derek Bairstow would – for O'Keefe – be yet more evidence of English treachery.

Cousins put the phone down.

'You think someone's doing O'Keefe a favour,' she asked, 'by killing Bairstow? Or do you think he's rather more involved than that?'

Cousins shrugged. 'I've no idea,' he said. 'That's why I asked you over. That's why I gave you the file. I think there's a link there.

That's my guess. I think O'Keefe had something to do with Bairstow's little accident. But how, or what, I don't know.'

'You want me to go to Ireland?'

'No, Birmingham.'

'Birmingham?' Annie gazed at him. 'Why Birmingham?'

'We have a guy up there. He's just back from Longford. We put him in a couple of weeks back, after they slotted Bairstow. You probably know him already, by reputation at least.' He paused. 'Eddie McCreadie.'

'Fat Eddie?'

'Yes.' He yawned. 'He knows the form, the names, the family tree. If there's anything obvious on the ground over there, he'll have found it. He came back last night. I talked to him on the phone and he knows you're coming.' He hesitated. 'He likes meets at the International Airport. The cops are armed up there and I think it makes him feel happier. There's a restaurant on the first floor. Half right at the top of the escalator. I've said you'll buy him supper.'

He produced a small black and white photo and gave it to Annie. It showed a cheerful middle-aged man in a polo neck sweater. He had a thick moustache and not much hair. Annie had never met him in person but recognised the face from the files. Fat Eddie. Once acting-quartermaster with the Belfast Brigade. Now enjoying an early retirement, courtesy of the relocation experts at the Field Research Unit. The man you go to for a little background, those times when you want to test a theory, or cross-check a fact or a face.

Cousins was on his feet again. 'The moustache has come off,' he said, 'but he tells me the rest looks the same. Give or take a stone or two.'

Annie nodded, still looking at the photo. 'I'm surprised he went,' she said. 'I thought he was past all that.'

'He is.'

'So what did it take?'

'A word in his ear. Plus a false name.' He nodded at the photo. 'Meet Sean McTiernan.'

'Am I supposed to use that name?'

'Up to you. Makes no odds.'

Annie looked at him a moment, marvelling at how easy it was when you were sat behind a desk. Then she slipped the photo into her bag. 'May I?' she said, gesturing at the file.

'Of course.' Cousins nodded at the pile on his desk. 'I've got plenty.'

'Are they all the same? Dupes?'

'Yes. As it happens.'

Annie bent for her bag, wondering what on earth Cousins was doing with so many copies of the same file. Then she stood up, smoothing her dress, aware of Cousins' eyes on her body, a frank appraisal. Cards on the table, she thought. Time to get one or two things straight.

'I'm a little vague,' she said carefully, 'about the line of command here.'

'Say again?'

'You and me. Where everything fits.' Annie smiled. 'Are you controller now? Have you taken over? Only they normally announce that kind of thing. Protocol, and so forth.'

Cousins looked briefly pained. Like many men, she detected a reluctance to deal with simple truths. He sat back in his chair, reaching for a pencil, tapping it lightly against the knuckles of his other hand.

'We've set up a task force,' he said, 'for the duration of this business. As you know, we have a special desk. Ring-fenced monies. Priority call on most facilities. You'll have been briefed on all that.'

'Of course.'

'Nominally, Francis Wren would be in charge. As Controller of 'T' Branch, that would make sense. He would be the line to the Directorate.'

'But?'

'There is no Francis Wren.'

'Meaning?'

'His position is vacant.' He smiled. 'Pending developments.'

'I see. So all this . . . the Sabbathman operation . . .'

Cousins nodded, watching her carefully again. 'Mine,' he agreed, 'as of yesterday.'

'And me?'

'You, too, I'm afraid. Until we slot the bugger.' He paused. 'I'm surprised Wren didn't mention it. Maybe he had other things on his mind. Still, if you don't object . . .'

'Not at all, of course not, I just' – Annie shrugged – 'wanted to know, that's all.'

Annie shouldered her bag and turned for the door. She was about to open it when Cousins called her back.

'This liaison business,' he said casually. 'You and your Plod friend.'

'Alan Kingdom?'

'Yes. Who's idea was that?'

'Wren's, as far as I know. I happened to fit the bill. Alan was the Yard's contribution. After my appointment.'

Cousins said nothing for a moment. The sunshine had reached Euston now, pouring in through the big plate-glass window, rimming his head in gold, casting his face into shadow. Annie wasn't sure but she thought he might be smiling.

'I've cancelled the arrangement,' he said at length. 'I thought it might make things easier for you.'

Annie hesitated, one hand still on the door handle. Cousins' use of innuendo was masterful. She thought she knew what he was saying but she was by no means sure so she decided to play it straight.

'He'll be pleased,' she said lightly. 'He's got troubles at home.'

Cousins was smiling now. Definitely. 'The wife?'

'His father. He has Alzheimer's. I think there's a problem with getting him looked after.' Annie paused, offering a smile of her own. 'And he's divorced, by the way, in case you'd got the wrong idea.'

Annie took a late afternoon train to Birmingham. At Cousins' suggestion, she'd been back to the flat and packed an overnight bag. From the station at the international airport, a monorail bridged the half-mile to the passenger terminal, and Annie found the restaurant up on the first floor, exactly as Cousins had described. There were a dozen or so tables, and a scattering of passengers bent over cups of tea. Of Eddie McCreadie, there was no sign.

Annie glanced at her watch and fetched a pot of coffee from the counter. A table near the back of the eating area offered a good view of the approach from the escalator, and she settled down to wait. On the train, she'd read through the rest of the Derek Bairstow file, trying to test Hugh Cousins' thesis against the known facts. The Fraud Squad file was exhaustive and it was plain that Bairstow had been under surveillance for the best part of a year. In all, according to bank statements recovered from his house after his death, he'd salted away more than £200,000 from a variety of contracts. In every case, the money had come from firms to whom he'd awarded PSA contracts, and these monies had been paid directly into a company account at the Zurich bank. The company, Nordvolk, had been held by Bairstow's wife in her maiden name, and she and Bairstow had made regular visits to Zurich to draw cash from the account.

Attached to the file had been a series of photographs. They'd included shots of Bairstow himself, both dead and alive, and a nicely framed view of his house, a modest semi at the cheaper end of Jesmond. Looking at the photo, Annie had wondered quite how the investigation had begun – there were no obvious signs of wealth – but reading on, she'd found a note of an interview filed by a detective called Gosling. The note, nearly a year old, appeared to have initiated the entire inquiry. Gosling had been phoned by the managing director of a marine engineering company in Aberdeen. The firm had tendered for a construction project out on the Northumberland coast and had lost. Suspecting foul play, the managing director had unearthed some evidence of his own, and handed it over. By itself, this evidence wasn't enough to secure a conviction but a year later the Fraud Squad were on the point of closing the trap. Pinned to the interview note was a photocopy of a letter from the same managing director. The letter was brisk. Six months after the interview, he was saying, nothing had been done. Bairstow wasn't only still working for the PSA, he'd actually been promoted. The signs, the managing director warned in the letter, were ominous. If a bent civil servant got promoted, where did the corruption end?

Annie had been amused by the tone of voice behind the terse interrogatives. She'd met men like this before – self-righteous, shrill, angry – and she wondered now whether O'Keefe came from the same mould. Had he written letters? Or phoned DC Gosling? Or had Cousins reached for his hi-lighter for some other reason? Because of the man's nationality? And because he fitted so neatly into the conspiracy they were all labouring to understand?

Annie shook her head, none the wiser, and when Fat Eddie finally turned up, nearly an hour later, she was no closer to an answer. He was a huge man, much bigger than the photo suggested, in ill-fitting brown trousers and a green Pringle sweater. He had a long, heavy jaw and a wary smile. Now, he sat behind a small mountain of pasta, winding spaghetti round his fork. The second bottle of Chianti was nearly empty, though Annie's glass was barely touched.

'So who briefed you?' she said. 'Who asked you to go?'

'Told me. Told me to go.'

'OK.' Annie conceded the point, 'So who was that?'

'Yer man down there.'

'Who?'

'Tall fella. Young looking. Had that way about him. You know what I'm saying? Nice enough now, but you wouldn't want to argue.'

Annie smiled, nodding. Hugh Cousins exactly. 'And you spent a fortnight there? In Longford?'

'Yes. I knew there were jobs going, you know, shite work, because he'd told me. I was staying at a grand little place out on the Newtown road there. I took the bus every morning.' He reached for the remains of the Chianti. 'Shite work.'

'Any faces you knew?'

'None. Every man a stranger. Every woman, too.'

'And the crack? In the evening?'

'Horses and politics and Gaelic football.' He frowned. 'And don't think I didn't put myself around. Because I did.'

'But nothing?'

'No. And no surprise, either. I told yer man before I went. I told him. Save your money, I said, there's no way, not in that town.'

'You'd been there before?'

'No, but that's not the point. Jeez now, Longford, there's a place the Irish are proud of. They've got jobs, prospects, the place works. The last thing those fellas need are us lunatics from the north. It's the same you'll find anywhere else there's a half-decent life. People down south don't want anything to do with the Provos. Especially not in a place like Longford.'

'And O'Keefe?'

'Least of all O'Keefe. Dessie's Mr Fianna Fail. He's mainstream. He's been at it most of his life and now they're in power again. They're running the place. Now why would he want to spoil any of that?'

He reached for a paper napkin and wiped his mouth. He had huge hands, and Annie watched him swallow the last of the wine, wondering about the wisdom of ordering another bottle. She'd rarely seen anyone so nervous. He'd refused even to sit down until they'd changed places. He'd said he needed to keep an eye on things. Looking at the wall gave him indigestion.

Now he was eyeing the clock beside the departures board.

'If that's all . . .' he began.

Annie reached out, restraining him. 'O'Keefe,' she said again. 'I need to know how sure you are. You know how the story goes?'

Eddie shook his head with such violence that his whole face wobbled. 'No,' he said firmly, 'and if it's all the same to you, I—'

'Listen,' Annie's hand was still on his arm, 'O'Keefe's been crossed in business. Man here on the mainland. It's cost him a lot of money. He asks his republican friends to teach the man a lesson. They do just that.'

'How?'

'By killing him.'

'How?'

'With a knife. At a football match.'

Eddie stared at her. His face, already red, had purpled. 'Provos?' he said. 'A knife? At a *football match*?'

'Yes.'

Eddie began to rock with laughter, the whole table shaking above his massive knees.

Annie steadied the empty bottle. 'Something I said?' she inquired. 'Something you find amusing?'

Annie phoned Cousins from a call-box half an hour later. She'd just escorted Fat Eddie back to his car, waving goodbye as he bumped away towards the pay booth. One of his back lights didn't work and she wondered how he'd make out if they stopped him on the way home. Even a frame that big couldn't hide two bottles of Chianti.

'Now, she bent to the phone. Cousins had told her he'd be waiting for her call. When his direct line didn't answer, she phoned the main switchboard, asking for him by name. The telephonist put the call through at once but the voice that answered, to Annie's surprise, belonged to Wren.

'You're after our new friend,' he said at once.

'How do you know?'

'Because I'm holding the fort.' he paused. 'He's gone down to Wales. He wants you to join him there.'

'Where?'

'Fishguard. You've to go to the customs people in the ferry port. They'll know where he is.'

'Why?' Annie said, 'What's happened?'

There was a brief silence at the other end. Then Wren was back again, chuckling softly to himself.

'They've intercepted ten kilos of Semtex. Plus some other goodies.' He paused. 'In a consignment of office furniture.'

EIGHT

INTERCEPT NOTE

Intercept Office: Gresham Street (BT)
Intercept date and time: Thursday 30 September, 14.37
Originating caller (OC): Conservative Chief Whip's Office, SW1
Call destination (CD): PPS Office, 10 Downing Street,SW1

OC: "Right. Absolutely right. The sums are horrible."

CD: "How horrible?"

OC: "Ghastly. All this business with Sinn Fein is starting
to surface. You know that as well as I do. If Molyneaux
gets the hump, if he thinks we're selling out to Dublin,
then we're down to single figures. <u>Single figures</u>.
One slip on fucking Europe, and we're looking at an
election . . ."

CD: "So what are you telling me?"

OC: "I'm telling you we can't do without the Proddies. Love
'em or hate 'em."

CD: "Can't do what"

OC: "Survive."

Annie was down at Fishguard by quarter to seven the following morning, stepping off the overnight train from Paddington. She'd dozed most of the way, huddled in the corner of an under-heated carriage, and when dawn came up she found herself in west Wales, a landscape of high stone walls, sheep-cropped upland fields, and the distant brown smudge of the Prescelly Mountains.

Fishguard itself was a pretty town, terracing the hills around a bay. A long stone jetty protected the harbour from the rolling swells of the Irish Sea, and at the landward end of the jetty there were berths for the big blue and white ferries that made the four-hour crossing to Rosslare. The railway station formed part of the ferryport, and the platform was dotted with passengers waiting for the connecting train to London.

Annie stood on the platform a moment, getting her bearings. It was windy by the sea and there was rain in the air. She stared out across the bay, watching gulls swooping over the stern of an incoming trawler, then she tried to shake the chill from her body and went to find the customs hall. The officer in charge occupied a tiny office beside the Nothing to Declare channel. A one-way mirror gave him a perfect view of the last of the exhausted foot-passengers, still plodding off the Rosslare ferry. Annie showed her MI5 pass and inquired about Cousins. Apparently he'd spent all night with a rummage crew in one of the freight sheds and had just retired to a hotel across the bay. The hotel was called St Athan's and it was evidently run by the customs official's sister.

'Good breakfast, mind,' he said, 'as long as you like mushrooms.'

A taxi took Annie to the hotel, a tall, grey building with a new slate roof and a full set of UPVC windows. She asked for Cousins at reception and a pretty girl in a pair of denim dungarees checked her name and then directed her to Room 214. Cousins, it seemed, had already ordered breakfast and Annie said yes when the girl asked whether she, too, would be eating.

Room 214 was on the second floor at the end of a long corridor. The big cast iron radiators were on full blast and for the first time in eight hours, Annie began to feel warm. At Cousins' door she paused and knocked. She could hear the hiss of a shower inside and the sound of someone singing. Eventually the door opened and Cousins appeared. He was still fastening a towel around his waist. His face and upper body were soaking wet and when he stepped back to let her in he left two perfect footprints on the nylon carpet.

'Welcome,' he said, 'You made it.'

Annie shut the door behind her and let Cousins take her overnight bag. The bed hadn't been slept in but the television was on and there were two used tea bags squashed flat in a saucer beside the electric kettle. Cousins put her bag on a chair by the window, told her to make herself at home, and disappeared into the shower. He didn't act like a man who'd been up all night. On the contrary, he seemed – if anything – refreshed.

Annie kicked off her shoes and lay full-length on the bed, her head against the pillow, half-watching the television. A reporter on the lake shore in Geneva was explaining something complicated about the latest push for peace in Bosnia. Annie did her best to follow the drift, thinking again how nice it was to be warm. Next thing she knew, Cousins was bent over the bed, a piece of toast in one hand and a cup of coffee in the other. He nodded at a tray on the table. He was fully dressed.

'Scrambled eggs,' he said cheerfully, 'and rather a lot of mushrooms.'

They ate steadily through the weather forecast before the eight o'clock news. When Annie asked Cousins about the customs seizure – what had happened – he shook his head, putting a finger to his lips, not taking his eyes off the TV screen. The news bulletin began. Second item, after a piece on a riot in South Africa, was a report about a big arms and explosives find at a ferry port in west Wales. Customs men had examined a container lorry from the Republic. Amongst other items, they'd discovered ten kilos of Semtex explosives, several automatic pistols, and a quantity of ammunition. The Garda in Dublin had been notified and investigations were under way on both sides of the Irish Sea. Annie glanced across at Cousins. He was sitting at the table by the window. When the next item started, he reached forward and turned the television off. He looked extremely pleased with himself.

'Excellent,' he said.

'What's excellent?'

'The coverage.' Cousins pushed his plate away and glanced at his watch. He was smartly dressed: beautifully cut suit, lightly striped shirt, plain blue tie.

'At ten o'clock,' he said, 'we get down to the serious work.'

'What's that?'

'Press conference.' He nodded out of the window, across the bay, towards the ferry port. 'Freight Shed "B". Our policeman friend's due down any time now from London. His show, of course. As far as Joe Soap's concerned.'

'Which policeman friend's that?'

'Allder, of course.' Cousins smiled. 'Who else?'

Cousins topped up his cup with coffee and reached for the sugar bowl. He said he'd taken a call from the customs investigation people late yesterday afternoon. They'd had a tip about an incoming consignment of office furniture due at Fishguard on the evening ferry. Cousins had left London at once, driving down to Wales, arriving in time to meet the boat. The target lorry had been one of the last vehicles off. They'd opened the container in Freight Shed 'B'. The container load had included a ton and a half of knockdown ready-to-assemble office furniture. In one of the packs, he and the customs rummagers had found explosives, hand-guns, ammunition and – most significant of all – a sniper scope and a map.

Annie was still finishing her breakfast. 'Map?'

Cousins nodded. 'Deal,' he said, sipping his coffee, 'in Kent.'

'Is that significant?'

'Yes. I think it probably is. Though God knows why.' He glanced across at her. 'I thought I'd let you handle that.'

'Thanks.' Annie finished the last of her scrambled egg and put the tray to one side. 'So tell me about this furniture. Where did it come from?'

Cousins was looking out of the window again. The ferry Annie had seen earlier was backing slowly away from the jetty.

'Where do you think?' Cousins said.

'Longford?'

'Right.'

'O'Keefe?'

'Of course.' He nodded at the television. 'Which is why our media friends will be so interested.'

Annie leaned back against the quilted bedhead. In six years with MI5, she'd never met anyone so publicity-conscious as Cousins. Normally, at Gower Street, the press and TV people were regarded as a necessary pain, an affliction, one of the curses that came with democracy. Controllers went to endless lengths to shield operations, to keep on-going inquiries under the tightest of wraps. Yet here was the new man, the coming force in 'T' Branch, positively eager to share the spoils with a wider public. Indeed, watching his face as he monitored the news broadcasts, he might easily have been a journalist himself, anticipating fresh twists to the story, bending it this way and that, examining it from every angle.

Annie looked across at Cousins, trying to sort through what he'd told her, the little basket of goodies he'd unwrapped overnight.

'This tip,' she began, 'to the customs guys.'

'Yes?'

'How come?'

Cousins glanced across at her, shrugging. 'Pass,' he said.

'But shouldn't we develop that? Ask the odd question?'

'Sure,' he smiled, 'I imagine they'll give you chapter and verse.'

'Me?'

'Yes.' He yawned. 'That's your baby. I'm giving it to you. Another one for your shopping list.'

A couple of minutes later, the last of the coffee gone, Annie asked to use the bathroom. Cousins was still sitting at the table, scribbling notes for a report.

'Sure,' he said, 'go ahead.'

Annie went into the bathroom and began to douse her face with cold water. Almost as an afterthought she called out, pulling open the door with her foot, telling Cousins about the conversation with Fat Eddie. The man had found nothing, she said. He'd looked, and he'd talked, and he'd asked around but there was nothing there. Cousins grunted from time to time, half-listening, and when she'd finished he put down his pen, got up, and crossed the room towards her. She eyed him in the mirror over the basin. He was leaning against the door jamb, watching her.

'Well?' he said. 'You believe him?'

Annie shrugged, wringing the water from the flannel and emptying the basin. 'I don't know,' she said, 'but on balance . . . yes.'

'You don't think he was covering his arse? You don't think the tip might have come from him?'

'But why? Why should he bother with all that?'

'I've no idea. Unless he wanted to keep a clean sheet with his Provo friends.'

'He has no Provo friends. He's past all that. That's why he wanted out. That's why he moved to Birmingham in the first place.'

'No Provo friends? Come, come. You know these guys. You've worked with them. It's a blood tie. Once you're in, you're in for good. Once a Provo, always a Provo.'

'Why do we bother with touts, then? Why spend all that money?'

'Eddie wasn't a tout. He hasn't taken a penny off us. Not one.'

'No, you're right.'

'So . . .' Cousins smiled. 'I suggest we take what he says with a pinch of salt. No?'

Annie turned round at last. A single blond hair had caught on Cousins' lapel. She reached out and brushed it off. Cousins didn't move. If anything, he looked amused.

'You know the trick in this game?' he said at last.

'No. Tell me.'

'It's two little words. Opportunity and timing. Knowing where to look and when.'

Annie nodded, searching for the ambiguities again, wondering what Cousins was really trying to say.

'Clever of you to remember the suit,' she said quietly, 'under the circumstances.'

Freight Shed 'B' formed part of the ferry port. It was a long, low windowless building with big sliding doors at either end to let the freight trucks through from the inbound ferries. When Annie and Cousins arrived, the shed was empty except for a single Scania truck parked in one corner. The rear doors of the big freight container were open and there were portable lights on collapsible stands shining directly into the back.

Carefully arranged on the oil-stained concrete beside the truck were several flat-packs of ready-to-assemble furniture. One of them had been opened along the line of heavy staples, the cardboard packaging folded back, exposing the lettered sections inside. Nestling amongst the lengths of conti-board and the plastic packs of handles and hinges were five packages wrapped in black polythene and then secured with brown adhesive tape. Four of the packages were about the size of a one-pound box of chocolates, and a fifth lay beside them, the black polythene scissored open, a block of something that looked like putty visible inside.

Cousins nodded to the customs official standing guard. 'Where's the rest of it?'

'Coming, sir.'

'Soon?'

'Any minute.'

Annie knelt beside the display, inspecting the unopened furniture packs. They all carried the same label, O'Keefe Discount Office Supplies, Longford, Eire. She glanced up, hearing the squeak of wheels. Two men had appeared with a trolley. On the trolley were a dozen or so collapsible chairs. The men began to arrange the chairs in a wide semi-circle around the cartons. Cousins was still talking to the customs official. When he'd finished, she stood up.

'Where were they hidden?' she said.

Cousins led her to the back of the truck. About a third of the contents had been offloaded and stacked against the wall of the freight shed.

Cousins peered inside the ribbed container. 'There,' he said, 'on the left-hand side.'

'Did you know what to look for?' Annie nodded at the display. 'Did you have box numbers? Some particular marking?'

'Yes,' he said, 'we had the product number. G26 something. The Space Saver Conference Desk.'

'But a particular box?'

'No, just the product number.'

'So how many of these desks were there? On board?'

'According to the manifest,' Cousins frowned, 'about twenty.'

'And you got lucky first time?'

'Christ, no.' He led Annie through a door into an adjoining office. Most of the office floor was knee-deep in scissored cardboard and bits of desk. 'We spent half the night with that lot. We must have gone through ten packs. At least.'

There were footsteps outside, then a movement in the open doorway behind them. Cousins looked round and for a fleeting moment, Annie saw the triumph in his eyes. She glanced over her shoulder, recognising the tiny figure she'd last seen on his feet in the Home Office meeting. Allder, she thought. Kingdom's boss.

Cousins stepped across the office, flattening rolls of corrugated cardboard and Allder accepted his handshake without visible enthusiasm. He hadn't bothered putting a coat over his three-piece suit and he was plainly freezing. Annie followed the two men back into the freight hall. They paused in front of the display while Cousins briefed Allder on developments overnight. The little policeman was making notes on a small leatherbound pad. The customs official had returned with an armful of automatic pistols, each one sealed in a polythene bag. He knelt by the display and began to arrange them round the blocks of plastic explosive. When he'd finished, he glanced up at Cousins for his approval. Cousins broke off a moment, viewing the effect from a number of angles, his eyes narrowed, and Annie watched Allder's face, sensing the rage behind the tight little smile.

Cousins told the customs official he needed more light on the display. Then he turned back to Allder.

Allder was looking at his notes. 'Bloke in Birmingham,' he muttered, 'Eddie McCreadie. Anything to do with you?'

Cousins was watching the customs official adjusting one of the lights. 'Yes,' he said, 'the name's familiar.'

'Used him recently at all?'

'Why?'

Cousins was signalling to the customs official, gesturing for him to bring the lamp a little closer. Allder was on the point of losing his temper.

'He's dead,' he said briefly, 'that's why.'

Cousins at last looked at Allder. So did Annie.

'Dead?'

'Yes.'

'How come? What happened?'

'Ran into the back of a parked truck. Last night. Pissed out of his brain.'

Cousins permitted himself a shake of the head. His eyes had gone back to the display.

'What time?' Annie said. 'What time did this happen?'

'I don't know. Before midnight, certainly.' Allder paused, looking at Annie. 'Why?'

Annie glanced at Cousins, then shook her head. 'Nothing,' she said.

A small group of men and women had appeared at the far end of the freight shed. One of them had a video camera and a big silver tripod. Another carried a microphone on a long pole. The rest, according to the customs official, were local journalists, called in at an hour's notice. After the press conference, they'd phone through their copy to the national papers.

Annie looked round for Cousins but he was already shaking hands with one of the journalists, a tall, dark-haired, rather saturnine young man in an expensive cashmere coat. Annie felt a pressure on her arm. It was Allder.

'Were you here last night?' he said gruffly. 'Were you part of all this?'

'No.'

'Know anything about the background? Where the information came from?'

Annie thought about Fat Eddie for a moment. Then she shook her head. 'No,' she said, 'I'm afraid not.'

'Anyone ever think to phone us at all? Or was it one of those private parties of yours? Invitation only?'

Annie looked down at him for the first time. She'd been watching Cousins, still deep in conversation with the man in the cashmere coat. She'd seen him before. She knew she had. Belfast again. Some other press conference. Some other post-mortem.

'I'm sorry?' she said.

Allder stared at her for a moment. He must have got up in a hurry because there were tiny nicks in his chin where the razor had slipped. He indicated the Semtex and the automatics. 'Don't tell me you didn't know,' he said, 'don't tell me you weren't expecting this lot.'

'I'm afraid I—'

'What's the story again? Some kind of customs tip-off?'

'Look, maybe you should—'

'Don't bother, love. It's OK. I don't suppose it's down to you.' He patted her arm and then fell silent, watching the approaching journalists. The TV crew began to set up their equipment. The rest were peering at the stuff on the floor. Cousins was still deep in conversation.

Annie nodded at the man in the cashmere coat. 'Who's that?' she said. 'I know I've seen him before.'

She glanced at Allder. Allder was frowning. A bad morning was clearly getting worse.

'His name's Devereaux,' he said tersely. 'He reports on security issues for *The Times*.' He glanced at Annie. 'Nice to see old mates together, eh?'

The press conference lasted less than half an hour. Allder stood in front of the tiny gathering, one hand in his pocket, and offered a brisk summary of the night's events. It was, he said, a significant find, yet more evidence that the Provisional IRA were willing and able to export their violence to the mainland UK. The Irish government, and his counterparts in the Irish Garda, had been notified and he anticipated some kind of statement from Dublin. In conclusion, he issued the usual plea for the public to be vigilant. Anything out of the ordinary, anything suspicious, should be reported at once. Only by enlisting the support of the ordinary man and woman in the street could the police hope to stay ahead in the battle against the terrorists.

At the end of his speech, Allder called for questions. A couple of local journalists asked for clarification about the source of the consignment. Allder spelled out the name of the Longford company – O'Keefe Discount – but added that it would be daft at this stage to jump to conclusions. The fact that Semtex had turned up in one of their boxes didn't necessarily point the finger at the Longford firm. There could be a thousand other explanations. At this point, he simply didn't know.

The journalist sat down, making a note on his pad, and Allder was about to bring proceedings to a close when the man from *The Times* raised a hand. He had a clipped, slightly disdainful manner and as soon as Annie heard his voice she remembered where she'd seen him before. Belfast, definitely. One of the ministerial briefings she'd been obliged to attend at Stormont.

'Anything else,' Devereaux was asking, 'Apart from the items on display?'

Allder did his best to duck the question, mumbling something about logistical back-up.

'What, exactly?'

'Bits and pieces. Nothing much.'

'But what? Can you not say?'

'No,' Allder shook his head, 'apologies, but no.'

Devereaux nodded, accepting the rebuff, and made a note on the back of a folded copy of *The Times*. Then he looked up again, indicating the arms cache with a nod of his head.

'Would you call this operation a success?' he said.

'Of course,' Allder said carefully, 'definitely.'

'A tribute to good police work?'

'A tribute to good intelligence.'

'So how much of that intelligence would you attribute to other agencies?'

Allder looked briefly confused. 'I've already mentioned the customs' involvement,' he said. 'That's where the information came from. That's how we got to know.'

'Of course,' Devereaux was smiling now, 'but what about other parts of the home team? MI5 for instance? To what degree were they involved?'

Annie glanced across at Cousins. He was standing in the shadows to one side, his hands in his pockets. He was smiling too, amused by the way Devereaux had skewered the little policeman. It was the perfect question, leaving Allder nowhere to hide, and Annie realised why the two men had earlier spent so long in conversation.

Allder, meanwhile, was playing the national security card. 'I'm afraid I can't comment,' he said coldly. 'You wouldn't expect me to answer that question, and I won't. Except to say that the operational campaign against the terrorists is police-led. Always has been. Always will be.'

'But intelligence is all-important, surely?'

'Of course.'

'Especially in a case like this.'

'Yes.' Allder did his best to smile. 'And we have our sources, too.'

'Too?'

'As well as . . .' He shrugged. 'Other agencies.'

'Like MI5?'

'Yes.' Allder nodded, impatient now. 'Of course.'

There was a silence. The other journalists were bent over their shorthand pads, scribbling. The TV cameraman began to prowl amongst the goodies on display, filming them from close quarters, while Allder pocketed his notes and accompanied one of the customs officials out of the shed. The truck driver was in Special Branch custody elsewhere in the ferry port, and Annie wondered how long Allder would devote to him before making his own way back to London. Strictly speaking she should pay him a visit too, though Allder was now in charge of all inquiries.

Annie was still watching the journalists drifting away when someone stifled a polite cough beside her. Devereaux. The man from *The Times*.

'Double top for Five, I'd say. You play darts at all?'

Annie shook her head. 'Never.'

'Pity. You've done well, you and Hugh. Though God knows what the Irish will say.'

'You mean O'Keefe?'

'Yes, but the Dublin Cabinet too. He knows most of them like brothers. In fact most of them owe him their jobs. That's going to make life difficult. With Dessie smuggling arms.' He beamed at the cameraman, still filming the little packets of Semtex. 'Hugh and I are stopping for a spot of lunch on the way back. Care to join us?'

Annie travelled back to London in Cousins' car, a brand new Volvo estate still smelling of the protective wax they injected at the factory. When she offered to share the driving, thinking he must be tired, he shook his head. Maybe after the pub, he said, depending on how much beer Devereaux forced down him.

They stopped for lunch at Carmarthen. It was market day and the pub was full of sheep farmers discussing the price of mutton. Devereaux found a table in the back lounge and insisted on buying the lunch. Cousins accompanied him to the bar, and watching the two men together, Annie realised that they must have known each other from way back. They had the same bone-dry sense of humour, communicating in half-sentences, the kind of code that only years of friendship can develop, and back at the table they both rocked with laughter when Devereaux recalled a mutual buddy who'd gone missing in the hills to the north. Apparently he'd been on some kind of Army survival test, and had finally reappeared three days overdue, but the point of the story was the abrupt change in the man's eating habits. Ever since his adventure in the hills, he'd refused point blank to touch lamb.

'Must have been a pretty one,' Devereaux mused over the last of his shepherd's pie, 'probably broke his heart.'

A couple of hours later, back in the car, Annie brought Devereaux up again.

'Was he one of your lot?' she asked, watching the lumpy Somerset hills roll past.

'My lot?'

'Yes.' She nodded. 'SAS.'

'You think I was SAS?'

'I know you were. I saw the tie you were wearing at the Home Office.' She glanced across at him. 'Or was that disinformation?'

'No,' he grinned, 'I wear it to intimidate the civil servants. It makes them nervous, keeps them in their proper place. They think we were the Wild Bunch. Poor fools.'

Annie smiled. 'So what about your chum? Devereaux? Was he in the Regiment, too?'

'Twenty-one. Not the real thing.'

'Good as, though. Eh?'

Cousins looked amused, conceding the point with another grin. Twenty-one SAS was the territorial battalion, part-time soldiers who trained at weekends. They did most of their recruiting in the City and the twelve-month selection course was famous for its brutality. Annie had once had an affair with a young Lloyds broker who'd got as far as the final dozen. The experience had turned him into a monster, prone to outbursts of extreme violence, and she still had a scar at the bottom of her spine from the evening she'd announced the affair was over. She told Cousins about it now, not bothering to hide a tone of wistful regret when it got to the ugly bits.

'I'm surprised,' Cousins said when she'd finished. 'The training's about self-control. You're supposed to be Mr Invisible at the end of it. The little mouse in the corner. The face that everyone forgets.' He smiled. 'That's why Devereaux never hacked it. He managed all the physical bits OK, tough guy and everything, but he hadn't got the temperament for it. They couldn't rope him down.'

'Did they rope you down?'

'They thought they did.'

'So what does that make you? Compared to Devereaux?'

'A better actor.' Cousins grinned again. 'No, Rupert's an extrovert. He has ambitions. Scribbling for *The Times* is just a step, as far as he's concerned. He's after greater things.'

'Like what?'

'Like Parliament, for a start. He's on the Central Office short list, believe it or not, the one they keep for by-elections. He tells me he's down for South-east Hampshire. He has to appear next week. In front of the local selection committee.' He laughed. 'He'll walk it. Bound to. All his bullshit.'

'South-east Hampshire was Carpenter's constituency,' Annie mused, 'the MP who got shot.'

'That's right.'

Annie glanced across. 'You think Devereaux might have done it? Subtle career move?'

Closer to London, Annie brought up Fat Eddie again. She'd been thinking about him all day. She couldn't get him out of her mind. She asked Cousins whether he knew anything more about his death – what time the accident had happened, whether he was alone or not, how much he'd had to drink – but Cousins said he didn't know. She told him again about the meeting they'd had, the way Eddie had dismissed any link between Bairstow's murder and the Provisionals, but when she began to think aloud about the implications Cousins changed the subject. The key thing now, he said, was focus. They had to concentrate on essentials and in his view the contents of the Fishguard arms haul were vital leads. Not simply the Semtex and the small arms but the rest of the stuff. The map. The sniperscope. Where did they belong? How might they advance the Sabbathman investigation?

Annie listened to him, saying nothing, playing the trusty lieutenant, making a note of a name he suggested at the Ministry of Defence. The map they'd found at Fishguard was a single page torn from a tourist guide to Kent. It showed the town of Deal. Deal was the home of the Royal Marines School of Music. In the eighties, the Provos had blown the place up, killing eleven bandsmen. Maybe they were planning a return visit, Cousins suggested, courtesy of the mysterious Mr Sabbathman. Or maybe it was something completely unrelated. Either way, the contact at the MoD might be able to help.

Annie circled the name, asking again about the call Cousins had taken from the customs people, the tip that had sent him racing down to Fishguard.

'How do you suggest I progress that?' she asked. 'Who else do you want me to talk to?'

Cousins didn't say anything for a while. They were passing Heathrow now, and there was traffic everywhere. Finally, he said it was tricky.

'What do you mean?'

'He's a shy bird, the guy I talked to. I'm not sure he'd welcome the attention.'

'Whose attention?'

'Yours.' Cousins braked sharply, making space for an intruder from the left. 'Ours.'

'Why not?'

'He operated in a sensitive area.'

'So do we.'

'That's not the point. We worked on the Matrix-Churchill business together. It's left a bruise or two. Nothing personal. On the contrary, we get on very well. It's just . . .' he shrugged. 'We tend to keep these things one on one.'

'You and him?'

'Yes.'

'So you don't want me to pursue it?'

'No, on second thoughts, best to leave the guy alone.' He glanced across. 'Sorry.'

'But I still don't understand. Why would anyone phone him? Out of the blue?'

'God knows.' Cousins dropped into third gear and then floored the accelerator. 'But I'm not complaining.'

Half an hour later, stuck in traffic on the Great West Road, Annie began to think about Devereaux again. In the pub, before they'd all said goodbye, she'd come back from the loo to find the two men deep in conversation. Devereaux had apparently been on the phone to the Features Editor at *The Times*. As well as a straight news report, he'd been given half a page the following day to tease out the implications. Thinking he meant O'Keefe and his Dublin political connections, Annie had been surprised to hear Devereaux speculating about the balance of power amongst the UK's rival security agencies. His feature piece, he confided to Cousins, would be in the nature of a half-time report. Given the editor's weakness for wordplay, he'd suggest some headline like 'FIVE ONE, YARD

NIL', plus – of course – the obligatory question mark. Cousins had laughed at the line, obviously delighted, and Annie remembered the two men walking out of the pub, still chuckling.

Now, she gazed out at the oncoming waves of rush hour traffic. 'Tell me something,' she said quietly, 'how come Devereaux made it down from London? In time for the press conference?'

Cousins was fiddling with the radio, trying to catch the five o'clock news headlines. 'I phoned him last night,' he said, 'before I went down there.'

'Knowing you might find nothing?'

'Of course.' He glanced across at her. 'Who dares wins, remember?'

Back at her desk in Gower Street, Annie found a sealed brown envelope carrying her name. She examined it a moment, recognising Francis Wren's careful handwriting. She opened the envelope. Inside was a thick sheaf of transcripts, pages and pages of single spaced typing on the distinctive yellow paper favoured by the transcription staff at Gresham Street. Attached to the transcripts was a breakdown of all outgoing calls on the Portsmouth number supplied by Kingdom. Annie glanced down the list of numbers. The transcribed calls were highlighted in green, standard procedure. Only two numbers had been subject to transcript, and the code NFA after the warrant termination date indicated that the yield from the interceptions had been zero.

Annie reached for the phone, glad that she was spared the chore of wading through the transcripts herself. Kingdom answered on the second ring, and Annie realised how glad she was to hear his voice. The last twenty-four hours had exhausted her.

'In the office?' she said. 'Nothing better to do?'

Kingdom favoured her with an obscenity or two and then asked at once about his transcripts. Annie told him what had turned up and said she was sorry he'd drawn a blank.

'Blank?'

'NFA,' she said, 'no further action. There's nothing there.'

She heard Kingdom yawning. Then he suggested a drink, a pub they sometimes used in Knightsbridge, the Pelham Arms. She glanced at her watch, wondering whether it was too late to phone the MoD. She told Kingdom she'd meet him in half an hour.

'OK,' he said, 'but bring the stuff anyway.'

'What stuff?'

'Those transcripts. And the call breakdowns.'

Annie hesitated a moment, looking at the stapled sheets of yellow paper. For the first time, she saw the note that Wren had added across the top. 'Old campaigners like me should know better,' he'd written, 'but good luck all the same.' She smiled to herself, reading it, barely registering the click in her ear as Kingdom hung up.

Ten minutes later, the phone rang. Annie was in the big office next door, trying to coax a full cup of coffee from one of the communal jugs. She returned to her desk, failing to recognise the voice at the other end. Definitely a man. Probably middle-aged. Plainly excited.

'Miss Meredith,' he said again.

'Yes.'

'The name's Dalzell. Hugh Cousins asked me to give you a ring.'

Annie remembered the name, and reached for her pad, confirming it. Bruce Dalzell. A middle-ranking civil servant in the MoD public relations set-up. The man she was to quiz about impending events at Deal.

'We've come across a map,' Annie began. 'It's all rather sensitive.'

'I know, I know. Hugh's been on already, about half an hour ago. I've had a chance to talk to the Palace now, and they've confirmed it.'

'Confirmed what?'

'The date.'

'I'm sorry,' Annie reached for the coffee, 'I'm not with you.'

Bruce Dalzell apologised and started again. The Royal Marine School of Music were hosting a Festival of Military Bands. The festival was to take place over the weekend of 16–17 October. The Colonel in command at the school was laying on a modest presentation on the Sunday. There'd be a field gun crew from Devonport, a tracked vehicle display, a mock-battle on the parade ground, and – of course – lots of music. For some of the regimental bands, due to disappear under MoD budget cuts, it would be a last opportunity to perform in front of royalty.

Annie blinked. 'Royalty? Who?'

'The Duke of York.'

'Anyone else?'

'Yes. The Secretary of State for Defence.' He paused. 'You should tell Hugh.'

'Yes,' Annie said, looking at her notes, remembering Cousins' description of the other items recovered from the Fishguard arms haul. One of them had been a sniperscope, the kind you fit to a high-velocity rifle. She hadn't seen the thing herself, but according to Cousins the scope had a low-light capability which meant nothing short of pitch darkness could hide a potential target.

She returned to the phone. 'When does this Sunday thing start?' she said. 'What time of day?'

'Oh, late, seven o'clock.' Dalzell sounded mortified. 'And I forgot to mention the firework display.'

Annie phoned Cousins the moment Dalzell hung up. When she finally got through to the office at Euston Tower, it was the secretary who answered. Annie gave her name and said it was urgent. The woman was sympathetic but explained that Cousins had already gone. She'd had a car standing by most of the afternoon, and he was at last on his way to the airport.

'Why?' Annie said blankly. 'Where's he going?'

The secretary hesitated a moment, then came back on the line. 'Belfast,' she said. 'I thought you knew.'

By the time Annie got to the Pelham Arms, Kingdom had been waiting for nearly an hour. He'd folded himself into a corner beside a tank of tropical fish. His glass was empty and he'd finished the crossword in the *Evening Standard*.

Annie kissed him on the lips, gave him Wren's envelope, and picked up his glass. By the time she returned with the drinks, the transcripts were back in the envelope. She could tell he'd flicked through them because there was green hi-lighter on his fingertips.

'Cheers,' she said, lifting her glass. 'Compliments of my ex-boss.'

Kingdom glanced up. He looked exhausted. 'Sacked? Retired? Run-over?' He paused. 'So Cousins can step in?'

'Something like that . . .' She hesitated a moment, before deciding there was no harm in going on. Wren was history, after all. 'They call him Jenny. His real name's Wren. That's something else I never thought was quite fair.'

'And he gave you these?'

'Yes. He's at Gresham Street now. Lashed to the transcription wheel.' She paused. 'It pays to have friends sometimes.'

'You'll miss him?'

'Yes.' Annie nodded, glancing at *The Evening Standard*, 'I will.'

Kingdom reached for his glass and swallowed a mouthful of beer. Annie was reading the paper now. The Fishguard arms haul was on the front page and there was a big piece inside about reaction from Dublin. The Garda were crawling all over O'Keefe's factory and the Taoiseach had called an emergency cabinet meeting. In a statement afterwards, the Minister of Justice had promised 'fullest co-operation' with UK investigators.

Annie read the story quickly and then looked up. Kingdom was smiling at her, Wren's envelope already tucked into the pocket of his trenchcoat.

'You should get over there,' he said, 'while they're still in the mood.'

'Where?'

'Dublin. You could cop a look at their files. I'm sure they'd show you everything.' He paused, reaching for his glass again. 'Seriously. You won't believe what they're offering. They were on to us this afternoon. They want Allder to go over there. I think they'd even send a plane, if he asked nicely.'

'Why? Why all the drama?'

'Embarrassment. They're as anti-Provo as the Brits and they want to prove it.'

'So they're calling for Allder?'

'Yeah. That's more or less it. Or that's what he says.'

Annie nodded, remembering her last glimpse of the man, storming off across the draughty freight shed.

'How is he? After this morning?'

'Choked. Pig sick.' Kingdom laughed. 'Cousins got him out of bed at four o'clock this morning. Gave him four hours to get to Fishguard. I've never seen him so angry, poor little bastard. Real stitch-up. Class bit of work.'

'You're saying we stole his thunder?'

'Yeah. Of course you did. Not that it matters. It's games, really, isn't it? Games for the big boys. When they've got fuck all else to do. Have you read this bit?'

Kingdom reached for the paper and found a paragraph at the bottom of page three. According to unnamed sources, the Fishguard arms haul was a tribute to MI5 intelligence.

Annie looked up. 'What's wrong with that?'

Kingdom laughed again. 'Nothing,' he said, 'except Allder doesn't believe it. Mind you, he doesn't believe anything.'

'But what is there to disbelieve? Does he think we make these things up?'

'God knows. I just tell it the way I see it. The man's rabid. Barking. Off his head about it all.'

Annie nodded, thinking about Devereaux again. If the Allder household took *The Times*, she'd recommend cancelling the order. She smiled at the thought, aware of Kingdom watching her.

'You hear about Fat Eddie?' he said at last.

Annie nodded. 'Yes.'

'Word is he'd been to a meet last night. Your lot.'

'Oh?'

'Nothing to do with you, by any chance?'

Annie looked away, not answering the question. The pub was filling up now, businessmen mainly, in twos and threes. 'When did it happen?' she said.

'Last night.'

'I know. But when, last night?'

'Late. Round eleven-thirty. The pubs had just shut.'

'And he'd been drinking? All evening?'

'Must have. He was loaded. Four times over the limit.'

'But specific pubs? Witnesses? Anyone with him? Anyone see him?'

'Dunno.' Kingdom was leaning forward now. 'Why?'

Annie shook her head, remembering Eddie's parting words as

he fumbled for change for the pay booth. He'd been keen to get home. It was his youngest's birthday. He'd promised to be back in time for the cake and the candles before wee Liam went to bed. She thought about it now, quite certain that Eddie McCreadie would have been as good as his word. Maybe he'd returned home, celebrated in style, and then gone out again. Or maybe something else had happened, an unplanned detour to some pub or other, a chance encounter with a friend, more drinks, more laughter, then a glance at his watch, and an oath or two, and the final dash to make it home for young Liam. Kingdom was still watching, still waiting for an explanation. She smiled at him and reached for her drink, changing the subject.

'That liaison arrangement,' she said brightly, 'you and me.'

'Yeah?'

'It's been cancelled.' She lifted her glass. 'Fancy an early night?'

They were back at her flat by nine. Annie lay on top of the big double bed. She'd lit a small scented candle and the warm, yellow light painted shadows across her naked body. She gazed up at the ceiling, waiting for Kingdom. He was still in the bathroom and she could hear the water sluicing out of the shower. After a while, the bathroom door opened and she heard his footsteps crossing the living room towards the open bedroom door. She closed her eyes, anticipating the next couple of hours, the games they'd play, the way they'd bury all the nonsense of the last few days.

In the hotel room, down on the south coast, she'd nearly lost him and she thought about it now, the gulf that had opened up between them, how angry she'd been, and then how sad. In a way, she knew it had been her fault. She'd never realised just how much his work mattered to him. In Belfast, he'd always seemed detached from it all, almost indifferent, shutting the bedroom door on the day's events, preferring to muse about the bundle of mistakes he called his private life. The closer they'd become, the more he'd opened up to her. She knew about his childhood, his mum and dad, his sister, and later his wife. She'd shared his passion for his kids, when they'd first arrived, and his bewilderment when the marriage began to go sour. He'd told her about the affairs he'd had, the answers they'd never given him, how easily he fell in love, how hopeless he was at finding the right woman. And when it dawned on her that he'd fallen in love again, with her this time, she'd let him talk about that, too.

She loved hearing him talk. She marvelled at his lack of inhibition, the way he gambled so recklessly with his feelings, telling her how much she mattered to him, how good she was in bed, how deeply she touched him. Curiously, unlike most men, he'd never asked for anything in return, respecting her reticence, her self-control, her mistrust of sentiment and easy passion. All that stuff she'd always hated. Words were like tissue paper, a wrapper for the real thing. They were disposable. You could screw them up and throw them away. A relationship, to her, was the sum total of what actually happened. Real things. Like passion, and laughter, and the treacly warmth that spread inside her when she and Kingdom made love. She smiled, feeling herself beginning to moisten, rolling over on her side, peering at the door.

'Alan?'

She waited for an answer. Maybe he was in the kitchen, poking around in the fridge. The man was always hungry. She'd never known anyone eat so much. She slipped out of bed and went to the door. Kingdom was sitting on the sofa in the living room. He had a towel round his waist. On his lap was the file she'd left by the telephone, the one that Cousins had given her about Bairstow. At the front of the file, she'd stapled a page of notes about her meeting with Eddie McCreadie and he seemed to be reading them now.

Annie crept back to bed and then called out again. She'd pretend she hadn't seen him. She'd pretend he'd never found the file. Good sex cured everything.

'Alan?'

She lay on the bed. Kingdom appeared at the door, still wearing the towel. She smiled up at him. She had the little bottles of body oil neatly lined up beside the candle.

'Anything,' she said. 'My treat.'

Kingdom sat down on the side of the bed. She'd always loved his hands, the way he used them, the way he sometimes touched her face, and she caught one of them now, trying to draw him down to her, making a big warm space for them both beneath the duvet.

'Alan?'

He felt stiff and cold and wooden. He didn't move from his perch on the side of the bed. Visitors did that, she thought. When you were sick.

'What's the matter?'

Kingdom shook his head, not answering.

'Is it your dad again?'

'No, I told you, he's OK.'

'You said he was upset.'

'He is. Yeah. But . . .' He shrugged. 'It's not that.'

'What is it then?'

Kingdom stared down at her. His hair was beginning to grow again, a dark, bristly shadow across his scalp. 'It's you,' he said.

'Me?'

'Yeah.' He reached down for her at last, tracing the line of her cheekbone.

She smiled again. 'You look very solemn,' she said. 'I thought we might . . .' She nodded at the waiting bottles of body oil. 'Whatever you want.'

'You. I want you.'

'Me?'

'Yes. You. All of you.'

'Terrific. Help yourself.' She paused. 'Alan?'

He was upright again, back on the edge of the bed, the candlelight shadowing his back.

'Listen,' he began, 'there are one or two things we ought to talk about.'

'I know. You get me wrong sometimes. I'm not just wanton. I know you think—'

'I didn't mean that.'

'No?'

'No.' He shook his head. 'I just don't want to see you hurt.'

'Hurt? How? You and me? That kind of hurt?'

Kingdom smiled for the first time and she reached up for him again, frightened of another gap, another gulf, more misunderstandings. Words, after all, had their uses.

'Look,' she said, 'don't get the wrong idea about all this. I might not say the things . . . you know . . . the things you want to hear, but that doesn't mean I don't . . .' She slipped under the duvet and pulled him in beside her. 'You understand what I'm saying?'

'Yes. But it's not that.'

'I know. But that's important, believe me, much more important than the rest of it. The rest of it I can handle. It's this that really matters.' She paused. 'Isn't it?'

They were very close now, nose to nose. He looked at her for a long time and she could see the conflict in his eyes, his need for her, his fears for her.

Finally he nodded. 'Yeah,' he said softly, 'it is.'

'OK.' She touched his lips with the tips of her fingers. 'So what would you really like? Go on, be honest, tell me.'

'I'd like to spend the rest of my life with you. I'd like to put you and this and all of it into some huge time warp. I'd like it to stay like this forever. Exactly this. Exactly now. Nothing else. Just this.'

'You're crazy.'

'I know.'

'It doesn't work that way.'

'I know. Your fault. You asked.'

'I did,' she kissed him, 'I did.'

She looked at him for a long time, the face beside her in the half-darkness, the candle nearly out. Then she began to kiss him again, very softly, exploring his mouth with her tongue, the gentlest of blessings. Then she nestled against him, folding the long hollows of his body around hers. The stiffness and the chill had gone. Whatever he'd wanted to say, whatever had taken him to the sofa and the file, had been forgotten. They were back where they'd always been, in the limitless space they'd made their own, a world of infinite possibility.

She reached for him, cupping his face in her hands. The question was a long time coming, and afterwards she sealed it with a kiss.

'The answer's yes,' she said softly, 'and I've loved you from the start.'

NINE

10 DOWNING STREET
LONDON SW1

TO: Hugh Cousins, PO Box 500
FROM: PPS
DATE: 1 October 1993

<u>STRICTLY CONFIDENTIAL</u>

I understand you are aware of recent developments in HMG's
dialogue with Republican sources in NI. In this context, the
Prime Minister would appreciate a supplementary briefing of
the kind you offered in your note of 15 September. The Prime
Minister would be obliged if these and any subsequent conversations remained strictly confidential, and to that end all
contacts will be conducted through myself. I suggest we meet
at the earliest opportunity.

Annie found Francis Wren on the top deck of the number seven tourist bus, exactly as he'd described. It was a glorious day, windless, warm, not a cloud in the sky, and Wren was sitting at the back, a folded cardigan on his knees, reading a copy of *The Times*.

Annie sat down beside him. He'd been in touch an hour earlier from a pay phone. He'd asked her to join the bus at a particular stop on the Chelsea Embankment and he'd given her a time to be there. When she'd asked why, he'd said something vague about a change of scenery. She'd made no comment but she'd suspected at once that the phrase referred to anything but geography. Wren had something to tell her. Something that he wouldn't risk on the phone, or even within the security of his own office.

The bus rumbled east, towards Westminster. The plane trees beside the river were scarlet with autumn and on the water a lone sculler was pulling hard against the ebbing tide. There were three other passengers on the top deck, all orientals. They huddled together near the front, trying to match the Japanese commentary to passing landmarks. Annie smiled, watching them. If you wanted somewhere confidential for a chat, a busful of foreigners wasn't a bad choice.

Annie glanced at Wren. He looked like someone up from the country, enjoying the first months of a well-earned retirement.

'Thanks for the transcripts,' she said lightly. 'I didn't want to embarrass you.'

'You didn't. Amusement would be closer. I always wondered why we bothered with procedures. With people like you on board.'

Annie blushed, recognising the reprimand for what it was. On occasions, like the Eton housemaster he'd very nearly become, Wren could be very stern indeed. Not that it mattered any more.

'I'm sorry,' she said quietly, 'I apologise.'

Wren didn't answer. His copy of *The Times* was carefully folded at the features section. Annie could see Devereaux's name beneath the half-page article. Since last night, to her surprise, she'd barely given him a thought. Wren tapped the article.

'You've read this?'

'No.'

'But you knew about it?'

'Yes. Cousins told me.' She smiled. 'What does it say?'

Wren was looking out at the view. Across the river, workmen were putting the finishing touches to MI6's new headquarters.

'It says that our little excitements down in Fishguard may be more important than they seem. It says there's blood on the walls at the Yard, and Moet by the crateload in Gower Street. It implies the war's over.'

'Do you think he's right?'

'No, I think he's being less than objective. In fact I'd put it even more strongly. I'd say he's being mischievous.'

Annie looked down at the paper, remembering Devereaux and Cousins at the pub in Carmarthen. Strictly speaking, she knew she should read the article but right now she didn't much want to. Kingdom had been right. Whichever way you looked at it, the thing was ludicrous, a waste of time and effort, a war within a war.

'So what's your view?' Annie said. 'You think we're winning? You think any of it matters?'

'Yes,' Wren nodded, 'I do.'

'Yes, we're winning? Or yes, it matters?'

'Both. The game's fixed, anyway. We all know that. It suits our masters nicely to put us in the driving seat. Saves them a great deal of anguish. We don't have to answer to anyone. We're effectively beyond reach. Now that's a very nice situation. From where the politicians sit.'

'And us?'

'We get on with it.' He smiled grimly, 'and we're duly grateful.'

'But aren't we more effective? Doesn't that matter?'

'Depends.'

'On what?'

'On what we're asked to do, and why we're asked to do it. It used to be simple. Queen and country. Even I could understand that. Now?' He shrugged, answering his own question. 'God knows. It's happened to the rest of the civil service. Why not us?'

The bus had stopped to pick up more passengers. Traffic was streaming over Lambeth Bridge. Wren put his hand briefly on Annie's knee, an almost fatherly gesture.

'A word in your ear about Cousins,' he said, 'while we're on the subject.' He glanced across at her. 'Lobby terms?'

'Of course.'

'Good.' He studied her briefly as the bus began to move again. 'Cousins and I are chalk and cheese. You doubtless know that. It's probably self-evident. Age, background, philosophy, all of it, really. But don't think I'm bitter or vindictive because I'm not. If it was as simple as that we wouldn't be here. I wouldn't have asked you and even if I had, you wouldn't have come. The dullest noise in the world is an old man having a moan. So believe me, this isn't a moan.' He paused. 'Cousins was in Belfast during the eighties. He was a major in 22 SAS and he spent a year or so trying to sort out some of the problems with 14th Intelligence. You're probably aware of all that.'

Annie nodded. She hadn't known the exact details but after the conversation with Cousins in the car she'd worked most of it out for herself. 14th Intelligence was an elite reconnaissance unit. It had been developed to give the Army its own intelligence source in Northern Ireland and it specialised in deep surveillance. It had taken a beating in the late eighties and the SAS had put in a couple of officers to stiffen morale. Cousins had evidently been one of them.

Wren had his head back now, letting the sunshine bathe his face. 'Cousins was a great fan of hard arrest. It's one of the reasons they put him into 14th. As long as the intelligence was good, as long as everyone was *sure*, then he saw no point in bothering with all the legal bits and pieces. You might say he favoured the bullet rather than the witness box. Saved a lot of time and money. Rather eighties, don't you think?'

Annie smiled at the way Wren phrased it. The language was

harsh but she recognised the picture he was trying to paint. Cousins was a true product of the Thatcher years, a real ultra, fuelled by self-belief and a certain smiling arrogance. She'd seen it in him yesterday, the way he'd humiliated Allder, landing him with a press conference about which he'd known virtually nothing.

Wren was watching her now, his head still back against the seat, one eye open.

'Hard arrest was policy,' Anne reminded him, 'not something Cousins invented.'

'I know that. But he was an enthusiast. Undeniably. And good at it, too.'

The bus drove into shadow and Annie felt a sudden chill in the air. Wren offered her the cardigan but she shook her head. Hard arrest was the Army's euphemism for shooting to kill. The SAS in Northern Ireland had perfected the art, ambushing suspected terrorists and cutting them down with overwhelming firepower. Time after time, they'd acted as judge, jury and executioner. The one item they never carried was a pair of handcuffs.

Annie glanced across at Wren. Towards the end of the eighties hard arrest had gone out of fashion, partly because of Operation Flavius, the Gibraltar debacle.

'So what happened to Cousins,' she asked, 'after the SAS?'

'He came to us.'

'In Belfast?'

'No, here, in London. He wrote position papers for the Directorate. They think very highly of him. They like the liberties he takes. They like his style, his lack of inhibition. They think he's slightly exotic, a creature from another planet. The phrase you'll hear in the executive dining room is *force majeur*. Our friend specialises in *force majeur*. It's one of the reasons he needs stopping.'

'Stopping?' Annie blinked. She'd never heard Wren speak this way before, declaring his hand with such quiet vehemence. He was looking ahead now, towards the Houses of Parliament, the Gothic stonework warm and honey-coloured after the recent renovations.

'Lawyers use *force majeur* when they mean an Act of God,' he said. 'In Cousins' case, the nuance is entirely appropriate.'

'You mean he thinks he's almighty?'

'Yes.' He nodded. 'And I suspect that's one of the reasons they're so frightened of him.'

'*Frightened?* Who?'

'The Directorate. Cousins comes with a certain reputation. They know where he's been, what he's done. They know the company he keeps too, the connections he uses, the way he plugs himself in . . .'

'Connections?'

'Friends,' Wren said. 'The man's a deeply political animal.'

'Friends where?'

Wren hesitated a moment, eyeing a covey of television technicians assembled around a tripod on the pavement. 'You could start with Tory Central Office,' he said at last, 'and keep going up.' He paused, still watching the TV people. 'That's what makes him so useful.'

'To whom?'

'To "T" Branch. That's where he pitched his tent, the moment he came back from Belfast. "T" Branch is rough trade, of course. We all accept that. And in my heart I suspect it needs someone like Cousins. But even so . . .' He picked at a loose end in his cardigan. 'There are limits.'

Annie nodded. 'Your job's up for grabs,' she said, 'and I gather he's favourite.'

'You gather correctly.' He offered her a chilly smile. 'But no decision's been taken. Not yet. Nothing final. Nothing binding.'

'So why are you telling me all this? Or is it rude of me to ask?'

Wren studied her a moment. He looked tired round the eyes and his face was slightly puffy. Poor diet, Annie thought. And not enough sleep.

'Are you asking me what's in it for you?' he said. 'Is that what you mean by "rude"?'

'Yes,' Annie nodded, 'crudely put, but yes.'

Wren said nothing, turning away. The usual queue had formed outside the House of Lords, foreigners mainly, marshalled by tour guides in gay blazers. Wren watched them as the bus inched past, stuck again in a traffic jam.

'You're young and you're highly thought of,' he said at last.

'Just like Cousins.'

'Yes.' He glanced across at her. 'And you're also a woman.'

'You think that's relevant?'

'Yes, I think maybe it is. These things go in cycles, of course, but just now it helps to wear a skirt.' He paused. 'There are great opportunities, that's all I want to say.'

Annie looked away. They were in Parliament Square and the bus had stopped again. Beside Great Palace Yard, two young policemen were bent over an old tramp. The tramp was sitting on the pavement, playing a jig on a battered tin whistle. Despite the noise of the traffic, Annie recognised the tune. 'The Wild Colonial Boy' she thought, one of Kingdom's favourites.

'Cousins is a fighter,' she said quietly. 'He doesn't take prisoners.'

'Precisely. That's what makes him so dangerous. That's why I'm here, talking to you.'

'Have you said anything to anyone else? Officially or otherwise?'

'No.'

'Why not?'

'Because there'd be no point. Once you're out of the loop, you're dead and buried. Make a fuss, raise your voice, and the whole thing just gets worse. So why compound grief with further insult? Why do that?'

'Grief?' Annie stared at him. 'Is it that bad?'

Wren offered her a bleak smile. Then he produced a small, silver-embossed card. On it was his home address and telephone number. 'I'm having a few people round,' he said, 'people I'll miss. People I'll treasure. Quite a small gathering. Nothing extravagant.' He touched her lightly on the arm. 'Might you come?'

Before Annie had a chance to say yes, he stood up. The bus was on the move again, turning onto the Embankment, pulling up outside the Norman Shaw building.

Annie gazed up at him. 'You're getting off?'

'Yes. Lunch appointment, I'm afraid.' He nodded towards the House of Commons. 'Good luck in Dublin, though.'

'What?'

Wren had turned and was making his way up the aisle. Annie caught him by the stairs.

'Where?' she said.

'Dublin.' Wren frowned, checking his watch. 'Hasn't anyone told you?'

Kingdom's flowers had arrived at Gower Street by the time Annie returned to her desk. The lady who patrolled with the tea trolley had brought them up and they were already in water, neatly arranged in a hideous brown vase. A card propped in her printer read *Time warps for no man. Except me*.

Annie picked the card up, fingering it, surprised and touched. Kingdom had never sent her flowers before. That kind of gesture just wasn't in his repertoire. Quite what it meant she didn't fully understand but she was still grinning when the phone began to trill. She recognised the voice at once, Cousins' secretary, over at Euston Tower. She sounded brisk.

'I've been calling for the last two hours.'

'I'm sorry. I've been out.'

'So I gather.' She paused, then suggested Annie get a pen.

The Fishguard seizure had evidently raised a diplomatic storm. Ulster Unionist MPs were accusing the Irish government of gun-running, and journalists on both sides of the Irish Sea were busy stirring the pot. The Taoiseach's office had spent most of the morning on the phone to Downing Street and were insisting that someone from British Intelligence be sent to Dublin to monitor the Garda's investigation. The invitation was pressing. It was an opportunity that 'T' Branch would be foolish to ignore.

'Of course,' Annie said, 'Hugh should do it.'

'Mr Cousins is in Belfast.'

'I know. Dublin's down the road. He could be there in a couple of hours.'

'Quite.' The secretary sounded icy now. 'But he's disappeared as well. I suggest you call here on the way to the airport. There's a full brief due anytime from the Home Office, and I've sorted out some extra numbers in Dublin. You're booked on the Aer Lingus flight. Half-past five.' She paused. 'Unless, of course, you'd prefer someone else to go.'

*

235

Annie got to Heathrow with five minutes to spare. She was last onto the aircraft and they were airborne before she had a real chance to take stock. At Euston Tower, she'd run into Andrew Hennessey, the head of Special Projects at Tory Central Office. He'd been sitting behind Cousins' desk, reading one of the Bairstow files that still formed a neat pile beside the blotter, yet another breach in the wall that was supposed to separate MI5 from the world of the politicians. Annie had already spent nearly an hour on the computer at Gower Street, updating herself on incoming source reports, and because time was now so short Hennessey had offered to brief her en route to Heathrow.

Annie thought about the conversation now, as Windsor Castle slipped beneath the starboard wing and the first streaks of cloud hid the ground from view. It was the first time she'd found herself at close quarters with Hennessey and she hadn't enjoyed the experience. He was thin and sallow with an abrupt manner and a nervous tic beneath one eye. He'd sat in the corner of the taxi, his briefcase on his knees, sketching in the background for the job she had to do. Annie recognised the technique from her exchanges with Wren, the way he carefully parcelled out the information, keeping the facts to the bare minimum, twitching the curtain from time to time, giving her just a glimpse of life backstage.

The thing was tricky, he seemed to be saying. Top secret 'conversations' were under way in Northern Ireland. These involved certain factions on the Provisional IRA Army Council and go-betweens reporting to Whitehall. Both the Unionists in the north, and the coalition government in Dublin, had scented the smoke in the wind, and neither party was happy. The Irish cabinet had been further incensed by the way the British were reporting the Sabbathman murders. Pointing the finger at the Republicans, implying that somehow an Irish hand lay behind the killings, had the ugliest possible implications, especially now, when there appeared to be prima facie evidence that a top Fianna Fail supporter was smuggling explosives into the UK. What were the Brits up to? Did they really believe that the Irish government – properly constituted, democratically elected, fellow members of the EEC – would really behave in this way? Where would the innuendo and the accusations lead? And when would they ever stop?

Hennessey had raised the questions in turn, emphasising the importance of each with a tiny chopping motion of his right hand, and when he'd finished he'd leant back against the corner of the cab.

'How much of that did you know already,' he'd said, 'as a matter of interest?'

'About the conversations? Sinn Fein? Whitehall?'

'Yes.'

'Most of it.'

'Who told you?'

'I was briefed. In fact I passed it on. To a journalist.'

'Who?'

'Willoughby Grant, off the record, of course. It was part of a negotiation. The lunch I described when we all met at Queen Anne's Gate.'

Hennessey had nodded, gazing out at the traffic. 'So who told you?' he'd asked again. 'Who authorised all that? I assume it was authorised?'

'Oh, yes.'

'So who was it?'

Annie had shaken her head, shielding Wren, under no obligation to do the bidding of some apparatchik from Smith Square, and when Hennessey had mentioned Wren himself, asking her for a simple yes or no, she'd once again declined to answer. The exchange had soured the rest of the journey, and when they'd finally pulled to a halt on the Departures ramp at Terminal One, and when she'd inquired about practical help – names, phone numbers – he'd simply handed her an envelope from his briefcase and then opened the door for her to get out. Standing on the kerbside, shaking the creases from her coat, she'd turned round to say goodbye, but the cab was already half-way down the ramp, looking for a gap in the traffic, heading back towards London.

Now, glad of the coffee at her elbow, Annie opened the envelope. The brief occupied a single sheet of paper. At the top, it was stamped 'SECRET: ADDRESSEE ONLY'. Annie read it through, recognising the odd echo here and there, phrases that Hennessey had already used in the taxi. The brief had come from his pen. Definitely. In essence, it boiled down to a single contact, an inspector in the Garda's Special Branch. The man's name was Dermot Reilly. He was based at SB headquarters in Harcourt Terrace. He'd be meeting her at the airport. He had access to the files on O'Keefe's business, and he was part of the team that was tracing every mile of the journey from Longford to Fishguard. If anyone had an answer it would be Dermot Reilly and he was under orders, for once, to share everything with London.

Annie reclined the seat a little, gazing down at the grey corrugations of the Irish Sea, wondering exactly where Hennessey fitted into the picture, and what gave him the right to the information he carried in his briefcase. Her hour on the computer at Gower Street had included a series of phone-calls to all the major intelligence sources for Northern Ireland. She'd anticipated, at the very least, reports of a rumour or two about new arms channels but wherever she'd gone, whoever she'd spoken to, the answer was always the same. The young Army captain on the intelligence co-ordination staff at Lisburn reported a total blank. The same went for MI5's own desk officer at Stormont. And when she'd phoned E3, the RUC's intelligence specialists at Knock, her inquiry had drawn a grim chuckle. They'd no advance knowledge of the seizure but there were hundreds of firms exporting from the Republic and all of them would be sitting ducks for the IRA quartermasters. O'Keefe's prominence in Fianna Fail, the fact that he had a high profile politically, simply made him an even sweeter proposition. 'Who'd ever dream of going through Dessie's stuff,' the inspector had asked, 'when the wee man has so much to lose?'

Dermot Reilly stepped aboard the aircraft the moment the cabin crew swung the big door open. He was younger than Annie had expected, with thick dark curly hair and a battered tweed jacket. His tie was loosened at the neck, the shirt button at the top undone. He had a fresh country complexion but there were signs of exhaustion around his eyes. Annie followed the stewardess up the aisle. The young detective had a farmer's handshake and the smile brought his face alive.

'You're supposed to be six foot nine with a moustache,' he said, 'the way I heard it.'

They stepped out of the aircraft. At the end of the access pier there was a door. While the rest of the passengers hurried towards the arrivals complex, Annie followed Reilly down two flights of wooden steps. Another door at the bottom opened onto the concrete apron. Annie stood in the gathering dusk. Coloured lights winked red and green and the air was heavy with the sweet tang of aviation fuel.

Reilly was standing by a battered Ford Sierra. 'The limo,' he said simply.

They drove beneath the arrival piers and out towards the perimeter road. Reilly kept a pair of glasses on the dashboard and he put them on now, peering uncertainly into the gloom. On the far side of the airfield, Annie could see some kind of trading estate, a collection of steel sheds, brightly-lit islands in a sea of black tarmac. There was a control point at the main gate. Reilly held his ID against the windscreen and a finger rose in salute as they drove through. One corner of the compound was occupied by a big green warehouse, slightly shabbier than the rest. Folding doors were concertinaed back and there was a line of container trailers parked inside. Men were working under the big overhead lights, transferring packages from one container to another, while a supervisor in a white coat scribbled notes on a clipboard.

Reilly stopped the car at the mouth of the warehouse and turned off the engine. They'd been talking about the consignment of office furniture, the packages from Longford that had rolled off the ferry at Fishguard. Reilly had spent the last eight hours at O'Keefe's factory, going over the workforce roll with the personnel manager, looking for employees with Republican sympathies, or family connections in the north, or some private problem serious enough to warrant risking a brief flirtation with the Provisionals. The factory, he said, was smaller than he'd expected, no more than sixty people, and most of them had been with the firm from the off. They'd known each other for years. They were like a family. There were few secrets. As Reilly talked, Annie was thinking about Fat Eddie's fortnight on the factory shop-floor. He'd said the same thing. Almost word for word.

She looked across at Reilly. He seemed half asleep. 'So what do you think,' she said, 'about Longford?'

'I can't believe it happened there. There's no evidence that I could find. No motive, either. O'Keefe's not an eejit. There's no votes in Semtex. Not any more.'

Annie smiled. She liked this man, his soft voice, his easy wit, and she believed him, too. She looked at the containers again. The woman with the clipboard was examining a pile of cardboard boxes.

'So what happens here?'

Reilly reached for a peppermint from an open roll on the shelf beneath the dashboard. He examined it for dust and hairs and then put it in his mouth.

'O'Keefe sends consignments all over,' he said. 'Anything for the UK comes here. There's usually not enough to fill a whole container so they off-load it from his wagon and add it to other part-loads. It's cheaper that way, and quicker. According to Dessie.'

'And?'

Reilly was still staring out through the windscreen. Annie found herself wondering when he'd last had a shave.

'There'd be no problem switching goods here. You could do it. You'd have to have another pack ready, another little parcel, like, with the same goods inside, plus whatever you wanted to get through. As long as you'd sorted it all out, there wouldn't be a problem.'

'But how would you lay hands on the replacement?'

'You could have bought one.'

'And leave a record? A name? An address?'

'Sure,' Reilly yawned, 'or you could steal one. Earlier. Weeks earlier. Months earlier. O'Keefe's stuff comes through here about every ten days. So you'd need to have been around a while.'

'So one consignment, an earlier consignment, would have been short. Is that what you're saying?'

'Yes.'

'And you've checked?'

Reilly smiled, reaching for another mint, returning the supervisor's wave when she caught sight of the car.

'Dessie,' he said at last, 'Dessie's checked.'

'O'Keefe?'

'Yes. It's his theory, the switch, not mine. But I don't blame him for that. Yes,' he yawned again, 'he checked and he found a customer in the UK, a Mr Perkins . . .'

His hand disappeared into his jacket and he produced a crumpled invoice. With it was a photocopy of a letter. He gave both documents to Annie and switched on the interior light over the windscreen. She peered at the letter. Mr Perkins ran an insurance agency in Gloucester. Three of the items he'd ordered from O'Keefe Discount had arrived. The fourth hadn't. Annie looked up. Reilly's head was resting on the steering wheel. His eyes were closed.

'I promise you,' he murmured, 'even the date makes sense.'

Annie looked at the invoice. Under 'Description of Item', against the missing piece of furniture, it read 'G26SSCD-47 Space Saver Conference Desk'.

She glanced up, her finger anchored on the form. 'You know how they found the stuff yesterday,' she said, 'at Fishguard?'

'Sure,' he nodded, 'we all read the English papers.'

'Same item number.'

'Yeah.'

'Same piece of furniture.'

'Sure.'

'Neat.'

Reilly said nothing, running a hand over his face and then leaning back against the seat.

Annie was looking at the invoice again. 'May,' she said. 'That's four months ago.'

'It is. It's plenty of time. You'd maybe need that.'

'But it's an age.'

'Exactly.'

She glanced across at him, frowning. 'So what are you saying?'

Reilly didn't answer but opened the door and got out. Annie did the same, following him across the warehouse to an office. The window of the office had been repaired with masking tape. Inside, the woman with the clipboard was sitting at a cluttered desk, adding up a list of figures on a calculator. Reilly shut the door behind him and introduced Annie. The woman's name was Mairead. She went to a drawer in the filing cabinet and produced a form. She gave it to Reilly and asked Annie if she'd like a cup of tea. When Annie said yes, she disappeared into a tiny kitchen next door.

Reilly gave Annie the form. Across the top, in heavy black letters, it read 'Flanagan and Co.'. Underneath, in childlike capitals, someone had filled in a series of personal details.

'Flanagan's the name of the shippers,' Reilly said. 'This place belongs to them. They're the ones you come to if you want to work here. And that form's the one you fill in if you want a job.'

Annie bent to the form. The man's name was Sean Quinlan. He was thirty-three years old, married, and had last worked for Centra Supermarkets.

'Where's Ballynoe Road?' Annie asked.

'North Dublin. Corporation housing. Working class area. Just down the road here.'

'But why's the address underlined?'

'It doesn't exist. Not 205.'

Annie looked up.

Mairead had reappeared in the open doorway. She was holding a spoon.

'Two, please,' Annie said.

She looked at the form again. Quinlan had started work in the warehouse in March. His timekeeping had evidently been exemplary.

'So where is he now?' she said.

'Gone.'

'Where?'

'No one knows. He didn't turn up for work yesterday and no one's seen him since. When we went looking for him this afternoon, that's what we found . . .' He smothered another yawn, indicating the heavy red line underneath the address.

'Does the firm have a photo?'

'Only the one for the ID badge. That's gone, too.'

'Nothing else?'

Mairead came in with the tea. She gave it to Annie. Annie sipped it, glad of the warmth. The office was freezing.

'There's one lead,' Reilly said at last. 'Quinlan made a friend here. Young lad. Name of Jimmy. They were both football crazy. Used to play against the far wall there, during lunchbreaks. So Mairead says . . .'

Annie looked across at Mairead.

She nodded. 'That's right,' she said, 'both of them mad for the game. More's the pity.'

'Pity?'

'My window.'

'Ah.' Annie grinned, looking at Reilly again. 'So? You've talked to this Jimmy?'

'Aye, I have. And it turns out yer man Quinlan may have been from the north. Talked about one of the Derry teams. Linfield. Knew Windsor Park as well.'

Annie nodded, looking at the form again. Windsor Park was the biggest stadium in Belfast. The Northern Ireland team played internationals there, and she'd been a couple of times, once with Kingdom.

'What else does Jimmy say?'

'Nothing. Except he thinks he may have a photo. One of the guys here was leaving, back in the summer, and they had a drink or two. Jimmy took some snaps. He thinks Quinlan may be in one of them.' Reilly smiled his soft country smile. 'Now how's that for starters?'

An hour and a half later, Annie and Dermot Reilly met Jimmy at a bar in Drumcondra, an inner-city area just north of the Liffey. The bar was shabby. The walls were yellowed with nicotine, and the floor was littered with discarded crisp packets. There were curling sausages in the hot cabinet on the counter and when Annie made her excuses and found the lavatory, the light bulb had been stolen. She sat in the dark, thinking about Reilly, and when she got back to the bar she found him talking to young Jimmy.

The boy had arrived late. He was barely sixteen: pale, thin, freckled, with a shock of red hair. His accent was even thicker than Reilly's and when Annie asked him what he wanted to drink, he settled for a Coke.

Annie got the drinks. Back at the table, the two men were bent over a handful of photos. They spread them over the greasy formica, peering at them one by one. Annie sipped her drink. The second Jamieson's was beginning to soften the pub's harder edges.

She looked down at the photos. Jimmy must have had problems with the flash on his camera because most of them were very dark, but she recognised the ghostly bulk of the big containers in the background, and Mairead's face under a green crêpe paper hat. Jimmy picked up one of the photos and showed it to Reilly. Reilly held it up to the light, nodding. Then he passed it to Annie.

'The one on the right,' he said. 'No marks for focus.'

Annie examined the photo. It had been taken outside the office where they'd been earlier. The window was intact, no masking tape. Two faces dominated the photograph, big men, clearly drunk, one holding a can of Harp lager. In the background, on the right of the photo, was another man. The focus was awful and his face was in near-darkness but there was enough to register certain features under the thinning hair. The mouth, for instance: wide, with fleshy, almost feminine lips. And the eyes, deep-set, with a startled expression.

Reilly was looking at the boy. 'Just the one photo? That's all you've got?'

Jimmy explained that Quinlan hated having his photo taken. Famous for it in the warehouse. Never looked a camera in the eye.

Annie gave the photo back to Reilly. 'How well did you know him?' she asked Jimmy.

The boy looked nervously at Reilly. Reilly told him to go ahead. He turned to Annie and explained they'd played football a lot, but not much else. He'd often suggested they went into the city together, maybe even get a ticket for one of the end-of-season cup games, but Quinlan had never been keen. He'd said his wife was an invalid. She needed looking after. She spent most of her time in a wheelchair.

'Did you ever see her?'

The boy shook his head. 'I don't even know where he lived,' he said. 'He never told us.'

'Wasn't that odd?'

Jimmy shrugged. A job was a job. People came and went, and it was just nice to kick a ball around with someone who really knew what they were doing. He gazed at his drink, uncomfortable again.

Annie watched him a moment, then nodded at the photo. 'Can

I keep that?' She found her bag and put an English ten-pound note on the table.

'Sure.' Jimmy brightened visibly. 'It's yours.'

Reilly drove Annie across the river and into the city centre. It was gone ten now but the streets were still busy. Cousins' secretary had booked Annie into a hotel by St Stephen's Green, and Reilly took her to a restaurant nearby, a newly-opened place he'd seen written up in something called *IT*. Annie said she insisted on paying but Reilly shook his head. Orders, he said, were orders. Nothing but the best. Courtesy of his bosses at Harcourt Terrace.

'What's *IT*?' Annie asked, settling behind a table near the back of the restaurant.

'It's a fancy magazine. *IT* stands for the *Irish Tatler*. I read it at the dentist's,' he winced, 'last week.'

'Ah,' Annie nodded, 'you spend a lot of time at the dentist's?'

'Too much.'

'Serves you right.'

'Why?'

'All those peppermints.'

The food was superb. They had a big dish of scallops and fillets of John Dory and a huge helping of buttered potatoes that the Irishman swore were the best he'd ever tasted. They talked about their respective jobs, what made the pulse quicken, what didn't, and they were onto the third bottle of Chablis when Reilly mentioned Sabbathman. Evidently the story was very big in Ireland. The government might be outraged but the rest of the country thought it was a gas.

'You solving that one too?' he said.

'Yes,' Annie grinned, 'me and a friend of mine.'

'Friend?'

'Boyfriend.'

'Intelligence? Like you?'

'No.' She shook her head. 'Special Branch. Like you.'

'Ah . . . then I was right.'

'About what?'

'That good taste of yours.'

He lifted the glass, a silent toast. He'd already told her he was married. His wife's name was Bridget. They had three kids and were saving up for a new second-hand car. Annie smiled at the phrase, thinking of Kingdom, what he was up to, who he might be with. She'd tried to phone to thank him for the flowers but apparently he was away for a couple of days. South Coast somewhere. Maybe Portsmouth. The name had made her stomach lurch and now she knew why. She missed him. Badly. She didn't want him talking to some pretty young doctor. She wanted him back home, in her bed, telling her how much she mattered. This was new territory, a journey she'd never risked before, and she found it oddly overwhelming.

Reilly had gone back to Sabbathman.

'You really think there's a link?' he was saying.

'To what?'

'To O'Keefe? To the north?'

'O'Keefe, no.' Annie shook her head. 'I don't see that at all. The north?' She shrugged. 'I like Quinlan. That sounds OK to me. You should put in for a commendation. Very neat. And very plausible.'

'We have a customer?'

'Definitely.'

'You'll be wanting it wrapped? To take home?'

'Please.'

Reilly beamed at her, lifting his glass again. '*Tiocfaidh ar la*,' he said, 'thank fuck for the armed struggle.'

TEN

SECURITY OFFICE
PO BOX 500, LONDON

TO: PPS, 10 Downing Street, SW1
FROM: Hugh Cousins
DATE: 1 October, 1993

<u>STRICTLY CONFIDENTIAL</u>

Thanks for the lunch. The Deal item I mentioned would now
appear to relate to the Secretary of State's forthcoming
visit to the Royal Marine School of Music. As you know, the
Deal barracks have already been subject to PIRA attack. The
temptation to have a second bite at the apple is wholly in
keeping with current PIRA strategy and would meet their
requirements for a spectacular mainland strike. I'd be grateful if you could include this intelligence when you talk to
the PM tomorrow. He may find it useful in the context of the
current conversations.

Annie awoke to the soft flutter of the bedside telephone. She struggled upright, peering at her watch. She had a headache. It was 07.38.

'Annie Meredith? Hugh Cousins.'

Annie settled back against the pillow. Outside the hotel, through the double-glazing, she could hear the growl of the morning traffic. She began to massage the ridge of pain above her eyes, giving Cousins a brief summary of what had happened. She was about to double-check the name of the head of the Garda Special Branch when he interrupted.

'You say you've got a photo?'

'Yes. It's not wonderful but I'm sure our guys can enhance it. All they need—'

'And you're saying the man's disappeared? Is that what you're saying?'

'Yes. A couple of days ago. According to the locals.' Annie closed her eyes, trying to will the pain away. 'I'm seeing Reilly again this morning. He's got some documentation for me. They're very keen. Give me a couple of days and God knows what they'll be offering. I'm serious. It's wine and roses. Literally. Reilly tells me—'

Cousins cut across her again. 'We need to meet,' he said quickly. 'Lunchtime would be best.'

'But—'

'Listen to me. Go to the airport. Get the first plane you can.'

'Plane?' Annie stared at the phone. Belfast was ninety miles up the road.

'I can take the train if it's that important,' she said, 'and be back here tonight.'

There was a silence at the other end. Then Cousins was giving her an address: 318 Queen's Gate Gardens.

Annie looked at it. 'That doesn't sound like Belfast,' she said.

'It isn't,' Cousins said briskly, 'it's London. I'm back home again.'

The flights out of Dublin were half empty and Annie had no trouble getting a seat on the 10.30. She sat near the back, still nursing the remains of the headache. Her bewilderment about Cousins had hardened into anger. She'd done well, she knew she had. She'd spent less than twenty-four hours on Irish soil and she had evidence that would probably connect the Fishguard explosives to sources in the north.

Politically, that was highly significant. It meant for one thing that someone at the sharp end of the republican movement had gone to enormous trouble to implicate the Irish government in an arms scandal. To clear their name, Dublin had offered unprecedented co-operation. Only yesterday, en route to Heathrow, Andrew Hennessey had told her how important it was to nurture this new openness. Dublin, he'd said, had always been pathological about the Brits. They'd never trusted a word we said. That made most negotiations a non-starter. It also made their security files a closed book. Anything, he'd said. Anything that might prise open the doors of Dublin Castle would be a major intelligence coup. *Major intelligence coup*. That had been his phrase. Exactly. So what on earth was she doing, airborne again, en route back to London? What could possibly be more important than staying in Dublin, knocking on doors, nurturing relationships, building up trust?

She thought about Dermot Reilly. Last night, at the end of the meal, she'd wondered aloud about buying a toothbrush and some spare underwear, and he'd offered to turn up the next day and take her to Dunne's, a big department store. Drunk or otherwise, that wasn't the kind of offer you turned down. Not if it came from a Special Branch inspector who probably fancied you. Not if you

252

were openly working for MI5. Not if you were serious about grabbing as much of this glorious windfall as you could. So why was Cousins calling her out of the orchard? What was suddenly so important it couldn't wait a day or two?

The British Airways flight landed at 11.45. Ignoring Cousins' instructions about lunch, Annie took a cab to her flat in Kew. The headache had gone now but she felt grubby and travel-worn. The least Cousins owed her was ten minutes in the shower and a clean pair of knickers.

She was still towelling herself dry when the chimes went on the front door. She slipped on a dressing gown, recognising Kingdom's long shape through the frosted glass. When he stepped inside, he was smiling. Pleased to see me, she thought. Definitely.

'I tried to raise you,' he said, 'first thing this morning.'

'I was in Dublin.'

'Dublin?'

'Yes.' She looked at him a moment, her hair still dripping wet. Then she reached up and kissed him, letting the dressing gown fall open, leaving the wet imprint of her body on his jeans. 'That was for the flowers,' she said, 'they were beautiful.'

Kingdom made coffee while she got dressed. He said he'd been down on the south coast but he didn't trouble her with any details. For once in their relationship, she found herself wanting to know more. She stood in the kitchen doorway, combing her hair back.

'Did you see your lady friend?' she said.

'What lady friend?'

'Your little doctor friend.'

Kingdom glanced round. He was heaping coffee into the cafetiere. She could tell how much the question had pleased him.

'Yes,' he said, 'since you ask.'

'In the line of duty?'

'Of course.'

'Fruitful?'

Kingdom laughed, turning back to the cafetiere, scalding the coffee with boiling water. 'If it was that great, I wouldn't be here, would I?' he said. 'If it was that great, I'd never have left.'

'I'm not sure I like that.'

'I'm not sure you're entitled to care.' He began to stir the coffee. 'Aren't there house rules about all this? You and me? Stuff we don't talk about, stuff we do?'

Annie eyed him a moment, wondering if her relationship with Cousins would sustain another hour or so's delay. Then she shrugged and turned away. 'OK, OK,' she said, 'just asking, you know, routine inquiries.'

She was back in the bedroom, applying a thin line of mascara under each eye, when Kingdom appeared with the coffee. He'd also found some croissants and they were piled on a tray beside an open half-pound of butter.

Annie looked at him in the mirror. 'They're stale,' she said.

'I put them under the tap. Then I grilled them.'

'Is that why I can smell burning?'

'Yes.'

She smiled at him, swopping the mascara for a lipstick. Stale croissants with this lovely man sounded infinitely nicer than lunch with Hugh Cousins. Kingdom was sitting on the bed. He'd kicked his shoes off and now he was undoing the buttons down the front of his shirt. Annie shook her head, finishing with the lipstick, testing the effect in the mirror.

'Can't,' she said.

'Why not?'

'Got to go out.'

'But you've only just come in.'

'I know.'

'And it's Saturday.'

'I know that too. You don't have to tell me. I'm supposed to be in Dublin. Buying silk underwear.'

Kingdom was looking at her in the mirror, trying to make up his mind whether she was joking or not.

She stood up, adjusting her skirt. She was thinking about Cousins again. 'You could hang on,' she said, 'until I come back.'

'Thanks.'

'Seriously.' She knelt down in front of him, running her fingers along the waistband of his jeans. 'Then we could do it justice.'

'Are you really going out?'

'Yes. Since when did I put lipstick on for you?'

She got up again, reaching for her coffee. Then she went into the lounge and dialled for a minicab. When the dispatcher asked where she wanted to go, she reached back with her foot, pushing the bedroom door closed before giving an address.

'About five minutes,' the dispatcher said, hanging up.

Annie sat on the sofa a moment, nursing her coffee. The clock on the mantelpiece was a quarter of an hour slow. That meant it was already 1.15. If the traffic was heavy, she'd be lucky to be at Cousins' place by two. She thought of blaming it on British Airways, then she shrugged. The summons back was crazy. Why should she apologise to a madman?

The bedroom door opened and Kingdom reappeared with the tray. She could read him like a book and she realised how disappointed he was. She got up and followed him into the kitchen, wondering for the second time exactly what had happened down in Portsmouth.

'I meant it about coming back,' she said. 'I'm not going to be long. You could settle in for the afternoon. We could go out somewhere tonight. Or just . . .' she shrugged, '. . .whatever.'

Kingdom put his arms round her. She nestled into him.

'What happened to those flowers?' he said.

'They're still at the office.'

'Why?'

'This is the first time I've been back since you sent them, since yesterday. I got back just now. Just before you arrived.' She looked up at him. 'Honestly.'

'And you've really been to Dublin? You're serious?'

Annie hesitated a moment, then nodded. Another rule broken, another dam breached. 'Yes,' she said, 'all of . . .' She frowned. 'Fourteen hours.'

'Productive?'

She nodded, her hands cupping his face, one finger sealing his lips. 'Very,' she said. 'But no more questions.'

'I love you.'

'That's different.'

'I know,' he grinned, 'just checking.'

The minicab came soon afterwards. Annie sorted quickly through her handbag and said goodbye at the door. When Kingdom reminded her to take the key, she said she had a spare one. If he fancied staying, she'd be back later. Otherwise, maybe he'd phone. She kissed him on tip-toes and touched him lightly on the face before heading for the stairs. At the bottom, in the communal hall, she looked back up at him.

'Me, too,' she said, 'if you're asking.'

Queen's Gate Gardens lay to the north of Gloucester Road, handsome mid-Victorian terraces around a rectangle of newly-mown grass. Number 318 was along from the Kuwaiti embassy and Annie recognised the yellow Volvo at the kerb. The car on the other side of the road looked familiar, too, though it wasn't until Rupert Devereaux opened the door of Cousins' flat that she realised where she'd seen it last. The Mercedes, she thought. The one he'd been driving in Fishguard.

Devereaux stepped aside, a long cheroot in one hand, inviting her in with an extravagant bow. Through an open archway Annie could see the main living room. It was somehow bigger than she'd anticipated, with tall French windows giving onto a small, sheltered patio. The room was cool and austere, grey walls, black leather chairs, and it was dominated by a long pine table. Cousins was sitting at one end, surrounded by the remains of lunch. There was a young child perched on his lap and he introduced the woman beside him with a casual wave of his right hand.

'Olivia,' he said, 'Rupert's wife.'

Annie shook hands. Through the open hatch into the kitchen she could see a pile of dirty plates stacked neatly beside the sink.

'We thought you'd gone astray,' Cousins said, 'so I'm afraid we got on with it.'

He looked up for a moment or two, the faintest smile on his face, then Devereaux sat down again and the two men resumed a conversation that Annie had obviously interrupted. They were talking about a sailing holiday they'd all taken a couple of months back. Somewhere in Greece. The way the conversation went, the jokes, the innuendos, the peals of laughter, it was obvious that the three of them spent a great deal of time together. Once or twice another name was mentioned, Colette, but it was a while before Annie began to suspect the truth of it: that Colette was Cousins' ex-wife, and that the marriage had only recently collapsed.

Cousins and Devereaux were drinking Armagnac. The bottle was three-quarters empty.

Devereaux offered some to Annie. 'Go on,' he said, 'puts hairs on your chest.'

Devereaux' wife exchanged glances with Annie and then left the table. Annie could hear her out in the kitchen, starting work on the dishes. Cousins had his mouth to the child's ear now, whispering some story or other, and Annie found herself wondering whether he had any kids of his own. There were no clues in the flat, no photographs or toys. On the contrary, the place was bare of the usual personal touches, as if Cousins had deliberately settled for a life without unnecessary ballast.

Devereaux drained his glass. He was looking at Annie. 'Time for the off,' he said. 'How's the traffic?'

'Fine. Are you going far?'

'Cotswolds. Chipping Campden.'

He crushed his cheroot in an ashtray and stood up. Then he took the child from Cousins, holding it awkwardly, like a parcel he didn't quite trust. His wife appeared from the kitchen, wearing a pair of yellow rubber gloves. Some signal passed between them and the woman nodded, peeling off the gloves. Annie was still sitting at the table when they both kissed Cousins goodbye. Evidently they were meeting again in a week's time. Their place this time. Some people Hugh might like to meet.

Annie heard the voices receding into the hall. Then the front door opened and closed and Hugh Cousins was back again, sinking into the chair across the table from Annie and reaching for the bottle of Armagnac.

'My godson,' he said absently. 'Lovely boy.'

Annie shook her head when Cousins pushed a brandy glass towards her. She had the photo she'd brought back from Dublin in her handbag. She laid it carefully on the table in front of Cousins and repeated the story she'd already told him on the phone. Cousins picked up the photo and gazed at it. When Annie had finished, he looked up.

'Which one?'

'On the right. In the background.'

Cousins frowned, examining the photo again.

Annie watched him carefully. 'You know who it is?'

'No, but,' the frown returned, 'what did the Garda say? Did they have a name? Apart from Quinlan?'

'Apparently not.'

'Nothing on file?'

'I don't know. I was about to find out but . . .' Annie shrugged, gesturing at the remains of the meal. 'You had other ideas.'

'You think they might know? You got that impression?'

'No. I got the impression they hadn't a clue. What matters is getting O'Keefe off the hook. Where Quinlan takes us is irrelevant. Just as long as it's in the north. That's all they care about.'

Cousins nodded. He was still fingering the photograph. 'Good,' he said, 'that's good.'

'Why?'

'Because they're in the clear. Good for them.' He nodded. 'And good for us.'

'You know who it is?' Annie said again. 'Only it might save us both a lot of time.'

Cousins glanced up at her, that same faint smile, and Annie began to wonder whether he ever relaxed. Once you got past the charm and the good looks, there was a chill about the man, an icy self-control that no amount of brandy or repartee seemed to penetrate. It went with this flat of his, its bareness, its lack of clutter. It spoke of self-discipline, and a tightly ordered life. Dawn circuits of Hyde Park, Annie thought, and half an hour in a cold bath afterwards.

Cousins was on his feet again. From a cupboard in the corner he produced a tin. On the lid it said 'Sharp's Toffees'.

'Are you sure you're not hungry?'

'Yes. It's OK, thanks. I had something on the plane.'

'Coffee? Tea?'

Annie shook her head. She wanted this to be over. She wanted to be back in her flat in Kew with Alan Kingdom, and a couple of bottles of good red wine, and nothing to think about but each other. Flowers, she thought. He sent me flowers.

Cousins sat down and opened the tin. Inside was a copy of one of the standard-issue contact notes in use at Gower Street.

'This might sound a bit brisk,' Cousins began, 'but there isn't much time.'

Annie looked across at the contact note. Upside down, she recognised the name. 'Bobby McCrudden?' she said. '*My* Bobby McCrudden?'

'Yes.' Cousins nodded.

Annie watched him leafing through other documents in the tin. Bobby McCrudden had been the best of the contacts she'd made during her last nine months in Belfast, a small, slight, crop-haired man with a huge pair of glasses and an almost permanent scowl. As a Sinn Fein councillor, he'd run a series of community programmes in Andersonstown and had taken a stand against pro-violence elements in the republican movement. He was tireless and extremely brave. Two of his brothers had been murdered by the Loyalists and his own home had been attacked at least twice. Since early summer, his wife and kids had been living behind steel shutters while Bobby himself moved from address to address every few days. The last time Annie had met him, he'd been wearing protective body armour, a Kevlar chest and backplate he'd acquired from the widow of a murdered IRA intelligence officer.

By now, Cousins had found what he was after. It looked like a map. He gave it to Annie. A small town near Portadown was circled in red.

'Tandragee?' she said.

'Yes. There's a bar called Flaherty's. It's across the road from the Catholic church. Everyone knows it. McCrudden will be there tonight. Half-past nine.'

'*Tonight?*'

Cousins nodded. He was looking at his watch. 'I spoke to him yesterday. He'd been in touch through Lisburn. Asking for you.'

'Why?'

'He says he needs to talk. But only to you.'

'What about?'

Cousins smiled. He was holding the photo, peering again at the face in the background. 'Our friend,' he said.

'Quinlan?'

'No.' Cousins shook his head. 'Sabbathman.'

'Bobby McCrudden? Wants to talk about Sabbathman?'

'That's what he says.'

'Are you serious?'

'Yes.'

Annie gazed at him, wanting to believe it. To the best of her knowledge, McCrudden's cover was still intact, partly because his commitment to the peaceful advance of the republican cause was so total. His dealings with Annie had always been on this basis. He wasn't a tout. He didn't take money. He wasn't under Brit control, hoovering up every scrap of information he could find. On the contrary, he was a dedicated grassroots politician who would, when it served the cause, do business with the Brits. But only with Annie. And only at a time and place of his own choosing.

'But what's the hurry?' Annie said. 'Why tonight?'

'I don't know.'

'How did he sound? On the phone?'

'Anxious.'

'He's always anxious.'

'Very anxious. He said he needed to get it over with.'

'What? Get what over with?'

Cousins was frowning now, visibly impatient. 'God knows,' he said, 'I imagine that's why he wants the meet.'

Annie nodded, accepting the logic. 'So you want me to go?' she said. 'You want me to be there?'

'Obviously.' Cousins got up and went to the phone. He dialled a number and waited for it to answer. 'The next shuttle's at five o'clock. I've got the duty major from Bessbrook on stand-by to meet you at Aldergrove. He's handling arrangements their end.'

The number answered. Cousins bent to the phone and asked for a minicab.

Annie was still looking at him. 'What arrangements?' she said.

'Tandragee for a start. There's no way you're walking into a meet like that without support. The duty major's organising five guys and a couple of cars. Two of the guys I know personally. They're first rate. At the airport you'll get radio frequencies and the full brief. The major's name's Mike Stanton, by the way. Little guy. Red hair.'

Annie looked at the map again, impressed by the planning. Cousins had thought the thing through. No doubt about it. She glanced up. 'Is this why you got me back from Dublin?'

'Yes.'

'So what are we expecting from McCrudden?'

'A name.'

'For Sabbathman?'

'Jackpot?' Cousins grinned. 'Yes.'

He looked at her a moment, then sat down again. The Green Slime, he said, had identified what they called 'the fault line' in the Provisional leadership. One faction, heavily represented in Sinn Fein, were not only talking to the Brits but to the loyalists too. The hard men, with no appetite for peace, were determined to wreck both sets of negotiations. To that end, they'd been planning a spectacular, something unusual, something on the mainland, something to truly focus the public's attention. On all three counts, Sabbathman fitted the bill. Thus, Cousins' excitement. And thus, now, the urgency. It was already Saturday. Tomorrow, Sabbathman would probably strike again.

Annie nodded. 'The Green Slime' was service slang for Army Intelligence. On occasions, they could be remarkably astute.

'And what about O'Keefe?' she said, picking up the photo. 'Where does all that fit?'

'Spoiling operation. Classic poison ivy. Peace depends on London talking to Dublin. If the Brits think Dublin are gun-running, where does that leave negotiations?' He nodded at the photo. 'Reilly's spot on. All it takes is a guy to switch consignments. The rest takes care of itself.'

'Thanks to your customs friend.'

'Yes.' Cousins smiled. 'Quite.'

Annie looked at the photo again, the fleshy lips, the startled expression. 'Poison Ivy' was the phrase you used in the intelligence game when you knew you were dealing with planted evidence. Cynics swore it flourished in Belfast. Something to do with green fingers and the incessant rain. Annie smiled. Cousins was right. If the hard men in the north wanted to strangle peace talks, they could do a whole lot worse than smearing Dublin.

Annie put the photo to one side and folded the map. 'Say he has a name tonight?' she said. 'Bobby McCrudden?'

'Then you pass it on. There and then. Stanton's boys have airborne assets at Bessbrook. They're tasked to move on ten minutes' notice.' He glanced at his watch. 'From 18.00 tonight.'

'Are you serious? You think we're that close?'

'Yes, otherwise . . .' he shrugged, '. . . I wouldn't be putting you through all this. Dublin's a bonus. You did well. Very well. But Belfast's where it begins and ends.' He stood up. 'I imagine you'll need a change of clothes. Under the circumstances.'

Annie gazed up at him. Clean knickers were the last thing on her mind. 'Yes,' she said. 'I suppose I will.'

'You've got a credit card?'

'Yes.'

'Use it at the airport. Keep the receipts. Anything up to . . .' He frowned. 'Say three hundred.'

'For underwear?'

'For whatever.' He paused. 'You've still got the combination for the safe house? Fitzroy Avenue?'

'Yes.'

'Good. It hasn't been changed. There's a hire car waiting for you at Aldergrove. Avis. Sort out the batting order with Mike, then go to the safe house. There's a holdall in the wardrobe in the top bedroom. Blue thing. You'll find a weapon inside, and some ammunition. The radio's there, too. But make sure you get the frequencies from Mike. OK?'

The doorbell chimed. Cousins was already half-way down the hall by the time Annie got to her feet. She put the map and the photo in her bag. The last ten minutes had left her feeling slightly dazed.

Outside, on the pavement, Cousins was holding the back door of the minicab open. He bent over her as she slid in. She could smell the brandy on his breath.

'Lucky thing,' he said, grinning, 'I feel quite envious.'

For the second time that day, Annie found herself at Heathrow. She tried to phone Kingdom at her flat but there was no answer.

She put the phone down, checking on the departures board again, wondering how best to kill the forty minutes before the five o'clock shuttle. At length, she dug in her bag and found the card that Francis Wren had given her on the bus. She'd been meaning to phone him since yesterday.

She dialled the number, taking the party invitation at face value, using his Christian name when he finally answered. She explained about Andrew Hennessey, the mysterious apparatchik from Smith Square. In the taxi, yesterday afternoon, he'd tried to pin her down about the approach to Willoughby Grant. He seemed to know that Wren had authorised the leak about the secret talks. When she paused for breath, Annie heard Wren chuckling. In the background, low, she recognised an aria from *Turandot*.

'You don't care,' she said, 'if Five know too?'

'Not in the slightest.'

'You know how vindictive they can be? The lengths they go to sometimes? Pensions and so forth?'

'Of course.'

'And none of that bothers you?'

Wren apologised, ever the gentleman. He said he was grateful for the trouble she'd taken. It had been kind of her to try and protect him, kinder still to make the call.

'No problem,' Annie said, 'I just thought it might have been important, that's all.'

'Oh, it is, it is.'

'Why?'

'Because I didn't authorise it. It wasn't my idea at all. In fact I was rather against the notion. Given the delicacy of the . . . ah . . . circumstances, I thought it was an extremely foolish thing to do.'

Annie was frowning now. There were bits of this conversation that didn't quite fit.

'So who authorised it?' she said, 'Who told you to brief me?'

The chuckle again. More Puccini. 'Hugh Cousins,' he said, 'who do you think?'

Half an hour later, the Belfast shuttle boarding, Annie was still trying to get through to Bobby McCrudden. She knew he was permanently on the move, two or three different addresses every week, but the one number she'd always trusted was the family home, the neat little council semi in Andersonstown where his wife and kids still lived. Annie had met McCrudden's wife, Darina, on a number of occasions. She was a handsome flame-haired woman with a slight limp from a teenage car accident, and she normally had a fair idea of her husband's whereabouts. If Bobby McCrudden was really in Tandragee, if the meet was genuine, then Darina would know.

There was a problem, though, with the number. The first time Annie tried it, she got a strange whine she'd never heard before. She dialled again, checking the number in her book, and this time she got a different tone, the signal that meant number unobtainable. Phoning Directory Enquiries would have been a waste of time because the home number had always been ex-directory, so Annie dialled Curzon House instead, getting through to Registry, checking in with her PIN code, and asking the girl on the duty desk to access McCrudden's file. She did so, returning within a minute with a six-digit number. Annie thanked her. The number was the same as the one she'd just tried so she dialled again, getting an identical tone, number unobtainable, and when she finally phoned the operator and got him to check the line, he too sounded puzzled.

'Doesn't ring in at all,' he said, 'can't think why.'

Annie thanked him, stooping to retrieve her bag and running across the concourse towards the Belfast gate. She'd phone again from Aldergrove, she thought. And if there was still a problem, she'd bring the operation to a halt until it was sorted out.

It was raining when Annie got to Belfast. The plane bumped down through low cloud and she barely had time to register a blur of sodden fields before they were swooping over the perimeter fence, the pilot throttling back as the wheels hissed on the wet tarmac.

Mike Stanton, the duty major from Bessbrook, was waiting for her at the arrivals gate. He was wearing civilian dress but there was a uniformed driver with him, a tall corporal with a thin pencil moustache and watchful eyes. Stanton led the way to a secure RUC interview room while the corporal went to the cafeteria for a tray of coffees. The interview room was small and bare and Annie was about to sit down at the single table when she spotted the phone on the wall.

'May I?'

Stanton, unpacking his briefcase, told her to go ahead and she dialled Bobby McCrudden's number again. This time, to her surprise, it began to ring. McCrudden's wife answered, a deep voice with a rich Belfast accent. Annie asked for McCrudden.

'He's not here. Who is this?'

Annie gave her name.

McCrudden's wife remembered her at once. 'Dear God,' she said, 'I thought you'd gone?'

'I have.' Annie paused. 'Had.'

'Back now, though? Can't leave it alone?'

'Something like that. Where's Bobby?'

'He's away to the west. In that car of his brother's.'

'Gone long?'

'Half an hour ago. You're unlucky not to catch him.'

'And back tonight?'

'Back in town, yes.'

Annie nodded, doing the calculations in her head. Bobby McCrudden's movements fitted perfectly. His brother's car was famous for breakdowns. To get down to Tandragee in time for the meet, he'd need to be on the road already and 'the west' was as close as he'd probably come to sharing the destination, even with his wife.

Annie bent to the phone again. She could hear the kids in the background and the signature tune from *Blind Date* on the television. Under the circumstances, it seemed nicely appropriate.

'By the way,' she said, 'your phone's been out of order.'

'I know. It went out this afternoon. Just for a couple of hours.' Darina laughed. 'Probably the rain.'

Annie returned to the table. Stanton was studying a large-scale map of Tandragee. The place was bigger than she'd expected and Flaherty's Bar was ringed in red chinagraph. Stanton pulled up a chair for her and began to run through the brief, indicating on the map where he intended to position his Q cars. The Q cars from

Bessbrook were mainly unmarked Escorts or Astras with Northern Ireland plates and a fancy radio set-up concealed in the dashboard. The evening's operational call-sign was to be 'Greenglass'. Annie would be 'Greenglass One'.

Annie listened to the briefing. The deployments were sensible and she said she anticipated no problems with McCrudden. Stanton nodded, glancing up from the map. He was quietly spoken, with a flat Home Counties accent. He didn't smile much, which Annie found oddly comforting. People who smiled a lot, she thought, often had things to hide.

The corporal arrived with the coffees. Stanton told him to pull up a chair, his finger still anchored on Flaherty's Bar, his eyes still on Annie. He had a terrible complexion, his skin pitted with acne scars.

'You're sure you don't want anyone inside?'

'Positive.' Annie nodded at the map. 'You've got line of sight front and back. I'm not that delicate.'

'And you're happy with the comms procedures?'

'Yes.'

Stanton grunted, spooning sugar into his coffee, running quickly through a pencilled checklist. If McCrudden came up with a name, Annie was to pass it on at once. The Q cars were in contact with Army headquarters at Lisburn and with the standing SAS detachment at Bessbrook. London had given the operation the highest priority, and a name would trigger an elaborate snatch operation. He didn't go into details but his manner left Annie in no doubt about the importance of what was about to happen. This was a weekend when reputations – perhaps even careers – would be made or lost.

'You'll be making your own way to Tandragee?' he said.

Annie nodded. 'No problem.'

Stanton hesitated a moment, ever the perfectionist, then reached for his briefcase and shrugged. 'OK,' he said, 'if that's what you prefer.'

The two soldiers escorted her out of the interview room and said goodbye on the concourse. When they'd disappeared towards the car park, Annie went to the Avis desk. She'd half-anticipated some kind of escort en route to Tandragee and she was glad that no one was insisting. The tricky parts of operational life in Northern Ireland were always the beginning and end of any journey. The end of this one – Flaherty's Bar in Tandragee – was now covered. She had total confidence in Stanton and the plans he'd made. That left the start of the journey, leaving the airport, and this she knew she could sort out herself. Her two years in Belfast had taught her a great deal, but the most important lesson of all was the absolute need for self-reliance. Keep things simple. And keep things to yourself. That way, most of the time, you'd get by.

At the Avis desk, she gave the girl her name. The girl consulted a board at the back of the booth. When she turned back, she offered Annie a key.

'It's a white Cavalier,' she said, 'out in the car park, off to your left.'

Annie smiled back, refusing the key. 'Some other car, please,' she said. 'I hate Cavaliers.'

'Really?' The girl looked startled but didn't argue. There were three rows of keys on the board at the back.

'Something a bit nippy, too,' Annie said, 'if you have it.'

'Same class?'

'Doesn't matter. Use my Visa if there's an authorisation problem.'

The girl looked at the board again. She gave Annie a key from the bottom row. 'Golf GTI,' she said, 'brand new.'

'Colour?'

The girl looked at the board again. 'Red.'

'Perfect,' Annie said, 'I hate white, too.'

Across from the car hire desks there was a small arcade of shops. Annie went to the counter selling rainwear and bought herself a big green anorak with a stiff turn-up collar. There was also a display of local knitwear and she found a flat tweed cap, the smallest size they had, putting it on and checking herself in the mirror. It wasn't a perfect fit but with the anorak it changed her silhouette completely and if she was unlucky enough to hit trouble, it might well buy her the couple of seconds she knew would count.

Outside the airport building, standing on the wet pavement, Annie waited until she'd spotted the Golf before hurrying out to the car park. She was wearing the anorak now, with the collar up and the tweed cap pulled low over her eyes. The car was, as promised, brand new. She experimented with the lights for a moment or two and then threaded her way onto the exit road, one eye on the rear view mirror. She drove round the one-way system twice, still checking for cars behind. Convinced she wasn't being followed, she finally took the road that left the airport, slowing for a wave-through from the armed RUC men at the security checkpoint.

It had stopped raining by now and the last of a cold, steel-grey dusk was settling on the line of hills to the west. On the motorway, traffic was still pouring out of the city, a flood of on-coming headlights, and Annie began to relax. If everything went according to plan, if Bobby McCrudden really had a name for Sabbathman, then she was hours away from giving her career a major lift. Events, for once, had put her at the very centre of a major national story and her bosses in Gower Street couldn't fail to take notice. Quite what shape her reward would take, she didn't know but the currency that really mattered in MI5 was battle honours, and just now they were extremely hard to come by. Sabbathman's was a scalp worth having. Even Alan Kingdom would admit that. The thought of him warmed her, and she slipped into the fast lane and took the Golf up to 95 mph as the lights of the city appeared ahead.

Minutes later, at the Grosvenor Road roundabout, Annie left the motorway. She drove up Victoria Street, past the Europa Hotel. A mile and a half further on, near the University, she made a series of left turns. The safe house lay in one of the avenues that ran down towards the river. She'd used it often, sometimes for converted terrorists in transit out of the province, sometimes to brief agents coming in. Once, at the start of their relationship, she'd even taken Kingdom there, making love in one of the bedrooms on the third floor. Kingdom had known it was a safe house from the start, recognising the wallpaper in the sitting room from a head and shoulders photo he'd seen in an RUC file. It was one of the first things she'd noticed about him, how perceptive he was, and how suspicious, searching the bedroom afterwards for hidden cameras.

Now, she parked the Golf three doors down from the safe house and walked back. The properties on either side of the safe house had been bought by an agency working on instructions from the Northern Ireland Office, and both had been converted into student lets. The safe house itself had a speaker phone by the front door with three buttons against three names. The device in fact acted as a security lock and Annie remembered the sequence without difficulty, three pushes on the middle button, one on the top, then two on the bottom. The door opened and she stepped inside, recognising at once the smell of the place, an unforgettable mixture of old fat, boiled sprouts, and the powerful disinfectant favoured by the woman who did the cleaning.

The house appeared to be empty. In a wardrobe in a bedroom upstairs, where Cousins had promised, she found a blue holdall. Inside, wrapped in a copy of the *Belfast Telegraph*, was a hand-gun, a Browning automatic, the sort she'd trained on and carried routinely throughout her tour in the province. Annie glanced at the paper. It carried yesterday's date, Friday 1 October, and she wondered for a moment whether Cousins himself had been here. Executives of his eminence rarely bothered themselves with the spadework but Cousins – as she'd begun to realise – was a law unto himself.

Annie picked up the gun again, checking the mechanism, working the action backwards and forwards. Then she loaded three clips with shells from the box of ammunition. Tandragee was about forty minutes out of Belfast, to the west. Cousins had arranged the meet for nine o'clock. McCrudden would wait for thirty minutes, no more. If she wasn't there by half-past nine, he'd leave. Annie slipped a full clip into the butt of the Browning and levelled the gun at a water colour of Lough Neagh on the wall. It was a beautifully balanced weapon, solid but not too heavy. Just holding it gave her instant confidence.

Annie put the automatic back in the holdall and took out the radio, entering the frequency Stanton had given her at the airport. Then she glanced at her watch. Nearly half-past eight. Already running late.

Outside, the street was empty, one or two parked cars, no other signs of life. Annie walked to the Golf and got in, stowing the holdall on the passenger seat beside her. At the end of the street, she turned right, making her way back to the main road. The traffic was much lighter now and once she'd rejoined the motorway, she took the Golf up to 80 mph. On the radio, she'd found a local programme called Classic Trax, an hour of music devoted to the seventies, and she eased her seat back, tapping out the rhythms with her fingertips, singing along to Chris Rea and Van Morrison. She smiled, thinking again of Kingdom. His kind of music. His kind of lyrics.

She was nearly at Lisburn when she realised she was being followed. The headlights in the rear-view mirror had slowly closed on her. Now they felt no more than a yard or so behind, the full beams dazzling her. She sank a little lower in the seat, going through the usual checks. She accelerated, way past the hundred mark, then she slowed again, down to sixty, fifty, but nothing made any difference. There was no attempt to overtake, no pulling back, just the harsh white glare in the rear-view mirror, and the miles unwinding to the end of the motorway. She was past her exit by now, way past, but that didn't matter. Bobby McCrudden could wait. Everything could wait. All that mattered now was putting darkness between her and the car behind.

She debated what to do, feeling her pulse at last beginning to steady. The Browning lay beside her, on top of the holdall. She reached for it, making sure it was still there, then she felt inside the holdall, pulling out the radio. The on/off switch was on the side of the set. She turned the radio on and held it close to her mouth.

'Greenglass One,' she said, using the call sign Stanton had given her at the airport. 'Does any one read me? Over?'

She listened for a moment, hearing no acknowledgements, wondering who else might be tuned in. Active operational channels were monitored constantly. She tried again, same message, the set tight to her mouth.

'Greenglass One, Greenglass One. Repeat. Emergency. Who reads me?'

Again, silence. She glanced down. Where a tiny red light normally confirmed working power, there was nothing. Only darkness. She switched quickly to receive, scanning through the channels, hearing nothing. The batteries were dead. There was no power. Annie closed her eyes a moment, cursing herself for not checking earlier, back in the safe house. She'd been too hasty. She'd put time before prudence, the cardinal sin, and now here she was, deaf and dumb, the speedo showing 89 mph and the headlights behind still rock-solid in the rear-view mirror. Provos, she thought, had to be. The hard-faced ultras from Cousins' scenario, the guys who wanted to strangle the peace talks at birth, the guys who'd do anything, take any life, to keep the province in a state of war. Somehow, they'd picked her up. Somewhere, they'd been waiting. Maybe at the safe house. Maybe somewhere else in the city. Either way, it was academic. All she had now was a full tank of petrol and 27 rounds of 9mm snubnose. The rest, unless she was very careful, would be all too predictable. She peered ahead. The rain had started again, flurries hitting the windscreen, greasing the surface of the road. That was good. That narrowed the odds a little. Head to head, she thought grimly. Who dares wins.

A big blue motorway sign flashed past, indicating the next exit. 'Armagh/Coalisland,' it said, '1 mile.' She took the Golf up to 110 mph, waiting for the line of green dots that would signal the beginning of the slip road. When they appeared, she left it as late as she dared and then swung left, feeling the back of the car starting to slide, correcting the skid with a flick of the wheel, then dropping two gears as the roundabout came up to meet her. The roundabout, mercifully, was empty. Behind, in the mirror, she could see the other car making a U-turn in the carriageway. Overshoot, she thought. At least three hundred yards in hand.

The country road to Armagh was unlit and she drove very fast into the wet darkness, trying to anticipate each corner, using the engine and the gearbox to glue the wheels to the road. Twice, she nearly came unstuck. The second time, a sharp left-hand bend took her by surprise and left her broadside in the wet, the wheels spinning, the engine screaming, the speedo still registering 73 mph. Behind her now there was nothing but darkness. Then a village appeared, a handful of houses and an empty-looking pub, and she slowed, looking for a telephone box. When she couldn't find one, she reversed quickly, backing the Golf into a narrow lane beside the pub. Before she left the car, she stuffed the Browning into the side pocket of the anorak. When she ran, she felt it banging against her hip.

The pub was deserted apart from an old man in the corner nodding over a pint of stout. A woman appeared behind the bar. Annie asked her about a pay phone and the woman indicated a door marked 'Toilets'. Outside the Ladies, she said, there was a phone. Would she be after any change? Annie nodded, taking no chances, swopping a pound for a handful of coins.

Out in the narrow passage, she found the phone. She began to dial the emergency number at Lisburn but then she stopped, spooling backwards in her mind, counting the number of turns she'd made, remembering the speed she'd maintained, and the distance she must have put between herself and the car behind. There was no way they'd find her. Phoning the emergency number was a surrender to panic. Soon enough there'd be time to report in. Just now, she needed a different kind of conversation.

She dialled her own number, the flat in Kew, just in case. When it didn't answer, she began dialling again, Kingdom's number this time, the little terrace house in Leytonstone where he lived with his father. Odds on, she'd find him there. Just the sound of his voice would be enough.

The number rang and rang and she was about to hang up when there was finally an answer, not Kingdom at all but an old voice, inquisitive, querulous, high-pitched.

'Alan?' she said. 'Is Alan there?'

'Who?'

'Alan? Alan Kingdom?'

'Who's that?'

'My name's Annie. He knows me. Is he there?'

Outside, faraway, she heard a car changing gear, the kind of urgent, violent gear change you make when you're going too fast into a corner. The voice was back again, lost, bewildered.

'Who do you want?'

'Alan? Your son? Only—'

The car was much closer now, just up the road, the tyres squealing in the wet.

'Who?'

'Alan. Alan Kingdom. Your son. Please—'

She shut her eyes as the car roared past. Then she heard the screech of brakes and the howl of the transmission as the driver reversed at speed. They've seen the Golf, she thought. They've seen it and they're coming back.

'He's asleep,' said the voice in her ear. 'Fast asleep.'

Annie heard a door slam. Then footsteps. She had the gun out now, levelled at the door. She should have phoned the emergency number. She knew it. She shouldn't have bothered with Kingdom. That was breaking the first rule. That was greed. And weakness. And stupidity. That was asking for it. She bent to the phone.

The voice was fainter now, as if losing interest. 'A friend, are you? Only—'

Annie dropped the phone, crouching low, waiting for the door to open. She could hear voices raised next door, someone knocking over a chair, someone cursing, then the door splintered around the handle and two men burst in. They looked like figures from a nightmare, anoraks, jeans, ski-masks. They both had hand-guns and she took the biggest first, the one on the left, the closest one, point blank range, aiming for the base of his throat. She squeezed the trigger. Nothing happened. She tried again. Another click.

The men were on her now, hauling her upright. She looked the smaller one in the eyes. His eyes were yellow. She could smell the whiskey on him. He hit her twice under the rib cage, big clumsy blows that drove the breath from her body. She heard the Browning clatter to the ground then skid across the lino as someone kicked it against the skirting board.

She was on her knees now, gasping with pain, and when she opened her eyes she saw the feet in front of her, the high-laced boots, the leather toecaps glistening with fresh mud, everything happening in slow motion. She caught the first kick on the side of her chest, turning her body side-on, trying to protect her face. Then something burst inside her head, a bright blinding light, and she felt a gloved hand on her mouth, muffling her screams. She was on her feet again, supported on either side, her chin on her chest, and before they dragged her away she saw the telephone, still dangling on the end of the cord, and she heard the voice, as bewildered as ever.

'Alan?' it was saying. 'You want Alan?'

Outside, she felt the rain on her face and she turned her head back towards the pub, trying to force another scream past the hand that gagged her mouth. The effort exhausted her but when the hand tightened she lashed out with her feet, making solid contact with the man behind. He began to curse her in the wet darkness, forcing her arm up her back until she knew her shoulder was on the point of dislocation. Her upper body had become suffused with pain, an almost liquid thing, swamping every other feeling. She heard a car door open. Then, abruptly, her feet left the ground and she was thrown head-first onto the rear seat. Someone clambered in beside her, sitting on her back, a terrible weight that drove the breath from her body. The engine started, the car accelerating hard, and before the darkness came she had time to marvel at the workings of her own brain, how detached it was, and how perceptive. Some kind of Ford, she thought. Not the VW at all.

When she came to, the car was travelling at speed. The weight on her back had gone but when she tried to move her hands, nothing happened. She tried again, pulling hard, realising that her wrists had been bound together beneath her body with some kind of tape. She got her head down, exploring it with her tongue, aware for the first time of her broken teeth. Her lips were swollen, the blood already beginning to scab, and the steady thump-thump in her head began to quicken as she strained again at the tape.

The car lurched into a bend and she peered up, trying to make sense of the shapes around her. She had the back seat to herself but she could smell the sharp, acrid tang of hand-rolled tobacco and when the car hit a bump in the road, making her gasp with pain, a face appeared in the gap between the two front seats, a featureless oval of white against the frieze of blurring trees beyond the windscreen.

'You OK?'

She recognised the accent, the harsh Belfast vowels.

The face was still looking at her. 'You'se want a cigarette?'

Without waiting for an answer, a gloved hand reached back, the tip of the roll-up glowing in the darkness. She shook her head, turning her face away, and then she heard another voice, the driver this time, something she didn't pick up. Then the car braked suddenly, the wheels locking, and when she looked again the face had disappeared.

One of the front doors opened. She heard another car, the VW this time, definitely. It pulled up alongside. The driver in the front was yelling now, telling someone else to hurry up. There were footsteps close by and she felt movement on the springs as someone rummaged in the boot behind her head. Then the rear door beside her opened and she smelled petrol, recognised the slosh of it in a can, and for a moment she closed her eyes, expecting the worst. They're going to pour it all over me, she thought. And then light a match.

The footsteps again, and the cough of an engine as the VW started. It pulled away and Annie heard the crunch of gravel beneath the tyres. The door beside her head was still open. The petrol smell had gone. She lifted her head, swamped with relief, listening hard as the VW bumped away, aware now of another sound. Water, she thought. A stream, or maybe even a river.

The two men in the front were talking, their voices very low, the conversation masked by music from the radio. From time to time, one of them laughed. They seemed relaxed, off-guard. When she began to move, first one leg, then the other, they didn't look round.

Annie closed her eyes, trying to slow her pulse, knowing that she had to get it right. In situations like these, they only gave you one chance, you only made one mistake. Screw this up, and there'd be no more open doors.

She tensed herself, both legs sliding off the narrow bench seat, both feet finding a purchase amongst the litter on the floor. Oblivious to the pain, she began to ease out of the car and as she did so she heard a whoosh in the darkness nearby, and saw a blossom of livid yellow silhouetting the trees across the road. The driver was laughing again, the man beside him too, both leaning across, gazing out at the burning shell of the VW, two kids on bonfire night, and for a moment, wriggling out onto the wet tarmac, Annie thought they hadn't seen her. Then she heard one of the men shouting, a car door opening, and the heavy thud of footsteps racing after her.

She scrambled into the trees across the road, searching blindly for a path. The river was closer than she'd thought, wide and sluggish, the flames dancing on the water. She ran as fast as she could, her hands still taped in front of her body, fighting to keep her balance. She followed the river, knowing that the men behind her were gaining with every step. She could hear them now, the rasp of their breaths, a muttered curse as one of them missed his footing in the wet bracken.

Up ahead, away from the burning car, the river was cloaked in darkness. Annie hesitated a moment, knowing it was her only chance, then she picked her way between the rocks and plunged in. The smack of the cold water took her breath away. The gravel beneath her feet softened into mud, then disappeared completely. She kicked hard with her legs, trying to stay afloat, then turned onto her back, still kicking. The first rock missed her head by inches. She half-saw it arching towards her in the darkness, closing her eyes as the water spouted beside her ear. Another came. Then she felt a terrifying pain in her knee, as abrupt as a gunshot wound, and she rolled her body over, trying to ease the agony. Face down in the water, she tried to raise her head, tried to breathe, her injured leg useless. For a moment or two she could taste the night air. Then her mouth began to fill with water and she held her breath as long as she could before giving up, aware of the darkness enveloping her, the icy kiss of the water in her lungs.

She came to on the river bank. Her cheek lay in a pool of vomit. Above her was a light of some kind, a torch, and a pair of faces peering down at her. One of the men was wringing water from his balaclava. The other was trying to light a cigarette. Annie groaned, reaching for her knee, trying to piece together the last few minutes, knowing that these men had stopped her drowning, probably saved her life, wondering why on earth they'd bothered. Then a third face appeared, much closer than the rest, and she blinked up at it. The thinning hair was as wet as her own, sodden through, but there was no mistaking the expression. She swallowed hard, tasting the vomit in her throat, not wanting to believe it. The wide, fleshy, almost feminine lips. The deep-set eyes. The face in the photo from the Dublin warehouse. The trophy she'd brought back to London.

Annie began to struggle upright, knowing that somehow she had to get away but a gloved hand reached out, restraining her. The voice belonged to the face in the photo.

'Take it easy now,' he murmured, 'we've lots to talk about.'

PHASE THREE

NORTHERN IRELAND SECURITY SERVICE
INTERNAL MEMORANDUM

TO: Director-General, Security Service, London
FROM: Director of Intelligence, Stormont, NI
DATE: 3 October 1993

I confirm a full news blackout on last night's incident. As
agreed, I have instituted an internal inquiry with a preliminary report deadline of 22 October. Until the full extent of
collateral penetration has been assessed, I have cancelled
all current and pending operations.

PRELUDE

He lay awake in his room, the bedside light still on, the curtains half-drawn, the Millwall FC mug on the window-sill, the agreed signal. He'd no real idea when it might happen but he'd raided his private supply of Le Carré novels in the library, and he'd no objection to reading half the night.

At eleven-fifteen, as usual, they'd secured the main door. He'd heard the key in the lock, first one turn, then another, then the precautionary tug on the handle, just in case. For weeks now, that had been the limit of their interest. No midnight checks. No patrols around the premises in the small hours of the morning. Nothing to disturb a decent stretch of solid kip. Maybe they were under-staffed again, he thought, or maybe it had something to do with yet another Home Office directive on rehabilitation. Extend a little trust. Offer a little responsibility. Change a man for life. What a joke.

He yawned, peering over the book at the bedside clock. Quite what excitements the stranger might bring he didn't know but only yesterday, in the visitors' room, Trish had confirmed the money. Five hundred in notes had been stuffed through the letterbox and she'd been sufficiently impressed to suggest he stayed inside a little longer. In a way, she had a point. It was, without doubt, the easiest money he'd ever earned.

He returned to the book. It was one of Le Carré's early efforts, and he'd read it before, but one of the things he'd noticed about this place was the tricks it played with your memory. The effect of even a modest stretch was almost chemical, like living on a permanent drip-feed of tranquillisers. Time hung heavy. The routines never changed. You ended up numbed, softly bludgeoned by the boredom of it all, longing for something, anything, to happen. He smiled to himself, turning back a page, trying to pick up the story. Yet another reason, he thought, for saying yes.

The knock at the window came an hour later. He sat upright, realising at once that he'd been asleep. He reached for the bedside lamp, turning it off. There were inspection panels inset in all the doors, and light from the corridor spilled into the room. He waited for a second or two, then eased himself out of bed, stepping across to the window and releasing the catch. With the window open, he could hear the wind in the trees. The wind felt cold against his naked flesh after the warmth of his bed and he began to shiver. This side of the block was shielded from the office beside the main gate and a row of bushes provided extra cover. It was one of the reasons, he assumed, that they'd chosen his room, one of the reasons he'd been tapped up for the favour.

He peered into the darkness, seeing nothing. Then a voice, very close, beneath the window-sill.

'Alright, then?'

The voice was light, amused with itself, an accent he'd grown up with.

'Yes,' he said. 'You coming in?'

He stepped back into the room, pulling the curtain aside. A slim, slight figure balanced for a moment on the window-sill, then stepped carefully into the room, pulling the window shut behind him. He was wearing jeans and a tight black roll-neck sweater. An olive balaclava masked his face. Mud from the worn Reeboks left a set of perfect prints across the grey lino. The visitor nodded at the bed.

'Get in. They tell you about this bit?'

'No.'

In one hand, the visitor carried a plastic bag. On the outside it said 'Debenhams'. He produced a length of cord and began to bind the prisoner's wrists together, working quickly. Another loop of cord and a knot secured his bound wrists to the bar at the head of the bed. The visitor was wearing gloves. He could feel the soft leather against his skin.

'That hurt?'

'Yeah.'

'Can you move at all?'

'No.'

The eyes behind the balaclava watched him for a moment, plainly sceptical. Then he produced a long knife, the kind you can buy at specialist kitchen stores. He cut the cord and began to bind his ankles together, stripping back the sheets at the bottom of the bed and securing the rope around the frame.

'That make it worse?'

'Yeah.'

'OK.'

He bent to both knots, easing them. 'Better?'

'A bit.'

'Sure?'

'Yeah.'

The face was very close now. His eyes, in the light from the corridor, were a pale blue.

'Which room?' he said.

'Twenty-six. Upstairs.'

'Towel?'

'In the drawer.'

He went to the chest of drawers. The towels were in the second drawer down. He chose an old one, barely any nap left, binding it tightly round the prisoner's mouth, knotting it at the back, checking to make sure he could still breathe through his nose. He stepped back a moment, reviewing his work, the knife still in his hand. Satisfied, he bent to the door, trying a number of keys from a ring in his pocket. When it finally opened, he looked out, up and down the corridor. Then he was gone.

ELEVEN

Kingdom was asleep again when the phone rang. He'd been up early, answering the call from his father's room, the spoon and empty cake tin routine they'd agreed for emergencies. It had still been dark, five in the morning, and he'd known at once what had happened. He could smell it from across the room, the sour pungent stench of urine, Ernie pissing himself again, half-awake, half-asleep, not knowing quite what to make of the spreading wetness between his legs.

Kingdom had told him it didn't matter, stripping the sheets off the bed, using the soiled pyjama bottoms to mop the mattress, but his father had taken it badly. He'd sat in the battered old armchair, naked below the waist, his head in his hands, making tiny gasping noises as if he couldn't breathe properly. When Kingdom had tried to comfort him, he'd clung onto his son's hand. He couldn't help it any more, he'd whispered. He'd tried and he'd tried but it just kept happening.

Now, half-asleep, Kingdom went down to the phone. He'd made up a bed on the sofa for his father and he was curled up beneath the spare duvet, only the top of his head visible. Lately, the last week or so, he seemed to have physically shrunk. With Barry no longer around, he'd stopped eating and the weight was falling off him. Very soon, Kingdom knew he'd have to find some kind of help but he was still no closer to working out exactly how. Even the social worker, it seemed, could offer nothing but forms.

Kingdom picked up the phone, wondering whether it might be Annie. He'd dialled the Kew number twice the previous evening,

291

trying to find out whether she'd returned, but both times there'd been no answer. By now, though, she might be back. Maybe she could come over for Sunday lunch. Maybe they could sort something out about Dad.

Kingdom kept his voice low, anxious not to wake his father. Instead of Annie, it was Allder.

'This is getting fucking silly,' he said at once.

Kingdom looked at his watch. It was later than he thought. Nearly eleven o'clock. 'What is, sir?'

'Our friend.'

'What friend?'

There was a moment's pause. Last time Kingdom had seen Allder was two days ago in the Assistant Commissioner's office at New Scotland Yard. The AC had convened an update conference on the Sabbathman killings, a family affair, Met CID and Special Branch only. There'd been fresh rumours out of Gower Street that the killings were definitely linked to some kind of split in the Provisional high command. No one at the Yard had access to any of their intelligence and there was now a perception that events were running out of control. If Sabbathman's strings were really pulled from Belfast, and arrests were imminent, then police involvement would have been zero. The meeting in the AC's office had lasted most of the afternoon, Allder's formal contributions punctuated by sullen asides for Kingdom's ears only. Kingdom had never seen him so dismissive and so bitter. MI5, in a newly appropriate phrase, was pissing all over them.

Now, Kingdom tried to shield the conversation with his body. The longer Ernie slept, the better. If Allder wanted to get anything else off his chest, it might take a while.

'Ford Open Prison,' Allder was saying. 'You know it at all?'

'Yes, sir. Sussex somewhere. Near Bognor.'

'That's right.' He paused. 'We're expected for lunch.'

'Why?'

'I'm sending a car. For you.'

'But why, sir?'

'Guess.'

Allder turned up half an hour later in the back of a brand new Daimler. The Assistant Commissioner had been emphatic about the Sabbathman inquiry having first call on resources, and Allder had evidently extended this largesse to the use of the AC's car.

They took the M25 clockwise, then headed south towards Brighton, the uniformed police driver hugging the outside lane, dismissing other traffic with brief bursts of main beam. At 110 mph the big car was rock-solid, the engine barely audible, leafy bits of Surrey racing past the tinted windows. Allder, to Kingdom's surprise, was unusually cheerful. In a fast-disintegrating world, he seemed to be saying, Sabbathman – at least – was someone you could rely on. A murder a week. Set your watch by it.

'Are we sure it's him?'

'Good as.'

'Why?'

They were passing Gatwick now. Allder was watching a big 747 fighting a cross wind as it wallowed in over the motorway.

'We've got a description, for starters,' he said at last. 'We know what he looks like. Height. Build. The stuff he was wearing. Matches the Carpenter job. Exactly.'

Kingdom nodded, watching the 747 disappear behind the embankment, remembering Clare Baxter, down in Hayling Island, and the candle she'd lit for Max Carpenter. She'd seen the MP's killer. She'd described him.

'Smallish?' Kingdom said. 'Slender build? Jeans? Cotton shirt? Balaclava?'

Allder nodded. 'Polo neck this time,' he said, 'but the rest's the same.'

Kingdom stretched out, rubbing his eyes, trying to concentrate, trying not to think too hard about Ernie. He'd asked his sister to take charge for the day but she'd said no. Since the collapse of Steve's firm, she'd become a virtual recluse. Her own world, she'd said, had fallen apart. The last thing she needed was more grief.

Kingdom blinked, suddenly aware that Allder was gazing at him. That smile again, something held back, something he had yet to mention.

'This bloke he stiffed,' Kingdom said, 'Marcus Wolfe.'

'Yes?'

'Was he asleep or what? Didn't anyone hear anything?'

'Nothing. Not a peep. No one saw or heard anything. Apart from chummy downstairs. The one he tied up. The one who got the description.'

'And you're saying he used a knife?'

'Yes. Cut Wolfe's throat and put a pillow on his face until he died. At least, that's what it looks like.'

'Blood?'

'Everywhere.'

'And . . .' Kingdom made a gesture with his right hand. He disliked the name Sabbathman. It was somehow a surrender, an acceptance of the script this weirdo was writing for himself.

Allder nodded, understanding at once. 'Yes,' he said, 'we're assuming he's probably covered in it.'

Kingdom looked away, still curious. Not about this latest killing, the sequence of events, what exactly had happened down in Sussex, but about Allder's mood, the reason for the grin he kept trying to suppress. Laughter just wasn't in his repertoire. Not, at least, until now.

'I'm missing something,' Kingdom said slowly, 'something obvious. Matey clocks on. Finds himself another victim. Only this time he's harder than usual to get at . . .' He glanced sideways at Allder. 'Yes?'

'Yes.'

'So he finds himself a way into the nick, a hole in the wall, whatever. Then he goes to the accommodation block, breaks in through someone's room, and does the business on this Marcus Wolfe.' He paused again. 'Am I getting warm?'

'Absolutely.'

'So it has to be an inside job, doesn't it? He has to know somebody. Somebody has to have marked his card, told him where Wolfe sleeps, how to find him, how best to get in, all that . . . no?'

'Of course.' Allder nodded. 'Logically, there's no other way. Unless he's been inside himself. But I have to say that's unlikely.'

'Why?'

'Because Wolfe's only been in Ford since the beginning of September. September the sixth to be precise. Before that he was up in the Scrubs. According to the prison people.'

'And by the sixth matey was already at it?'

'Exactly.'

Kingdom nodded. Allder was right. The Sabbathman killings had started on 5 September, the day that Sir Peter Blanche was shot at his home in Jersey. If Sabbathman really existed, if the same man was really responsible for five consecutive deaths, then he'd hardly be banged up between killings.

'So we have a lead at last?' Kingdom said. 'An accomplice? Is that it? Is that why we're off down there?'

Allder beamed at him. 'Of course,' he said, 'of course.'

The little man was perched on the edge of the seat now, his body turned sideways. He looked absurdly pleased with himself. Something else, Kingdom thought, something else he's yet to tell me.

'Wolfe,' he said carefully, 'anything there?'

'Apart from the obvious, no.'

Kingdom nodded. Marcus Wolfe was doing five years for fraud and embezzlement. The trial had been high-profile, daily reports in all the national newspapers, yet another eighties legend exposed as a swindler and a crook. Wolfe had been selling high-yield retirement bonds through a series of international tax havens and he'd squandered hundreds of millions of pounds in the process. When his empire had finally collapsed, there'd been nothing left. No deposits. No assets. Nothing. Given the number of investors he'd reduced to near-poverty, the list of potential killers probably ran to five figures.

Kingdom was still looking at Allder. Despite the differences in rank and age, the frustrations of the inquiry had drawn them together. Sometimes, just sometimes, he almost liked the man.

'OK then,' he said, 'I give up.'

'Give up what?'

'Give up trying to guess what's got into you.' He paused. 'Sir.'

Allder reached across, patting him lightly on the thigh. 'Our witness,' he said, 'the one who got tied up.'

'You think he's the accomplice?'

'I don't know. Maybe. Maybe not. But that's hardly the point. Not according to the conversations I've had so far.'

Kingdom gazed at him for a moment, trying to think the thing through, trying to imagine the local CID boys arriving at the prison, assessing the scene, interviewing the witness, nailing down the obvious, getting it on tape, putting it on paper. That's the way you always did it. Simple things first. Nothing complicated. Nothing fancy.

'He spoke,' Kingdom said slowly, 'matey opened his mouth. Said something.'

'Yes. Exactly.'

'And he had an accent?'

'Correct.'

'And it wasn't Irish?'

'No.' Allder sat back at last, exultant. 'Since when have the Provos been using cockney hit men?'

Ford Open Prison is south of Arundel, a sprawling collection of huts and brick-built accommodation blocks surrounded by an eight-foot wire fence. The Daimler swung into the main gate and stopped for a security check. The uniformed driver showed his Met ID and the prison officer touched his cap briefly before bending to the window and giving instructions on where to find the governor. Parked inside the gate, on a square of oily tarmac, was an untidy line of media vehicles. Kingdom counted them while they waited to move off. There were five in all: estate cars belonging to TV news crews, local radio cars, even one of the bigger outside broadcast vans capable of transmitting live reports from the scene of major incidents. Since Hayling Island, Kingdom thought, Sabbathman had acquired a major following.

The prison governor occupied a shabby office in the administration complex. He'd evidently been at his desk since dawn. Empty styrofoam cups ringed his telephone and the pad beside his elbow was covered in angry doodles. He was a small, thickset man with a greying moustache and the beginnings of a double chin. According to Allder, he had a reputation as a liberal, one of a crop of high-flying seventies recruits who still believed in rehabilitation.

Allder asked for an update and the governor stared glumly at his pad for a moment. Wolfe's body, he said, had been discovered by a fellow prisoner at five in the morning. On the way to the lavatory, he'd spotted blood in the corridor. The trail had led back to Wolfe's room, and the prisoner had raised the alarm. A CID team from Chichester had arrived by seven, and they'd made themselves a temporary home in one of the prison's two classrooms. To his knowledge, they were still at work in the accommodation block where Wolfe had been quartered. Two rooms had been sealed off. One was Wolfe's. The other belonged to the prisoner who'd been gagged and tied up.

Allder stirred. He'd been gazing through the window at a group of prisoners standing outside on the footpath. They were locked in conversation, muttering to each other, grim-faced.

'Who was he, then,' Allder inquired, 'this bloke who got tied up?'

The governor reached back, closing the window behind him. The prisoner's name was Weymes, he said. He'd been inside for nearly a year and he had another eighteen months to serve. In civilian life he'd been a freelance journalist.

'What's he down for?' Allder asked. 'What did he do?'

'Is that strictly relevant?'

'Yes,' Allder nodded, 'it probably is.'

The governor hesitated a moment, clearly uncomfortable, mother hen to his flock of nervous chicks. This prison, like any other, was a closed world and he obviously resented interference.

'Well?' Allder said. He had a pad out now, and he was uncapping his fountain pen with his teeth.

The governor shrugged. 'Mortgage fraud,' he said. 'I understand he raised a lot of money on the same property.'

'How much money?'

'A quarter of a million. Give or take.' He paused. 'Eight loans, to you or me.'

'Whereabouts? Where does he live? Where does he come from?'

The governor opened a drawer and pulled out a file. He peered at it for a moment or two. 'Peckham,' he said at last, 'I believe the place he bought was up in Greenwich.'

Allder nodded, making a note. Then he looked up. 'So how's he been since? Any trouble?'

The governor shook his head, emphatic, not bothering to consult the file this time.

'No bother at all,' he said, 'good as gold. Runs the library for us. Bloody good at it, too.'

'Mates? Anyone in particular?'

'Of course. But no one you'd look twice at,' the governor touched the file, 'if you mean what I think you mean.'

'Visitors? Recently?'

'His wife. Every fortnight.'

'Anyone else?'

'Not according to the records.'

'Letters?'

'His wife again. Twice a week. Regular as clockwork.'

'You read them at all?'

'Good Lord no. Why should we?'

Allder gazed at him a moment, amused. Then he stood up, pulling his coat around him. The governor stood up, too, visibly relieved that yet another ordeal was over. Then he nodded at the window. A couple more prisoners had joined the group on the footpath. The discussion, if anything, was even more heated.

'This is an open prison,' the governor said, 'Category C blokes, Category D. We're flexible here. We give them a lot of scope. It's not a holiday camp, far from it, but it does work, believe me. And that's partly because we're seen to care.' He leaned forward, angry now, fixing Allder with an accusing stare. 'And you know what's happened? This morning? Since all this?'

Allder shook his head, pocketing the fountain pen. 'No,' he said.

The governor rocked on his heels a moment, then looked away, gesturing limply at a list of names on his pad. 'Seven,' he said, 'seven requests. All after the same thing.'

'What? What do they want?'

'A transfer.' The governor shook his head. 'Back to what they call a real prison.'

Allder and Kingdom found the detective in charge of the murder hunt standing by his car outside the building which housed the prison classrooms. Via a handset, he was talking to force head-quarters. Evidently he needed someone to deal with the media.

Unlike Arthur Sperring, in neighbouring Hampshire, he regarded them as a pain in the arse. Spotting Allder, he brought the conversation to an end. The two men were obviously old friends.

'Tricky Mickey,' he said, 'the man himself.'

For the next hour or so, the three detectives toured the prison. Allder introduced the local man as Brian Macintosh. He now held the rank of Detective Chief Superintendent, but he'd spent nine years in the Met and for some of that time he'd occupied an adjoining office to Allder when they were both DIs. Despairing of promotion in London, he'd finally transferred to West Sussex. The life, he said, was pleasant enough but undemanding. Once in a blue moon you stumbled on a half-decent piece of villainy and he was pleased to say that the Wolfe killing showed every sign of being exactly that.

As far as he could judge, the killer had entered the prison grounds at the south-east corner of the compound. Here, in a sheltered corner where two fences met, there was a breach in the wire. It was always under repair because prisoners routinely used it on shopping expeditions to nearby Littlehampton. They'd leave after dark, spend the evening at one of the town's pubs, and return after closing time with a bagful of tinnies from the off-licence. The cash they'd get from selling these back in the prison would, it seemed, fund the evening's drinking.

By now, they'd reached the spot in the perimeter fence that Macintosh had described. It lay in a hollow on the far side of a football pitch. The nearest building, a long low wooden hut, was seventy metres away. Allder squatted by the fence. A pair of angle irons braced the post where the two fences met and the wire sagged at the top where men had obviously climbed over. Allder was still examining the soft mud below. At least three pairs of footprints were plainly visible. He glanced up at Macintosh.

'You say you've got prints from the room?'

'Yeah. Perfect set.'

'And they match?'

'Yeah.' He indicated the smallest of the three prints. 'That one.'

Allder nodded, standing up again. A prisoner had appeared on the football pitch. He was young, crop-haired, wearing a track suit and trainers. He had a ball with him and he began to chip shots into one of the two goals. Kingdom watched him for a moment or two, listening to Allder outlining progress on the serial killings. A communiqué to *The Citizen*, he said, would clinch it but from where he stood Wolfe was another Sabbathman victim. Definitely. The timing, for a start – a Sunday – and the choice of target. Macintosh looked a bit askance at this but Allder patted him on the arm and told him to have faith. After five murders, he said, he'd begun to get inside the man's head. Sabbathman was choosy. He went after public hate figures, the rich and the powerful, people to whom society owed nothing.

Macintosh gazed at him, more sceptical than ever. 'Mr Angry?' he said. 'Is that what you're telling me?'

'Yes,' Allder nodded, 'something like that.'

'You pulling my pisser?'

'No,' Alder beamed, 'definitely not.'

He went on to compare the five killings, the care the killer had taken in his preparations, how neat he was, how painstaking. Once, just once, he used the word 'executions'. At this, even Kingdom looked surprised, catching Macintosh's eye and permitting himself a quiet smile. Since the news about the killer's accent, Allder had become positively evangelical. Offered an alternative to the MI5 line, he was now determined to bury the long shadow of Provisional involvement.

Allder nodded at Kingdom. 'My friend here's been developing another line,' he said. 'According to him, we should be thinking green.'

'Thinking what?'

Allder turned away, examining the wire again, while Kingdom explained what he'd been up to. The Max Carpenter killing, in his view, had been somehow linked to the protests over Twyford Down. It was a big step from stopping bulldozers to cold-blooded murder but times were changing fast and if you cared to listen there was an audible rage at the direction the country had taken.

'You can stand this up?' Macintosh inquired drily. 'You've got names?'

'No. Nothing firm.'

'But it's looking promising?'

Kingdom hesitated a moment. He'd spent the last four days

exploring various arms of the ecological movement. The transcripts Annie had got hold of on Jo Hubbard's number had given him three or four names, moving spirits in the battle for Twyford Down, but all the conversations she'd conducted on the phone had stopped well short of homicide. In fact the closest anyone had got to discussing direct action was a hint from the *Anarchists' Cook Book* that earth-moving plant could be crippled by tipping sugar in the fuel tank, but even this suggestion had been hastily withdrawn. 'NERVOUS LAUGHTER,' the transcribing clerk had noted, 'CONVERSATION TERMINATES.'

Macintosh was still waiting for an answer. 'Well? What do you reckon?'

Kingdom shrugged. 'Dunno,' he said truthfully, 'but I'm starting to doubt it.'

Allder chuckled and took Macintosh by the arm again, leading him back towards the football pitch, and Kingdom followed at a distance, listening to the little policeman completing the brief. Sabbathman was obviously a professional. He knew a great deal about violence. He applied it with great skill. Accordingly, one or two of Allder's blokes were talking to people in the private security world. They were also doing a trawl of known hit-men, underworld specialists with certain talents for sale. They'd even begun to compile a list of mercenaries, ex-soldiers taking a break from Bosnia, in the belief that this might be fruitful.

Kingdom ticked off the various lines of inquiry in his mind. They were all sensible, and Allder would have been negligent not to pursue them, but he somehow doubted that anything would turn up. In his own opinion, the key to the puzzle lay closer to home. He'd been back to Hayling Island twice in the last week, and he was now reasonably certain he'd answered two key questions about the Max Carpenter killing. The first was access: just how had the killer got into Clare Baxter's house? The second was equally bewildering: what had happened to him afterwards? Where had he gone? How come he'd simply disappeared? On both counts, Kingdom now considered that he was close to the truth. So far, prudently, he'd said nothing to Allder but soon, he knew, he'd have to declare his hand.

He was crossing the football pitch by now, ten yards or so

behind the two detectives. The prisoner in the tracksuit was juggling the ball from foot to foot. After thirty seconds or so he pivoted on one leg and floated the ball neatly into the net. He punched the air, grinning to himself, then looked up, catching Kingdom's eye as he walked past.

Kingdom paused a moment. 'Playing this afternoon?' he said. 'Got a game?'

The prisoner shook his head, bending to adjust one of his socks. 'Cancelled,' he said briefly.

'Why's that?'

The prisoner stood up again. The disgust showed on his face. 'Mark of respect for Wolfie,' he said. 'Fat little yid.'

By mid-afternoon, the scenes-of-crime team had finished with the ground floor room where the killer had gained access. The white tape across the door had come down and the room's occupant was back inside. Kingdom found him sitting at the desk beside the bed, scribbling notes on a lined pad. He looked up as Kingdom stepped inside. The expression on his face was at once curious and wary, a half-smile deadened by exhaustion.

'Press?' he said at once.

Kingdom shook his head. 'Alan Kingdom,' he said, extending his hand. 'Special Branch.'

'Local?'

'Met.'

'Ah . . .' He pushed his chair back and got up. 'Peter Weymes. Glad to meet you.'

Kingdom sat down in the single armchair, refusing the offer of tea or coffee. Weymes was in early middle age. He had neatly cut blond hair, slightly receding, and a pair of wire-rimmed glasses on a cord around his neck. Like everyone else in the prison, he was wearing dark grey trousers with an open-necked blue shirt. The shirt was on the small side and too many helpings of chips had begun to strain the bottom buttons. Back at the desk, he leaned forward, the pose of a man eager to get one or two things straight. He had a strong cockney accent.

'You part of the team,' he said, 'or is that a leading question?'

'What team?'

'This Sabbathman thing. Mr Angry.'

'What makes you think it's got anything to do with him?'

'Nothing . . .' He hesitated, more cautious now. 'Except the guys out there can't talk about anything else.'

He gestured vaguely at the window. A camera crew were shooting the prison governor emerging from the dining hall. When something went wrong with the first take they asked him to do it again. Kingdom watched them for a moment longer, then turned back into the room.

'I thought you lot had been gagged,' he said. 'No talking to the press?'

'We have.' Weymes returned the grin. 'But it's Sunday.'

'So what?'

'They're working the weekend roster and they're understaffed as it is. It's a numbers game here, just like any nick. You'd know that, surely . . .'

Kingdom conceded the point with a rueful nod. Weymes had an easy warmth coupled with a natural curiosity, striking up a rapport at once, his questions heavily larded with a thick layer of bonhomie. Before you'd know it, Kingdom thought, this man would be your friend. And after that, you'd find yourself in cold print, a list of quotes, half of them probably fictitious.

Kingdom leaned back in the chair. The room was small. A line of paperbacks on a shelf included three slim novels by Elmore Leonard. Kingdom was grinning again. 'What's it like then,' he said, 'easy bird? Like everyone says?'

'Here?'

'Yes.'

'It's fine. Dull, but OK. There's things you miss but I suppose it could be worse.'

Kingdom nodded, looking at the desk. The photo propped against the Millwall mug showed a pretty redhead. She was wearing the bottom half of a bikini and a huge pair of sunglasses. Behind her, on the beach, was an Arab on a camel.

'That your missus?'

'Partner. Trish.' Weymes glanced over his shoulder at the photo. 'We went to Monastir a couple of years back. Tunisia's a steal. Ridiculous prices.'

Kingdom nodded. 'Nice,' he said.

'Yeah. If you like couscous.'

'I meant your friend.' He smiled. 'Trish.'

Weymes looked nonplussed for a second and Kingdom leaned forward, stifling a yawn. 'Second thoughts,' he said, 'maybe a coffee would be nice.'

Weymes got up and left the room. Kingdom could hear him in the kitchen down the corridor, filling a kettle. Kingdom was on his feet now, inspecting the desk. His knowledge of shorthand didn't extend to the scribble on Weymes' pad but when he flicked back through the pages he found what he was after, a central London number, 071-675 1234. He made a note of it, leaving the pad the way he'd found it, returning to the armchair. Of all the prisoners on site, Weymes – more than any of them – would know the value of the story unfolding outside in the pale autumn sunshine.

Weymes came back with two mugs.

'I read the statement you gave the CID blokes about last night,' Kingdom said. 'You must have been shitting yourself.'

'When the fella came in?'

'Yeah.'

'I was. Bet your life I was. It's not my style, all this. I'm a journo outside. White collar job. Closest I normally get to the sharp end is talking to blokes in pubs.' He shook his head, tipped milk from a plastic screw top bottle into the steaming mugs. 'No kidding,' he said again, 'frightened me silly.'

'So why did he choose' – Kingdom made a loose gesture with his right hand – 'your room?'

'That's what the CID guys asked.'

'I know. And you told them you hadn't a clue.'

'It's true.'

'Really?'

'Yeah.' He shrugged. 'There's a dozen other rooms on the ground floor. You tell me.'

'Pure chance? Is that what you're saying?'

'Has to be. Except mine's the only window that opens right

up. Most of them have little catches, just here.' Weymes was at the window now, indicating a metal stop half-way up the bottom frame. The windows were of the sliding type, double-glazed. Kingdom followed Weymes' pointing finger. The window frames had been dusted by the SOCO and a greasy white powder still clung to the bare metal.

'Yours broken?' Kingdom asked.

Weymes nodded. 'Since last week.'

'Aren't they fussy about that kind of thing? Don't they check?'

'Never. Or very rarely.'

'But aren't you supposed to report something like that?'

'Yeah, but . . .' Weymes shrugged, returning to the desk. 'You forget sometimes, don't you? Plus, to be honest, I like fresh air. These rooms are centrally heated. It's like a sauna sometimes.'

'You're telling me you broke it?'

'No,' Weymes shook his head, 'I'm telling you it doesn't work. Just like everything else around here.'

Kingdom smiled, sipping the coffee. 'I understand you run the library,' he said at last. 'Blokes in here do a lot of reading, do they? Banged up all day?'

'Too right. The ones that know how.'

'And what sells? What's popular?'

'Crime, believe it or not. And war. War's huge, the Falklands especially. Very big with the head-bangers, believe me. When I get out, I'm going to—' He broke off. 'Huge,' he repeated, 'colossal.'

Kingdom nodded, getting up, going to the window. Outside, the camera crew were packing up their gear. Kingdom put his coffee on the window-sill and fingered the metal stop. It was loose to the touch, sliding up and down at the slightest pressure.

'You might be right about this Sabbathman bloke,' he mused. 'Wolfe's a dead ringer, for a start. Right up his street.'

'That's what the blokes outside say.'

'They're probably right.' Kingdom turned round. 'You know Wolfe at all? Ever talk to him?'

'Not really. We played backgammon a couple of times but the bastard was always cheating.' He laughed. 'Even for matchsticks he'd cheat. Pathetic, isn't it?'

305

'Was he popular?'

'So, so. One or two of the guys would tap him up for financial advice and I gather he'd give them the odd tip. But he wasn't a nice man. You'd know that, just by looking at him.'

'And would that be enough . . .?' Kingdom glanced back over his shoulder, nodding down at the bed.

'To get his throat cut? Christ no, do me a favour. This is an open prison. Not Palermo. Jesus,' he shook his head again, 'no way.'

'So what do you think?'

'What do *I* think?'

'Yes. You're an intelligent man. You must read the papers in that library of yours. I expect you get to see a lot of television, listen to the radio. You've got time on your hands . . .' He paused. 'So what are we dealing with here? A lunatic? A terrorist? A psychopath? Or what?'

Weymes shrugged, sitting with his back to the desk, one elbow shielding his pad. 'Pass,' he said. 'How would I know?'

'Because you've met him. You've seen him. You're not telling me you haven't thought about it since? You're not telling me you haven't got a theory or two?'

Weymes was on the defensive now, his face wooden, the smile quite gone. 'Pass,' he said again. 'I'm just glad he didn't beat the shit out of me. That's all. Saved the knife for fatso upstairs.'

Kingdom looked thoughtful for a moment. 'I gather Wolfe moved rooms last week. Something about a dust problem. Some allergy or other.' He paused. 'Is that right?'

'No idea.'

'You didn't know?'

'No.' Weymes looked blank. 'Why should I?'

Kingdom studied him a moment, then shrugged, a gesture of regret. 'Just wondering,' he said, picking up his mug and draining the last of the coffee.

He crossed the room again, leaving the empty mug on Weymes' desk. Weymes was watching him carefully. By the time Kingdom got to the door, he was frowning.

'Is that all?' he said. 'No more questions?'

Kingdom grinned, nodding at the pad on the desk. 'Hate to interrupt a man when he's working.'

Kingdom was still in the prison library when Allder finally found him. He rapped at the door. Kingdom unlocked it, returning at once to the desk under the window where Weymes kept his paperwork.

Allder stood in the doorway, his coat buttoned. 'What's this then?' he said impatiently.

Kingdom glanced up, explaining briefly about Weymes. The ledger he'd found recorded all loans, going back to the beginning of the year, a painstaking hand-written list of book titles with lenders' details attached.

'What does that give us?' Allder demanded.

'Names,' Kingdom said, 'and where each bloke is billeted.'

'So?'

Kingdom got up and took the ledger to the ancient photocopier. The machine was already switched on and there was a neat pile of photocopies beside it. Allder peered at them.

'Still not with you,' he said, 'what's this got to do with Wolfe?'

Kingdom put the last page of the ledger under the photocopier and pressed the button on the side. An over-inked copy appeared almost at once. Kingdom held it at arm's length. His fingers were black with toner.

'Wolfe moved rooms last week,' he said, 'and Weymes told me he didn't know. Wolfe made the move on Tuesday. That was the 28th.' He stopped waving the photocopy and beckoned Allder closer. All the entries were in the same handwriting. Friday had been especially busy. The third title booked out had gone to Marcus Wolfe. Beside the name, in capital letters, Weymes had noted 'A26'.

Allder was frowning. 'A26 is where Wolfe died,' he said.

'Exactly. A26 was his new room.'

Allder looked up. 'So what made you check?'

Kingdom returned to the desk. A library book lay beside the ledger. He picked it up. 'This was in Wolfe's room. The SOCO had it down on his list. Wolfe had probably been reading it last night.' He opened the back of the book and showed Allder the return-by stamp. 'You can keep a book for three weeks. This one's due back on 22nd October. That means Wolfe must have taken it out on Friday.' He shrugged. 'Weymes dug the hole. All I had to do was give him a nudge.'

Allder nodded, pulling on his leather gloves. Despite the scowl, he was visibly impressed. 'Clever,' he muttered, 'fucking clever.'

It was late afternoon before Allder and Kingdom left the prison. Kingdom had assumed they'd be returning to London but when they got to the main east-west coast road, Allder told the driver to turn left. Kingdom peered at the first of the big green roadside signs. 'A27,' it read, 'Portsmouth.'

He glanced across at Allder. 'Why Pompey?' he asked.

Allder was staring out of the window. 'We're going to Arthur's place,' he said vaguely, 'we're invited for tea.'

Arthur Sperring's house occupied a quarter-acre plot on a new executive mainland estate across the creek from Hayling Island. The site was still under development and contractor's plant littered the end of the newly-surfaced cul-de-sac.

Allder pointed out the house and told the driver to turn the Daimler round and wait. A note on the front door told callers that Sperring was in the garden at the back, and Kingdom followed Allder round the big two-car garage and along the strip of muddy concrete that edged the side of the house. Sperring was at the bottom of the garden, nailing a length of fencing to stout timber posts. He was wearing overalls and a greasy flat cap, and he had his back to the house. Allder picked his way carefully across the newly-laid turfs and tapped him lightly on the shoulder but Sperring finished driving in the nail before turning round.

'Thank fuck for that,' he said, 'an excuse to bloody stop at last.'

They had tea in the lounge that stretched the full width of the house at the back. Sperring occupied the biggest of the three wing armchairs, and Allder sat beside him on one end of the sofa, helping himself to ham sandwiches, telling the Hampshire DCS what had been happening along the coast at Ford. Before they'd left, easing their way through the cordon of media vans, the governor had agreed to keep an eye on Weymes. Allder wanted to know who his friends were, who he talked to, who he was phoning. The governor had also agreed to compile a complete list of prisoners with brief details on each. At first, weighing Allder's request, he'd been less than eager but when Allder pointed out that the Home Office would be only too willing to oblige, he'd changed his mind. Already, according to the radio news, they'd caved in to pressure for a full inquiry. Clearly, it was in the governor's interests to co-operate.

Sperring listened to Allder's account. At the first mention of the Home Office, he reached for a cigarette and Kingdom remembered the last time they'd met in the smoky, overheated office Sperring occupied at Havant Police Station. The Home Office were part of the conspiracy that had hatched the Sheehy Report. That made them enemy number one.

'Wankers,' Sperring growled when Allder had finished.

'Who?'

'The Home fucking Office.' He tapped his cigarette into an ash-tray beside his foot. The new carpet around his chair was already cratered with small brown holes. 'Weymes, then, is it?'

Allder nodded. 'For starters,' he peeled the bread off another ham sandwich and spread on more mustard, 'we'll put a wire on his girlfriend's phone. See what she has to say for herself. Tomorrow might be interesting, too.'

'Why?'

'Kingdom here thinks he's sold his story to *The Citizen*. Our friend Willoughby Grant. We found their number on Weymes' pad. He'd obviously been talking to the media blokes first thing. Soon as they arrived.'

'But what's he going to say?'

'God knows. That's what makes it interesting.' He paused, demolishing the middle of the sandwich with a single bite. 'Then there's the usual. Our friend Mr S. Monday's publication day for him too, another little *billet doux*. Assuming we've got it right. Assuming it was him.'

Sperring looked up sharply. 'No fucking doubt, is there?'

'No, not that I can see.'

Sperring grunted, reaching for his tea, brooding again. Beneath the bluster and the blasphemies, Kingdom was beginning to understand what a proud man he was. The lack of progress over the Carpenter murder, coupled with the enormous publicity, had wounded him deeply. Sabbathman's only saving grace, in his eyes, was the fact that he kept on getting away with it. Every fresh killing made his own failure just a little easier to bear.

Sperring sipped his tea. He was gazing at Allder again. 'Your lad there had a theory. He tell you about that?'

'Twyford Down?' Allder shook his head, 'Don't see it.'

Sperring looked briefly at Kingdom, realising the *faux pas*.

'It's not Twyford Down,' Kingdom said quickly, 'it's something else.'

Allder stared at him, the remains of the sandwich half-way to his mouth, his face beginning to darken. 'What?' he said.

Kingdom glanced across at Sperring.

Sperring was trying to mask a smile. 'Listen,' he began, 'us country coppers . . .'

'*What*?' Allder said again, his eyes still locked on Kingdom.

Kingdom shifted his long frame in the armchair. Sperring's wife had reappeared with a plate of fresh scones. Allder's passion for clotted cream was legendary. She put them carefully on the table beside him. Allder didn't take his eyes off Kingdom.

'What theory?' he said.

Kingdom was looking at the scones. He hadn't had time for lunch at the prison and he realised he was starving.

'I've been concentrating on the Carpenter hit,' he said carefully, 'as you know.'

'And?'

'I've been trying to get a line on how chummy got off the island, how he got away. Turns out he went by boat. Rubber dinghy, to be exact. Probably one of those Zodiac things. Big outboard. Terrific performance.'

Allder was frowning. 'Impossible,' he said, looking at Sperring. 'You told me you had the harbour mouth covered.'

'We did.'

'Then I don't understand.'

Kingdom reached forward, helping himself to a couple of scones. They were open already and warm to the touch, melting the cream he spooned on top. Allder's gaze wavered for a second, then he pulled at the crease in his trousers, a sure sign that he was losing his temper.

'You're saying this man escaped by sea?'

Kingdom shook his head. 'By boat.'

'Same thing, isn't it?'

'No. You escape by sea, you go out through the harbour mouth. I'm saying he went the other way.'

Allder looked blank. '*Inland*?'

'Yes. Across the harbour. You need to see it. There's miles of water until you hit the mainland, and even then there's a creek that takes you round the top of Pompey. With the right boat, the right engine . . .' Kingdom shrugged. 'You could be the other side of Portsmouth in half an hour. I've walked the course. I've talked to the locals. Believe me, you could do it.'

'But have you got evidence? Something concrete?'

'Yes. Sinah Lane ends in a close of houses. I went back there. Bloke in number six thinks he may have heard something that Sunday morning. Around half-ten.'

'Like what?'

'Like an outboard.'

'Where?'

'Just down from his garden. Where the harbour starts. There's plenty of water at high tide.'

'You looked?'

'Yes.'

'You find anything?'

'No,' Kingdom shook his head, 'but we're talking a couple of weeks after the event.'

'But what about at the time?' Allder looked at Sperring. 'Did your blokes talk to this witness? Whatever his name is?'

Sperring, who'd clearly been anticipating the question, nodded. 'Of course we talked to him. It's on the computer. But he didn't say bugger all.'

'Nothing about an outboard?'

'Nothing about anything.'

Allder fell silent for a moment. When it came to exposing supposition or argument to the cold test of logic he had an unfailing instinct for the weakest point. It was one of the talents, Kingdom supposed, that had taken him to command of the Anti-Terrorist Squad.

He was frowning now. 'Big outboard, you say? Premium on speed?'

Kingdom nodded. 'No question.'

'So how come your man never heard anything' – he looked at Sperring – 'at the first time of asking?'

Sperring shrugged. 'No idea,' he said.

Kingdom reached for another scone. They were delicious. 'Outboards can be silenced,' he said slowly, 'even big ones you can muffle. Not completely. But enough to do the job.'

'So how come your man had second thoughts?'

'He has a dog. Big thing. Collie cross. He takes it out on the harbour sometimes, in his own dinghy. When he goes fishing.'

'And?'

'That morning the dog went ape. Barked and barked.' Kingdom paused. 'Dogs have a different register to humans. They hear things we don't. Like muffled outboards.'

'So did he look out of the window? This bloke of yours? Did he see anything?'

'Nothing. He was in bed. At the front of the house.'

Allder nodded slowly, teasing the theory out, acknowledging for the first time the plate of scones.

Kingdom passed the jam. 'Getting hold of these engines,' he said, 'isn't easy.'

Allder reached for a scone. 'So who do we look for?' he said. 'Who'd know where to find one?'

Kingdom and Sperring exchanged glances. They'd been through most of this on the phone, though at greater length and with less precision.

'Special forces,' Kingdom murmured, taking the last scone, 'SAS or Royal Marines.'

Allder and Kingdom left Sperring's house forty minutes later. Kingdom had been explaining the other conclusion he'd reached, his provisional answer to the question of access. How, exactly, had the killer got into Clare Baxter's house? How come he'd found, or already possessed, a key? Kingdom had pondered these questions. Then, on his third visit to Sinah Lane, he'd stood beside Clare Baxter's front door and made a list of all the houses with direct line of sight. In all, there were four. Inquiries at the first three drew a blank. The occupants had been here for years. They knew Clare Baxter well. They'd hardly be part of any conspiracy to kill their local MP.

At the fourth house, though, Kingdom had drawn a very different response. The young couple who owned it had only just moved in. The house had been on the market for more than a year and for most of that time it had been empty. Upstairs, the smaller of the two front bedrooms offered a perfect view of the tiny bed of shrubs where Clare Baxter hid her key.

Armed with the name of the selling agent, Kingdom had pursued the inquiry. One of the three partners in the agency had handled all dealings on the house. Because of the area, it had attracted a good deal of interest. Normally, inspections of the property were accompanied. Occasionally, when things got busy, prospective buyers were handed a key and invited to take a look for themselves. On these occasions, as a precaution, the agency took a covert note of the buyer's vehicle registration number.

In the case of the property in Sinah Lane, there'd been two such buyers. One of them, a young married executive from IBM, had used the place at lunchtimes to make love to his secretary. He'd done it twice before the agency cottoned on. The second buyer, a middle-aged woman, had spent an hour or so looking round and then returned with the key, explaining that it wasn't quite what she'd expected.

In the agency, Kingdom had asked for details. What was the woman's name? When had this happened? Was there anywhere local where she could, if need be, get a key cut? The answer to the last question was straightforward. There were two shops which had the equipment, and both could supply spare keys within ten minutes. The woman's name and address, though, were more problematic. Normally, this kind of information was kept on file for at least two years but the agency was in the process of moving to smaller premises and some of the paperwork, the agent confessed, was a mess. If the inquiry was important, she'd certainly have a root around but she couldn't promise anything.

Kingdom had thanked her, leaving Sperring's name and the telephone number of the Havant Incident Room in case anything turned up. Twice since then he'd phoned the agency but both times he'd got no further than an embarrassed apology. Times were difficult, the agent had explained. Staff had been laid off. She'd have a proper look as soon as she could.

Kingdom finished the story there, raising his shoulders in a shrug, offering an apology of his own. It had, he said, been a long shot. Maybe this woman had got herself a key cut. Maybe someone had been at the house – upstairs – on Sunday mornings. Maybe they'd kept Clare Baxter's house under surveillance. Maybe they'd seen where she hid the key. He still didn't know but there was certainly nothing in Sabbathman's track record to discredit the thesis. Here was a man who evidently covered every angle, a guy with a real taste for the tiniest detail. To date, he'd probably killed five men and not once had he made a mistake. Given time, and patience, and money, there was no reason to think he couldn't kill again. Indeed, he could conceivably go on and on until he either tired of it all or – less likely – he simply ran out of victims.

At this, Allder reached for his coat. He had infinite respect for detailed detective work and none at all for long speeches. They were in the hall, looking at one of Mrs Sperring's water-colours, when Sperring himself took Kingdom's arm. The front door was already open, the police driver reaching for his ignition key.

'She phoned back yesterday,' Sperring said. 'That's why I invited you over.'

Kingdom paused. The painting was awful, a landscape the colour of Brussels sprouts.

'Who phoned back?'

'Your woman at the agency. She found the name. And an address.'

'And?'

'They were fake. I had them both checked.'

Kingdom looked at him for the first time. Allder was already at the door, but he'd stopped too.

'Was there a car?' Allder said. 'Did she take the registration?'

Sperring nodded. 'Yes,' he said, 'and we checked that too. Her real name's Feasey.' Sperring took a folded square of paper from the pocket of his shirt and offered it to Kingdom. 'Her address and her phone number.' He smiled. 'With my compliments.' Kingdom was staring at him now. Sperring was still holding out his precious piece of paper.

'Ethne Feasey?' Kingdom asked. 'From the Isle of Wight?'

Sperring's grin disappeared. 'Yes,' he said heavily. 'How the fuck did you know that?'

TWELVE

CONSERVATIVE CENTRAL OFFICE

32 SMITH SQUARE, LONDON SW1P 3HH
TELEPHONE: 071 222 9000

<u>VIA FAX</u>

To: Hugh Cousins, PO Box 500, London
From: Andrew Hennessey
Date: 4 October 1993

Thanks for your letter of 29 Sept. The Willoughby Grant
issue has to be decided one way or another, and I suspect
these things are best discussed face to face. Usual place?
Tonight? Around ten?

They were north of Hindhead, returning to London, when the call came through. The Daimler had a mobile phone, as well as the standard force radio, and the driver passed the handset back between the two front seats.

'For DI Kingdom, sir. Sounds urgent.'

Allder gave the phone to Kingdom. Kingdom heard a male voice he didn't recognise and it took him several seconds to realise just who the voice was talking about.

'Ernest Kingdom?' he said. 'You mean my father?'

'That's right.'

'And who are you?'

'The name's Farrar. King's College Hospital. Senior Houseman in the A and E Department.'

Kingdom frowned. King's College was a big London hospital south of the river. What on earth had Ernie been up to? The doctor was talking again, explaining that the injury was serious but not life-threatening. The old man had evidently wandered into the path of a Transit van. He'd been queueing for a bus on the Old Kent Road and for no reason at all he'd stepped out into the traffic. The van driver had braked at once but the force of the blow had been enough to shatter his right leg. The femur was broken in two places and the knee was a mess. With luck, he might be on his feet again within a month or two.

'A month or two?' Kingdom blinked.

'I'm afraid so.' The doctor paused. 'Your father's out of theatre now. We've pinned the leg. I'm sure he'd like to see you.'

'Of course.'

Kingdom glanced sideways at Allder. Allder was still reading the telephone transcripts Kingdom had given him earlier.

'We'll go there now,' Allder said without looking up. 'Tell him an hour or so.'

King's College Hospital stands on Denmark Hill, a gaunt, Victorian redbrick building with the usual twentieth-century additions. The Daimler dropped Kingdom outside the Accident and Emergency Department and Allder leaned across as he bent to the rear window. They'd already agreed the programme for tomorrow. Kingdom would return to the south coast and take the ferry to the Isle of Wight. Allder would be in his office at the Yard, awaiting an update. Now, Allder fingered the button that controlled the rear window. The window purred down.

'Give him my best,' he said. 'Hope he's still smiling.'

'Yeah . . .' Kingdom pulled a face. 'Daft old sod.'

Kingdom found his father in a corridor behind the A and E Department, one of half a dozen patients occupying trolleys tidied into a neat line against the wall. The young student nurse who'd collected him from reception glanced up. Clearly she hadn't a clue who to look for.

'I'll leave you to it,' she said brightly, 'he's bound to be one of these.'

Ernie's trolley was up the far end, several steps from the lavatory for the disabled. He lay under a blanket, flat on his back, his eyes closed, his face the colour of chalk. The graze across his forehead was already beginning to scab and one side of his face was purpled with bruising. A tube on a stand by the trolley dripped fluid into his forearm.

Kingdom bent to the trolley, the back of his hand brushing his father's face. His cheek felt stubbly where he hadn't shaved.

'Dad?'

The old man stirred, groaned, licked his lips. Then one eye opened. He looked blankly up at Kingdom.

'What happened, Dad?'

'Eh?'

'What happened? What've you been up to?'

The old man tried to move, struggling upright on the trolley, but when the pain hit him he screwed his eyes shut and collapsed back onto the mattress. When he tried again, Kingdom restrained him gently, reaching over, both hands, feeling his father's ribcage beneath the surgical smock. Thin, he thought. Just a shadow of the man he'd once known.

'Dad?' he said again.

Ernie acknowledged him this time, one bony hand crabbing across the blanket, finding Kingdom's, holding on tight. 'My fault,' he said at length.

'You remember what happened?'

'Yeah.'

'So why . . .' Kingdom bent closer. 'What were you doing down there?'

'Yeah,' he nodded, 'Yeah.'

'No, Dad, I'm asking you why.'

'Why?'

'Why you were in the Old Kent Road. Why you were waiting for the bus.'

The old man looked vague, then startled, then vague again. Finally his eyes began to film with tears. 'Barry?' he whispered.

'What?'

'You think he'll mind?'

'Mind what?'

'Me coming like this?'

'You were going to Barry's? Is that what you're saying?'

'Eh?' He was trying to get up again, as helpless as a baby. 'You know him? You know Barry?'

For the first time it occurred to Kingdom that his father hadn't a clue who he was, just another passing stranger, someone who'd paused for a chat.

'It's me, Dad. Me. Alan. Your son.'

'Who?'

The old man moistened his lips again and Kingdom glanced round, looking for a nurse, a doctor, anyone who might be able to explain what was going on. Had the houseman on the phone got it right? Had they really operated? And if so, would he be getting a bed of some kind? In a proper ward? Or was Kingdom supposed to borrow the trolley and push him back to Leytonstone?

At the end of the corridor was a pair of swing doors that led back to the A and E Department. In an office beside the nurses' rest room he found the sister in charge. She was sitting behind a desk listening to someone on the telephone. She looked exhausted.

Kingdom stood in the doorway until the conversation was over. When he introduced himself, the sister got to her feet at once, telling him to close the door. She was a small, compact, pretty woman in her late thirties. A pot of coffee bubbled on a hot ring in the corner. She poured him a cup without asking.

'Someone should have explained,' she said, 'before you saw him.'

'Explained what?'

'The situation. We ran out of beds. I'm afraid it's always happening. People we admit, patients like your father, have to wait their turn.' She nodded at the telephone. 'We managed to get him into theatre but there's nowhere for him afterwards. Couple of hours? Tonight maybe? Who knows . . .'

'But how is he? How did it go?'

The sister looked at him for a moment, then she said she didn't know. Clinical prognosis was in the hands of the orthopaedic consultant. It was his job to talk about the medical details.

'Bloke called Farrar?'

'No, he's the houseman. The consultant is a Mr Ellis-Jones.'

'Where do I find him?'

The sister glanced at her watch. 'At home, I expect. Or back at his private clinic.'

'So what happens to Dad?'

'He'll go up to a ward. As soon as a bed's available.'

'You're serious?'

'Yes.' Her eyes strayed towards the phone again. 'It shouldn't be too long. I've got two definites on one of the general wards and a possible on Gynae. Gynae isn't ideal, of course, not for your father, but . . .' She shrugged, reaching for her coffee. 'If needs must . . .'

'But is he OK where he is? Out there? In the corridor?'

'Yes.' She frowned. 'We pop down and keep an eye on things whenever we can. It's not quite as bad as it looks.'

The phone began to ring. She picked it up, listening to the voice at the other end. The conversation over, she smiled at

Kingdom. 'That was the general ward,' she said. 'We're in luck. One of the definites just died.'

Kingdom returned to his father. The sister came with him. She'd made up a glucose drink in a plastic cup and she gave Kingdom a bendy straw to feed it to the old man. After the operation, she said, he'd be thirsty. The more fluids he took, the better it would be.

Ernie's eyes were closed again. Kingdom held his hand a moment, asking him whether he'd like a drink. When he nodded, he took the cup and teased the straw between the old man's lips. Ernie began to suck, a tiny moist sipping, the noise an injured animal makes. After a while, he stopped.

'Enough?'

Ernie nodded and Kingdom returned the cup to the sister. The old man was beginning to groan, turning his face to the wall.

'What's the matter? Dad?'

The old man shook his head, refusing to say, and Kingdom glanced up at the sister. She'd already warned Kingdom that the post-operative drugs would soon wear off. Any break in the femur, she said, was bad. The pain would be excruciating. Kingdom turned back to his father, wondering what might help. Something to distract him. Something to take his mind off the pain.

'Dad?' he whispered. 'Why did you do it?'

Ernie eased his head round. He was drowsy now, barely able to focus. 'Do what?'

'Go and find Barry . . . or try to.'

Ernie stared up, barely acknowledging the question. Then he tried to smile, a small rueful grin. 'Miss him,' he whispered, closing his eyes.

Kingdom stayed beside the trolley for another hour and a half, watching the steady rise and fall of his father's chest. When he checked beneath the blanket he saw that they'd plastered his right leg, hip to ankle. There was a dressing on his left leg, too, pinked with fresh blood. Soon, Kingdom thought, they'll come and take him away. Then he'll have a proper bed, clean sheets, a fresh dressing, a nurse on call to make sure he was comfortable.

When nothing happened, Kingdom went to find the sister again. She was back in her office, eating a salad sandwich.

'Ten minutes,' she said at once, 'the porters just phoned.'

'He'll get a bed?'

'Yes.'

'But will he stay? Or what?'

'I honestly don't know. You'll have to talk to admin. And the consultant, of course. He's OK for the time being, though.' She offered Kingdom a bleak smile. 'Until we get someone worse.'

'But what then? What happens then?'

'I told you, I'm sorry, I don't know.'

'Will they send him home?'

'Of course. In the end.'

'When's that?' Kingdom forced a smile. 'Rough guess?'

The sister tidied the crumbs on the plate, refusing to answer. Finally, she looked up. 'He's a bit of a mess,' she conceded. 'It may take weeks.'

'Weeks? The doctor said months. Or a month, at least.'

'Yes.' The sister was frowning now. 'Does he live alone, your father?'

'No. I'm there too.'

'All the time?'

'Some of the time.'

'But can he cope by himself?'

'No. Definitely not.'

'Is that why we found the card in his pocket? Your name? And that number we had to phone? Scotland Yard?'

'Yes.'

'Is that where you work? Full time?'

'Yes.'

The sister nodded. She was gazing out through the glass partition, watching a staff nurse bending over a black youth in the cubicle beside the door. There was a deep gash under his left eye and every time she approached with her kidney bowl and her balls of cotton wool, he turned his head away.

'Is he incontinent? Your father?'

'Yes. Just recently.' Kingdom nodded, Yes.'

'Confused?'

'Definitely.'

'At risk, then? You'd say?'

'Yes.'

The sister fell silent and for the first time Kingdom realised what it was that awaited his father. After all his attempts to raise money, to somehow make it possible for Barry to take over full time, there was nothing left but residential care. He'd already discussed the possibility with the social worker who'd called round, and he knew now that Charlie Truman had been right. The house would have to go. And so would Ernie's meagre savings. In exchange for that, the old man would get a bed in some nursing home or other, three meals a day, and a limitless supply of television. It wouldn't last long, this half-life, because the old man wouldn't let it. He'd never allowed his wings to be clipped. He'd always loved his freedom. That's what he'd been doing in the Old Kent Road. God knows, that's probably why he gave up waiting at the bus stop and tried to leg it across the road. Old and mad, a nursing home would kill him.

Kingdom stood up. The sister was looking speculatively at the coffee pot. Did Kingdom have room for another cup? Kingdom shook his head and thanked her for her help. She'd been very patient. He'd say goodbye to his father and then he'd go. She nodded, extending a hand.

'You're welcome,' she said. 'I wish you luck.'

Kingdom returned to the corridor. The queue of trolleys had lengthened but where his father had been there was now a gap. He looked at the trolleys for a moment, the blank empty faces, the patched-up wounds, the busy little woman hurrying past with an armful of files. Then he turned on his heel and left.

Allder rang at midnight. Kingdom was back home in Leytonstone. The house was damp and cold and stank of urine. Even in the depths of his divorce he'd never felt so depressed.

'How's your dad?' Allder asked at once.

Kingdom explained what had happened at the hospital. Ernie had been through a major operation and would slowly get better.

Sooner rather than later they'd doubtless chuck him out. By which time the social workers would have found a drawer that more or less fitted him.

'Drawer?' Allder said blankly.

'Nursing home,' Kingdom said, 'some fucking bin or other.'

'Ah . . .'

Allder abruptly changed the subject, his manner warmed by some fresh excitement, and as he talked Kingdom realised that for the last six hours he hadn't once thought about the job. The Sabbathman killings had become utterly remote, momentary interference he'd be more than happy to tune out of his life. Allder was talking about MI5 again. Apparently their ship had hit the rocks and Allder was gleeful at the prospects.

'Why?' Kingdom inquired. 'What's happened?'

'Don't know. Something's gone wrong in Belfast. No one seems quite sure what but that's no surprise. Those bastards always play it tight. This time maybe too tight.'

At the mention of Belfast, Kingdom began to concentrate again. Annie would know, he thought.

'You want me to find out?' he said. 'Is that why you've phoned?'

There was a brief silence. Then he heard Allder chuckling. If the man had a saving grace, Kingdom thought, then it would have to be a sense of total shamelessness. Sympathy was a wonderful thing. But it didn't solve serial killings.

'Please,' he said, 'soon as you can.'

Kingdom rang Annie's flat the moment Allder put the phone down. When there was no answer he hung up, standing in the lounge for a full minute, wondering what to do. Without Ernie, the house had become a shell, a husk, the remains of a life which he knew in his heart had gone. If he stayed the night, if he trailed upstairs to the narrow little bedroom and tried to sleep, he knew he'd regret it. The place was beginning to haunt him. Too many ghosts. Too many memories.

He reached for his coat and checked the pockets. Annie's key was still there and Ernie's Wolseley was in the lock-up across the street. This time of night, he could be over in Kew in less than an hour. Whether Annie was there or not, it was a better prospect than a night by himself in this icy mausoleum.

Kingdom left the house and retrieved the Wolseley from the lock-up. He hadn't touched it since getting it back from the local CID and there was still half a tank of petrol. He drove south, through largely empty streets, turning onto the Embankment at Blackfriars and following the river as far as Kew Bridge. By half-past one, he was outside Annie's flat.

He turned off the engine, peering up at the first-floor windows. The curtains in the lounge were still pulled back, the way he'd left them, and there was no sign of Annie's car. Kingdom got out of the Wolseley and crossed the road. One of the keys on Annie's ring let him in through the communal front door. He found the time switch on the wall and climbed the stairs. At the top there were two more doors. The one on the left belonged to Annie. He rang the bell twice, in case she'd returned. When there was no response, he used the key to get in.

He knew at once the place had been wrecked. The coats on the hooks in the tiny hall were strewn across the floor and there was a strong smell of perfume. Kingdom paused a moment in the half-darkness, looking left through the open door into the living room. Light from the street lamp outside spilled in through the uncur-tained window, bathing the living room in a livid orange. Cushions from the sofa were scattered on the carpet and a bookcase had been overturned. Against the far wall was a small pine Welsh dresser. The audio stack Annie kept on the top had gone and the drawers were hanging out, their contents emptied onto the floor beneath.

Kingdom stepped into the room and pulled the curtains. Then he switched on the light. A framed print of the Galway coast lay at his feet, the glass smashed. There were books everywhere, paper-backs mostly. Even the brass scuttle on the hearth had been upturned and shaken empty, and the wind-gnarled bits of drift-wood Annie had collected from visits to various beaches lay heaped on the white shag rug.

Kingdom went to the dresser. In one of the drawers, Annie kept her CDs. She had a sizable collection but when he knelt to inspect the bits and pieces on the floor he knew at once that they'd gone. He glanced round. The television usually stood on a small table in the far corner, but that had gone, too. Kingdom got up and peered at the books again, stirring the pile with one foot, not touching anything with his hands. Superficially, it looked like a standard B and E. The intruder had been through all the books just like any half-decent thief. Paperbacks were where most people hid their spare cash, and their building society accounts, and other stuff like savings certificates. If you knew what you were after, that's exactly where you'd look first.

Kingdom returned to the hall and checked the two bedrooms. Annie's was a mess. The bed had been stripped and the built-in wardrobe had been emptied. There was a small mountain of clothes beside the open door and both drawers in the dressing table had been torn from their runners and upturned over the bare mattress.

Kingdom sat on the bed for a moment, looking at the contents of the drawers. The cap was off the bottle of L'Air du Temps and most of the perfume had spilled over a corner of the mattress. Kingdom closed his eyes, smelling Annie in the room, imagining her sprawled on the bed, that mischievous half-smile she reserved for the wilder nights. Half of him wanted to know where she was, what she was up to, who she was with. But the other half of him knew it was better that he'd been the one to find the flat in this state. At least, before she returned, he could get the place tidied up. No one deserved to walk back into this.

Kingdom quickly checked the rest of the flat. The spare bedroom, bare of furniture, seemed untouched. Ditto, for some reason, the kitchen. He returned to the living room. On the kitchen window-sill he'd found an old cassette, an Andy Shepperd recording that Annie had treasured, and when he'd carefully opened the cupboard beside the fridge, there was the ancient Sony radio-cassette recorder she often listened to when she was cooking. He put the radio on the Welsh dresser and loaded the cassette. It was Annie who'd introduced him to Andy Shepperd and there was a particular track on this album – sax, piano, double bass – that still haunted him. He played it now, circling that flat, a glass of Rioja in his hand from the bottle he'd been saving for her return. The bottle, out in the kitchen in plain view, was something else that hadn't gone, and the more he thought about it, the odder the break-in began to seem. Alcohol was usually a prime target, easy to carry, nice to celebrate with afterwards. So why hadn't they taken that?

Kingdom chased the questions around his head for nearly an hour. When the bottle was empty, he picked his way across the living room and up the hall. Tonight, he'd kip in the spare bedroom. Tomorrow, before he drove south again, he'd get Allder to sort something out about the flat. The local boys would botch it. The place needed a thorough going-over, a real seeing-to. At the door, he remembered the file he'd read a couple of days back, the one Annie had left on the table beside the sofa. It had been there yesterday, too. He knew because he'd seen it.

He stepped back into the room, knowing already that it had gone but quartering the carpet again, just in case. Not finding it, he went to Annie's bedroom. He'd need some bedding for the room next door and he was in the process of gathering up the big double duvet when he saw the photographs. There were a handful of them, colour prints, sticking out of an air mail envelope.

He sank onto the mattress. The wine had made him less fussy about disturbing the evidence and he held up the envelope by one corner, letting the prints fall onto the bed. There were four in all. Three of them showed a man in his middle thirties. He was on a boat of some kind, leaning against a rail. He was tall and good-looking with a strong open face and a quiet smile. He carried a jacket, looped on one finger over his shoulder, and the sleeves on the crisp white shirt were rolled up. In the background, beyond the river bank, there were mountains, summer-green. Kingdom looked at the fourth photo. It showed the same man – an almost identical pose – but this time he had a companion, smaller, slighter, tucked in beside him. Her head was on his shoulder. She had the same cropped blonde hair, the same tight white singlet, but it was the smile on her face that Kingdom found hardest to take. Annie Meredith. Looking pleased with herself.

Kingdom turned the photo over. There was a line or two in German that he didn't understand, and a name. He peered at the name. It might have been Bernd. He couldn't tell. He reached for the envelope. The stamp was German and the town on the postmark was smudged, but the date was still legible: 8/86, it said. August, 1986.

Kingdom put the photos back in the envelope, half-wishing he'd never found them. Another cupboard Annie had never wanted him to open. Another part of her life that belonged to nobody but her. Kingdom hesitated a moment, looking down at the envelope. Should he ask her about it? When the time was right? When they were next together? Maybe in this flat? Maybe in this very bed? Should he bring it up, a chance comment, a joke maybe, smuggling himself into her previous life? Or should he simply forget it? Accept the relationship for what it was? No baggage? No ghosts? Every day a glad return to Year Zero?

He shook his head, not knowing the answer. In these moods he knew he could be utterly self-indulgent. The best surrenders, he'd always told himself, were to your own emotions, your own bewilderment, your own despair. Annie, sharp as ever, had recognised this swampy part of him from the start, and when she thought it mattered she went along with it. Other times, though, she'd pull him up short, the rider on his horse, telling him it was all bollocks. Life was difficult. Life was complex. Life was very frequently unfair. But the last thing you ever did was moan. 'Moan' was Annie's code for pausing, for reflecting, for letting yourself have doubts, three cardinal sins she simply never permitted herself to commit. They were, she'd always told him, the prelude to giving in. And once you'd done that, you were history.

Next morning, Kingdom was on the phone to Allder the moment he got into the office. He explained about the break-in and the state of Annie's flat and when Allder put the obvious question – anyone we know? – Kingdom said he wasn't sure.

'There's a file gone, though,' he said.

'What file?'

Kingdom told Allder about the Bairstow file. When he'd left the flat on Saturday, it had been there. Now it had disappeared.

'What's in it? You get a look?'

'Yes.'

'Anything interesting?'

Kingdom hesitated a moment. Most of the material he'd seen before, documents sent down from Newcastle at his own request, but one piece of correspondence had been new to him.

'There were a couple of letters from a bloke in Aberdeen,' he said. 'Runs an engineering business. The file contact was a copper called Gosling. DC Gosling.'

'And?'

'I just wondered why they weren't in the file I got.'

'Where's the file you got?'

'In my desk. At the office.'

'You want me to talk to them? Up in Newcastle?'

Kingdom smiled. Doing favours wasn't something Allder normally had much time for. Too matey. Too demeaning.

'Yes, please,' he said, 'and I thought we might get someone half-decent to take a look at this place. They make mistakes sometimes, you never know . . .'

'Who? Who make mistakes?'

'The bad guys,' Kingdom smiled, 'who else?'

He gave Allder details about where he'd leave the key to the flat. Then he said he was off to look for Ethne Feasey. He'd be in touch again when he had something to report. He paused. 'Anything else, sir?' he said.

'Yes,' Allder grunted, 'get yourself a copy of *The Citizen*.'

Kingdom read *The Citizen* on the last stage of his journey to the Isle of Wight. It was late morning. He'd driven down to Portsmouth and taken the Wolseley aboard the big slab-side car ferry that made the forty-minute crossing to Fishbourne. It was a beautiful day, still, sunny, windless, and he found himself a corner on the upper deck as the ferry slipped out through the harbour mouth on a falling tide.

The nation's favourite serial killer had been in touch with *The Citizen* again and the paper had featured his latest communiqué on the second page. The note had evidently arrived in time for the Monday first editions which meant, by Kingdom's calculations, that it must have been delivered some time Sunday evening, presumably by hand, possibly in person, a piece of *brio* somehow typical of the man who'd now increased his personal body count to five. '*Marcus Wolfe,*' it ran, '*offered 16,000 punters the earth. Greedy they might have been but how were they to judge a man licensed by the DTI? Turns out he robbed them all. Leaving little me to stick the knife in.*' The note had been signed, once again, '*Sabbathman*', though everywhere else the paper had substituted its own invention, Mr Angry.

Kingdom read the note for a second time, as intrigued as ever by the tone of voice this strange killer had chosen to adopt. The murders themselves signalled a certain icy professionalism, but added to this was an attitude of almost biblical contempt. What this man was doing, in note after note, was to redefine the crime he'd just committed. He wasn't involved in murder but in punishment. The men he'd killed weren't victims, but corrupt and greedy individuals who'd earned their just rewards. If Sabbathman didn't do the dirty work, the notes seemed to be saying, then society would be somehow robbed of justice.

The Citizen, way ahead of the rest of the press, had become part of this beguiling nonsense and was busy beating the drum that their own Mr Angry had supplied. The paper's centre pages were devoted to a feature on the Marcus Wolfe scandal and an accompanying piece listed individual reactions from investors who'd suffered at his hands. Most of them were pensioners, some of them reduced to bankruptcy, and in every case they applauded what had happened. 'THUMBS UP FOR MR ANGRY', the headline read, 'NO TEARS FOR MARCUS WOLFE'.

Kingdom turned back to the front page. It was dominated by another headline and a huge, hand-drawn footprint. The headline, in a rich aside to a tabloid rival, screamed 'GOTCHA!' and underneath the footprint was a first-person account from 'the man who could have been victim number six'. Peter Weymes wasn't mentioned by name but reading the flurry of breathless paragraphs, Kingdom had no doubt that the piece was his. He'd been woken up in the middle of the night. He'd found himself looking at a stranger. He'd been forced back to bed at knife-point. He'd been tied and gagged. The account was strangely lacking in physical detail – 'In the pitch darkness I couldn't see him. But the voice was enough to tell me he meant business' – a precaution, Kingdom assumed, to minimise any subsequent risks, but Weymes had obviously been clever enough to make a copy of the footprint on his lino before the cleaners got to work, and it was clearly this that had closed the deal. Kingdom studied the footprint now, wondering how much he'd asked, how much they'd settled for, and how – exactly – he'd smuggled the drawing out. With supervision so lax, he suspected it wouldn't have been a major problem. Not if a few quid were involved.

Kingdom flicked through the rest of the paper. With the inside track on the day's biggest news story, everything else had been relegated to the barest details but a piece on page six caught his eye. Under a grainy photograph of a Ford Cortina, there were a couple of sentences about an incident in Northern Ireland. A Sinn Fein councillor had been lured to a meeting in a pub in Tandragee. Outside, in the car park, he'd been shot. Unusually, the loyalists had denied responsibility. So had the Provisional IRA. 'WHO DUNNIT?' ran the headline, 'BOTH SIDES PLAY DUMB'.

Kingdom's eyes lingered on the photo a moment. The councillor's body was half out of the car. Blood had pooled beneath his head. At first sight, it looked as if he was being sick but closer inspection revealed the bullet holes in the car door, and the fragments of broken glass on the muddy gravel. Kingdom shivered, his eyes drifting across to the paper's editorial on the facing page, an abrupt return to the fairy-tale world of Mr Angry. 'The spivs and the con men must be worried,' thundered *The Citizen*, 'and so must the thousands of guilty men who've betrayed the public's trust. We can't name them and we won't. But Mr Angry has a list. You bet your life he does!'

The car ferry docked at Fishbourne at ten past one. Kingdom eased the Wolseley off the landing ramp and followed the queue of traffic up through the car park. According to both Arthur Sperring, and the transcripts Annie had given him, Ethne Feasey lived in the middle of the island, near the village of Merstone. Her name and address had been neatly typed by the transcribing clerk beside the telephone number Jo Hubbard had dialled, back in March.

As far as Kingdom could judge from the transcript of the conversation, Jo was responding to a letter that Ethne had written. She'd asked for contacts, some of the Twyford Down people, and on the phone Jo had obliged with the numbers of a couple of solicitors in Winchester who were helping organise opposition to the cutting through the hill. Ethne apparently had a son, Douglas, who wanted to enlist in the cause. He was at a loose end after university and he was keen to put his time to good use. He'd flirted with various left-wing organisations and he was, in Ethne's phrase, 'aggressively green'. This passage in the conversation had attracted the attention of the Gower Street analyst. 'Transferred to master file TWYD006,' read the terse note, 'NFA.'

The conversation between the two women had gone on for a couple of minutes afterwards and there'd been various references to 'hell on earth' and 'up there'. A number of Christian names had been mentioned and reading the transcripts, Kingdom got the impression that the friendship between the two women was recent and had probably been formed on some kind of holiday. Jo had done most of the talking and one or two of the phrases she'd used had reminded him of the Scottish adventure course she'd mentioned when he'd first met her at the hospital. Since then, he'd met her again at greater length but the conversation on that occasion had been devoted almost entirely to the battle for Twyford Down. If only for the purposes of elimination, Kingdom had still wanted to be sure that the Sabbathman murders weren't the work of some radical green hit-team, and the fact that Jo herself was so obviously sceptical was one of the reasons he'd finally dismissed the theory. 'These people just aren't like that,' she'd kept saying, 'violence appals them. That's what Twyford Down's all about. That's why they're protesting in the first place. I know you want to find your Sabbathman, but they're the last people you should be thinking about.'

It took Kingdom less than twenty minutes to get down to Merstone. He'd never been to the Isle of Wight before and he liked it at once, keeping to the minor roads, marvelling at the absence of traffic. It was a landscape that was made for the Wolseley, a glimpse of a different age, and Kingdom sat back behind the wheel, the window down, the hedgerows thick with cow parsley and fuchsia, the pastures dotted with fat brown cows. The address he had for Ethne Feasey was Garland's Nursery, and when he got to Merstone he stopped outside the village store which doubled as the Post Office. A plump woman was serving behind the counter. The place smelled of fresh flowers and cheese.

'Garlands?' she queried, peering at Kingdom's scrap of paper. 'Up the road. Less than a mile. Past the pub on the left.' She paused. 'Mrs Feasey's gone, though. You won't find her there.'

'Gone where?'

She shook her head. 'No idea,' she said. 'Nice woman, though.'

Kingdom drove on through the village. Past the pub, as promised, he found a gate. Beyond the gate was a rutted track and a levelled half-acre that must – once – have been a car park. Beside it was a long wooden glasshouse, perhaps thirty yards by fifteen. The paintwork on the window frames was peeling and several of the panes of glass were either broken or missing entirely. Inside, where there must once have been rows and rows of plants, the long slatted wooden tables were empty.

Kingdom left the Wolseley and followed a path through knee-high grass around the end of the glasshouse. Hidden from the car park by a line of spindly fir trees was a small bungalow. Like the glasshouse, the bungalow had seen better days. Tiles had begun to slip on the roof and there were damp stains on the brickwork beneath the eaves. Kingdom circled the bungalow, peering in through the windows. As far as he could judge, the place was empty. No furniture. No carpets. Just bare light bulbs hanging on twists of flex, and bare floorboards beneath. Out of curiosity, he rapped on the front door. A pair of rooks rose from the tallest of the fir trees and flapped away towards the road but there was no response from inside.

Behind the bungalow, the land fell gently away towards the south and there was evidence of cultivation, long strips of turned soil, newly surrendered to the weeds. Every now and again there were plastic hoops in the soil, a foot or so in height, and he was about to explore further when he heard a diesel engine and the crunch of tyres.

Kingdom returned to the car park. Beside the Wolseley was a small blue flat-bed truck. On the door, in white letters, it said

'CHRIS WELLS, LANDSCAPE GARDENER'. On the back of the truck, amongst the litter of garden tools, was an electric concrete mixer and a stack of bricks. The van door opened and a man got out. He wore an ancient pink sweatshirt with 'Newport Harriers' across the chest and a pair of old shorts. The mud on his boots had dried where he'd obviously been working, and there were holes in the calf-length socks. He looked young, no more than twenty-five. He greeted Kingdom with a grin.

'Yours?' he said, nodding at the Wolseley.

'Yeah.'

'Lovely.' He walked across to the old car, running a finger along the line of the rear fin. 'Wonderful.'

Kingdom joined him beside the Wolseley. He said he was looking for Mrs Feasey.

'Ethne?'

'Yeah.'

'No chance.' He shook his head. 'She went in April.'

He walked back to the truck and retrieved a mobile phone from the cab. He put the phone on the bonnet and then sorted through the pile of bricks until he found the one he wanted. He gave it to Kingdom, nodding at the rest of the pile.

'Fareham reds,' he said, 'just feel the weight of that.'

Kingdom agreed it was a nice brick. He knew nothing about bricks. 'Are you Chris Wells?' he said. 'Your truck? Your business?'

'That's right.'

The young gardener returned the brick to the back of the truck and set off towards the glasshouse, happy to talk. The place, he said, had once been a working nursery. Now it belonged to the bank. If the price was right, he was thinking of buying. The soil wasn't bad and trade on the island was there for the taking. He'd proved that himself, moving from job to job, redesigning people's gardens.

'People retire here,' he explained. 'They're at the time of life when they want to get things right. And they've got the money to do it.'

They were standing in the glasshouse. The young gardener had the key and now he bent to inspect the big oil-fired heater that kept the place warm on sunless days.

'What happened?' Kingdom inquired, looking round. 'What went wrong?'

Wells produced a screwdriver and began to dismantle a valve at the bottom of the boiler. 'More or less everything,' he said at last. 'They borrowed at the wrong time, they tried to over-expand, and then it all got sticky.' He eased the cover off the valve and inserted a finger. When he pulled it out, it was black with grease and dirt. He sniffed it, frowning. 'Common enough story,' he said. 'You raise a hundred thousand, say. Interest rates look reasonable. Then, next year, up they go. Bang.'

'When was this?'

He glanced up. 'End of '90. Early '91. They were unlucky, mind.'

'How?'

'Fireblight.' He stood up, wiping his finger on his shorts. He had watchful eyes and a wonderful complexion. He was gazing at the boiler. 'It's a notifiable disease. Cotoneasters. Pyracanthas. Affects the ends, the growing tips. Once you've got it, you have to burn or bury the lot.'

'And that's what they did?'

'Had to. The Ministry check up.'

'Ah,' Kingdom followed Wells out into the sunshine, 'Nasty.'

The young gardener was examining a standpipe now, trying to turn on the tap. Kingdom offered to help.

Wells shook his head. 'Knackered,' he said.

The mobile phone began to ring and they returned to the truck. The conversation on the phone was brief and when Wells replaced the receiver, his face was wreathed in smiles.

'Customer of mine,' he explained, 'just dug her a pond. Wants to know if I can train frogs.'

He looked at Kingdom a moment then set off down the path towards the bungalow, moving quickly, his eyes missing nothing. Kingdom caught him up by the bungalow. Another set of keys opened the front door. They stood together in the kitchen. The place smelled musty. The young gardener dropped to his knees, peering at a pile of droppings by the skirting board.

'Mice,' he said briefly.

Kingdom was looking out of the window. From the kitchen,

he had a clear view of the cultivated strips that led down towards the bottom of the property.

'What happened out there,' he said, 'as a matter of interest?'

Wells was back on his feet again. He didn't bother looking out of the window. 'Beds,' he said briefly. 'One for growing. The other for selling. You cover them with polythene. We call it multispan. You get a kind of tunnel effect and you blow hot air through to bring the plants on.' He paused, gazing up, inspecting the mould on the ceiling. 'Costs a fortune, too. That wouldn't have helped.'

He shook his head, tut-tutting at the state of the ceiling, then returned to the hall. A door at the end led to a bedroom. Kingdom found him on his hands and knees again, examining the lead pipe that fed the hand basin. The basin was suspended in a metal cradle. The porcelain was cracked and there were brown rust marks around the single tap.

Kingdom stood by the door. This room, unlike the kitchen, was sunless. 'Ethne Feasey,' he began, 'she lived here? She ran the place?'

'Yes.' Wells had a knife out now and was hacking away at something under the sink. 'She and her husband. They'd put everything into it. The lot. Worked bloody hard, too. From what I hear.'

'And the business collapsed? Is that what you're saying?'

'Yes. Start of the year. I think she hung on as long as she could but once you get behind the game . . .' He stood up, shaking his head again. 'Banks can be bloody evil.'

'So where are they now?'

'They?' Wells looked up.

'Yes. Ethne Feasey. And her husband.'

The young gardener examined a cut on his finger a moment, then closed the blade on the penknife. 'She's working in Shanklin,' he said at last. 'I've got a number if you want.'

'And her husband?'

'He's dead. Shot himself. Just about where you're standing. It all got too—' He broke off, cocking an ear, looking out of the window, back towards the car park. 'Sorry,' he said, heading for the door, 'I think that's the mobile again.'

THIRTEEN

CABINET OFFICE
70 WHITEHALL, LONDON SW1A 2AS

The Home Secretary
50 Queen Anne's Gate
London SW1H 9AT

4 October 1993

Subject: "Sabbathman"

The implications of the enclosed note, received by mail yesterday, are extremely troubling. The Prime Minister insists
that the note's existence remain confidential but should it
prove authentic it of course adds a considerable degree of
urgency to the current investigations.

I need hardly point out that the swift resolution of this
matter will have an important bearing on the demarcation
issue between the police and the Security Service. As you
can see, I have copied this note to the Metropolitan
Commissioner but you may well decide to raise the matter
with him personally.

Back in the village, Kingdom phoned the number he'd been given for Ethne Feasey. The young gardener had been vague about exactly what it was she now did, but suspected it might have been something to do with nursing. In the event, he was right.

'St Boniface Rest Home,' a voice said. 'Can I help you?'

Kingdom asked for Ethne Feasey. The woman at the other end said she wasn't on the premises. Evidently, she worked nights. Kingdom might like to call back around eleven. Otherwise, he could find her at home.

'Where's that?' Kingdom asked.

'5b Pitwell Avenue,' she said briskly, 'that's in Shanklin, of course.'

'And does she sleep during the day? Only—'

'Until mid-afternoon, I believe. I'm sure tea-time would be suitable.'

Kingdom thanked her and hung up, checking his watch. It was barely half-past two. He stood in the phone box a moment, then reached for the directory. The Isle of Wight's only newspaper was published from offices in Newport. The town, according to signs he'd passed, was less than ten miles away. Kingdom pushed out of the phone box, still thinking about Ethne Feasey, glad of the chance to conduct a little extra research.

The newspaper offices were in the middle of Newport, a three-minute walk from the car park where Kingdom had tucked away the Wolseley. The front office dealt with classified adverts and general inquiries. Kingdom said he was interested in back numbers.

The old man behind the desk peered up at him. An empty

sandwich box stood beside his phone and there were crumbs everywhere.

'Any particular date?' he said.

Kingdom mentioned Ethne Feasey. Her husband had shot himself. Back towards the end of last year. The old man frowned. The name rang a bell, he said. Something to do with a garden centre?

'Garland's Nursery,' Kingdom said, 'at Merstone.'

The old man nodded and got up. The bottoms of his trousers were tucked into his socks. He crossed the room and pulled open a drawer in a big mahogany chest. The drawer was full of news-papers. The old man called Kingdom over.

'November and December,' he said, 'help yourself.'

Kingdom found the reports he wanted almost immediately. There were three in all, spanning five weeks. On 15 November, Patrick Feasey had put a shotgun in his mouth and killed himself. On the 18th, the coroner had released his body for burial. And on 21 December, the inquest had passed a formal verdict of suicide.

The last report had included two paragraphs on Feasey's business difficulties. Evidently the bank had foreclosed on the couple after two disastrous trading years, and Feasey had been obliged to declare himself bankrupt. An accompanying story referred to other nurseries on the island in similar circumstances and quoted a local businessman's warning about the risks of moving into this particular sector. With luck, and a good accoun-tant, you could make a fortune. But get the thing wrong, for any one of a thousand reasons, and the consequences could be catastrophic.

Kingdom looked up, thinking about the semi-derelict site he'd just toured with the young gardener. On an island like this he could see the attractions of having a go. Outdoor life. Mild climate. Lots of prospective customers. No hassles with commuter trains or office politics. Ideal for someone with drive, and energy, and a helping or two of self-belief.

He glanced down at the paper again. Beside the report on the inquest, there were two photos. One was a head and shoulders shot of Patrick Feasey. His eyes were shadowed by the flat cap pulled low against the sun but there was no mistaking the grin on his face.

He looked buoyed-up, eager, a healthy middle-aged man embarking on a huge adventure. The other photo pictured the story's end, Feasey's widow following her husband's coffin to the grave. She was a big woman, blonde, bareheaded, handsome. She was wearing a long white trench-coat and a pair of wellington boots, a strange outfit for a funeral, but looking at her Kingdom got the impression that this wouldn't have mattered in the slightest. She'd come to bury her husband, her partner, and the normal protocols – how one behaved, what one wore – would have been quite irrelevant. Kingdom gazed at the photograph for a long time. The expression on her face told it all, he thought. A mixture of grief, betrayal, and cold fury. He glanced up as a shadow fell across the page. The old man had spotted the date.

'Funny thing about suicides,' he said, 'they always do it round Christmas.'

Kingdom phoned Allder from a phone box beside the car park.

'Anyone been to Annie's place?'

Allder said yes. He'd arranged for a forensic specialist and a photographer as soon as Kingdom had told him what had happened. The two men had been at the flat all day and had already phoned in with a preliminary report. Without an inventory, it was obviously difficult to gauge what was missing, but the job was certainly the work of an expert. They'd managed to isolate two sets of prints – Annie's and, Allder assumed, Kingdom's – but after that the trail went cold. There were no rogue finger or palm prints. None of the neighbours had reported anything unusual. And the exact mode of entry remained a total mystery. They'd even taken the front door locks apart in the hope of finding scratch marks but, once again, they'd drawn a blank.

'What about the Bairstow business?' Kingdom said. 'Are they sending down those letters?'

'Yeah. When they find them.'

'They've *lost* them?'

'That's what they're saying. For now.' He paused. 'Did you get hold of a paper? Your friend Weymes?'

'I did.'

'Bit swift, wasn't he?'

Kingdom laughed. 'Swift', in Allder's book, was high praise. It described a talent for spotting the right opportunities and taking maximum advantage. The best criminals had it. And so, in Kingdom's opinion, did the best coppers.

'How much did he get?' Kingdom asked. 'Anyone been to see his missus? She'd know.'

'Pass,' Allder grunted, 'but I hope it cheers him up.'

'Why's that?'

'Someone at Ford had a go at him. This morning. Did his knees with a hammer and cut his face up. He's in hospital now. Under armed guard.'

'Shit.' Kingdom blinked. 'Do we know who?'

'No, that's the problem. The governor's flapping around blaming it all on the media. Says he hates violence. One day it might dawn on him he's running a prison.'

'Yeah.' Kingdom was frowning now. 'But this is important. Find out who did Weymes, and we're starting to get somewhere.'

'Quite.'

'So who's down there? Who's at the hospital? Who's waiting for a name?'

'One of Macintosh's blokes.'

'And?'

'Apparently Weymes isn't talking. Not yet, anyway.'

Kingdom was all too aware of the damage the journalist had probably suffered. In the right hands, as he'd seen in Northern Ireland, fifteen seconds with a hammer could cripple a man for life. Taking a Stanley knife to his face was just an extra, a little something for him to carry home and show the wife. Allder was talking about Gower Street now. Apparently MI5's domestic crisis had deepened.

'How?' Kingdom asked.

'No one knows,' Allder chuckled, 'but I'm seeing the Commissioner in an hour.'

*

Kingdom drove east across the island to Shanklin. For reasons he couldn't quite identify, Allder's parting phrase had disturbed him. MI5, as far as he was concerned, had always been a race apart, men and women who'd been schooled for a very different war. By and large, the people he'd had to work with had been unimpressive: over-cautious, bureaucratic, determined to maintain the lowest of profiles. They hugged the shadows. They rarely took risks. They even mistrusted each other. In this respect, Annie had always been the exception rather than the rule – headstrong, flamboyant, loyal – and the very fact that she and Kingdom had always got on so naturally together made Kingdom wonder just how well she fitted in at Gower Street. He knew how ambitious she was, and how single-minded, and he knew as well how easily that could make her enemies. MI5 people could be truly vicious. They operated in a world without rules, especially where each other were concerned.

Kingdom slowed for the outskirts of Shanklin, trying to rid his mind of the darker fears. Annie, he told himself, could handle most situations. She had stamina and she had guts. In a couple of days, she'd be back in Kew, harassing the insurance company for compensation, demanding Kingdom's attendance at some department store or other. There'd be the telly to replace. CDs to buy. Ernie to visit. Real life, he thought. And the odd half-day to enjoy it.

Shanklin turned out to be a sprawling Victorian resort, built around a wide sweep of bay. The bay was flanked by headlands, north and south, and a stubby pier bisected the miles of sandy beach. Kingdom drove slowly along the sea-front, looking for Pitwell Avenue. According to the street map he'd bought in Newport, it lay at right angles to the promenade, leading in towards the town's railway station. Kingdom spotted the street sign, pulling the Wolseley into a parking bay and killing the engine. While he still had daylight he wanted to take a good look at the property where Ethne Feasey had made her new home. Meeting her could wait until tomorrow. By then, if he turned up in the morning, she'd be exhausted. Tonight, once she'd left for work, he'd go through the flat.

Kingdom locked the car door and strolled up Pitwell Avenue.

Most of the properties, at street level, had been converted into shops. Number five was an Indian restaurant, the New Bengal. Kingdom paused outside, studying the menu. In a recessed entrance beside the restaurant door there was a speakerphone. The phone had three buttons; 5b was labelled 'E. Feasey'. Kingdom stepped back into the street and gazed briefly up at the face of the building. Above the restaurant, there were three stories. The curtains in all the windows were open. If Ethne Feasey was still asleep, then the bedroom was probably at the back.

Kingdom walked on down the street and found the alley at the back. Access to the rear of the restaurant was barred by a high brick wall and a locked door but there were knotholes in the woodwork and Kingdom bent to peer through. A tiny paved yard lay inside. At the end of the yard was a newish extension which obviously housed the kitchen. On top of the flat roof, zigzagging up the brickwork, was an iron fire escape. Kingdom smiled. He'd had some easy B & Es in his time, but nothing quite as simple as this. He studied the windows at the back of the building. If the flats went sequentially upwards then Ethne Feasey lived on the second floor. In one of the two windows, the curtains were pulled. The bedroom, Kingdom thought, wondering whether she might be the kind of person to take extravagant security precautions. Somehow, remembering the photo in the paper, he doubted it.

Shanklin was full of signs for bed and breakfast. Kingdom booked into a quiet boarding-house behind the sea-front and spent the early part of the evening at the cinema. At nine o'clock, bored and hungry, he slipped out and returned to Pitwell Avenue. At the New Bengal, the table in the window was empty. Kingdom ordered a chicken Madras curry and an assortment of side dishes. He'd bought the *Daily Telegraph* earlier, and when he'd finished the meal he asked for a second coffee and settled down to wait. At half-past ten, he heard footsteps on the staircase beside the restaurant. Then there was a squeal of unoiled hinges and a shadow lingered briefly in the street, pulling the door shut. Right height, Kingdom thought, watching the white trench coat hurrying past.

He waited in the restaurant for another hour. The hot towel in the wicker basket slowly cooled. When the waiter asked him for the third time whether he wanted anything else to eat, he glanced up.

'What time do you close?' he asked, 'as a matter of interest?'

'One o'clock, sir.'

'People upstairs not mind? All the noise? From the kitchen?'

The waiter looked confused. Then he understood. 'No, sir, not at all. Very old people, most of them.' He put his fingers in his ears, smiling sheepishly, miming deafness.

Kingdom walked the beach until two in the morning. Then he retraced his steps to the alley behind Pitwell Avenue. Someone had left the lid off the dustbin outside the back of the restaurant and there were two cats fighting over the carcass of a chicken. Kingdom shooed them away, replacing the lid and using the dustbin to lever himself over the wall. The tiny square of backyard was thick with spilled grease and he stood in the shadows for a full minute, watching the darkened windows at the rear of the property.

When nothing happened, he skirted the bicycles propped against the wall and crouched beside the kitchen extension. One of the louvre windows was open and he could hear the slow drip-drip of a leaking tap. There was an iron ladder inset into the brickwork, part of the fire escape, and he climbed up. The fire escape proper started on the roof. The rungs felt cold and scabby to the touch and outside the window on the first floor he narrowly missed stepping in a saucer full of milk.

Seconds later, he was another flight up, squatting beside the window he'd earlier seen curtained. Now the curtains were drawn back and in the faint glow from the street lamps at the end of the alley he could see a glimmer of light in a mirror and the outlines of what looked like a dressing table. The window was sash design, open at the top. He reached up, pulling it down. It moved a little, then stuck. Kingdom cursed, exerting more leverage, beginning to sweat, but the harder he pulled, the more firmly the window bedded itself in. He bent down, trying the bottom frame, but nothing he could do would move it. Finally he gave up, squatting on his haunches, his back to the brickwork, feeling horribly exposed. The least he could do for Mrs Feasey, he thought, was warn her about the state of her sashes. If the place caught fire, she wouldn't have a prayer.

He crept to the end of the fire escape. The other window on the second floor was narrower, sash design again, with a couple of feet of sill. This time the bottom sash was open and from where he stood Kingdom could smell the resinous scent of shower gel. He leaned out as far as he dared, one hand against the cold brickwork, trying to measure the distance in the half-darkness. His legs, he knew, were long enough to reach the window but at some point he'd have to transfer his whole weight onto the sill, his hands reaching for the bottom of the open window frame, and if anything went wrong then nothing would prevent him falling backwards. He peered down, over the edge of the fire escape. The kitchen extension didn't stretch the full width of the property and he could just make out more dustbins in the well of the courtyard below. More half-eaten curries, he thought grimly, wiping the sweat from his face.

He shut his eyes a moment, taking a series of shallow breaths. Then he inched to the edge of the fire escape. He bent forward and his left foot found the window-sill. Then, for a split second, he was in mid-air, unsupported, his hands reaching for the underside of the open window. He grabbed it, hanging on, his other shoe finding a foothold on the pitted stonework. Then, too late, he remembered the grease from the yard below, the stuff all over the soles of his shoes, and his feet began to slip, his whole body falling backwards. He fought the urge to scream, prickly tides of adrenalin swamping his system. The window-frame was beginning to shake and he twisted sideways, one foot slipping off the window-sill entirely, his body dangling over the drop. Then he made a final lunge, all caution gone, his head smashing against the thick glass, one shoulder at last inside the room, the rest of him following in a tangle of arms and legs.

He lay on the floor, gasping. He could feel wetness beneath his cheek and a pain in his chest and he thought for a moment that he was having a heart attack. After a while, he got to his feet, feeling his way across the room, finding the toilet beside the bath. He bent over it, vomiting, wiping his mouth with the back of his hand when the last of the chicken Madras had gone. Some fucking entrance, he thought, fumbling with the door handle, wondering vaguely about the smells he'd made.

The first room he searched was at the front of the flat. He pulled the curtains tight, keeping the door open, using the light from the hall outside. The living room was shabby. The nylon carpet was worn bare round the door and the fireplace, and the paper on the walls was beginning to peel. The furniture looked as if it had come from some house clearance or other and the scent of fresh flowers from the vase on the mantelpiece failed to hide the smell of damp. The smell hung like a physical presence in the flat, something you could almost taste, and when Kingdom rearranged the curtains, tucking them in around the bottom of the bay window, he found wads of sodden newsprint stuffed in cracks in the woodwork. He stepped back, wiping his hands on his trousers, remembering a similar smell in the bungalow where Patrick Feasey had taken his life. Maybe damp was something you got used to. Maybe it was something that stuck with you for life.

Except for a clipframe over the mantelpiece, the room was bare of ornament. The clipframe held a montage of photos, jigsawed together, some cropped, others full-sized, and Kingdom recognised bits of the nursery over at Merstone. The contrast to what he'd seen earlier was absolute. Here was a thriving business, the car park full, the glasshouse newly painted, trays of bedding plants, rows of shrubs, every photo busy with customers. Another shot had been taken from the room at the back of the bungalow, a view dominated by the long polythene growing tunnels, and looking at it Kingdom remembered Chris Wells telling him about the size of the investment these people had made, what you needed, how much it cost. Kingdom stepped back a moment, standing in the middle of the room, trying to imagine what it took to live with a statement like this, a reminder of the days when the gamble had worked, when the risks and the hard graft were paying off, when every morning saw a fresh queue at the cash till, when nothing could ever go wrong. It was a gesture, he thought, at once brave and defiant. That was us once. Bugger what came next.

In one corner of the room was a cheap plastic table, the kind you buy for patio barbeques. On the table were two cardboard boxes, full of business files. Kingdom began to unpack them, piling the files on the table, opening each one, quickly aware of their importance. This was the small print of the story he'd pieced together during the day, the invoices, and tax returns, and VAT statements, and endless other bits of paper that charted the path from the busy idyll over the fireplace to the chilly adieu at Patrick Feasey's graveside. Kingdom hesitated a moment, knowing at once that he couldn't possibly go through all the paperwork. Only an accountant or a lawyer could do justice to the whole story. All he could manage was a sample, a hasty dip into the wreckage of two lives.

He skimmed quickly through one file, then another, trying to keep the chronology in his head. The key to the early days was a bank loan. For £140,000, the Feaseys had evidently pledged everything: their little house in Ventnor, their two cars, even a sailing dinghy. In return, they'd bought a twenty-five-year lease on the Merstone nursery, plus the hundred and one other items they'd need to start a proper business.

Kingdom picked up another file, then a fourth. The eighties ended with a half-decent balance sheet and the prospect, quite soon, of pushing the business into the black. Then Kingdom found a press cutting. It came from the paper he'd visited in Newport. The date was February 1990. A storm had swept across the Isle of Wight and amongst the many casualties were the Feaseys' precious polythene growing tunnels. A photograph showed them shredded, the surrounding meadow littered with scraps of flailing plastic. Beside the photo, in black biro, was a line or two of rueful arithmetic. '£9000 each for new ones!' someone had written. 'Plus stock!'

The new decade got worse. The miracle economy faltered. Interest rates soared. Thatcher's England shuddered to a halt. 'Dear Mr Feasey,' wrote the Newport branch bank manager, 'once again I must draw your attention to the state of your business account. Any further failure to meet due payments will, I'm afraid, meet with . . .' The letters got briefer, more terse. A soaring overdraft multiplied the unpaid interest. By August 1992, Patrick Feasey owed the bank £197,768. In the words of his solicitor, himself owed thousands, the game was up.

Kingdom leaned back at the table. He'd found a small Angle-poise and the light pooled on the pile of correspondence. He knew there was nothing unusual about this story. Something similar had happened to thousands of other small businessmen, naive enough to believe that eighteen-hour days and a good product would somehow earn success, trusting enough to let the bankers bind them hand and foot. Quite where fireblight belonged in all this, the killer disease mentioned by the young gardener, Kingdom didn't know but he could imagine how devastating yet more bad news would be. Was that what had driven Patrick Feasey to the comforts of his 12-bore shotgun? Was that what had made him pull the trigger?

Kingdom opened the last of the files. On top was a handwritten letter on Garland's headed notepaper. It was addressed to the chairman of the bank where the Feaseys had kept their business account. Kingdom was on the second paragraph before his eyes returned to the name of the addressee. 'Sir Peter Blanche,' it read, '7 Leadenhall Street, London EC3.' Kingdom stopped a moment, his finger on the name. Blanche was the first of the Sabbathman victims. Blanche was the man who'd been sitting on his Jersey patio in the warm September sunshine when someone put a bullet through his throat. Blanche was where the trail began.

Kingdom read the rest of the letter. It came from Ethne Feasey. Unlike everything else he'd read, it wasn't measured out in carefully balanced paragraphs. It didn't talk of negative cash flow and factoring contracts. It didn't make pleas about debt moratoriums or rolled-up interest payments. Instead, it simply stated the obvious. She and her husband had worked hard. They'd done their best. Nature had been less than kind and the recession wasn't their fault but they were still enthusiastic, still willing, still strong. All they needed was time. Time, and a little faith. The letter ended, 'I know there's a way, and I know you'll help us find it. Yours truly, Ethne Feasey.' Kingdom read the letter again and then checked the date: 22 October. Almost exactly a month before Patrick Feasey had taken his life.

He put the letter to one side. Facing him, on top of the file, was the reply. It came not from Blanche himself but from one of his 'personal assistants'. It occupied half a page. It said that Sir

Peter was distressed to learn of the Feaseys' situation but regretted that he was powerless to help. Inquiries to the bank's loan department had revealed a very substantial debt. In view of the bank's duty to its shareholders, it had no choice but to press for full and prompt settlement. Should that not be forthcoming, it would press for liquidation. 'Please accept,' the letter ended, 'our good wishes for the future.'

What future? Kingdom got up, chilled to the bone. The letter was devastating, a bullet between the eyes. If Patrick Feasey had ever read it, suicide must have seemed an almost welcome release. A proud man, bankruptcy would have finished him. And what about his wife? How must she have felt? Getting a letter like this?

Kingdom began to repack the files, replacing them in the cardboard boxes, numbed by the way the tragedy had unfolded in front of his eyes; remorselessly, out of control, two lives skewered by some remote capitalist's duty to his shareholders. Marx had a point, he thought, reaching for the second box. It's all about greed, and fear, and exploitation. It's all about hard-faced men who haven't got the time, or the imagination, or the simple humanity to think beyond their precious balance sheets. Hand society to these guys, put them in charge, and that's what you end up with. A pile of fucking mouse droppings where Patrick Feasey took his life.

Kingdom was about to slip a handful of files into the second box when he noticed a plastic bag full of photos in the bottom. He made a space on the table and shook them out. The landscape looked wild, water everywhere, big brown mountains, torn strips of cloud, peat bogs studded with outcrops of wet rock. Most of the photos featured little groups of people, in threes and fours. They were all dressed for the weather – anoraks, woolly hats, overtrousers, stout boots – and the first face Kingdom saw made him edge the photo into the light. The big, open grin. The pudding-basin haircut. No doubt about it. Jo Hubbard.

Kingdom began to sort through the photos. There were dozens of them. Some featured Ethne herself. He recognised her face from the photo he'd seen in the paper and he began to wonder when, exactly, this holiday had happened. Various references in the phone transcripts would place it around March, and looking at the weather, and the double layers of clothing, that would seem about right. The wind was clearly arctic, even when the sun was out.

Kingdom looked up, aware for the first time of noises in the flat below. Someone was making a phone call. He could hear the voice. It sounded old, faintly querulous. Kingdom glanced at his watch. Ten past three. Someone's heard me, he thought. Someone's heard me breaking in. They've lain in bed. They've had a long think. And now they've summoned the bottle to do something about it. Ten past three in the morning. Who else would you phone but the police?

Kingdom worked quickly, putting the photos back in the box, replacing the files on top. Then he circled the living room, drawing the curtains, shutting the door, retreating down the hall to the bathroom. The bathroom still stank of chicken Madras but he knew there was nothing he could do about it so he stepped into the bedroom, turning on the light. The room was dominated by a double bed. Against the wall, facing the window, was a cheap dressing table with a single drawer. On the floor by the bed was a flannel nightshirt, and Kingdom picked it up, using it to cover his hands while he pulled out the drawer. Emptying the contents on the floor, he crossed quickly to the window. The window was still stuck fast. He stepped back and began to kick out the lower pane. When most of the glass had gone, he wriggled carefully through.

A light came on in the property next door and someone opened a window. Hugging the shadows, Kingdom clattered down the fire escape, pausing for a moment before tackling the ladder. The temptation was to look up but he kept his head down, taking the iron rings two at a time. At the end of the courtyard he tried the door. It was bolted at the top. Seconds later, the bolt undone, he was off down the alleyway. Only when he was back on the seafront, in sight of the Wolseley, did he see the first of the Panda cars moving at speed towards Pitwell Avenue. He glanced at his watch, impressed. Twelve minutes, he thought. Not at all bad.

Kingdom phoned Allder next morning from a call box in the town centre. The weather had changed overnight and in the gale force wind the rain was nearly horizontal. Kingdom peered out through the smeary glass. A man with a dog was chasing his hat along the promenade.

Allder came on at last, and Kingdom knew at once that something had happened. He sounded as gruff as ever but there was a new note in his voice, a tone that Kingdom had never heard before, a brittleness that sounded close to anxiety.

Kingdom frowned, still watching the man with the dog. 'What's wrong, sir?'

'Nothing. Why?'

'I just . . .' Kingdom hesitated, wondering how far to push it. 'I got the feeling that . . .'

Allder interrupted. 'Where are you?'

'Shanklin.'

'Phone secure?'

Kingdom blinked, looking around the freezing box. To his knowledge, public phones were rarely tapped. Allder was still waiting for an answer. 'Yes, sir,' Kingdom said, feeding in another pound coin, 'as far as I know.'

'OK.' Allder paused. 'I was with the Commissioner last night. I think I might have mentioned it.'

'Yeah,' Kingdom nodded, 'you did.'

'He'd been over to Downing Street. Seems they got a billet doux from our friend.'

'*Sabbathman?*'

'Yeah. Arrived in the mail. London postmark. Strictly confidential. Heart to heart job.'

'What did he say?'

'He told them to take care, watch their step. He said he was putting them all on report, best behaviour, that kind of thing.' He paused while Kingdom tried to stifle his laughter. 'If you think that's funny, think again. This bloke delivers, and they know it. He says he has a list. It starts with the PM. Home Secretary's number three, after the Defence Secretary. They're all shitting themselves. Believe me.'

'And?'

'God knows. They've put the squeeze on the Commissioner and he's put the squeeze on me. We have an ultimatum. From Downing Street. We have to come up with a result.'

'Or?'

'Or they take Five off the leash.'

'But Five are in the shit. You told me yesterday. Grief, you said.'

'Sure, but this latest thing's got to them. The Commissioner thinks they've lost their bottle. You know these people. You've been with them, protected them. They lose touch. They live in a different world. They're shielded from the likes of you and me. Our friend's got through all that. They think he's some kind of force of nature. They want him stopped, binned, taken care of. They want someone to turn the lights on and pull back the curtains and tell them it's going to be all right.' He paused. 'Nightmare time. You getting the drift?'

'Of course, sir.' Kingdom was still smiling. 'But what about the Commissioner? What did he say?'

'He said we've got ten days.'

'Is he serious?'

'Very.'

'And if nothing happens?'

'Then we're looking at a lot of Charlie.'

'Me?'

'Us.'

'Charlie' was Allder's private code for 'Charlie Romeo' or 'Career Reassessment', itself a cheerless euphemism for the leaving party and the P45. Life in the A–T Squad was a grand prix without pit stops. If you didn't deliver, if you couldn't stay with the pace, you were retired. Simple as that. Kingdom bent to the phone again. In these situations, you always went back to detail. Always. 'What about Weymes,' he said, 'has he coughed yet?'

Allder said nothing for a moment, then laughed. He'd got what he wanted to say off his chest. He'd established the deadline. He'd made the price of failure plain. Now, as ever, it was back to work.

'No, but his missus has.' He paused. 'The lovely Trish.'

Kingdom hesitated a moment, remembering the redhead in the photo on Weymes' desk. Always the women, he thought. Never the men. 'What did she say?'

'We've got a name. Bloke at the nick. Apparently Weymes told her a week or so ago. She's furious.'

'Who is he?'

'Bloke called Pelanski. Doing time for flogging dodgy MOTs.' Allder paused. 'Weymes mention him at all? During your little chat?'

Kingdom began to doodle the name in the condensation on the cold glass, trying to remember where he'd seen it last. 'Yeah,' he said at last, 'it was down in Weymes' register at the library. Bloke had borrowed some books last week. Made me laugh because of what Weymes had been saying about the Falklands.'

'What?' When Allder was puzzled it often came out as irritation.

'The Falklands,' Kingdom said again. 'Weymes was telling me how popular books about war were. The Falklands especially. This bloke took out four books. Everything Weymes had left. The lot.'

'Really?' Allder's voice was warmer now, even enthusiastic. 'You know anything about the war? Units? Who went down there?'

'A bit.' Kingdom frowned. 'Why?'

'Apparently this Pelanski got a medal there, 3 Para.' He paused. 'That mean anything to you?'

Kingdom was back outside the New Bengal restaurant by half-past eleven. He'd been watching the property for an hour, sitting in the Wolseley across the street, waiting for the young policewoman to finish her paperwork. When she finally got in the Panda and drove away, Kingdom crossed the road and rang the doorbell. Nothing happened. He rang again. Then a second time. At length, there were footsteps down the staircase and a wrench at the door.

'Mrs Feasey?'

'Yes.'

'Alan Kingdom. Police Special Branch.'

Kingdom showed her his ID. She inspected it carefully, then looked up. She was tall for a woman, nearly six foot, and her complexion wasn't quite as flawless as Kingdom had somehow imagined. She was wearing a dressing gown, belted at the waist, and a pair of thick woolly socks. She smelled faintly of shower gel.

'Are you with the girl,' she said, 'the one who just left? Only I'd quite like some sleep.'

'No, I'm not.' Kingdom feigned surprise. 'What girl's that?'

Mrs Feasey studied him for a moment, then told him to come in. Kingdom left a trail of wet footprints up the stairs. At the top, with some reluctance, she took his coat. She had a faintly foreign accent, German or Scandinavian, barely perceptible. She was extremely direct.

'I've had a break-in. Did you know that?'

'No.'

'Early this morning. While I was at work. You might as well take a look since you're here.'

She led him into the bedroom. The broken window had been roughly boarded up with a sheet of plywood and there was a line of china bowls on the carpet to catch the drips. The duvet on the bed had been folded back and the nightshirt Kingdom had used earlier was lying on the pillow.

'You lose much?' Kingdom inquired.

'Nothing. That's what's so strange.'

'Someone raise the alarm?'

'Yes, the woman downstairs. Scared her to death.'

'Lucky for you, though, eh?'

Mrs Feasey stepped away from the window, stooping to pick up a tiny shard of glass. She was frowning. 'Lucky?' she said.

'Not losing anything.'

Mrs Feasey studied Kingdom a moment then pulled out the drawer in the dressing table. Amongst the balls of cotton wool and the jars of skin cream was a man's leather wallet. She opened it with both hands, like a book. Inside, plainly visible, was a sheaf of credit cards.

'Open, like this,' she said, 'on the floor. Couldn't miss it. Unless you were blind.'

Kingdom looked at the credit cards. 'Lucky,' he said again.

They went through to the living room, Mrs Feasey standing beside the mantelpiece, her arms crossed over her chest, waiting for Kingdom to explain what he wanted. Kingdom sat down, uninvited, eyeing the unlit gas fire. The room was freezing and above the howl of the wind he could hear the slow drip of water from the holes around the windows. For someone who'd lost everything, he couldn't think of a more depressing place to live. It was the living evidence that life, inconceivably, could always get worse.

'Been here long?' he said.

'Six months. Why do you ask?'

'Ever think of moving at all?'

Mrs Feasey said nothing, her face quite expressionless. She must have been stunning once, Kingdom thought, and even now, even here, she had enormous presence, the kind of strength you saw in certain paintings. Her cheekbones. The line of her chin. The way she carried herself, straight-backed, erect, undaunted. Kingdom nodded at the other chair. Dirty yellow sponge bulged through a rip in the vinyl cover.

'Why don't you sit down? This needn't take long.'

'I'm about to go to bed,' Mrs Feasey said again. 'I'm quite happy as I am. Just tell me what you want.'

Kingdom was looking at the cardboard boxes on the table across the room. He'd spent most of the morning anticipating this conversation, wondering just where to start.

'You went to look at a house,' he said slowly, 'back in the summer.'

'Did I?'

'Yes, on Hayling Island.' He paused. 'The agency were called Saulet and Babcock. As it happened, they remember you well.' He smiled. 'June 7th. In case dates are a problem.'

Mrs Feasey nodded. 'You're right,' she said, 'I remember now.'

'Number sixty-five. Sinah Lane.'

'Yes, something like that.'

'Did you want to buy it?'

'It was a possibility. This place has its charms but,' she smiled thinly, 'a change would be nice.'

'I'm sure.' Kingdom frowned, spotting a tiny curry stain on his trousers, looking up again. 'They wanted quite a lot of money. £175,000 in fact.'

'Was it that much?'

'Yes.'

'Then no wonder I turned it down.'

'Quite.' Kingdom looked at her a moment. 'Were you serious? When you went to look?'

Mrs Feasey shrugged. Smudges of colour had appeared in her cheeks. Irritation rather than embarrassment. 'I'm not entirely clear what you're asking me,' she said coldly. 'Is it against the law to look at a house?'

'Not at all. But I was asking you whether you were serious.'

'Of course I was serious.'

'You wanted to buy it?'

'I wanted to see it.'

'With a view to buying it?'

'With a view to making a decision.' She nodded. 'Yes, of course.'

'And the decision was no?'

'Obviously.'

'But it could easily have been yes?'

'Of course.'

Kingdom nodded, taking his time now. 'You left a false name with the agency,' he said carefully. 'You called yourself Anderson. Elaine Anderson. You left a false address, too. Up in Guildford. The road you mentioned doesn't even exist.'

'Doesn't it?'

'No.'

Mrs Feasey nodded, saying nothing. The irritation had gone now. She'd become wary, watchful, one hand straying to a tiny mole, just visible beneath her left ear. She fingered it, waiting for Kingdom's next question, and the moment he asked it, he knew she'd already prepared the answer.

'So why?' he said. 'Why the false name?'

'I . . .' She shrugged. 'It's difficult.'

'Tell me,' Kingdom smiled, 'please.'

'I've been through . . .' She shook her head. 'Things have been difficult. There's been publicity. My name's been in the paper. You get nervous about people recognising you, recognising the name. I know it's unreasonable but there you are. It makes you want to hide. It must seem terribly devious but that's all it was, really. A little white lie.'

363

'But what would have happened had you liked the house? What would you have done then?'

'I don't know. You don't think these things through. They just happen. I suppose . . .' She frowned, then shook her head. 'I honestly don't know.'

Kingdom shifted his weight in the chair. One of the springs was on the point of collapse. 'Let's go back to the money,' he suggested.

'What money?'

'The money you'd need to pay for the house. Assuming you'd liked it.'

Mrs Feasey nodded. Her eyes had settled on the photo montage over the mantelpiece. Her face had softened. She looked wistful and a little lost. 'This is a game,' she said quietly. 'You know the answers already.'

'What answers?'

'Me,' she nodded at the photographs, 'Paddy. What happened to the business. That's why you weren't surprised next door, when I showed you the credit cards. You know I'm a bankrupt. You know the cards are worthless. You know I didn't have the money to pay for that house.' She paused. 'What else did Chris tell you?'

Kingdom gazed up at her. 'Who?'

'Chris. Chris Wells. The young man you met out at the nursery yesterday.'

'You've talked to him?'

'He phoned me, last night, saying he'd met someone. You fit the description.' She paused, fumbling in the pocket of the dressing gown for a cigarette. 'It's called friendship,' she said bitterly, 'in case you were wondering.'

Kingdom sat back in the chair, saying nothing. Rain drummed at the window. At length he bent forward, offering Mrs Feasey a match, smelling the shower gel again. She must have been ready for bed, he thought. She might even have been half-asleep when he started ringing the front door bell.

'Tell me about the house,' he said softly. 'I want to know about the house.'

'There's nothing to tell.'

'I don't believe you.'

'You don't?'

She looked down at him a moment then finally sank into the chair opposite. A tiny flicker beneath her left eye betrayed her exhaustion and Kingdom began to wonder exactly how much stress the average human being could take. This woman's last couple of years would have been enough for anyone. It was a miracle she was still in one piece. Strength, Kingdom thought again. And immense courage.

'You had the key for an hour,' he said. 'Were you alone?'

'Yes, of course.'

'Why of course?'

'I don't know.' She shook her head vigorously, as if to dislodge something. 'I don't know.'

'So what did you do with the key?'

'I looked round the house.'

'But why do that? If you couldn't buy it?'

She glanced up at him, then away again. She looked haunted now, and the accent in her voice was a little stronger.

'Someone else,' she muttered, 'I was looking on behalf of someone else.'

'Why?'

She shrugged. 'They wanted a second opinion.'

'A woman's view?'

'Yes.'

'I see.' Kingdom nodded. 'So who was he?'

There was a long silence. Then she shook her head. 'I can't tell you.'

'Why not?'

'Please. Don't.'

She was on her feet again, looking at the photos, and it took Kingdom a moment or two to realise that the tears were genuine. Real grief. Real despair.

'Someone's husband?' he said. 'Is that what you're saying?'

She nodded, turning her head away, covering her eyes with her hand. 'Yes, she whispered. 'Something like that.'

*

Kingdom left the flat an hour and a half later. He'd led her back to the house on Hayling Island a thousand times, trying to pin her down, asking for a name, an address, just a little more information about this mystery friend for whom she'd been doing a favour. But the blunter his questions became, the more reluctant she was to continue the conversation. The man's wife, she implied, had been a good friend. Nothing had happened. Nothing would ever happen. But the woman concerned was jealous by nature and deeply vulnerable. The last thing she wanted to do was hurt her.

At last, recognising the futility of pressing any harder, Kingdom had changed the subject. Without explaining why, he asked her about her movements in recent weeks. Specifically, he was interested in weekends. How did she normally spend her Saturday nights? Who could vouch for her whereabouts on Sundays? Composed again, Mrs Feasey had answered the questions with a weary indifference. Saturday nights, she said, were easy. She'd been at work. As for Sundays . . . She'd shrugged, shepherding Kingdom out into the narrow, dark little hall, handing him his coat, indicating the open bedroom door, explaining that daytimes were reserved for sleeping. Sundays included. Kingdom had asked for corroboration, the name of someone who could confirm the arrangement, but she'd shaken her head. How can I do that, she'd asked coldly, when I sleep alone?

Now, Kingdom found a phone box. Allder, according to his secretary, was still at lunch. After that, he had a meeting at the Home Office. The earliest he'd be back was four. He thanked her and dialled another number, police headquarters in Winchester. The switchboard answered and he asked for Special Branch. The line went dead for a moment, then the duty sergeant came on.

'Rob Scarman, please,' Kingdom said. 'Tell him it's urgent.'

Scarman came to the phone at once. The two men exchanged greetings and Scarman mentioned Arthur Sperring. Apparently he'd been boasting about some lead or other, crumbs he'd tossed to Micky Allder.

'He's right,' Kingdom said grimly, 'more right than he fucking knows.'

366

He explained about Ethne Feasey. He said he had nothing concrete but he was certain she'd repay a little further investment. Kingdom began to describe one or two bits of the conversation he'd just had but Scarman cut him short.

'What are we talking?' he said. 'What do you need?'

'I want her watched. And I want a tap.'

'When?'

'Soon as possible.'

'Have you got a warrant? For the tap?'

'You're joking. I've only just left her.'

Scarman put the phone down a moment and Kingdom heard him talking to someone else. Then he came back.

'OK,' he said, 'Leave it to me.'

Kingdom gave him the address and the phone number he'd memorised during his visit to the flat. The phone number would save a lot of time with the telephone tap. With the right authority, both incoming and outgoing calls could be intercepted at the exchange.

Kingdom paused. 'Got all that?'

Scarman said yes. 'Arthur's worried,' he added, 'thinks you're not to be trusted.'

'Is that a problem?'

'Christ, no. Quite the reverse. Means he thinks you might be getting somewhere.' Scarman began to laugh and then put the phone down.

Kingdom was still grinning when he got through to his next number. The receptionist at the Queen Alexandra Accident and Emergency Department confirmed that Dr Hubbard was on duty. She answered her bleep within seconds.

'Jo? Alan . . .'

'Hi.'

Kingdom's grin widened. Their last encounter hadn't quite exhausted her patience. 'Listen,' he said, 'I'm in Pompey tonight. Thought we might eat.'

'Oh? Why?'

'I'm interested in that Scottish thing you mentioned. That adventure course. Remember?'

'Yes.'

'Thought I might try it myself. You take any snaps at all?'

'Loads.'

'Great.' He paused, gazing out at the rain. 'Then why don't you bring them along?'

FOURTEEN

10 DOWNING STREET
LONDON SW1

TO: Chairman, Conservative Central Office, Smith Square, SW1
FROM: PPS
DATE: 5 October 1993

Subject: Sabbathman

The Prime Minister has asked me to drop you a formal line
about the extension of security restrictions on ministerial
public appearances. While he knows how irksome and disruptive
these restrictions will be, he believes he has no choice but
to accept the advice of those charged with the security of
himself, and of others.

He has also asked me to assure you that maximum pressure is
being exerted on the Metropolitan Commissioner to bring this
extraordinary episode to an early end. I understand the
Commissioner has been left in no doubt about the long-term
consequences of a protracted, or unsuccessful, inquiry. In
his own phrase, the Prime Minister believes it is totally
unacceptable to have to tailor his public and private lives
to the demands of some deranged criminal.

On a more personal note, the Prime Minister much appreciated
your remark about Walworth Road and the activities of our
Sabbathman friend. Desperate though HM's Opposition may be,
he doesn't think they'd stoop to political assassination to
square the odds in Parliament. Indeed, he suspects an initia-
tive that effective is probably beyond them.

'Are you serious about going to Scotland? Do you know what you'd be in for?'

'No,' Kingdom grinned, 'tell me.'

They were sitting in a harbour-side pub in Old Portsmouth. It was still early, half-past six, and the last of the sunshine gilded the churning tide beneath the big picture windows. Jo Hubbard selected one of the photos she'd spread on the table between them. It showed a sweep of broken rock climbing steeply towards a leaden sky. Looking at the photo, Kingdom could count six shades of grey.

'Day one,' Jo said, 'Ben Leacach.'

'What's that?'

'A mountain. Bloody big one, too. You climb it before lunch. All of you. Regardless.'

'Of what?'

'The weather. The wind, especially.' She took the photo out of his hand and studied it fondly. 'That day wasn't too bad. Twenty, twenty-five knots. Apparently it gets tricky when you can't stand up.'

'But you got to the top?'

'Of course.' She looked genuinely startled. 'Too right we did.'

Kingdom reached for his beer. He'd picked her up half an hour earlier. She'd just got in from the hospital and he'd waited in the car outside the neat little terrace house while she fed the cats and changed into jeans and a big old rollneck sweater. The more he saw of her, he thought, the more he liked her. She was always so cheerful and uncomplicated. She had a sense of optimism so powerful it was almost catching.

'Then there's this,' she said, selecting another photo and passing it across.

Kingdom studied it. Half a dozen people stood knee-deep in peaty brown water. Floating amongst them were a gaggle of single-seat canoes. Kingdom peered at the faces. Ethne Feasey's wet-suit was black and purple and she'd tied her hair in a tight blonde bun at the back. Another storm was looming over the mountains in the distance and she looked less than happy.

'So what kind of people go on these courses?' Kingdom asked. 'What should I expect?'

'All sorts. Young, old, men, women . . .' Jo shrugged. 'You all muck in. There's nothing fancy up there. You just get on with it. All you really need is a sense of humour. And a reasonable degree of fitness, of course. That helps.'

'But why do people go? What makes them want to do these things?' Kingdom fingered another of Jo's photos. A man in his forties was hanging off a cliff face, supported by a harness and two lengths of rope. The sea boiled on the rocks several hundred feet below.

Jo grinned. 'People like that guy have no choice,' she said. 'He was volunteered.'

'Who by?'

'His firm. The centre runs leadership courses for key managers. Companies decide who they want to send along and the people at the centre do the rest. They swear it's character-forming.'

'And is it?'

'Depends who you talk to.' She nodded at the photo. 'He'd tell you it was a waste of time.'

Kingdom inspected the photo again. The man on the cliff looked terrified. His glasses were pebbled with rain and his knuckles were white with strain.

'Was this some kind of punishment?' Kingdom inquired. 'What exactly had the guy done?'

'Nothing. His big mistake was owning up.'

'To what?'

'Vertigo.'

Kingdom blinked. 'Are you serious?'

'Yes. If you've got a weak spot, they'll find it. It's almost part of the contract.'

'And this was a *holiday*?'

'Yeah, for people like me it was. You don't have to be on one of these leadership courses. You can just go for the ride. Choose what you want to do. Design yourself an individual course. They call it "Pick and Mix".'

'And you enjoyed it?'

'Loved it. It was a laugh. A rage. Totally brilliant.'

'They didn't find your weak spot?'

'I haven't got one.'

'I don't believe you.'

'Well,' Jo grinned, looking down at the photos again, 'only snakes, and there aren't too many of those in Scotland.'

She passed him more shots. She'd seen a feature on the place, she said, in one of the Sunday magazines. It was tucked away on the Isle of Skye, miles from anywhere, the brainchild of an ex-soldier. He'd been running it now for nearly fifteen years, and it was still known by the name he'd given the place when he first settled.

'What was that?'

'*An Carraig*. It's Gaelic for the rock. You'll understand when you get there. The place is a real wilderness.'

Kingdom nodded, thinking of Ethne Feasey again, wondering how she'd ended up at a place like this. Jo was telling him about the routines, the demands the course made on you, the unspoken acceptance that you were there to do your best, to stretch yourself in ways you'd never done before. The living conditions, she said, were frankly spartan and the weather was frequently awful. Each new day brought a fresh set of physical challenges, most of them terrifying, but the instructors were excellent and after a while it began to dawn on you that you might survive. After that, you began to get the hang of it. And after that, if you were lucky, something rather magical happened.

'What?' Kingdom inquired drily.

Jo was looking out of the window now. There'd been some kind of race offshore and a line of dinghies were making their way back into the harbour, the wind behind them, their sails gull-winged. In the gathering dusk, they looked like birds.

'It's hard,' she said at last, 'to describe.'

'Try.'

'I don't know.' She shook her head. 'It's got something to do with self-belief, self-respect. At least, that's what they tell you. But it's more than that. Much more. It's like' – she frowned – 'you've opened a box and taken a look inside. Until you've done it, until it's happened to you, you didn't even know the box existed.' She shrugged. 'But now it just makes everything different, somehow. It's very raw, very powerful. You just know you've been there and done it. It's very special.'

'Very private?'

'No, not really, not when you're with other people, because they've got the box too, and they can look inside. Maybe that's what makes it so special. While you're there you get close, really close. Yeah . . .' She nodded, still gazing out at the dinghies.

Kingdom picked up a photo he'd had his eye on for some time. Three people were squatting in a group in front of a small ridge tent. One of them was Ethne Feasey. Another, Jo. The third, an older man, knelt between them, his arms around both of them.

'Is that what you're talking about?'

Kingdom passed the photo across, indicating the same huge grin on both women's faces.

Jo glanced at the photo and nodded. 'Exactly. That's it exactly. The last day, day ten. We'd made it. We'd got there. You can see it, can't you?'

Kingdom smiled, understanding perfectly. 'And do you keep up afterwards?' he asked. 'Friends for life?'

'You mean this woman? And me?'

'Yes.'

Jo looked at the photo again. 'Off and on,' she said. 'We've certainly been in touch.'

'And does she feel the way you do? The box? The magic?'

Jo hesitated a moment. 'I'm not sure,' she said. 'To be honest I think that particular lady's had a few problems. It's nothing she's said but, you know . . . you sometimes get the feeling . . .'

'Really?'

'Yes.'

'But didn't you get close? Isn't that what you just said?'

'Yes, of course. But some things, private things, I dunno . . . I got the impression with her that the holiday was some kind of present, maybe from her son, something to cheer her up. I think her husband had left her but it wasn't something she ever wanted to talk about . . .'

'And you'd respect that?'

'Of course.'

Kingdom nodded. One of the Isle of Wight car ferries was pushing out against the tide. He could see the passengers queueing at the bar.

'When were you up there,' he said, 'as a matter of interest?'

'March.'

Kingdom nodded, his earlier guess confirmed. By that time, he thought, Ethne Feasey had been a widow for four months, and a bankrupt for slightly longer. With that much grief, most people would have welcomed a shoulder to cry on, but Ethne wasn't one of them. Of that, Kingdom was certain. She had too much pride, too much self-respect. He'd seen it only hours ago, talking to her in that Godforsaken room.

'You've seen her a lot, you say? Since?'

'Once.'

'And you got the photos out? Compared notes?'

Jo said nothing, reaching for her beer. She was on her second pint, a warm, nutty, slightly sweet brew that Kingdom had never tasted before. She took a couple of mouthfuls, eyeing the photos. Then she put her glass down and sat back against the padded seat.

'Are you really going to Scotland?' she said quietly. 'Only you might as well be honest.'

'Me? You mean why am I here?'

'Yes.'

Kingdom looked at her for a long time. Too many questions about Ethne Feasey, he thought. Too obvious. Too crude. 'What else might I be doing?' he asked lightly.

'I don't know. I can think of a couple of things.'

'Such as?'

She shrugged. 'There's the obvious, I suppose. You might . . . fancy your chances.'

'With you, you mean?'

'Yes.'

'Or?' Kingdom smiled. 'Is there another option?'

'I dunno.' She shrugged again. 'You're a policeman, a detective. It must be your living, asking questions. You tell me.'

Kingdom frowned, turning his head away, not answering. He'd toyed all afternoon with coming clean about his interest in the photos but his instincts told him to hold off. The direct line to the mountain top was seldom the best route up. As Jo would doubtless know.

'I'm not here to make a pass at you,' he said, 'if that's the worry.'

'Good.'

'Why good?'

'Because it would be a shame to spoil all this', she grinned at him, gesturing at the photos and the beer, 'when I'm enjoying it so much.'

'Quite.' Kingdom toasted her with his glass. 'Boyfriend?' he inquired. 'Husband?'

'Neither.' She hesitated for a moment, 'I'm gay.'

'Ah . . .' Kingdom nodded, feeling suddenly foolish. 'Silly me.'

'You hadn't guessed?'

'No, not at all.' He paused. 'On the contrary.'

'Good. Not that it matters, eh?'

'No, absolutely not.'

'Good,' she said again, 'just thought I'd clear it up, that's all. Just in case . . .' She beamed at him across the table, bright-eyed again, mischievous, and for a moment Kingdom wondered whether she was lying. He'd never heard of women pretending they were gay, not under these circumstances, but he could see how effective the tactic might be. He reached for the photograph of the threesome outside the tent.

'I'm not being nosey,' he said, 'but you and this lady . . . you weren't . . .'

Jo followed his pointing finger, then began to laugh. 'Ethne? And me? No, definitely not.' She shook her head. 'No way.'

'Not interested?'

'Not remotely. Quite the reverse, in fact. Can't you see?'

She nodded at the photo and Kingdom picked it up again, taking a second look at the man kneeling between the two women. He seemed older than both of them, early fifties perhaps. He had a big, windburned face and the lean, spare features of someone who exercised a great deal. He was wearing an old green sweatshirt and his legs were bare under the khaki shorts. His hair, greying but cropped brutally short, gave the smile a certain edge.

'Who is he?' Kingdom asked. 'Volunteer or pressed man?'

'Neither.' Jo laughed, still gazing at the photo. 'Ethne called him Akela. Used to drive him nuts. She was great that way. Nothing fazed her. Absolutely nothing. Whatever he made her do, no matter how tough it was, she just took it in her stride. Imagine. A middle-aged woman. Diving. Abseiling. Running up and down mountains. Whatever it was, she just got on with it, gave it her best shot. No wonder he . . . .' she began to laugh again as Kingdom completed the sentence.

'. . . fell for her?'

'Yes.' She nodded vigorously. 'Head over heels. Complete infatuation.'

'And did they . . .?'

'Get it on?'

Kingdon nodded.

'I honestly don't know. Maybe not. But that wasn't the point. He was besotted with her. I'd never seen it quite like that before. He just couldn't get enough of her. Looking at her. Being with her. Talking to her. Showing her how to do things. Incredible. Potty about her. Absolutely nuts.'

'She's an attractive woman,' Kingdom pointed out, not bothering to look at the photograph.

'I know. I know. She is. We all thought that. But even so . . .'

'What?'

'I dunno. He was just . . .' She shrugged. 'Like a puppy. That's what made it so funny, I suppose. Here was this big butch man, you know, Mr Tough Guy. Been everywhere, seen it all, done it all, waded through the muck and bullets, trust him with your life. All that. And along comes dear old Ethne and he starts behaving like a two-year-old. Sweet, really . . .' She shook her head, thinking about it, then swallowed another mouthful of beer.

Kingdom was watching her carefully. Take it easy, he told himself. You're simply here to look at a handful of holiday snaps. End of a busy day. Act knackered. He began to flick through some of the other photos, smothering a yawn.

'So was he an instructor, this bloke? Does he work at the place?' Kingdom glanced up, aware of Jo looking at him.

The expression on her face was a mixture of amusement and pity. 'Akela?' she prompted. 'You ever read Kipling?'

'No.'

'Then you should. Akela's the leader. The boss. The one in charge. What Akela says, goes.'

'So chummy here . . .' Kingdom tried to find the photo.

Jo was nodding now, all smiles. 'Exactly,' she said, 'he's the one who owns the place. He's the one' – she spotted the photo and picked it up – 'who started it all.'

A couple of minutes later, Jo left the table and went to the lavatory. While she was gone, Kingdom sorted quickly through the photographs. The shot outside the tent he put in his pocket. The rest he began to shuffle into a pile. In doing so he came across another photo he hadn't seen before. It featured half a dozen or so people milling around the end of a stone quay. Moored to the quay was a white motor cruiser. It was broad in the beam, with a long cabin forward. It looked tough and workmanlike and there was a sizable rubber dinghy tied up alongside. Across the stern, in blue letters, the motor cruiser carried the name *Catherine May*, and the man Ethne had called Akela was standing in the well. He was bigger than the first photo had suggested, at least six feet tall, powerfully built. By now, Kingdom knew his real name. Jo had written it down for him, along with the address of the adventure centre. Dave, she'd said, Dave Gifford. He was the one to write to if Kingdom was serious about putting himself to the test.

Kingdom was studying the photo when Jo returned.

'His pride and joy,' she said, looking over Kingdom's shoulder. 'He even let Ethne have a go.'

'Off by themselves? Into the sunset?'

'Hardly. We were all on board.' She nodded at the group on the quay. 'But only Ethne got to steer the thing.'

She turned away, reaching for her coat, and Kingdom palmed the second print into his pocket. Then he put the rest of the photos into Jo's envelope and touched her lightly on the arm.

'Here,' he said, 'let's go eat.'

The restaurant was across the road. Outside the pub they stood for a moment by the water. It was nearly dark now and one of the big cross-Channel ferries was nosing out through the narrow harbour mouth. The ship looked brand new, a wall of white steel towering above them. There were passengers clustered at the rail, dim black dots up on the top decks, and Jo lifted an arm, waving at them. Kingdom was amused, watching her.

'They won't be able to see you,' he pointed out, 'not down here.'

'So what?' she said, still waving.

The restaurant specialised in local fish. Over sea bass and braised vegetables, Kingdom talked about his father. He'd managed to get through to the hospital again, while he'd waited for the car ferry on the Isle of Wight, and the consultant had told him a little more about the operation. They'd had to insert a metal rod into Ernie's shattered thigh bone, reconnecting the severed ends. Kingdom thought he'd used a German word.

'Kuntscher,' Jo said, mopping the juices on her plate with a slice of French bread. 'It's called a Kuntscher nail. It's standard procedure, a case like that.'

Kingdom nodded, recognising the phrase. 'So what's the outcome?' he said. 'What happens next?'

'He'll stay there for a bit while they try and mobilise it. He'll need lots of physio. It'll be bloody painful. Really nasty. Poor man.'

'But how long will they keep him?'

Jo shrugged. 'Depends. They tend to be very aggressive these days. Get people on their feet as soon as possible. It's beds, really. They need throughput to keep the accountants happy. It's called productivity.'

'He's seventy-three,' Kingdom pointed out. 'Does that make any difference?'

'Of course it does. It means he'll be there longer. That makes him a management nightmare. Daring to be injured at that age . . .'

She shook her head, refusing to take the conversation any further, and Kingdom thought of the last time he'd seen his father, grey with pain on a stretcher in some hospital corridor. They'd wheeled Ernie away when he wasn't looking, and in his bleaker moments Kingdom wondered whether he'd ever see the old man again.

Jo reached for another piece of bread and Kingdom tried to rid his mind of the image of his father. Motor cruiser, he told himself. With an inflatable dinghy.

'This guy Dave Gifford,' he said casually, 'Mr Akela. What exactly did he do? In the Army?'

'Not sure. There was a kind of bunkhouse they'd built where we had our meals and there was some regimental stuff up on the walls. Photos, the odd shield.' She frowned. 'Royal Marines? That sound about right?'

'Yes. Could be. Or the SAS. Or the Paras.'

'No,' Jo shook her head, emphatic, 'it definitely wasn't the Paras. That was his son. His son had been in the Paras. They were always going on about it. The son used to call him a cabbagehead. No,' she shook her head again, 'Dave Gifford must have been in the Marines. I'm sure of it.'

Kingdom was leaning forward now, newly alert. Another Gifford. Another ex-soldier. But younger. 'Son?' he said idly.

'Yes, he had a boy, Andy. I say boy. He must have been in his late twenties, maybe older. It was hard to tell. He had one of those faces.'

'And built like his dad, I expect. Brick shit-house.'

'No,' she said, 'Andy was much smaller, slighter. Not much taller than me, actually. That's why he'd gone into the Paras. That's why Dave couldn't resist all the little digs.' She looked up. 'Dave used to call him "PS" when Andy said he was a cabbagehead.'

'PS?'

'Yes. We all assumed it was something to do with an after-thought, you know, a kid that comes along late in a marriage. But it turned out to stand for Pint Sized. Didn't do too much for Andy, as you might imagine. He was nice, actually. What I saw of him. Very quiet. Very thoughtful. Not like Dave at all.'

'And is he in these snaps? The ones you took?'

'No.' She shook her head. 'He wasn't around that much. He helped on one or two of the abseiling days but not much else. Apparently he was writing a book of some kind. I think he was just up in Skye for a couple of months. His real home was in London.'

Kingdom nodded, saying nothing. One more question, he thought. One more tiny question. He looked at Jo. Her mouth was shiny with melted butter. He reached across with his napkin, wiping it away, deciding that it no longer mattered about cover, about his fantasy trip to Scotland. Not now, not this far down the road.'

'Tell me,' he said carefully, 'this Andy's eyes. What colour were they?'

Jo stared at him a moment. Her fingertips stopped exploring the corner of her mouth. 'Blue,' she said. 'You couldn't miss them.'

Kingdom phoned Rob Scarman at midnight. Scarman was in bed with his wife. Kingdom didn't waste time on apologies.

'Did the tap go on?'

'What?'

'Mrs Feasey's place. In Shanklin.'

There was a long pause. Kingdom heard the squeal of bed-springs and the pad of Scarman's footsteps as he went to another extension. When he came back on the line his voice was icy.

'You never mentioned she'd been wired before,' he said.

'I didn't know.'

'Well, she's already on line. In fact we nearly ended up with two taps.'

'Great,' Kingdom laughed, 'stereo.'

'Very funny. Gower Street are taking first bite, though when I asked they seemed surprised we should be interested.'

'That's their way of saying fuck off,' Kingdom muttered. 'Don't be fooled.'

'You sound like Allder.'

'Yeah,' Kingdom nodded, 'occupational hazard.' He paused. 'So when do we get transcripts? And what about your guys outside? What's she up to? What's she been doing?'

Scarman swallowed a yawn. He said he'd found room in the budget to send two DCs. One of them was first-rate, a real flier. The other one was brand new. So far they'd not been in touch but between them Scarman was sure they had the job sorted. As for the phone tap, he was expecting the first cassette in the morning's internal post. Under the circumstances, he'd skipped the formality of a properly-typed transcript. A waste of time, he said heavily, and a waste of money.

'Couldn't agree more,' Kingdom said. 'When shall I phone again?'

'Tomorrow morning.' Scarman yawned for the second time. 'On the office number.'

The phone down, Kingdom dialled Annie's flat again. He'd been trying off and on all day, increasingly anxious, but still there was no answer. He let the phone ring and ring, thinking she might be asleep, wondering why Gower Street had any kind of interest in Ethne Feasey. The only possible link he could think of was her son's involvement in the Twyford Down campaign. MI5 were always on the look-out for fresh conquests to add to their empire, and eco-terrorism – just now – seemed promising. Protest groups were springing up all over the country and sooner or later someone would pursue the debate with Semtex, rather than letters to the *Guardian*. Maybe they'd both been shaking the same tree, Kingdom thought, though he was now certain in his own mind that there was nothing remotely green about Sabbathman.

He waited another minute, listening to the burr-burr on Annie's line. When there was still no answer, he put the phone down. By tomorrow, she'd have been gone four days. Quite a while, he thought, when she'd only popped out for lunch.

Next morning, after a night in another bed and breakfast, Kingdom was back in Old Portsmouth. He drove slowly round the area, getting his bearings. The city's first settlements had sprung up around the harbour mouth. A medieval stone tower guarded the

harbour entrance and a warren of cobbled streets led away from
the waterfront. Between this finger of land and the city's cathedral
was a pocket of water known locally as the Camber Dock. Protected
on three sides, it had served as the town's first harbour and even
now it was still busy with shipping of all descriptions.

Kingdom parked the Wolseley on the dockside and got out. It
was a bright, windy day and a trawler was berthing alongside a tall
line of sheds. Forward of the wheelhouse, beneath a cloud of
seagulls, men were already working in the hold, stacking the plastic
crates of fish while a fork-lift truck whined to and fro on the
quayside, depositing wooden pallets. Kingdom watched for a
moment, as fascinated as ever by the life these men must lead. In
reality, he knew it was probably a terrible job – long hours,
indifferent pay, lousy working conditions – but in his heart he'd
always wanted to go to sea. It had long been a dream of his, a door
that would open to limitless freedom. At sea, he thought, they'd
never get you. At sea, at last, you could be safe.

The first crates of fish swung out of the hold and Kingdom
picked his way around the waiting pallets. In another part of the
Camber, away from the trawlers and the big Isle of Wight car
ferries, developers were building a small marina, floating walkways
quartering the oily water. It was here, according to the manager
Kingdom had already talked to on the phone, that visiting boats
would tie up. Kingdom looked at the neat rows of moored yachts,
wondering what the next few minutes would turn up. The manager
had told him to try knocking at the Berthing Master's door. Behind
the Keyhaven Restaurant, he'd said helpfully, next to the Pilot's
Office.

Kingdom found the restaurant. The Berthing Master had just
arrived for work. Kingdom showed him his ID and took the
proferred seat while the Berthing Master sorted himself out. He
was a small, balding man with a slight squint. The badge on his
blazer said 'Royal Yachting Association'. He finished unpacking his
briefcase while Kingdom explained what he was after.

The Berthing Master opened a drawer and took out a clipboard.
'Do we have a date in mind?'

Kingdom nodded. He knew the chronology by heart now, the
stepping stones that led from a banker's clifftop estate in Jersey to

room 26, block A, Ford Open Prison. 'Around the weekend of the 18th and 19th September,' he said. 'That's last month.'

The Berthing Master flicked back through a sheaf of computer print-outs clipped to the board. He extracted the entries for the relevant weekend and ran a finger down the list.

'And the name again? The boat?'

'*Catherine May.*'

The Berthing Master nodded, showing Kingdom the list. A motor cruiser called the *Catherine May* had berthed on Thursday 16 September. She'd left again three days later, on Sunday 19. Dues of £20 had been paid in cash.

Kingdom produced the photograph of the boat he'd removed from Jo Hubbard's collection. He showed it to the Berthing Master. 'Is this the one? Would you recognise it?'

The Berthing Master glanced at the photo, then shook his head. 'I was on leave,' he said. 'You need to talk to Harry.'

Harry turned out to work as a book-keeper for a local crane company. They were based in one of the sheds on the quayside, and Kingdom found him bent over an electric fire in the glass-partitioned office at the back of the building. He introduced himself and explained about the boat. Harry peered at the photo. He was a stout, cheerful man in his late fifties. His ginger beard was greying but there was nothing wrong with his eyes.

'Yep,' he nodded, 'that's her.'

'You sure?'

'Positive. I went on board.'

'You met the owner?'

'Yep.' He nodded again, indicating the figure in the photo. 'Him. That one. I collected the money and we had a chat.'

'When? When did he pay?'

'Up front, as soon as he arrived. I gave him a berth over by the pub. He knew he was going on Sunday, see, so he paid the twenty quid up front. Cash in hand, like.'

Kingdom bent over the desk, feeling his pulse beginning to slow again. In any investigation there came a moment when you knew, with total certainty, that you were closing on the truth.

'Was he alone?' Kingdom asked.

'No. He had another chap with him, a younger chap. Didn't say a lot, mind.'

'Big? Small?'

Harry glanced up. The tea at his elbow was getting cold. 'Titch,' he said, 'half your size.'

'And younger, you say?'

'Yep. 'Bout thirty odd. Sandy hair.' He looked at the photo again. 'Nice boat, mind.'

Kingdom took out his notepad, scribbling Harry's name and address. Later, he told him, someone would return for a full statement. It was possible, at some future date, that he might have to appear as a witness in court.

Harry began to look troubled. 'Don't know about that,' he mumbled. 'What's he done? This bloke?'

Kingdom ignored the question. He still had the photo. 'What about the inflatable?' he said. 'Did you see that as well?'

'On the cabin roof, lashed down.'

'Did they use it at all?'

'Dunno.' He shrugged. 'Might have done.'

'But you're not sure.'

'No.'

Kingdom pocketed the note-pad and thanked Harry for his time. As he began to back out of the hot little office, Harry looked up.

'You try the museum at all?' he said.

'What museum?'

'The Royal Marine place. Up at Eastney. Only he got me to phone a cab for him. Take him there. That first day he arrived.'

The Royal Marine Museum lay at the other end of the sea-front, part of the original barracks that had once housed thousands of serving troops. Kingdom found it without difficulty, turning into the car park beneath a ten-foot statue of a patrolling trooper. The car park was empty. A path led through a litter of Marine trophies to an imposing flight of steps. Inside the tall glass doors was a reception desk. Kingdom showed his ID again and asked to see the officer in charge. At length, an archivist appeared, a tall young man in a checked shirt. Kingdom explained his interest. Bloke called Gifford. Probably an ex-Marine. Thursday 16 September. Might have popped in for a chat, or a beer, or simply a look-round.

The archivist was frowning. The name, he said, sounded familiar. He led the way down to a basement office. Bookshelves lined the walls. The archivist waved Kingdom into a chair and produced a blue visitors' book, and Kingdom watched him checking back through September, marvelling at the footprints Gifford had left behind him. Always the same, he thought. If you know where to look, everyone makes mistakes.

At length the archivist glanced up. 'You're right,' he said, 'Dave Gifford. He had an inquiry about an oppo he'd served with. I remember now.'

'And?' Kingdom had his notepad out again.

'Couldn't help him, really. They'd served together in 45 Commando, mainly in Aden. His mate had done something heroic in one of the Crater riots. I gather this bloke had just died and Gifford had been contacted by the widow. She'd never been clear about the details of the incident and she wanted something official to show the son. Gifford said he'd oblige.'

'But you couldn't help?'

'No. I got out some of the standard reference but I think he was after something more personal. Field reports, maybe even a citation if a medal was involved. He seemed a bit vague about that.'

'So what did you say to him?'

'I told him to go to the Public Records Office.'

Kingdom nodded, making a note. 'How did he behave when he was here? How did he seem to you?'

'Fine.' The archivist shrugged. 'Fit for his age. Big man. Said he missed it. Like they all do.'

'Missed what?'

'The Corps.' He paused. 'It's quite a blow for some of them, leaving it all behind. He'd been out for a while, '78 I think he said, but it's often hard, making the adjustment. Life can be physically tough inside, but you're well protected. Money. Food. Heating. Mates. They miss all that. You can tell.'

'You're talking about Gifford now? Dave?'

'Any of them really. They can get a bit . . .' He frowned, searching for the right word. 'Lost. That's all. Marines are funny people. Very black and white. Give a Marine a job to do and you've never met a happier bloke. Give him his gratuity, cut him adrift, and who knows?'

He pushed the visitors' book across the desk, asking Kingdom to sign it. While Kingdom was scribbling his name, he sat back, brooding, and Kingdom wondered just how many of these conversations he'd had, old campaigners dropping by, inquiring about mates, reminiscing about favourite postings, trying to puzzle out the world to which they now belonged.

Kingdom closed the visitors' book.

The archivist rubbed his eyes. 'You know this man Gifford?' he asked.

'No.'

'You know his son at all? Andy?'

'No.'

'You should.' He smiled at last. 'He's quite a talent.'

Kingdom waited, his notepad open in front of him. 'Talent?' he said.

'Yes.' The archivist nodded. 'He was down in the Falklands. The Paras, not the Marines. He was involved on Longdon and wrote some stuff about it. Got published too, much to some people's disgust.'

'Published?' Kingdom blinked, remembering Jo Hubbard's line about the son writing some kind of book. The communiqués, he thought, Sabbathman's regular post-mortems. Nicely done. Neat turns of phrase. Kingdom picked up his pen. 'So what did he write about? This Andy Gifford?'

'The truth, as far as I can make out. How bloody dreadful the whole thing was.' He paused. 'Interesting guy. Interesting job, too.'

'In the Paras?'

'Yes.'

'What did he do?'

The archivist yawned, glancing at his watch. 'He was a sniper,' he said, getting up, 'good at it too, according to the stuff I read.'

*

389

Kingdom was in Winchester by lunchtime. He found Rob Scarman at his desk in the big fifth-floor office, halfway through a pile of corned beef sandwiches. Beside the sandwiches was a thermos of hot consommé and an audio-cassette. He tossed the cassette to Kingdom.

'It's been here since ten,' he said reproachfully. 'I cancelled a haircut because of you.'

Kingdom eyed the sandwiches, realising how hungry he was. Scarman pushed them across.

'You got a player for this?' Kingdom indicated the cassette.

'Over there. In the corner.'

Kingdom crossed the room, sinking his teeth into the sand-wich, wiping crumbs off the brand new Sony tape machine. When he pressed the play button there was a crackle or two on the sound-track then the long hollow sound of a telephone line interrupted by the burr-burr of an incoming call. Someone picked up the receiver. Then Kingdom heard a woman's voice.

'Four-eight-five-six-seven-four,' she said.

Scarman was looking at Kingdom. 'That her? Your Mrs Feasey?'

'Yeah.'

A man's voice was talking now, rougher than Kingdom had anticipated, a flat, ugly southern accent, Essex maybe, or Kent. The conversation was brief. He called Ethne 'luv'. He said she was to phone back. The line went dead. Kingdom looked up, crossing the room for another sandwich.

'What happened?' he asked.

'She went out. Almost immediately.'

'Where?'

'Call box on the sea-front.' Scarman shrugged. 'She reversed the charges. That's all we know.'

'Anyone been on to the exchange?'

'Yes. But we haven't heard back yet. And there won't be a tape. Just the number.'

'Was she on long?'

'Ten minutes. Give or take.'

'Then what?'

'She went home again.'

'And?'

'We think she's asleep. The curtains at the back are pulled.' Scarman paused. 'I gather she works nights.'

Kingdom looked up, startled. 'How did you know that?'

'There's another call on there.' Scarman nodded at the tape machine. 'Her this time. She's talking to her boss as far as I can make out, apologising really. It seems she had a break-in last night. Someone called the Bill and the uniformed boys turned up at the place she works at four in the morning. The management weren't best pleased.' Scarman paused, gazing at the remains of his lunch. 'Did you have to kick her window in?' he said at last, 'Or was that just for effect?'

FIFTEEN

TO: Home Secretary, Queen Anne's Gate, London, SW1
FROM: Commissioner, Metropolitan Police
DATE: 6 October 1993

Subject: "Sabbathman"

Further to our discussion this morning, I have now received
a detailed report from Commander Allder. In the light of
this report, I have the fullest confidence that vigorous and
comprehensive inquiries are proceeding and will bring the
matter to a satisfactory conclusion. I will, of course, keep
you informed of further developments on a day-to-day basis.

I understand that you have now been fully briefed on the
special security arrangements in place for next, and successive, Sundays. While we naturally regret the disruption to
your domestic arrangements, we believe it best that you and
your family remain at home under close police protection
until the present situation is resolved. This also, of
course, applies to your colleagues.

The helicopter looked brand new. It chattered out of a clear blue sky and settled gently onto the painted white 'H' on the parade ground behind Hampshire police headquarters. Kingdom was waiting in the shelter of the main building, his trench-coat buttoned against a keen north-easterly wind. He watched the pilot shut down the engine and leaned across to release the passenger door. The tiny figure beside him clambered out and hurried across the tarmac. Kingdom grinned, his hands plunged deep inside the pockets of his coat. On the phone last night, Allder had sounded guarded, even sceptical. Now, for whatever reason, he looked euphoric.

He stood in front of Kingdom, eyeing him up and down. The sudden cold was making his nose run. He jerked his head back towards the waiting helicopter. On the side, in blue letters, it said 'Metropolitan Police'.

'Traffic want it back by lunchtime,' he said, 'so why don't you talk me through it?'

Kingdom wondered about cancelling the car and the driver he'd arranged, then thought better of it. Instead, he accompanied Allder back to the landing pad. The helicopter was a Jet Ranger, two seats up front, two behind. Allder told Kingdom to get in behind the pilot and tell him where to go. Airspace around the Solent was evidently crowded. The man would need to file some kind of flight plan.

Kingdom slipped into the left-hand seat and agreed a route while Allder made himself comfortable in the back. Within five minutes they were airborne again, the pilot holding the hover at the level of the fourth floor long enough for Kingdom to give Arthur Sperring a smile and a wave. The DCS had been in conference with the Chief Constable since eight, passing on what little Kingdom had seen fit to tell him. Now, back in his office, he glared out at the helicopter, deeply suspicious.

The pilot nudged the joystick forward and the nose dipped as the helicopter gathered speed. Then he pulled the machine into a tight climbing turn, levelling out at eight hundred feet, the squat grey bulk of the cathedral slipping beneath them.

Kingdom felt a hand on his shoulder. He half-turned in the seat, restrained by the safety harness. Allder was offering him a newspaper. Both men were wearing headphones.

'Special edition,' Allder said, 'hot off the presses.'

Kingdom glanced down at the paper. *The Citizen*'s front page, yet again, was devoted to Mr Angry. The page was dominated by a photograph of the cabinet. The photograph had been taken in the aftermath of the 1992 election and at some point someone must have put it in an envelope because the fold marks – one up, one across – were clearly visible. Beneath the photo, in bold type, was the text of a message newly received by the newspaper. '*Blanche and co,*' it read, '*had one thing in common. Greed. None of them knew when to stop. And all of them paid the price. Which is why this bunch of comedians should start worrying about their just deserts. Politics should be about leadership. Not another four-year wallow in the trough. Know how the rest of us feel? Pig-sick . . .*'

Kingdom glanced up a moment. The back of the sun visor over the windscreen was mirrored, and he could see the top half of Allder's face. He was looking down at the huge chalk cutting gouged in the flank of Twyford Down. The contractors were pushing into the hill from both ends, the big yellow graders bumping back and forth, dragging behind them long plumes of grey-white dust. On the neighbouring by-pass the traffic was nose-to-tail and as the helicopter banked onto a new heading, Kingdom could see the raised chalk embankment where the motorway would sweep across the water meadows, and on towards the distant blue shadows of Southampton.

Allder's voice crackled in his ear. 'What do you think of it?'

'I think it's hideous.'

'I meant the paper.'

Kingdom glanced down at *The Citizen* again. The headline above the rows of smiling cabinet faces read 'GOVERNMENT HEALTH WARNING?'. Kingdom smiled, thinking of the conversation he'd had with the archivist at the Eastney museum. *The Citizen*'s sub-editors had begun to ape the mystery killer. Sabbathman himself might have penned the headline.

'Nice turn of phrase,' he said, 'our Mr Angry.'

'Quite.'

'Is this the one he sent to Downing Street?'

'No, but the thought's the same. And so is their reaction. They've been talking to Gower Street again. Five are insisting on operational primacy.'

'And the Commissioner?'

'He's trying to fight them off.'

'And?'

'We'll win.'

Kingdom said nothing, looking down at the construction site. The contractors had built a compound beside the line of the motorway, a small city of portakabins webbed with muddy tyre tracks. From two thousand feet, the landscape resembled a patient in hospital, the victim of some particularly vicious attack. Wherever you looked, there were fresh wounds. Max Carpenter had a neat little phrase for it. You can't make omelettes, he'd said, without breaking eggs. Too right, Kingdom thought, watching a line of diggers tearing at the exposed chalk.

They flew south-east, towards the coast. North of Portsmouth, the ground rose beneath them, another chalk escarpment, and then fell away again, the southerly slope of the hill covered with the sprawl of a housing estate. Ahead, silhouetted against the glare of the sun, was the city itself, street after street of terraced houses, high-rise council blocks, and the towering gantry cranes in the naval dockyard. The harbour was bisected by the incoming motorway, and one of the big white cross-Channel ferries was nosing past a line of anchored warships. The helicopter began to lose height. Where the harbour narrowed at its seaward end, Kingdom could see the Camber Dock. The trawler he'd watched unloading yesterday was still there, the fish hold empty, the orange nets spread across the quayside.

Kingdom signalled to Allder as the pilot brought the helicopter into the hover. 'This is where we start,' he said. 'Gifford turned up on the Thursday. With his son.'

'Andy? The one you told me about?'

'Yeah.'

'We can prove that?'

'Yeah. He took a berth down there. The boat's booked in. I've seen the entry. Talked to the guy who took the money.'

Kingdom gave Allder a moment to get his bearings. The altimeter was showing 150 feet now and the pilot was slowly rotating the Jet Ranger on its axis, giving Allder a panoramic view. Beneath them, on the promontory outside the pub, Kingdom could see faces upturned, coats flapping in the downdraft, eyes shielded against the bright sunlight.

'OK,' Allder said, 'what next?'

'Hayling Island.' Kingdom glanced at the pilot.

The nose dipped again, and bits of the sea-front began to race past as they flew east, still low, the funfair empty, the long promenade dotted with joggers and mothers with pushchairs. Past Southsea Castle, the pilot climbed to 500 feet, and Kingdom felt the machine juddering as the rotor blades bit into the airstream.

'This is guesswork,' he said, 'but I think Gifford's son took the inflatable over to Hayling Island on the Saturday night. He probably came this way, offshore. There's an anti-submarine bar-rage here, goes out about a mile, but you'd be safe enough at high water.'

'When was that?'

'Nine thirty-five.'

'After dark?'

'Yes.'

'Wouldn't that have been a problem?'

'No,' Kingdom shook his head, 'not if the boy knew what he was doing.'

Kingdom glanced up at the mirror. Allder was looking down

at the sea-front, totally absorbed. The Royal Marine Museum was clearly visible now, the shadow of the statue at the gate falling across the newly surfaced access road. The pilot began to lose height again as the foreshore curled away at the mouth of Langstone Harbour.

'Here's where he comes back in,' Kingdom told Allder. 'With me, sir?'

'Yeah.'

The pilot was back at the hover now, still losing height, the downwash from the rotor blades feathering the water below. The tiny snubnose ferry that chugged back and forth across the harbour mouth had just berthed alongside the Hayling Island landing stage, and half a dozen passengers were filing off. From here, a single road snaked away towards the built-up areas of the island, perhaps a mile to the east.

Kingdom exchanged glances with the pilot. They'd discussed the next manoeuvre, back on the ground at Winchester.

Allder tapped Kingdom on the shoulder. 'What's that?' he said.

Kingdom followed his pointing finger. Across the road from the landing stage was a squat, two-storied building, painted yellow.

'It's a pub, sir.'

'Busy on Saturday nights?'

'Packed. According to the locals.'

'And you think our friend's on the move around half-nine? Ten?'

'Best guess,' Kingdom nodded, 'yeah.'

'And no one heard anything? In the pub?'

'I don't know, sir. This is supposition. Arthur's boys can do the legwork.' He paused, still looking at the pub. 'And in any case, the outboard's muffled . . .' He shrugged. 'Dark night, noisy pub, I'd be amazed if anyone bothered even looking.'

Allder was silent for a moment. 'OK,' he said at last, 'what next?'

The pilot glanced at Kingdom and then eased the joystick forward. The helicopter was low again, no more than fifty feet, skirting the pebble beach that edged the harbour mouth. Beyond the landing stage, he banked to the right, following the shoreline as the pebbles gave way to marshland. They clattered past a holiday camp, frightening a dog. A minute or so later they were at the hover again while Kingdom twisted in his seat, pointing down.

'Do you see?'

'See what?'

'That close of houses. That's where the guy I mentioned remembered his dog going barmy. The next morning. The Sunday morning. So what I'm saying is chummy came in at high water Saturday night and left the inflatable down there, on the saltings.'

Allder grunted. Kingdom could see his face pressed against the cold perspex. 'And?' he said.

Kingdom nodded to the pilot and the helicopter dipped slightly as they began to follow the road south.

'This is where it becomes Sinah Lane,' Kingdom shouted, 'just here.'

Allder hadn't moved. 'So where's the house you mentioned? The one you're saying our friend used?'

'Down there. The white one.'

Kingdom pointed again, indicating the house that had been for sale. The trees in the garden had lost a lot of leaves in the past ten days and the property was clearly visible. Allder had unbuckled his harness now, trying to get a better view.

'And Clare Baxter's place?'

Kingdom glanced across at the pilot, circling his finger, and the helicopter began to revolve, bringing the other side of the road into Allder's field of view. Kingdom could tell from his tone of voice that he was beginning to enjoy himself.

'Is that the one?' he was saying. 'The one with the skylight in the roof?'

Kingdom peered down. He could see a curl of blue smoke from a bonfire in the back garden. The only sign of Clare Baxter herself was a tea towel pegged to the clothes line. 'That's it, sir,' he said.

'And you're saying our friend holed up over the road? Saturday night?'

'Yes, sir.'

'Waited for Carpenter Sunday morning? Knowing he'd be along?'

'Yes, sir.' Kingdom paused. 'He's got a copy of the key because he knows where she keeps it and he's taken an impression some previous weekend when he was doing the recce. Piece of piss. She used to put it out last thing Saturday night. She told me that herself. Just in case she overslept next day. Lazy cow.'

He heard Allder chuckling in the back. The pilot was smiling, too, and Kingdom wondered for the first time exactly what he was making of all this.

'So he has the key,' Allder was saying, 'and lover boy's arrived.'

'Yeah.' Kingdom picked up the story. 'So chummy nips across the road, lets himself in, goes upstairs, does the business—'

'Yeah, yeah,' Allder sounded impatient now, 'but then what?'

'Afterwards?'

'Yeah.'

Kingdom looked at the pilot, and the pilot grinned back, tightening his grip on the controls. The helicopter shuddered for a moment, climbing fast then surging forward as it gained speed. The browns and yellows beneath them began to blur and then they were over the water again, flying low, maximum speed, racing across the flat blue expanses of Langstone Harbour. Ahead, on the mainland, Kingdom could already see traffic on the east/west motorway. Seconds later, the pilot banked sharply to the west where mudbanks and marshland narrowed the harbour to a tidal creek. The creek ran alongside the motorway, perhaps fifty metres wide. A dual carriageway flashed beneath them, choked with traffic, then a railway line. Allder was peering down, his eyes locked on the silver strip of water until it disappeared briefly beneath an enormous roundabout. At this point, the pilot pulled the helicopter into a steep climb, rolling the machine off the top and offering Allder a view back along the length of the tidal creek. Kingdom looked across at the pilot. The manoeuvre had been perfect, a real piece of theatre. He was full of admiration, miming applause.

In the back, Kingdom heard Allder refastening his harness.

'An island,' he said thoughtfully, 'I see what you mean.'

'You do?'

'Yes.' He paused a moment. 'And you think he came this way? That morning? In the inflatable?'

'Yes.'

'You can stand it up? You've got witnesses?'

'Not yet, sir. Give me time. People fish along here, take their dogs for a walk, go cycling. It's a big city. Someone must have seen him.'

Allder grunted, saying nothing. His nose was back at the window. They were much higher now, back at two thousand feet, and Kingdom could see the whole city laid out before them, the long oblong shape of the island, the image he wanted Allder to take away with him. Allder was frowning now, shielding his eyes with his hand. Beyond Portsmouth lay the Solent and the dark swell of the Isle of Wight.

'You think the woman was involved?' he mused. 'Your Mrs Feasey? You think she came over at all? That weekend?'

'She says not, sir. Says she spends Sundays in bed.'

'Witnesses?'

'None.'

'Kips alone?'

'Apparently.'

Allder nodded, falling silent again, then the pilot broke into the circuit, talking for the first time.

'Eleven-twenty, sir,' he murmured, 'you're off the clock.'

They landed back at Winchester fifteen minutes later. The pilot kept the rotors turning, telling them to duck their heads when they left the aircraft, and Kingdom was still debating whether to offer him a tip when Allder opened his door and tugged him onto the tarmac. When they got to the grass, Arthur Sperring was there to meet them. Allder looked up at him. A camera had appeared in his hand.

'Here,' he said, giving Sperring the camera.

The DCS looked at it blankly. Allder took Kingdom by the arm, glancing back over his shoulder, manoeuvring their bodies to get the helicopter in the background. The pilot was already easing the machine off the ground. The noise was deafening.

'Take a picture,' Allder shouted at Sperring, 'before he goes.'

Sperring lifted the camera to his eye, doing what he was told. By the time he gave the camera back, the helicopter had gone.

404

'What the fuck was all that about?' he said.

Allder looked at him a moment, then pocketed the camera. 'One for the book,' he said, 'when I get round to writing it.'

Rob Scarman was waiting for them upstairs. A WPC was sitting at a desk in the corner of his office, tapping data into the HOLMES computer. When all three men had settled round the conference table, Scarman asked her to leave. Allder was looking out of the window. The last forty minutes had raised the colour in his face, but when the door finally closed behind the departing WPC he was as brisk and businesslike as ever. The anxiety, the self-doubt, had definitely gone.

'Number one,' he said, 'who's talked to Jersey?'

Scarman was toying with a pencil. He picked it up. 'Me, sir,' he said.

'And?'

'Gifford's boat was in the St Helier marina on . . .' He consulted the pad at his elbow. 'The 3rd of September. That was a Friday. Left again two days later. Sunday the 5th.'

'Was he alone?'

'No, there was someone else with him. They had a couple of meals at one of the local bistros. We've got a description. Sounds like the son.'

Allder nodded, his eyes still fixed on Scarman. If he was pleased, Kingdom thought, it didn't show. Arthur Sperring leaned forward, uncapping his pen, an unopened box of Marlboro at his elbow. He was scowling again, the expression of a man with an acute sense of trespass, and watching him, Kingdom wondered when the explosion would happen. Sperring's temper was legendary. Grown men had wept.

Allder, oblivious, was still looking at Scarman. 'How about the Bairstow job?' he said. 'Anything on that?'

Scarman smiled, and Kingdom realised for the first time how much he was enjoying himself. The inquiry had been bogged down for far too long. At last he had some answers.

'I've been talking to VISA,' he said carefully. 'Both the Giffords have cards. That's how we managed to point the Jersey boys at the bistro in St Helier.' He got up and fetched a fax from his desk. Back at the table, he spread it carefully beside the pad. 'On the

10th, Andy Gifford bought a railway ticket. The Visa entry only records the amount and the issuing office. The entry was for sixty-seven pounds. He bought the ticket at Southampton.' Scarman paused, glancing up. 'Sixty-seven pounds is the price of a return to Newcastle, and that's where Bairstow died.'

Sperring grunted, saying nothing.

Allder looked visibly impressed. 'What else did he use the card for?' he inquired, 'that weekend?'

'Nothing. Just the ticket.'

'Are there any marinas in Southampton?'

'Yes. Huge place. Ocean Village.'

'And?'

'Nothing. Gifford's boat definitely wasn't there. I checked Hamble, too. And Warsash. Nothing. However,' he leaned back in his chair, 'one of our blokes was onto the people in Cowes.'

'Cowes?' Allder blew his nose. 'Where's that?'

'Isle of Wight,' Sperring growled.

Scarman glanced across at Kingdom and Kingdom nodded, thinking of Ethne Feasey again as Scarman confirmed that Gifford had hidden himself away in a berth on the Medina River, upstream from Cowes, the dates of his stay neatly bridging the gap between Jersey and his arrival in the Camber Dock.

Allder's eyes were still on Scarman. 'It's all circumstantial,' he said, 'so far.'

Sperring nodded, spotting his opening. 'Too fucking right.'

'But persuasive,' Allder looked at Sperring for the first time, 'don't you think, Arthur?'

Sperring said nothing for a moment. Kingdom was trying to work out whether it was real anger or just a pose.

'Yeah,' he muttered at last, 'but why? Why would he do it? What's in it for him? Them?'

'I don't know. But that's hardly a question we need bother about. Not yet, anyway. It's method that interests me, not motive.'

'You think the son's this Sabbathman?'

'I think he's the killer.'

'Same thing.' Sperring frowned. 'Isn't it?'

'Not necessarily.'

'What's that supposed to mean?' He glared at Allder, trying to provoke him, but Allder refused to take the bait. Finally, Sperring leaned forward, his huge hands flat on the table, the honest provincial copper, tired of this Metropolitan flannel. 'If you think you've got the evidence,' he said slowly, 'why don't we pick them both up?'

Allder considered the proposition for a moment or two. Then he shook his head. 'It's Wednesday,' he said, 'we've got a bit of time yet.'

'Time for what?'

'Time before the next one. If there is a next one.' He paused. 'Mind you, the kind of blokes he's knocked off so far, I'm not sure it matters.'

Sperring frowned, uncertain whether Allder was taking the piss or not. Finally, he threw his pen on the table and sat back. 'If it's that fucking obvious,' he said, 'you should pick them up. And if you don't, I should.'

'No, you won't.' Allder shook his head. 'Gifford's back in Scotland. We checked this morning. So is his son. Under the Home Office arrangements, I have lead authority. So until I say different, we keep pulling in the evidence.' Allder looked directly at Sperring. 'Understood?'

Kingdom gave Allder a lift back to London in the Wolseley. The traffic was heavy on the M3 and a tanker spill near Basingstoke brought all three lanes to a halt. Kingdom fed another cassette into the slot beneath the radio. Chris Rea, he thought. One of Annie's favourites.

Allder had his head back against the scuffed leather neckrest. He'd been asleep for nearly half an hour and Kingdom wondered whether he'd spent the entire night in the office. They'd had a couple of lengthy phone conferences the previous afternoon, Kingdom still down in Winchester telling Allder exactly what he'd been up to, adding light and shade to the version of events which seemed – to him – to make most sense. Ethne Feasey, he'd kept saying. Ethne Feasey is where it begins and ends. A woman with a story. A woman who'd touched Dave Gifford's heart. A woman whose grief had turned to fury, and whose finger pointed squarely at Sir Peter Blanche. Kingdom had told Allder about the letter the woman had written to the banker. More important still, he'd said, was the reply. A letter like that, in his opinion, was a gun to Patrick Feasey's head. As far as his wife was concerned, the man had probably died at Blanche's hand, not his own.

On the phone, Allder had been unconvinced. Like Arthur Sperring, he preferred to deal in hard facts, solid motivations, not something as subtle and complex as this. Why should Gifford go to so much trouble? And why should the settling of Ethne Feasey's account extend to four more bodies? Kingdom, knowing Allder's impatience with half-baked speculation, had admitted at once that he didn't know. The son, Andy, had apparently suffered some trauma or other in the Falklands. He'd written about it since, though Kingdom had yet to lay hands on the piece. Maybe it was something overtly political. Maybe it was quite the reverse. But either way it was now beyond doubt that the man was perfectly qualified to undertake the Sabbathman killings.

From Winchester, Kingdom had been able to check with the regimental depot in Aldershot. Back in 1981, Corporal Gifford had been on the NATO sniper's course, down at the commando training base in Devon, and – according to the 3 Para adjutant – he'd done extremely well. On Gifford's file, he'd found a copy of the Instructing Officer's report. After six weeks, Gifford had passed all the badge tests with flying colours – observation, map reading, concealment, stalking, target work, the lot. Kingdom had interrupted at this point, asking the obvious question, wasn't '81 a long time ago? But the adjutant had said no, chuckling quietly on the phone. Snipers, he'd told Kingdom, were a breed apart. You had to be dispassionate. You had to be a loner. You had to have a taste for hardship and extreme conditions. And above all, you had to be able to kill, to take a man's life, without any trace of remorse or emotion. The course taught certain skills, but what really mattered was temperament. If you had the right temperament, the skills – once mastered – would never go.

The traffic began to move again, and Allder jerked awake. He rubbed his face, peering up at the lorry cab beside them, and Kingdom marvelled again at the way his guv'nor had so completely regained his nerve. Here was a man barely a week away from losing his job. Yet the deadline scarcely seemed to have touched him.

'Thirsty?' Allder said, stretching his tiny arms and yawning.

They pulled in at the next services complex. Kingdom queued for a pot of tea and a plate of scones while Allder found a table by the window. When he sat down, Allder reached for the tiny plastic pots of strawberry jam. Kingdom had bought six, just in case.

'I'm arranging for you to go to Scotland,' he said at once, building a mountain of jam on the side of his plate.

'Where?'

'Scotland. I've organised some discreet inquiries. They've got plenty of room, you can leave on Monday.'

Kingdom frowned. 'I'm not with you, sir.'

Allder began to spoon the jam onto the first of his scones. He looked distracted for a moment, licking his fingers.

'Arthur Sperring's right,' he said at last, 'we have to crack the motivation. That means talking to the man. Being with him. Listening to what he has to say for himself.'

'Easy. We pull him in.'

'No.' Allder shook his head. 'It's got to be better than that. It should be his place, not ours. I want the truth, not some bloody statement or other. Tape recorders. Attending solicitors. All that.'

Kingdom was still frowning. A helping or two of Jo Hubbard's kind of holiday was the last thing he wanted. Autumn would be like spring. Non-stop gales and rain every hour.

'Why?' he said. 'Why dress it up? Why make it so hard for ourselves? Why not go in mob-handed, turn the place over, pull them both in?'

Allder took another mouthful of scone and a tiny sip of tea. Then he gestured at a couple two tables away. They were sitting side by side, their heads together, engrossed in the front page of *The Citizen*. Kingdom recognised the photo on the front, the '92 cabinet posed in the garden of Number 10, the same old faces digging in for yet another term of office.

'We have to get this right,' Allder was saying, 'and thanks to you we're not far off. Five are in the shit. I don't know what's happened but it isn't pretty. The buggers are there for the taking.

They're still talking Northern Ireland so that means we have to come up with the full story, every dot and comma of it. That's you, son. Getting up there. Signing on. Getting to know the bloke. Getting to know what makes him tick. The thicker the file we hand the DPP, the more we shaft these Gower Street bastards.'

'Sunday's four days away,' Kingdom pointed out. 'What happens if Arthur's right? What happens if they disappear and slot someone else? We'd look pretty silly, wouldn't we? Not pulling them in?'

Allder shook his head, reaching for another scone. 'Won't happen.'

'Why not?'

'I've got blokes up there. Since early this morning. The place is the other side of Skye. There's one road out, and we have it covered.'

'Boat?' Kingdom said bleakly.

'Nothing there. Apart from some canoes.'

'Not the motor cruiser? The *Catherine May*?'

'No, definitely not. In fact I've ordered an all-marina alert. As of this morning.'

Kingdom nodded, saying nothing, telling himself to look on the bright side. Allder, at the very least, appeared to have accepted his version of events: Dave Gifford, the man of action, exacting revenge for a woman who'd clearly come to obsess him. Kingdom swallowed a mouthful of tea. The story, he thought, belonged in some paperback or other. If he'd listened harder at school, it might even have made him a bob or two. He glanced up, thinking of Peter Weymes, and the price he was paying for his precious front-page lead.

'This bloke Pelanski you mentioned,' he began, 'anyone talked to him yet?'

Allder nodded. 'Yes. Couple of Mac's boys.'

'And?'

'He's not talking, not so far, anyway, says it's all a fit-up.' He paused, frowning. 'I've been onto the Serious Fraud Squad, though.'

'Oh?'

'Yes.' He nodded. 'Those bonds that Marcus Wolfe was flogging, they've got a full client list, the people who really got clobbered, the ones who lost everything.'

'And?'

'One of them was a woman called Dorothy Gifford.' He reached for the last pot of jam. 'Our friend's mother.'

Kingdom dropped Allder at New Scotland Yard, pausing long enough to check for messages. Before midday, everything had been rerouted down to Winchester and the afternoon had produced nothing new. Kingdom checked as well in the L-shaped administrative office one floor below Allder's. The woman in charge had been one of the first to pick up the gossip from Belfast when Kingdom and Annie had originally met, and ever since then she'd appointed herself keeper of Kingdom's secrets.

'Nothing from Five?' he inquired. 'No calls?'

'Afraid not.' She glanced up. 'The lady gone missing again?'

'Yeah.'

'No postcards?'

'Not one.'

'Heartless cow.'

Kingdom closed the door on the cackle of raucous laughter and walked down the corridor to the lifts. Allder had spent the last part of the drive back to London clarifying what he expected from Kingdom's visit to Skye. The Monday course lasted until the following weekend. The enrolment forms were being completed in the name of Gordon Travis, and he'd be posing as a freelance journalist in need of a break. The course, by all accounts, was rugged and Kingdom might be wise to take a day or two off. Plenty of kip. Plenty of good, solid food. Easy on the fags. Not too much to drink.

Kingdom had sat in the Wolseley, still wondering whether Allder could possibly be serious. Time was precious. Even if Dave Gifford turned out to be Sabbathman, there were a thousand loose ends to tie up but when he pointed this out, Allder seemed unconcerned. Kingdom, he'd said with sudden warmth, had cracked it. He'd come up with a couple of names and enough circumstantial evidence to fit the known facts. There were hundreds of other bodies on the Branch who could deal with the supplementary inquiries. What mattered now, he said again and again, was motive. Why would the Giffords have done it? Why would they have launched this extraordinary conspiracy?

Kingdom left the office at five. The traffic was solid down Victoria Street and he decided to leave the Wolseley in the underground car park at the Yard, taking the tube to Brixton. The walk to King's College Hospital took less than five minutes, and when he asked for Ernie at the reception desk in the A and E Department, a woman directed him to a ward on the second floor.

Kingdom took the lift. The ward was crowded, half a dozen or so beds down either side of the room, lines of blank old faces staring into space. There was a television on a shelf at the end of the ward but no one seemed to be taking very much notice. A young nurse spotted Kingdom by the door. She was holding a bedpan in one hand and a plate of uneaten food in the other. Kingdom asked her where he might find his father and she indicated a bed beside the window.

'I might be wrong,' she said, 'but I think he's asleep.'

Kingdom sat beside his father's bed for nearly an hour. In the last few days, Ernie had aged ten years. His face seemed to have shrunk to the shape of his skull and his scalp showed white through the thinning hair. There were cuts on his chin where someone had tried to shave him, and wisps of cotton wool clung to the scabs of clotted blood. Except for a glass of water, the cabinet beside the bed was quite bare – no flowers, no books, no cards – and Kingdom realised how empty his life had become. This old man had nothing. No peace, no dignity, not even the comfort of a memory or two. The one person who might have made a difference – Barry – was denied him and the best he could now expect was another bed like this in some Godforsaken nursing home or other until the big heart stopped altogether.

Kingdom felt for his father's hand. The nails were long and cleaner than he'd ever seen them, not Ernie's nails at all. Kingdom reached out, touching his face, and the old man grunted, some private thought disturbed. He turned his head and a thin trickle of saliva found a path to the pillow. Kingdom wiped his mouth with a corner of the sheet, his lips close to his father's ear.

'Dad?' he whispered.

The old man's eyes opened. They were filmy and moist and the pain showed at once, the way he screwed his face up.

'You OK?'

The old man blinked, not understanding the question, not understanding anything, only the pain. The consultant had warned that it might be this way. The anaesthetic, he'd said, could play havoc with the remaining brain cells.

'Dad?'

The eyes closed again and the mouth fell open. After a while, the breathing resumed, shallow, half-hearted, the chest barely rising under the cotton sheet. Kingdom stayed for a while, hoping his father would wake up. Finally, he tucked the hand underneath the blanket, and left. No point, he thought, walking away from the ward, trying to make sense of the blur of signs in the corridor outside.

Kingdom walked back to Scotland Yard. Before he reached the river, he called at a pub near the Elephant and Castle. He drank three pints of Guinness, each with a chaser of Bells. By the time he was back beside the Wolseley, the alcohol was beginning to work. Anaesthetic, he thought, sliding in behind the wheel.

He was halfway up the exit ramp before he spotted the note on the windscreen. It was tucked behind the wiper on the passenger side. He pulled up at once, leaving the engine on, getting out of the car, retrieving the fold of yellow paper. It was dark now, and he stood beside the Wolseley, oblivious of the patrol car stalled on the ramp behind him, the barp on the horn, the impatient frown beneath the uniformed cap.

'Room 1807,' the note said, 'before you leave.'

Kingdom got back in the car. Room 1807 was Allder's office. The note was in Allder's handwriting. What did the man want now?'

Kingdom took the lift to the nineteenth floor. The door to Allder's outer office was half-open. Inside, through the ribbed glass on the inner door, Kingdom could see the outline of his diminutive figure behind the big desk by the window. Allder was on the

413

phone. He could hear the rasp of his voice. He hesitated a moment, then knocked and walked in. Allder peered across the room at him, bringing the conversation to an abrupt end. He put the phone down and stood up. He was in his shirtsleeves, his jacket over the chair by the cocktail cabinet.

'Drink?' he said at once.

Kingdom sank into the chair in front of the desk. He could hear Allder behind him, pouring the drink. It sounded enormous.

'Here.'

He put the crystal goblet in Kingdom's hands. Then he circled the desk and sat down. There was an inch or so of Scotch left in the bottom of the bottle. Most of it went into the glass at his elbow.

'Cheers.' he said.

Kingdom raised his glass, echoing the toast, wondering whether the Commissioner had been on again, a new deadline, an even shorter piece of rope for Allder to hang himself with.

Allder nodded at the telephone. 'Belfast,' he said.

'Sir?'

'Just now. Your mates from Knock. Just to say . . .' He tried to end the sentence but couldn't, turning his face away, revolving the chair towards the window, the glass to his lips again. Kingdom, watching him, felt a sudden chill, an icy hand inside him, encircling his heart. Annie, he thought numbly. It's about Annie.

'What's happened?' he said quietly. 'Just tell me.'

Allder got up, his back still turned to Kingdom. 'The army people found a body. This morning. Down in Armagh somewhere. Crossmaglen.'

'Annie's? Annie Meredith's?'

'Yes.' He nodded. 'They think so.'

'*Think* so?' Kingdom stared at him. Lisburn had photographs, fingerprints, everything. It was standard procedure, positive ID in case the army ended up shooting the wrong people. 'Sir?'

Allder turned round at last. The glass was empty, his face quite expressionless. 'They have a problem. They're saying the body's incomplete. They're saying . . .' He made a vague circular movement in the air with the empty glass. 'You're the one who'd know best.'

SIXTEEN

SECURITY OFFICE
PO BOX 500, LONDON

INTERNAL MEMORANDUM

TO: Director of Intelligence, Stormont, NI
FROM: Hugh Cousins
DATE: 7 October 1993

<u>VIA FAX</u>
U R G E N T ,   P R I O R I T Y

Whilst I of course accept the formal requirement for
identification, and the regrettable difficulties in this
instance, is there <u>no one</u> else with the required level of
intimate knowledge? I need hardly spell out the potential
consequences of sharing hard-won intelligence with our
Metropolitan friends.

Kingdom read Andy Gifford's book on the plane. In a way, as he quickly realised, it was better than alcohol or tranquillisers. Here was a pain as deep as his own, and an anger no less savage.

Andy Gifford, as Kingdom already knew, had served in 3 Para. As a nineteen-year-old, he'd been shipped south to the Falklands with the rest of the Task Force, and found himself walking across ninety miles of sodden, windswept bog. Every bone in his body had ached from the weight he was carrying. He'd suffered trench foot and periodic bouts of dysentery. But by the eve of battle, in his heart, he'd known that he was ready for it. After three weeks in the open, the men were like animals. They'd shed their excess weight. They'd hardened themselves to the cold and the wet. Battle would now be an overwhelming release. 'Swift and hard,' Gifford wrote, 'that was our mantra.'

Three Para were assigned a feature called Mount Longdon, a long ridge of rocky outcrops guarding one flank of the road to Stanley. On top of Longdon sat a large number of Argentinian troops, some of them highly trained special forces. They had radar, mortars, 106 mm rifles, heavy machine guns and limitless ammunition. Most important of all, they'd had the time to bed themselves in, to dig their trenches, to site their heavy weapons. Geography and sheer weight of numbers piled the odds against the Paras. In technical terms, they were crazy even to plan an attack. But insanity, as Gifford acknowledged, was part of the contract. 'We came from the Planet Zilch,' he wrote, 'though none of us yet knew what deep space really meant.'

The attack on Mount Longdon started at half-past midnight.

The Paras attacked from two directions. Andy Gifford, as part of 'B' company, went up the long forward slope of the mountain. Men around him were dying in some numbers, the work of snipers hidden in the rocks above. Life on the receiving end, as Gifford drily noted, could be 'fucking unpleasant'.

It got worse. 'B' company fought its way to the top of the mountain. Amongst the crags and gullies, the carnage started in earnest. There were bodies everywhere, both British and Argentinian, and seeing people they knew blown away stung the Paras to yet greater violence. Fuelled by fear and the primitive drive for revenge, they pushed on through the rocks, clearing bunker after bunker. Much of the fighting was hand to hand. The Argentinians were wearing heavy winter clothing. To kill with the bayonet, you went in through the eye. There was little time to take prisoners.

By daybreak, half the mountain had fallen but the battle for the rest was still in progress. By now, Argentinian gunners in Stanley had the range of the Paras. The incoming artillery shells screamed towards them, sucking the air from the mountain top. Gifford, crouched behind a rock, saw one of his closest mates caught in the open. The shell exploded, red-hot fragments of shrapnel everywhere. Covered in earth, trembling uncontrollably, Gifford lifted his head. The lower half of his mate's body lay in a heap beside the charred edges of the shell hole. Blue smoke was curling from his combat trousers. The left-hand side of his face clung to a nearby rock. The rest had gone.

Later, the battle over, the Paras tidied up. The smell was appalling. There was shit and bodies everywhere. Many of the surviving Argentinians were kids, teenagers. In their pockets, the Paras found letters from home, photos of their mothers, rosary beads. Occasionally, the big guns in Stanley would open up again and a round or two would rasp towards the mountain and the cry 'Incoming!' would send men diving for cover. On one such occasion, curled in a shell scrape, Andy Gifford watched two injured men sitting with their backs against a wall of rock. One was Argentinian, the other a Para. Both just sat there, helpless, unable to move, like spectators at some insane international.

Victory was sweet release but for Gifford nothing would ever be the same again. 'Politicians,' he wrote, 'blame war on events.

They say it's diplomacy by other means. They say it's something you get into when everything else has failed. That's maybe true but it begs a couple of questions. The first is about war itself. War is the real enemy. It breaks you inside. It takes your pity away. In a single night we became old men, changed forever. If you bothered to look hard enough, you could see it when we got back home. All the flags, and the bands, and the banners, and the cheering, what was all that about? Us? Where we'd been? What we'd done? What we'd seen? Was that why people were *celebrating*? War is a conjuring trick. It depends on keeping your mouth shut afterwards, on not giving the game away, on maintaining the illusion. The illusion is simple. It says that it's somehow honourable and necessary to deprive a mother of her son, a wife of her husband, a child of its father. But it isn't. It's none of those things. It's depraved and ugly, and if you've been there and seen it and done it, it fucks you up for life. Nothing ever touches you, troubles you, ever again. You're immune. You're dead. You're the creature from the Planet Zilch, an alien on earth, forever . . .'

Andy Gifford's book was short, no more than 120 pages, and Kingdom was reading the postscript when the outskirts of Belfast appeared through a tear in the clouds and the captain announced the final approach to Aldergrove airport. Kingdom reached for his seat belt, not realising that it was still fastened from take-off, his eyes returning to the book. After the war was over, the defeated Argentinians were corralled on Stanley airfield. Soon afterwards, they were marched onto two civilian ships for the 400-mile crossing to Argentina. One of the prisoners, a young conscript, was stopped and searched. In his rucksack, in pieces, were the week-old remains of his brother. He was taking him home. To be buried. Kingdom shut his eyes as the aircraft bumped down through the cloud. This incident had evidently become instant legend. On the voyage back to Ascension, the paras had sung about it. 'Pack up your brother in your old kit bag,' went the chant, 'and smile, smile, smile . . .'

The major from Bessbrook that Allder had mentioned was waiting for Kingdom at the airport. He said his name was Stanton. The driver beside him took Kingdom's bag and they walked straight out to the car park. Stanton, thought Kingdom, had an old man's face. He couldn't have been more than thirty, probably less, but life seemed already to have walled him in. Sitting in the back of the unmarked Cavalier, Kingdom asked him how much he knew about Annie's death.

'Bits and pieces,' he said, 'not the whole story.'

'What does that mean?'

Stanton didn't answer, lifting a hand as they swept out through the security checkpoint. Finally he turned round in the seat, looking at Kingdom over the headrest. He had terrible skin, cratered with the burnt-out remains of a savage acne attack.

'I'm sorry,' he said, 'I understand you two were close.'

'That wasn't my question.'

'I know but . . .' He shrugged. 'I'm still sorry.'

Kingdom nodded, sensing at once the man's reluctance to talk. Allder, earlier, had warned him it would be this way. The thing had obviously been a gigantic fuck-up, and whatever had happened to Annie lay at the very middle of it. No one would say more than they had to. Kingdom's job was simply identification. Nothing more.

Kingdom gazed out of the window. Annie occupied a shelf in the fridge in the mortuary at the Musgrave Park Hospital. That's where they were going now. Afterwards, as Stanton had tactfully put it, there'd be the option of lunch and maybe, just maybe, a chat. Then the ride back to Aldergrove, and another ninety minutes or so in the company of Andy Gifford.

Kingdom thought about him now. He'd called the book *Enemy Territory*. It was an exact phrase. It cropped up time and time again. It referred not just to the looming shadows of Mount Longdon, but also to the world to which Gifford and his mates had returned. Another book, authored by a fellow-Para, had contained allegations that Argentinian prisoners had been slaughtered in cold blood after the battle. These allegations were now being investigated by Scotland Yard. Conceivably, if the inquiry ran its course, ex-paratroopers could find themselves on trial for murder. It was a prospect that had, according to Gifford, reduced the men who'd fought there to helpless laughter. But there was a serious point to be made as well. 'They'd loved the headlines, those politicians,' Gifford had written, 'and the victory parades, and all the stuff on television, but they'd never wanted to pick up the bill.

So we got it instead. Once by going to war, and again by being wicked enough to kill the enemy. "Blood? You spilled blood? Oh my God . . . arrest that man at once!"'

Enemy territory. Kingdom sat back as the motorway in from the airport unrolled before them. He'd already been onto some of his Belfast police contacts, phoning a series of unlisted numbers at RUC headquarters at Knock. He'd left a lot of goodwill behind him after his year in the city but none of the men he'd talked to could help him about Annie. Her body had been found wrapped in black polythene in the back of a car on a country road down near the border. There was evidence that the car had been abandoned in a hurry. There was a can of petrol on the back seat and an unprimed grenade. The grenade had been traced to a consignment listed as stolen from an Irish Army depot across the border. The car, too, had been stolen, this time from a quiet street near the university. But that, regretfully, was about the sum of it. The body had been retained by the British Army. Further inquiries were in the hands of the Director of Intelligence at Stormont Castle. The body, subject to confirmation, belonged to one of the British security agencies. The investigation, therefore, was a strictly family affair.

The outskirts of Belfast appeared, the tower blocks veiled in drifting rain. Kingdom stirred. Since Allder had given him the news, he'd been trying to piece together Annie's last known movements.

'She must have been over for a meet,' he said, 'that night.'

Stanton didn't bother to turn round this time. 'So I understand.'

'Somewhere in the city? Belfast somewhere?'

Stanton didn't say anything. Kingdom asked the question again.

'I'm afraid I don't know,' Stanton said at last, 'I've not seen the file.'

'Would that be the Sabbathman file?'

'The what?'

'Sabbathman? Our serial killer?'

Stanton shook his head. 'I'm afraid I can't help you.'

'Can't? Or won't?'

Kingdom waited for an answer, knowing already that there wouldn't be one. Finally he sat back, not bothering to hide his contempt.

'Forget it,' he said, 'I'm sorry I asked.'

The hospital was still being repaired after a successful IRA bomb attack months earlier. They parked outside the military wing and went straight down to the mortuary. In an outer office, a woman in a white coat sat behind a metal desk. The in-tray was piled high with paperwork and on top lay a pair of white latex gloves. Kingdom couldn't take his eyes off them.

'Dr Tomlinson,' Stanton said, doing the introductions, 'our pathologist.'

The woman stood up and offered Kingdom a limp handshake. She smelled of bleach.

'I'm afraid this won't be pleasant,' she said at once, 'I apologise in advance.'

'Not your fault,' Kingdom said automatically, his eyes going back to the gloves.

The doctor took him through to a long white room adjoining the theatre where she performed post-mortems. Everything was tiled except for a bank of fridges along one wall. The smell of bleach was stronger, despite the steady hum of the big extractor fans recessed in the ceiling. The pathologist paused a moment, explaining that Annie had been dead a couple of days before the body had been found.

Kingdom caught the drift at once. 'You mean she's . . .' He shrugged. 'Gone off?'

'Decomposing.' The doctor nodded. 'We're thinking central heating. Wherever she was kept must have been pretty warm. You'll appreciate it isn't easy to be precise about these things but, well . . .' She offered Kingdom a tight little smile. 'You'd better see for yourself.'

Kingdom nodded, glancing at Stanton. The legal position had begun to bother him. 'Say it's her,' he began, 'who do I tell?'

'Me.'

'Is that enough?' Kingdom frowned. 'Isn't there a procedure here? A formal statement? Something for me to sign?'

Stanton and the pathologist exchanged glances. Then the

pathologist walked across to the bank of fridges and opened a door at the end. The fridge was full of bodies wrapped in white plastic shrouds. The runners squealed as she pulled out a tray near the bottom. Kingdom looked down at it. Annie's parcel was much smaller than the rest.

The pathologist glanced up at him. She'd produced a pair of scissors from the top pocket of her coat.

'OK?'

Kingdom nodded. Last night, for the first time in months, he hadn't had a drink. Nothing would help, he'd told himself, not when it came to this. The pathologist bent to the tray again and began to snip the tapes securing the parcel. Then she unwrapped it, stepping back. The smell bubbled up towards them and Kingdom heard a shuffle of footsteps behind him as Stanton turned away. The pathologist was still looking at Kingdom, an almost forensic interest in his reaction.

Kingdom took his time. The body had no head. The hands and feet had gone too, hack-sawed off, but there was no mistaking the rest. Kingdom knelt quickly beside the tray. This was what gangsters did, he thought. Remove every trace of identity, every fingerprint, every tooth, every feature, until nothing remained but a bloated torso and the stench of death.

Kingdom looked up at the doctor, indicating a series of brown marks across Annie's chest. The marks all intersected at broadly the same point, although bits of the tiny rose tattoo that Annie kept between her breasts were still visible.

'What are they?' he asked.

'Burns.'

'Before or after?'

'I'm sorry?'

'Was she dead or alive,' he nodded at the marks, 'when they did that?'

The pathologist, for the first time, looked uncomfortable. 'It's hard to be—'

Kingdom was on his feet again, his face so close to the pathologist's that he could see the contact lenses swimming in her eyes. 'A straight answer,' he said softly, 'please.'

The pathologist stared at him for a moment or two, then

glanced at Annie's remains. The smell was overpowering now, the sweet cheesiness of decomposition.

'Before,' she muttered, 'just.'

Kingdom sat in a bar in Great Victoria Street. Two women were comparing divorces in a cubicle near the window. Kingdom watched them, emptying his second pint of Guinness, trying to sluice away the memory of the last couple of hours, but every time he lifted the glass to his lips, the smell of the mortuary returned. He'd been to the lavatory twice already, soaping his hands under the scalding water, but the foulness seemed to have penetrated his very flesh. Once they'd returned Annie to the fridge, he'd found Stanton on the phone in the pathologist's office. Kingdom had stayed long enough to confirm that the body was Annie's and to ask about the funeral. The remains were evidently being air-freighted to London. Arrangements for whatever happened there-after was obviously in the hands of relatives.

Kingdom had been standing in the open doorway. 'What relatives?'

'Her parents, I imagine . . .' Stanton had tried to soften his awkwardness. 'And people like your good self.'

After his second pint, Kingdom went to the telephone. He'd used this pub regularly during his time in Belfast and he knew the phone was on a shelf beside the Streetfighter II console. While he waited for Allder to answer, his fingers found the Fire and Move buttons and the phrase came back to him yet again. Enemy territory, he thought, Annie had strayed into enemy territory. And ended up in pieces.

Allder's secretary plugged the call through at once. 'Well?' he asked.

'It's her. Definitely.'

Allder said he was very sorry. Then he began to talk about Dublin but Kingdom interrupted. Until he heard the sound of his own voice, he didn't realise how angry he was.

'They won't talk about it,' he was telling Allder, 'they won't say a word, not a fucking word. Not where it happened, where she was going, what she was up to, who she was with, not a fucking dicky bird.'

'Who did you ask?'

'The guy who met me, the one they sent to the airport. He knows. I know he knows. And he knows I know he knows. But I might as well have been some punter off the street . . .' He paused, letting the anger drain out of him, shaking his head. 'Is this war, or what?' he said at last. 'Only it might be helpful to fucking know.'

'War,' he heard Allder saying, 'definitely war.'

'Us? Us and Five? Us and Five and the Army people? Us and the rest of the fucking universe? Only from where I sit—'

'I don't know,' Allder said quickly, 'but it's getting clearer.'

'Yeah? Tell me about it.'

'I will, but listen. I've been talking to our friends in Dublin. The Special Branch people in Harcourt Terrace. The ones I mentioned before, the ones who wanted me to go over when the Fishguard thing blew up.'

'Yeah?' Kingdom couldn't wrench his mind away from the mortuary. The tattoo, he kept thinking, Annie's precious rose. How many times had he touched it? Kissed it? How many times had she offered it to him, enfolding him between her breasts, moulding herself to him? Grief, real grief, smelled of body oil lightly tainted with bleach. He shuddered, hearing Allder again. 'His name's Dermot Reilly,' he was saying, 'He met Annie last week. Did she mention a photo at all?'

'What?'

'A photo? Blokes at some piss-up or other?'

'No.' Kingdom shook his head, trying to concentrate. 'Nothing like that. She said she'd been to Dublin, though. Before she went off.'

'Went off where?'

'Fuck knows. She took a . . .'

Kingdom stopped in mid-sentence. The relays in his brain weren't working too well. The fuseboard kept tripping out, thoughts forming and re-forming, memories getting muddled up, no coherent pattern emerging, no sense. But this was different. Allder was onto something. The cab company. The lot who'd sent a car for Annie. They'd have records, dockets, a print-out of some description. He frowned, thinking hard now, letting Allder prattle on in the background, something else about Dermot Reilly. Annie had phoned the cab company from the flat while he'd been in the bedroom. He remembered her closing the bedroom door with her foot when it came to her giving these guys the address where she wanted to go. They were a local firm. He'd seen the logo on the car door when he'd acknowledged her farewell wave from the front bedroom window. Kingston Cabs? Kingston Mini-cabs? Kingston something. He was sure of it.

Allder was still talking. 'You get that?' he said, 'Harcourt Terrace? Six-thirty? Dermot Reilly?'

Kingdom took the train to Dublin. He'd phoned the Irishman from Belfast. He'd explained about the train and Reilly had given him the name of a bar in O'Connell Street. The service from Belfast was often late. He'd be sat at a table in the back of the bar. If Kingdom had nothing better to do then they might as well make a night of it. He was sorry, he added, about Annie. He'd got the gist of it from Allder.

Reilly was right about the train. It was over an hour late and it was nearly eight o'clock before Kingdom found the bar. It was crowded with drinkers, a mix of businessmen and students, and Kingdom picked his way between them, looking for the table beneath the Murphy's calendar that Reilly had described. For the first time that day, it occurred to him that he'd had nothing to eat.

Reilly was on his feet at once as Kingdom emerged from the scrum of drinkers round the bar. He leaned across the table, extending a hand, a rumpled figure, younger than Kingdom had expected, with thick black curly hair and a ruddy smile. Sitting opposite was an older woman, thin, slightly dessicated, wearing a smart tweed jacket with a plaid bow tie. Reilly introduced her as Siobhan, no surname, disappearing to the bar to buy a round of drinks.

Kingdom sat down, aware of the woman watching him. At her elbow was the remains of what looked like an orange juice. Around her neck was a neat gold crucifix. After a while, she leaned forward and Kingdom realised that she was even older than he'd first imagined. Late fifties, he thought. Easily.

'Bless you,' she said.

Kingdom thanked her for the thought, aware of her hands on his. Her hands were warm and dry, an inexplicable comfort. Kingdom looked up. Reilly had returned with the drinks. He gave Kingdom a tumbler of Jamieson's, explaining that the Guinness would take a while to settle. Then he nodded at the woman.

'We have a little team over here in Dublin. You might have heard. Keeps an eye on the fellas from MI5.' He smiled. 'Siobhan runs it.'

They stayed in the pub all evening. Kingdom did most of the talking, progressively detached from any real sense of time or place, gladder than he could say to have the company of strangers. He owed these people no apologies. They had no prior ties. He could start from square one, and all they need contribute was patience and a listening ear.

He felt, he said at the outset, like a refugee. He had no secrets to trade, no gossip even, just an overwhelming sense of bewilderment, a bottomless grief that threatened to swamp his little boat entirely. Dermot, he knew, had met Annie. Allder had told him so. Maybe he'd had a drink or two with her, spent the evening together, shared one or two laughs, glimpsed the kind of person she could be. Given all that, he'd maybe understand. And if he understood, then maybe he could also explain a thing or two. Like where had she gone? And what had she been up to? And why, please God, hadn't someone been there to protect her?

Dermot Reilly, and the woman he called Siobhan, listened to Kingdom, offering sympathy and a steady supply of Guinness. Towards the end of the evening, when Kingdom was trying to work out why he still felt so sober, why so much alcohol had made so little impression, Dermot began to steer the conversation in a new direction, tossing in bits of information, watching to see what Kingdom made of them. MI5 had become a major force, he said, in the Republic. Using the usual mix of blackmail and hard cash, they'd managed to penetrate both the IRA and Sinn Fein. MI5 had always maintained a presence at the British Embassy at Ballsbridge, the so-called 'Irish station', but this latest operation was run directly from London and was different in scale to anything they'd mounted before. It was obvious, said Dermot, that they were desperate for trophies and it had come as no surprise that the first Brit to appear after the Fishguard debacle had been from Five.

It was late now, the bar beginning to empty. Kingdom was looking at Dermot, following every word. 'You mean Annie?' he said. 'My Annie?'

'Sure.'

'And you're saying you expected someone else? Someone from the Branch? Me, for instance? Or my guv'nor?'

'Not expected, no. We expected someone from Five. That's the whole point of it. They're hungry. They're quick on the draw, like. You know what I mean?'

Kingdom was still thinking of Annie, smiling for the first time. Quick on the draw was a nice phrase. It fitted her exactly. 'Yeah,' he said. 'I know what you mean.'

Dermot nodded. It was a shame, he said, that Special Branch, or CID, or some other representative from the police hadn't got to Dublin first. The government had never been so co-operative. The opportunity had been there for the taking. The fact that one of Cousins' people should have turned up first had simply confirmed what Harcourt Terrace had been suspecting for some time. That the battle for turf was over. That Five had won.

Kingdom was looking at the bar. His glass was empty. 'Who?' he said numbly.

'Five.'

'No,' he shook his head, 'the name you mentioned.'

'Ah,' Dermot Reilly smiled, 'Cousins. The famous Mr Hugh.'

They took Kingdom to a French restaurant on the bay-front at Blackrock. Through the window, Kingdom could see the car ferry unloading under the big arc lights at Dun Laoghaire. When they asked him what he wanted to eat, he waved the offer away but when the woman insisted, he asked for fish and chips. The order made the waiter's eyebrows rise but Kingdom didn't care. Offered a choice between turbot and John Dory, he left it to the chef's discretion. What happened with Annie? he kept asking. What did you tell her when she came across?

Dermot took him through it. He explained about the cargo

shed on the airport site, and the import/export firm. He outlined Dessie O'Keefe's theory about the switch and he described the employee who'd abruptly gone missing. The man was rumoured to have come from the north. The dates he'd enrolled in the firm fitted Dessie's theory. The story had been strong enough to get the Irish cabinet off the hook and everyone at Harcourt Terrace had agreed that the photo had been a fine stroke of luck.

'Photo?' Kingdom was picking at his bread roll, trying to remember what Allder had said about it. 'What photo?'

'The photo we gave to your girl, Annie.'

Dermot explained about the photo. It included a mug shot of the missing employee. Nothing brilliant, mind, but OK. Good enough for enhancement. Good enough for Hugh Cousins.

'And she took it?'

'Of course.'

'Back to England?'

'Where else?'

Kingdom nodded, remembering Annie in the flat last Saturday, her bag never far from her side, her insistence that she had to disappear again for a few hours. She'd had the photo, he thought. She'd had the photo and she was under orders to hand it over. Either that, or she thought she'd cracked it single-handed. Ambition, after all, was what had made her engine run.

The waiter arrived with a bottle of Chablis. Kingdom asked for Guinness. He went away again.

'This photo,' he asked slowly, 'where did it come from?'

Dermot explained about a youth in the import/export company. He'd taken a whole roll of shots. Dermot had seen them all. So had Annie.

'Where? Where did you see them?'

'In a pub. In Drumcondra.'

'And where's the lad now?'

'God knows.'

'So how do I get to him? How do I lay hand on these pictures?'

Dermot glanced at the woman. She was rummaging in her handbag. Eventually she produced a colour photograph. She gave it to Kingdom. It showed two big men. They looked very drunk, leering at the camera. Dermot leaned forward, indicating another

431

face in the background. Kingdom peered at it. Thinning hair. A big, fleshy mouth. Funny eyes.

'This him?'

'Yes.' Dermot nodded.

'And can I keep it?'

'Sure. You can have as many as you like.'

'How come?'

Dermot grinned, leaning back as the waiter returned with Kingdom's Guinness. 'I helped myself to the negatives,' he said cheerfully, 'the night we talked to the young lad.'

Kingdom was back in London by early afternoon next day. Allder had told him to come straight to his office at New Scotland Yard, and he was waiting when Kingdom arrived. It was a Saturday and instead of the usual suit Allder was wearing corduroy trousers and a mustard yellow Pringle sweater. He must have been shopping on the way to the office because there was a plastic bag on the floor beside his chair. On the side it said 'Wimbledon Seedlings'.

'Gardening again, sir?' Kingdom inquired, putting Reilly's photo squarely on the desk and sinking into the waiting chair.

Allder ignored the question, reaching at once for the photo. After a while, he looked up. 'They gave you this?'

'Yes.'

Kingdom briefed Allder on the story and indicated the face in the background.

Allder nodded, examining the photo again. 'They know who he is?'

'No, sir. Not that they'd say.'

'Do you know?'

'No.'

'But it went to Cousins? Is that what you're saying?'

Kingdom nodded. He'd lain awake for most of the night in his Dublin hotel room, haunted by Cousins' face. He'd been the man in the pub, the evening Annie had gone to the PYTHON meet at the Home Office. Kingdom had watched them together in the corner of the lounge bar, Annie leaning towards him across the table, the quicksilver smile, the gestures with the hands, the way she used her face and body to make the points that mattered. He'd seen her at this kind of game before. It meant that Cousins had something she wanted, something that she considered rightfully hers. Probably a seat at the top table, a job of some kind, more status, a bigger desk.

Allder asked Kingdom whether he wanted a coffee. Kingdom was still thinking about the pub.

'This Cousins bloke, he's Controller now, isn't he? "T" Branch?'

'Controller-Designate,' Allder said, 'yet to be confirmed. The guy who used to run it has been put out to grass. Bloke called Wren. Old school. Clever bastard but very cautious. Not at all what they're after now.'

Kingdom nodded, remembering Annie mentioning the name. In the office they apparently called him Jenny but she'd got rather fond of him.

'And Cousins?' he said.

'Younger. Smarter. Right pedigree, ex-SAS, all that Action Man bollocks.'

'But any good?'

'Yes, if you don't look too hard at the small print.'

'Meaning?'

Kingdom let the question hang in the air, wanting to know more. Allder's humiliation at the Fishguard press conference had done the rounds at the Yard, and it was clear from the expression on the little man's face that he wasn't in the business of forgiveness.

'Connections,' he said slowly, 'it's all down to connections. Who he's lobbied, who he's been talking to, who's impressed by all that SAS shit. Know what I mean?'

'No, sir,' Kingdom said woodenly.

Allder frowned, trying to mask his indignation. He reached for a paper clip, trying to unbend it in his tiny fingers. 'High places,' he said at last, 'friends in high places.'

'How high?'

'Very high.' He tossed the paperclip into the bin. 'How do you think he landed the plum job? "T" Branch? The crown bloody jewels?'

'Dunno.' Kingdom shrugged.

'Because it suits their purposes. That's why.'

'Whose purposes?'

Allder gazed at him, more irritated than ever, not quite believing how slow he could be.

Kingdom returned the stare, determined to get it out, to get it on the record. 'Whose purposes?' he said again.

'The Home Office, of course. And Downing Street. They've been after Five forever, like every government there ever was. Cousins will give it to them on a plate, theirs for the asking, as long as they put him in charge.' He offered Kingdom an icy smile. 'The outlaws back in the corral, and no Mr Sheehy to raise the dust. Neat, don't you think?'

Kingdom nodded, reaching for the photo again. There were aspects of Allder's paranoia that were frankly beyond him. Not because he couldn't follow the logic but because he didn't care. Politicians dealt in power. Power corrupted. If you believed anything else, you were a fool. Kingdom gazed at the face in the photo. The eyes. The startled expression. The slack, fleshy mouth.

'So what was Annie doing in Belfast?' Kingdom said after a while.

'I've no idea.'

'Have you asked?'

'Of course I have.'

'And?'

'No one's talking. She was obviously there. I imagine she'd gone for a meet of some kind. Maybe our friend in the photo. Maybe someone else. Either way, I'm afraid she's still dead.'

'Yes, but who slotted her?'

'I'd be guessing at this stage.' Allder was frowning now, tapping the desktop with his pen. 'Some Provo faction or other. Pro-talks, anti-talks. The peacemongers, the wild bunch . . . who knows?'

'Sure,' Kingdom said, 'but there's a procedure to these things. You have a meet, you take precautions. You don't just step in. Not if you know what you're doing.'

'And she did? She knew the score? Is that what you're saying?'

'Yes,' Kingdom said, 'she was bloody good at it. She took the odd gamble, the odd risk, but nothing really silly, nothing that would explain . . .' he broke off, turning away, the smell of bleach in his nostrils again, the sickening moment when the pathologist bent down with her scissors. 'Someone fucked up,' he said at last. 'I know they did.'

'Cousins would have sent her,' Allder pointed out, 'almost certainly.'

Kingdom said nothing, looking at the photo again for the last time. Then he gave it back to Allder.

'So how do I get hold of him,' he said, 'this Cousins?'

'No idea. You could do what I do. You could try phoning Gower Street. But apart from that . . .' He shrugged. 'Why?'

'I'd like to talk to him, find out what happened.'

'You think he'd tell you?'

'I think he might.'

'What does that mean?'

Kingdom looked at him a moment, then shook his head, refusing to answer. The little man shrugged again, pulling open a drawer. Inside was a sheaf of transcripts. He slid it across the desk.

'You ought to read this before we talk about Monday,' he said, 'before you go to Skye.'

'What is it?'

'Phone transcripts. Faxed through this morning. Rob Scarman's compliments.'

'Ethne Feasey? More calls?'

'Sort of.'

Kingdom reached for the transcripts. Across the top, standard format, was the number of the tapped telephone: 0983 456734. Kingdom frowned. It was an Isle of Wight number but it didn't belong to Ethne Feasey. He was sure of it. He began to read the transcript. It was the record of the call she'd made after the brief exchange he'd listened to in Rob Scarman's office. The guy with the rough voice. The one who'd told her to call back. She'd gone out immediately afterwards. Scarman's boys had followed her.

Kingdom looked up. 'The phone box on the sea-front?'

Allder nodded. 'Yes.'

'Tapped?'

'So it seems.'

'For how long?'

Allder smiled at last, leaning forward. 'At least three months,' he said, 'according to the BT people.'

Kingdom phoned for a mini-cab from his own desk. He'd been through Yellow Pages and he was certain he'd found the right firm. The dispatcher from Kingston Cabhire promised him a driver within half an hour, and Kingdom thanked her with a quiet smile, returning to the notes he'd made prior to Allder's departure. Their conference had ended at three in the afternoon, the little man seizing his bargains from the garden centre and shepherding Kingdom towards the door. With luck, he mumbled, he'd have them in before nightfall. Providing, of course, the rain held off.

Now, Kingdom studied his list of notes. Most of them were simply updates, more bits of the Sabbathman jigsaw. News from Tyneside about the Bairstow inquiry. A fax from the Devon and Cornwall CID boys establishing that Dave Gifford's motor cruiser had recently visited the Torquay marina. Another conversation with the Aldershot adjutant confirming that Andy Gifford and the guy in Ford Open Prison who'd crippled Peter Weymes had been very close buddies in 3 Para. More and more bricks in the wall that would finally encircle Sabbathman,

Allder, it now seemed, needed no more convincing that the serial killings were down to Dave Gifford and his son, and he'd therefore reinforced surveillance on the Scottish west coast landfalls from Skye. To his certain knowledge, both men were still on the island, weathered in at *An Carraig*. According to a phonecall from one of the Special Branch team at Kyle of Lochalsh, the whole area lay under a heavy blanket of cloud, with the winds gusting to sixty knots and the mountains largely invisible. Conditions like these, said Allder, were a blessing and the forecast was even better. Another deep depression was racing east, across the Atlantic. By Monday, the weather on Skye would be horrible.

Kingdom sat back, pushing his list to one side. All of it was important, he knew it was, but what preoccupied him now was the news about the phone box on the Shanklin sea-front. It was more than possible that Ethne Feasey had been using it for some time to talk to Dave Gifford. For a man with a lot to hide, it would have been an obvious precaution, especially if he'd thought that Ethne Feasey's own line might have been tapped. Her son, after all, had got himself involved with the Twyford Down people and Dave Gifford would have been experienced enough to suspect a tap on these grounds alone. So far, so good. But what Dave Gifford couldn't have known was that the public phone box had also been bugged. Which meant that someone, somewhere would have a complete record of all calls on the sea-front number.

Kingdom toyed with his pen, exploring the implications. Men as love-struck as Dave Gifford had loose tongues. If he was campaigning – killing – on Ethne Feasey's behalf, he may well have shared the secret with her. God knows, they may even have been in it together, and if so, the transcripts of their conversations would have provided a blueprint for the entire campaign. So who had ordered the transcripts in the first place? And exactly how revealing had they been?

Kingdom was still pondering the questions when the phone rang on his desk. The mini-cab had arrived from Kingston. It was waiting for him downstairs. Kingdom rode the lift to the ground floor, still thinking about the transcripts. The mini-cab was a dirty blue Datsun with 93,000 miles on the clock. The driver, a young Moroccan, was yawning behind the wheel. Kingdom got in beside him. The man looked half-asleep.

'Kew,' he confirmed, giving Annie's address.

They drove west, towards Hammersmith, the traffic heavy for a Saturday. By the time they'd crossed the river at Chiswick, Kingdom and the young driver had become friends, both over-worked, both underpaid, both completely knackered. When they got to Annie's turning, the driver began to indicate left. Kingdom reached across, cancelling the indicator. Then he nodded at the two-way radio under the dashboard, a constant stream of messages from the dispatcher.

'Take me to your leader,' he said, 'change of plan.'

Kingston Cabhire operated from premises behind the railway station. The dispatcher, a middle-aged woman, was too busy to answer Kingdom's questions and told him to talk to the boss. The boss, just now, was having a snack in the Wimpy Bar round the corner. Kingdom found him at a table beside the deep fryer, a thick-set, middle-aged man with a day's growth of beard and a collarless shirt, open at the neck. His half-pounder dripped with ketchup and after every mouthful he carefully wiped his chin with the back of his hand.

Kingdom slipped into the seat opposite. He showed his ID long enough to register the look in the man's eyes. Someone's been here before, he thought. Someone's told him to expect me.

Kingdom helped himself to a chip. 'Customer of yours from Kew,' he said, 'a woman called Annie Meredith.'

'Yeah?'

'Last Saturday. You'd have the records.'

'Yeah?'

'I want to know where she went. The address.'

The man looked at Kingdom for a moment or two. The remains of the burger lay on his plate. Kingdom wondered briefly about ordering one himself, then thought better of it.

'Well,' he said, 'shall we go back to the office?'

'No point.'

'Why not?'

'We don't . . . ah . . . keep records.'

'At all?'

'Of the destinations?' The man shook his head. 'Never.'

'Then maybe you'll tell me who took her. I'm sure you've got a record of that.'

The man frowned a moment, reaching for a paper napkin, buying time. 'Bloke's left,' he announced at last, 'gone.'

'Disappeared?'

'Yeah.' He finished with his chin and started on his forehead, leaving a thin film of ketchup below the hairline. 'Fucking typical. These days.'

Kingdom nodded, saying nothing. Then he sat back, smothering a yawn, a smile on his face. 'You pay your drivers shit,' he said at last, 'they're all on the black. No stamps. No NI. Half the poor bastards are foreign, and I'm sure most of them don't even have work permits.' He reached for another chip. 'You've got ten minutes to tell me what I want to know. Otherwise . . .' He shrugged. 'It might get heavy.'

'How heavy?'

Kingdom licked his fingers, taking his time. 'Inland Revenue. The VAT people. DSS. The Immigration lot . . .' He smiled. 'Then me again.'

Kingdom took the train back into Central London. By half-past six he was standing outside Gloucester Road tube station, watching the Saturday traffic inching past, wondering quite how late he should leave it. According to the A-Z, Queen's Gate Gardens was five minutes away. If Cousins was at home, then now would be as good a time as any to knock on the door. If nothing else, they had Annie in common. The least the man owed him was some kind of clue, some kind of indication about how and why she'd died. With that, he told himself, he could begin to make his peace.

Kingdom crossed the Cromwell Road, heading north towards Hyde Park. Queen's Gate Gardens was next on the right, a handsome square of tall mid-Victorian houses, each entrance with its separate portico. Kingdom mounted the steps to number 318 and paused beside the wall-mounted speakerphone. Cousins, to his surprise, had used his own name. Second bell. Ground floor flat.

Kingdom rang the bell a couple of times. Nothing happened. He rang it again. Finally it answered, a man's voice. Kingdom gave his name and asked for Hugh Cousins.

'Who are you again?'

'A colleague.'

There was a pause and then the lock slid back in the big front door and Kingdom stepped through into the carpeted hall. The flats smelled of money: fresh flowers, expensive perfume, and the skins of very young animals. A door at the end of the hall opened and a tall figure stood waiting for him. He was wearing jeans and a nicely-cut white shirt. He had dark, curly hair and a quizzical smile. The handshake was light, the merest touch of flesh on flesh.

'Hugh's away,' he said at once, 'back tomorrow afternoon.'

Kingdom registered his disappointment with a scowl. He could smell burning toast now.

'Shit,' the man said, 'hang on.'

He turned on his heel and disappeared. Kingdom ran his fingers over the lock. Double mortice, he thought. The best you can buy. He peered around, looking for the tell-tale signs of a security system – photoelectric sensors, pressure pads – knowing already that he'd have to come back tonight, and lay the ghost the proper way. No flannel. Nothing face to face. Just a thorough search of the flat on the off-chance that he might find something worth the effort and the risk. Men like Cousins often made mistakes that way, leaving stuff around, and Kingdom remembered his face again in the pub. He'd had that look, that arrogance.

The man who'd opened the door now was back again, newly apologetic. 'I'd ask you in,' he said, 'but I'm off out.'

'Back later?'

'No.'

'I meant Hugh.'

'No.' The man was frowning now, studying Kingdom a little harder. 'I thought I told you. He's away until tomorrow.'

Kingdom grinned, stepping back into the hall, saying he'd phone Hugh in a day or two. The man at the door was still watching him as he paused at the end of the hall and let himself out.

It was dark before Kingdom saw him again. He emerged from the flats, pulling the front door shut behind him and testing it to make sure it was locked. He was wearing a suit now and when he got to the pavement he put on a long black raincoat, turning up the collar against the blustery wind that was stirring the leaves in the garden which occupied the middle of the square. He set off towards Gloucester Road, then paused, patting the pockets of the raincoat. Standing in the shadows across the road, Kingdom heard the soft curse as he turned back to the flat, running up the steps to the front door, pausing to let himself in. A minute later he was out again, pocketing the keys, walking briskly in the direction of Earl's Court.

For a minute or two, half an hour later, Kingdom thought he'd lost him. They were walking east along the Brompton Road, and the pavement was thick with pedestrians. Scaffolding covered a parade of shopfronts, with a walkway underneath, and by the time Kingdom emerged, Cousins' friend had vanished. Kingdom began to run, stepping out into the road, hugging the kerb, careful not to find himself suddenly abreast of the man. Maybe he's taken a cab,

he thought. Or maybe he's ducked into one of the several res-
taurants he'd already passed. Then he spotted him again, the other
side of the road this time, just the back of the long black raincoat
as he disappeared into the lobby of a big hotel.

Kingdom waited for less than a minute. Inside the hotel, the
lobby was crowded with guests. Cousins' friend was nowhere to be
seen. Kingdom paused at the reception desk. The girl gave him
directions to the cloakroom. He followed the stairs to the basement. Cousins' friend was standing beside the counter. He had a
ticket in his hand and the attendant was busy putting his coat onto
a hanger. Kingdom slipped past, pushing open the door to the
men's lavatory. Locked in a cubicle, he waited a full minute,
emptying his coat pockets. When he emerged again, Cousins'
friend had gone.

At the cloakroom counter, Kingdom handed over his coat. The
attendant gave him a ticket.

Kingdom smiled at him. 'Expecting a busy night?'

The attendant was young. The broad Geordie accent sat oddly
with the pressed brown uniform. 'I'm off out, sir,' he said, 'as soon
as the relief arrives.'

Beside the lobby was a small cocktail bar. Kingdom limited
himself to a single Pils before he returned to the cloakroom. The
attendant who'd given him his ticket had gone. In his place was a
much older man. Kingdom stood at the counter, turning out his
pockets. The ticket he'd collected for his own coat was number 92.
When the attendant shot him a sympathetic smile, he shook his
head.

'Gone,' he said.

'Number, sir? Can you remember?'

'Ninety-one. My wife's age,' he grinned, 'last birthday.'

The attendant offered a dutiful chuckle, then disappeared into
the line of coats. 'Can you describe it, sir?' he called.

'Black raincoat. Ankle-length.'

'Make, sir?'

'Pass,' Kingdom grunted, 'The missus, again. Never look too
hard at a present. Never know what you might find. My theory,
not hers.'

The attendant emerged with the raincoat. Kingdom gave

him a pound before he folded it over his arm and made for the stairs.

The keys were still in the pocket. Kingdom took a taxi from the hotel forecourt, and was outside Cousins' flat again less than ten minutes later. There were seven keys on the ring, including one for a Mercedes. By this time, he'd also found a number of other objects in the pockets of the raincoat. They included a pair of leather gloves and a balled-up credit card sales slip. The signature was a scrawl, but Kingdom finally deciphered the name Devereaux.

Kingdom paused outside the big front door, trying the keys, one after the other. A newish Yale finally did the trick and he stepped into the empty hall, closing the door behind him. At the door to Cousins' flat, he went through the keys again. Within a minute he was inside, wondering about the security, whether or not Cousins had a system, and if so whether it was fully activated.

A small table lamp in the living room was already on, light spilling through the open arch in front of him. Kingdom dropped to his knees, crawling carefully forward. A small square of Afghan rug lay on the carpet in front of him, and when he lifted it he found the pressure pad beneath. He paused, scanning the pale grey walls, looking for the tiny glass eyes that would indicate a sensor system. Somewhere, he thought, there'd be a master switch, a way of turning off the security alarms. He examined the bunch of keys again, knowing that Devereaux would have the same problem. Then he began to search the area round the front door, aware that most systems work on a time delay. Once the front door had been opened, the occupant would have a pre-set period of grace to deactivate the system, otherwise the alarm would sound.

Kingdom worked quickly, first one wall, then another. Beside the arch was a shelved recess. The shelves were bare except for a couple of railway timetables and junk mail from the AA. At the back of the middle shelf, painted the same colour as the wall, was a small square flap. Kingdom pulled on Devereaux' gloves and opened it. Inside was a time clock and an electrical switch. The switch was down. Kingdom peered at the clock. It had been pre-set on a two-minute delay and a neat little digital read-out was counting down to the moment when the system would signal an intruder. With seven seconds left, Kingdom reached for the switch and deactivated the system. The digital read-out stopped and then returned to two minutes. Kingdom watched it, his finger still on the master switch. When nothing happened, he began to relax.

The flat was spacious. Kingdom moved from room to room, pulling the curtains, getting the feel of the place. As far as he could judge, Cousins lived here alone and everywhere Kingdom looked he found more evidence for the neat, tightly ordered life this man must lead. The Marks and Spencer ready-to-eat meals in the freezer. The tidy piles of newly-ironed shirts in the airing cupboard. The membership card for a Bayswater health club tucked behind the black and white digital clock on the mantelpiece. The copies of *The Economist* carefully indexed beside the Technics audio stack. The flat had a cool sense of function. There were no photographs, no souvenirs, no silly knick-knacks. It wasn't a place you'd find it easy to relax in.

Kingdom finished with the living room and moved into the bedroom. It was at the back, beside the bathroom. The window was barred on the outside and security lights flooded the tiny courtyard. Kingdom pulled down the calico blind and turned back into the room. There was a plain black duvet on the low single bed and three pairs of trainers in a line by the built-in wardrobe. Beside the bed was a cabinet, knee-high. On top, propped against the clock radio, was a notepad. Kingdom picked it up. Someone had made a series of jottings on the pad and then torn off the top leaf. They must have pressed hard because he could still read the indentures left by the pen on the sheet below. Kingdom removed the sheet and held it up against the light. 'A1,' it said. Then there was an arrow to another scribble, 'A6136', then a second arrow, 'B6270', with the word 'Muker' beside it. Road directions, Kingdom thought, folding the torn-off sheet and slipping it into his pocket.

Kingdom paused for a moment. A framed photographic print hung on the wall facing the bed. It was an image he'd seen before, Ayers Rock in Australia. The photo had been taken in low sunlight, the beginning or the end of the day, and it showed an orange, alien place, a landscape the colour of Mars, the dead heart of an entire continent. Kingdom looked at it, wondering what kind of man would want to wake up to a picture like this. It spoke of something fierce and implacable, at once arid and overwhelming.

Kingdom shrugged, turning back to the cabinet. In the drawer, beside a box of Kleenex tissues, was a Jiffy bag. He took it out. It was addressed, in a child-like hand, to 'Mr Cousins' and it had been sent from Belfast only two days ago. Kingdom peered inside, shaking out the contents. A single audio cassette fell onto the duvet, no box, no letter, not even a note. He looked at it a moment, wondering whether or not it was important. On the evidence of the postmark alone, he knew he had to find out.

In the living room, part of the audio set-up, was a cassette player. Kingdom slipped the cassette into the machine. There was a dubbing option on the control panel and Kingdom began to go through the drawers below again, looking for the cassettes he'd examined earlier. Cousins kept a couple of dozen of them, mostly recordings from Radio Four, each neatly labelled. Kingdom found one at the back marked *File On Four: Nato in a Changing World*. He loaded it into the machine's auxiliary cassette port, winding it back, hoping that Cousins wouldn't miss it. This way, if the Belfast cassette was important, he'd be able to leave with a copy.

On top of the audio stack was a pair of lightweight headphones. Kingdom plugged them in, knowing that the machine would now play mute. The last thing he wanted was visitors. He reached forward, checking the audio levels, then pressed the play and record buttons. He was sitting on the floor now, his back to the wall beside the machine, his long legs reaching out towards the sofa. On the sound track he heard a rumble, then someone coughing. A door opened and closed again. Something fell over, something big, and a voice began to curse. It was a man's voice, a rich Belfast accent, slightly slurred. Someone else was in the room, another man. He was laughing. A radio was turned on, very loud, then the same voice cursed again.

'You'll fucking turn it off,' he said, 'we'll need the plug.'

The door opened again and someone else came in. Then the recording stopped. Seconds later, it started again. Kingdom had no idea how long the real gap had been but that didn't matter because the situation had now become abruptly clear. Two men, both of them with Belfast accents, and someone else who was refusing to talk.

'You'll tell me,' one of the voices kept saying, 'so help me God, you'll tell me.'

The voice was low, almost a hiss, the tone you might use with a child who wouldn't eat his breakfast, or a dog which wouldn't sit down.

'Fucking do it, do it, fucking tell me.'

Kingdom flinched as the first blow fell, the smack of knuckle against flesh, of knuckle against bone. Then the questioner again, more insistent.

'Who did you show? Who else saw it?'

A brief silence. The sound of a passing car. Then another blow, much heavier than the last, and a gasp of pain. Kingdom stiffened, reaching for the controls, wanting to stop the tape, wanting to rewind it, play the last few seconds again, make sure he hadn't got it wrong. A woman, he thought. A woman in there. Taking the punishment. Absorbing the pain.

The interrogation went on and on, the questioner beginning to lose his temper. The woman had something, something important, something no one else should see. Had she kept it to herself? Or had she shared this mysterious secret?

From the woman, so far, there was nothing. The odd gasp, the odd little cry, but nothing they could seize on, exploit, pull and twist until the truth came tumbling out. Whoever she is, Kingdom thought, she's playing these animals at their own game, refusing to say a single word, refusing to even acknowledge them.

The man with the questions, the one in charge, was angry now and Kingdom could hear slurping noises from time to time, regular pulls from some bottle or other. Finally, getting nowhere, the man came up with a new suggestion.

'Light the fucking gas,' he said thickly, 'and fetch the poker.'

'But—'

'Just fucking do it.'

The door opened. The other man went out. Then he came back in again.

'It's lit.'

'OK.'

'It'll be a while.'

'Sure. Take her top off.'

'You.'

'No, you fucking do it.'

The two men argued. Kingdom sat on the floor, his mouth dry now, a terrible certainty growing inside him. There was a tear of clothing and one of the men whistled. Kingdom shut his eyes, trying hard not to turn the sound-track into pictures, desperate not to visualise the way it must have been. The woman naked from the waist up. Tied to some poxy chair or other. Waiting for these animals with their red hot poker. One of the men was out of the room again. When he came back there was a moment's pause. Then the low, gruff Belfast voice.

'Fucking do it, before it gets cold.'

'Where?'

'Wherever you like.' Pause. 'There. That tattoo there. Yeah, that's right, just move them.'

Kingdom reached up for the controls. He should stop the tape. He knew he should. Before he wrecked the flat, broke it up, piece by piece, starting with this hideous piece of machinery, an orgy of violence that would only be over once he'd got his hands on Cousins. The man must have listened to this tape. He must have sat here, just like Kingdom, eavesdropping. That was unforgivable. That was worse, in a way, than even inflicting the pain in the first place. Ayers Rock, he thought. The dead heart.

Annie Meredith spoke for the first time. She sounded calm, in control of herself. Only Kingdom could recognise the tiny tremor in her voice, undetectable unless you knew her well.

'It'll make no difference.' she was saying, 'I promise you.'

'We'll fucking see about that.'

'I meant the whisky. It won't help. If you do it, you'll never forget it. It'll be with you forever.'

'And you, cunt.'

The men began to laugh and then there was a new sound, a high-pitched scream, unforgettable, and another and another, and Kingdom shook his head, trying to block out the noise, trying not to make the obvious connection, the poker, Annie's naked flesh, the rose tattoo scorching and bubbling under the red hot metal.

'Stop, for fuck's sake. You'll kill her.'

'Piss off.'

There was the thud of another heavy blow, the guy with the whisky out of control, then Annie again, the screaming louder and louder, then abruptly cut-off. Kingdom drew his knees to his chin, hearing her beginning to choke, recognising the low gurgling sound for what it was, hands around her throat, her life ebbing away.

The tape ended a minute or so later, silence in the room, the Belfast voice very close to the microphone. The man was out of breath. He had a message for the boss.

'You're in the clear, so you are. The wee girl's gone.'

ENDEX

SECURITY OFFICE
PO BOX 500, LONDON

Andrew Hennessey
Conservative Central Office
Smith Square
London SW1

8 October 1993

Dear Andy,

Thanks for the invite to "Der Rosenkavalier". It was a kind
thought and you'll forgive me for not being able to accept.
As far as Mr Grant is concerned, I'm afraid our hands are
tied. His freedom to publish nonsense (and make oodles of
money) is as fundamental as our freedom to curse him for it.
Perhaps, one day, he'll get the come-uppance he so richly
deserves.

Yours ever,

Hugh Cousins

PRELUDE

It was nearly midday before he saw the Range Rover. It came bumping around the shoulder of the hill across the valley, travelling slowly, halting every ten yards or so while the driver inspected another obstacle. The overnight rain, draining from the moorland slopes above, had filled the deep potholes in the track and the Rover's paintwork was blotched with mud.

He eased his position in the wet heather, reaching for the rifle beside him. He'd expected them much earlier, around ten, ten-thirty, and the fitful sunshine had done nothing for the chill that had seeped through the layers of clothing beneath the thin camouflage smock.

The Range Rover had stopped now, another hundred yards down the track. The doors were opening and the men inside were getting out. There were five of them, and when he tucked the wooden stock of the Enforcer into his shoulder and lowered his eye to the sniperscope, he recognised at once the face of the man he'd come to kill. He stood in the middle of the group, a slight figure, dressed for his weekend in the country. He had a shotgun tucked under his arm and the flat tweed cap was pulled low over his eyes but the sun was out again and there was no mistaking the milky paleness of his skin, nor the rash of freckles, nor the diffident smile he offered to the man at his side.

A cocker spaniel had appeared from the back of the Range Rover, barking with excitement, and the shooting party began to walk along the track, deep in conversation. After a couple of yards, someone pointed out a path up the hill and they turned onto it, single file, winding upwards through the heather.

He leaned into the rifle, the stock cold against his cheek. He'd already estimated the range at 550 yards but the men were walking away now and every step they took widened the gap. The target was number four in the line, the cleanest of kills, but he had no taste for shooting a man in the back and he waited patiently for the party to turn round to enjoy the view. A head shot would be best, full frontal, anywhere between the hairline and the base of the throat. Just like Jersey, just like Blanche. He smiled.

Across the valley, the five men toiled upwards. Only when they were close to the top of the hill did they pause and look back. Through the sniperscope, their breaths clouded on the cold air. Unfit, he thought, as his finger curled around the trigger.

The target had something in his eye. When he'd sorted it out, he took off the tweed cap and wiped the sweat from his forehead. As his face tilted up again, the cross-hairs in the scope came to rest. The other men were already on the move again. The target was still enjoying the view.

His finger tightened on the trigger and he waited another second or two, taking the lightest of breaths. The sun went in as he fired, the cloud patterning the valley floor. The noise of the single shot rolled across the empty moor and seconds later the dog began to bark, sniffing at the fallen body, calling back the men above.

SEVENTEEN

Allder had taken a room in a hotel in Kyle of Lochalsh. It was Monday morning and he'd been in residence just five minutes, scuttling in from the car, trying to avoid the torrential rain.

Kingdom had already been in the hotel almost twelve hours. Now, he joined the four other men who'd been summoned to the room Allder had hired, picking his way past the pile of soaking waterproofs heaped by the door. Allder appeared from the bathroom, mopping his face with a towel. The drive across from Inverness had done nothing for his temper.

He retrieved his briefcase from the floor beside the bed. Inside was a copy of *The Citizen*. Monday's edition had yet to find its way to north-west Scotland but Allder had bought a copy at Heathrow and he gave it to Kingdom now. Kingdom looked at it. He'd heard the news on the radio, first thing, and he'd wondered then quite how *The Citizen* would cope.

The other men in the room joined him on the bed. Three of them had been out on the coast for four days now, part of the Special Branch surveillance team seconded to the Sabbathman inquiry from Clydebank Police HQ in Glasgow. They'd been watching the Skye ferries in six-hour shifts, one team down in Mallaig, the other here at Kyle. It was on the basis of their reports that Allder had felt relaxed about delaying Kingdom's visit until now.

Kingdom was still reading the paper. The front page had been devoted to a head and shoulders photo of Willoughby Grant. The portrait was edged in black. Beneath it, the single headline,

459

'SLAIN!' *The Citizen*'s chickens had come home to roost. Mr Angry had shot the editor.

Kingdom turned over. Amongst the testimonials and the hand-wringing he could find no trace of the usual communiqué.

He glanced up. 'No word from the man himself?' he queried. 'Nothing in writing?' Allder produced an envelope from the briefcase and tossed it across. 'It's a photocopy,' he said curtly, 'you can keep it.'

Kingdom nodded, sliding a single sheet of paper from the envelope. The message, as ever, was brief. He opened the paper on his knee, letting everyone read it. *'Papers like yours,'* it ran, *'use other people's grief to make a profit. Your Mr Angry was a bit fed up about all that but profits obviously matter to people like you so I decided to make a little contribution of my own. The boss died smiling, by the way. Nice day. Clean air. Wonderful views. Over and out. Sabbathman.'*

Kingdom read the message again, hearing the men beside him beginning to chuckle. No wonder they hadn't printed it, he thought. He peered hard at the lines of type. It had come from a manual machine, like the other communiqués, but there was something subtly different about the typeface. He looked up.

Allder was watching him carefully. He nodded. 'Different machine,' he said.

'Meaning?'

Allder shrugged. He was looking now at the oldest of the surveillance team, a tough, balding inner-city Glaswegian called George who'd been in charge of the operation since Thursday. Kingdom had been talking to him most of the morning. He'd been tramping the Highlands since adolescence and he knew the area backwards. Now he answered Allder's unvoiced question about the Giffords.

'Dunno, boss,' he said, 'just dunno.'

'You watched every ferry? And you didn't spot him?'

'Aye.'

'Absolutely certain?'

'Aye.' He paused. 'He could have crossed in the boot of someone's car, of course. Or maybe in disguise.'

Allder eyed him for a moment. 'Balaclava?' he inquired drily. 'Ski mask?'

George didn't answer. He looked exhausted.

'What about using a fishing boat? Or a dinghy? Inflatable of some kind?' Allder was saying. 'There must be a thousand places they could have nipped across.'

George shook his head. 'Not in this weather,' he said, 'not if you wanted to survive.'

'So it had to be one of the ferries?'

'Aye, and even they were finding it tough going.' He shook his head again. 'He must have come across on Friday or first thing Saturday. Thursday he was definitely over there, like I said on the phone.'

'You're sure?'

George was looking at the youngest of the four detectives. He was sitting on the carpet beside the television with his back against the wall. The rain had plastered his hair to his scalp and the ends were still dripping.

He mustered a tired nod. 'I was over on Thursday,' he said. 'There's a wee hill this side of the centre. You can look down on the place, see everything. It's a tidy view.'

Allder raised an eyebrow. 'And you're saying you saw him? The young one? Andy?'

'Aye. I was there in the morning and he was in and out of the house, loading stuff into a van, mainly cardboard boxes.' He patted the binoculars at his side. 'It was definitely him. We've all got the mug shots. He was wearing one of those waxed jackets.'

'And has the van been over on the ferry? Since?'

The young detective shrugged, looking at George. George shook his head. 'It's still there, sir. Still at *An Carraig*.'

'So he couldn't have come across in the van?'

'No.'

'And he definitely hasn't been back?'

'No.' George nodded at the rain still streaming down the window. 'There were no boats yesterday. Nor this morning, so far.'

Allder leaned back, warming himself on the radiator, and Kingdom could see him doing the calculations. Grant had been killed on the Yorkshire Moors, around midday Sunday. Unless he'd used a helicopter or a light aircraft, the journey up to Skye would have taken at least six hours.

Allder rubbed his face. 'So it's just the old man over there, Dave Gifford,' he said. 'Is that what you're saying?'

George shrugged. 'That's the way it looks, boss.'

'But are you even sure of that? Has anyone been over?'

'How? When there aren't any ferries?'

There was a long silence.

Kingdom stirred. 'I phoned this morning,' he said, 'just to check the booking.'

'And?'

'Dave Gifford's definitely there.'

'Are you sure?'

'Yes.' Kingdom nodded. 'I talked to him about gear, making sure I've got the right boots.' He paused. 'It's the same guy who talked on the phone to Ethne Feasey. Same voice. Definitely.'

Allder looked thoughtful and Kingdom began to wonder what his last twelve hours must have been like. Arthur Sperring, for one, would have been asking some of the harder questions. Like why the Anti-Terrorist Squad were amassing piles of evidence and then doing nothing about it. And why they'd allowed a suspected serial killer to add another body to his list. Questions like this would be yet more bullets for Downing Street's gun. Assuming it was still cocked.

'Well?' Allder was saying. 'What's next? Any bright ideas?'

Kingdom eased some of the stiffness from his long frame. The mattress on the bed in his own room had been far too soft and he'd spent most of the night on the floor.

'I'll still go across,' he said. 'The boy's bound to come back sooner or later.'

'Like when?'

'Dunno.' Kingdom paused. 'But Dave Gifford's there. He'll do for starters.'

Allder looked at him, saying nothing, then he turned his back on the room and gazed out of the window. The Isle of Skye, half a mile away across the water, was invisible. Kingdom waited for a decision. This was the moment, he thought, when Allder would have to reveal himself. Was the trust between them real? Had the odd grudging compliment been sincere? Or would it turn out like most of the other operations he'd been on? A wild zig-zag through the evidence? Everyone covering their own backs? He thought of the Commissioner again, and Allder's career in the balance. Allder was still at the window, staring out at the gloom.

'Let's talk about the comms,' he said at last. 'How are we going to work this?'

Mid-afternoon, the rain stopped. Livid shafts of sunlight lanced through the holes in the cloud and the glistening black shoulders of the island appeared across the water. The wind had veered to the north-west, bringing with it the smell of winter, but in the sudden bursts of sunshine the place looked utterly different. Gulls wheeled and dived over a gardener at the back of a nearby croft. Fishing boats danced at their moorings in the Sound. And away to the right, beyond the uncompleted sweep of the new bridge, was the dramatic backdrop of the Cuillin Hills, the kind of mountains a child might draw, shadowed by the racing clouds.

Kingdom watched from the top deck of the ferry, the wind tearing at his anorak. He'd once listened to Annie talking about the west coast of Ireland, how special it was and how remote, and he thought of her now as the ferry nosed against the ramp on the island side of the crossing. Kerry and Galway must have been like this, he thought. He should have listened harder. They should have gone there. He should have taken up her suggestion, called her bluff. They should have settled down. Had dozens of kids. Never come back.

Kingdom clattered down the steel ladder to the lower deck, shouldering his rucksack as he went. Allder was back at the hotel. He'd been up at the bedroom window now, watching the ferry through his new Zeiss binoculars. His mood had changed with the weather. His indecision, his gloom, had gone. He'd left the detailed back-up planning to George, stipulating only that Kingdom's safety was paramount. At least two members of the surveillance team were to be on standby on the island night and day. The men, like Kingdom himself, were armed. Everyone had a radio and there were a series of emergency code-words for denoting various degrees of what George drily termed 'fuck-up'.

Watching Allder as he'd drawn the briefing to a close, Kingdom had sensed the little man's need for a result. He had an almost animal hunger for victory, an absolute determination that decent policework, what he called 'honest coppering', should bring this extraordinary episode to an end. Leaving the hotel, he'd touched Kingdom lightly on the arm, wishing him luck. Kingdom had looked down at him, faintly uncomfortable, and Allder had patted him again, an almost fatherly gesture, asking him whether there was anything he needed, anything he hadn't covered in the briefing.

Kingdom had nodded. 'That photo I gave you. The one from Dublin.'

'Yes?'

'What are we doing about it? Where's it gone?'

Allder had smiled, stepping out of the hotel lobby, accompanying him down the hill towards the ferry. The photo had gone to the RUC boys, he'd explained. If the face was on file, if it belonged to a known player, he'd have a reply within days. Kingdom had looked sceptical at this, knowing all too well that life was seldom that simple in Belfast. People had their own agendas. The guy might be a tout, an informer, someone highly placed, a prime Provisional source. That would mean protection, a shield from prying eyes, the return of the photo with an apologetic little note. 'NK,' someone would have scribbled. 'Not Known.' They'd stopped by now, Allder curious, wanting to know more.

'That bother you?' he'd said. 'The photo?'

Kingdom had nodded, turning away towards the loading ramp. 'Yes,' he'd said.

Now, he trudged off the ferry. Up ahead, he could see the minibus from the Adventure Centre, parked by the first shop as Dave Gifford had promised on the phone. So far, Kingdom hadn't told Allder anything about his visit to Cousins' flat, the cassette he'd found there, the voices in his head that refused to go away. Not because he didn't trust the man but because it had become so overwhelmingly personal. Allder had been right all along. He'd involved himself in a war.

The minibus was empty except for the driver. Kingdom could see his silhouette, watching the passengers from the ferry in the rear-view mirror. Kingdom went to the rear door and knocked on the window. The driver leaned back, reaching full length, releasing the lock. He was wearing jeans and a thick white roll-neck sweater.

He had delicate, almost feminine hands and a pleasant, open face. He looked about thirty.

'Mr Travis?'

Kingdom nodded, throwing his rucksack across the long bench seat and getting in behind it. The driver had a London accent, flat and slightly nasal.

'Amazing weather,' Kingdom said, pulling the door shut.

The minibus bumped away towards the mountains, following the metalled road that skirted the coast. Kingdom made himself comfortable, his back against the rucksack, using the full width of the seat. There was a portable cassette-radio in the front and the driver was singing along to an old Paul Simon album. He had a soft, tuneless voice and he gave up on the high bits to point out passing items of local interest.

The island, he said, had once supported a population of more than twenty thousand but now the numbers were down by two thirds. In the last century, the place had taken a battering from the old clan chiefs who'd driven the people off the land and replaced them with sheep. Many of the islanders, impoverished and starving, had been forced onto the lumber ships, exchanging everything they had for a passage to Newfoundland or Canada. Many of the ships were falling apart and had gone down en route but those who'd stayed behind had faced a constant battle to even put food in their mouths. The driver laughed, a high mirthless giggle. It was the old imperial story, he said. The landlords screwing the natives for everything they could help produce – kelp, wool, fish while the big guys who controlled the markets down south got richer and richer.

They were approaching a village now, a light dusting of cheerless roadside bungalows, and the driver indicated an area off to the right wedged between the road and the sea. Here, he said, one of the island's lairds had established a crofting township. One hundred and fifty years later, the locals were still trying to coax a living from the soil but it was tough going. The land was too soft for cattle and too wet for hay and the peats never dried properly. The driver caught Kingdom's eye in the mirror.

'Buggered then and buggered now,' he said. 'Know what I mean?'

He hauled the minibus round a corner and changed down a couple of gears as the road began to climb the flank of a mountain. The mountain towered above them, the summit shrouded in cloud, and Kingdom peered up at it, wondering what he'd let himself in for.

'You busy this week?' he said. 'Only I expected other people on the ferry.'

The driver was back with Paul Simon and the warm African melodies of *Graceland*. 'Not really,' he said.

'So how many have you got room for?'

'Max? If we really need it? Around twenty-four, twenty-five, but that's a pain, believe me. You end up spending all day in the kitchen. Not my idea of heaven.'

Kingdom offered a dutiful laugh, still looking for the top of the mountain. 'So how many this week? All up?'

The driver laughed. He was rolling a cigarette now, steering with his knees. To the right, across a sheet of black water, was a stand of fir trees.

'Three,' he said at last.

'*Three?*' Kingdom looked at him for a moment. 'Plenty of individual attention, then?'

'Sure,' the driver laughed again, 'so if you're expecting a skive, think again.'

A little later, they emerged on the edge of a sea loch, pausing to let a couple of sheep cross the road in front of them. The landscape was wild and empty, even more forbidding than Jo Hubbard's photos had suggested, and the wind howled down from the mountains, squalling across the waters of the loch, making the minibus rock on its springs. At the head of the loch, high above a stony beach, a burn was in spate and the torrent of falling water shredded in the wind, blowing like smoke across the bare brown mountainside.

The driver had turned the music off now. Like Kingdom, he sat in silence, waiting for the sheep, gazing at the view.

'Been up here long?' Kingdom asked.

'Me?' the driver laughed. 'I'm in and out of the place. Back and forth. Strictly part-time.'

'You can do that?'

'Sure. No problem.'

'And you like it? The work? The island?'

'Yeah . . .' He sounded reflective now. 'Yeah, I do. I like the peace of the place. And the weather, too, believe it or not. Drives some people mad, the wind especially, but I love it. You get the odd day off, you know, when the old man's feeling generous, and you can be in the hills all day and not see a soul. Just the sheep. Magic.'

Kingdom nodded. 'The old man?' he said lightly.

'Dave. Dave Gifford.'

'And he runs the place?'

'Yeah. You talked to him this morning. About those boots of yours.'

'Of course,' Kingdom nodded. 'So what's he like? Patient? Only I haven't done this kind of thing for a while.'

The driver looked at Kingdom in the mirror again. The light was beginning to fade but there was no mistaking the smile that curled his lips.

'Dave?' he said lightly. 'I'm the last person to ask.'

Kingdom frowned, not understanding. 'Why's that?'

The driver didn't answer for a moment. Then he turned round in the seat, extending a hand. 'My name's Andy,' he said. 'I'm Dave's son.'

It took another forty minutes to get to the Adventure Centre. Kingdom spent most of the journey with his eyes shut and his head bumping against the window. He'd established in minutes that Andy Gifford had spent the entire weekend at *An Carraig*. They'd had trouble with the wellhead pump they used to supply the bunkhouses with fresh water and it had been his job to help one of the instructors sort the problem out. They'd stripped the thing down and traced the fault to a crack in one of the metal seatings but the weather had slowed them down and even if they'd fancied a wild night in the fleshpots of Kyle, it would have been out of the question. The last ferry on Saturday had left at five o'clock and after that the island had effectively been cut off. Kingdom had followed the story nut by nut, bolt by bolt, knowing that it must be true. When Willoughby Grant was shot, Andy Gifford had been 300 miles away, helping to mend a dodgy water pump. So who on earth had been out on the moor? Who had pulled the trigger? Sent the note? Added yet another notch to Sabbathman's gun?

The Adventure Centre, *An Carraig*, lay in a bowl between the mountains and the sea, a collection of stout timber huts roughly fortified against the weather. Sheep cropped the surrounding grass and there were a couple of dogs chained to a post beside the cindered hard-standing where Andy brought the minibus to a halt. He helped Kingdom from the bus, stooping to pat one of the dogs. Upright again, he grinned and suggested a drink. Kingdom grinned back. There was still enough light to get his first good look at Andy's face. The eyes, as both Clare Baxter and Jo Hubbard had mentioned, were the palest blue.

Kingdom followed Andy towards a small white house beyond the huts. Away to the left, a heavy swell was breaking on a pebble beach. The beach was protected by rocky headlands on both flanks and there was a tidy line of canoes upturned on the rising ground beyond the high-water mark. Mountains rose beyond the headlands, a depthless black against the darkening sky. The wind had died now, and apart from the growl of the breakers, the silence was unbroken.

Andy paused outside the house, stamping the mud from his boots. There were a couple of lobster creels propped against the wall and above them, on the window-sill, someone had left a hand-line, the kind you use for mackerel fishing, the hooks baited with feathers. Beside the door, roughly chiselled in blue-grey slate, was the name of the house, '*An Carraig*', and from somewhere deep inside came the voice of a BBC newscaster. Sarajevo, he was saying, was under renewed bombardment.

Kingdom followed Andy into the house. The front door opened into a narrow, stone-flagged hall. Yellow waterproofs hung on a line of hooks. Beyond the hooks, through another door, was the living room. A large man occupied the only armchair. He was wearing a pair of ancient tracksuit bottoms and a faded blue denim shirt and his feet were bare. Copies of *National Geographic* lay in a pile beside his chair and a huge mug of tea was steaming on top. The sock on his left hand was in even worse shape than the tracksuit bottoms and he was attacking the biggest hole with stabs from a darning needle. He grunted at Andy and looked up as

Kingdom came in. Except for the glasses, the face hadn't changed since he'd posed outside the tent back in March with Ethne and Jo Hubbard. The same lean features, hollowed by exercise, leathered by wind and rain. The same watchfulness in the eyes. Dave Gifford. Definitely.

'Quietened down nicely,' he growled.

'What?'

'The weather, son.'

Kingdom looked around, recognising the gruffness in the voice, the flat Kentish accent. The room was undeniably cosy. Framed photos hung on the rough stone walls, souvenir shots from summers gone by, and there was wood everywhere, polished boards underfoot, tongue and groove panelling overhead, shelf after shelf of books. Handcarved pieces of driftwood necklaced the fireplace. Peat glowed in the hearth. A cat sprawled on a square of raffia matting. If home's as good as this, Kingdom asked himself, why are these men putting it all at risk?

Andy completed the introductions and fetched a chair from the room across the hall. When he came back for the second time, he carried four cans of McEwans. Dave Gifford had a map out now, Ordnance Survey, 2½-inch to the mile, and was quizzing Kingdom on what he wanted to do. It took him about a minute to realise that Kingdom's thoughts on the matter were less than precise, and he didn't bother to hide his impatience.

'Fresh air and a bit of exercise?' he repeated. 'You could have got that in Hyde Park. The exercise, anyway.'

Kingdom tried hard not to look foolish. He was better at playing the callow journalist than he'd expected.

'Well . . .' He shrugged. 'You know . . .'

'Done this before?'

'A bit.'

'Where?'

Kingdom blinked at the tone of voice. With the half-moon glasses and the piercing stare, this man could be truly intimidating. Sergeant-Major Gifford, he thought. The toast of the Aden mess.

'West Country,' he said limply, 'Dartmoor.'

Gifford grunted, refusing his son's offer of a beer. Kingdom's eyes were back on the map. Wherever you looked, there were brown contour lines, painfully close together. Gifford's finger was anchored on the Adventure Centre.

'You free tomorrow?' he was saying to his son.

'Sure.'

'Packing done?'

'More or less. There's another van-load to go, but there's no rush.'

'What about Hughie?'

'He's with the girls. They're taking the canoes out tomorrow. Over to Soay, weather permitting.'

Gifford nodded, looking sharply at Kingdom again. 'Canoeing?' he said. 'That appeal at all?'

Kingdom reached for a beer and ripped off the ring-pull. 'No,' he said, 'I'd prefer dry land.'

'OK.' He nodded again. 'Andy'll take you up Sgurr Fasach. Give you an appetite, if nothing else. You bring a camera?'

'Yes.'

'Then take it. Brilliant views. As long as the rain holds off.'

Gifford reached for his darning, the conversation evidently over. Andy had disappeared without a word and from the back of the house Kingdom recognised the sound of a washing machine.

'I hear you had problems with the plumbing,' he said, 'over the weekend.'

'Yeah?' Gifford was bent over the darning, the needle tugging together the wreckage of the sock. He looked up, as gruff as ever, a man with little time for either courtesy or conversation.

'Andy mentioned it. Said there'd been some problem with a pump.'

'He's right. Hughie could have done it single-handed, with his background. But he had a touch of flu.'

'Hughie?'

'One of our instructors. Came from down your way. Devon somewhere. Used to work for the water people before they took it private. Bloody useful round here. Good bloke, too. I'll miss him.'

'Is he leaving?'

'We all are.'

'Really?'

'Yeah.' The needle paused and Gifford looked up again. 'The place is fucked. You're the last person I should be telling, your line of country, but too bad. Nothing wrong with the truth, is there?'

The question came out like a challenge, terse, angry, full of bitterness, and for the first time Kingdom began to sense what was missing. The room was clean and warm. It spoke of a life rooted in this remote, solitary place, of memories gathered in and harboured, of good times photographed and framed, but there was no softness, no plants, no flowers. What it needed, what it didn't seem to have, was a woman.

'Business bad?' Kingdom asked. 'Recession? Is that it?'

'Not really. It's been OK, no worse than anywhere else. No,' he shook his head, 'it's not that.'

'Then I don't understand. Is the lease up or something? Doesn't the place belong to you?'

'Here, you mean? This house?'

'Yes.'

'No,' he dismissed the point, 'it's always been ours. Ours to buy. Ours to develop. And now ours to sell. You interested, then? Fancy it, do you?'

Kingdom said he wouldn't know where to start. He had trouble wiring plugs. Gifford got on with his darning.

'Any chance of a buyer?' Kingdom inquired after a while. 'Anyone turned up?'

'We think so.'

'Someone local? In the same game?'

'Fuck, no. The locals think we're barmy, always have done. No. There's a bloke up from London. Phoned through this morning. Due across Wednesday. Says he wants to do what we did . . .' He began to laugh, a derisive cackle, the darning thrown aside, one huge hand reaching for a can of beer.

'What's that then?' Kingdom asked. 'Wants to do what?'

Gifford was gazing at him now, his eyes tinged with yellow, hostile, unblinking, the stare of a man with an uncertain hold on reality. 'Get away from it all,' he said softly. 'Isn't that the phrase? Wasn't that what you said on the phone? This morning? Good to be up here? Good to get away from it all?'

'That's right.' Kingdom nodded, beginning to tire of the aggression and the rudeness. 'And I meant it, too. If you live where I live, this could be the moon.'

'Yeah, once maybe. Now?' Gifford tipped the can to his mouth and took a long pull at the beer. 'Who knows? If these bastards have their way, we'll be a theme park. Like the rest of this fucking country.'

'Which bastards?'

A shadow fell between them. Andy had reappeared with an armful of peats. He knelt in front of the fire, busying himself, playing the housewife, asking his father whether he wanted to bother with soup. He was baking trout for supper, with loads of potatoes and greens. Afterwards, there was the remains of last night's crumble. Listening to the exchange, Kingdom had the strong impression that Andy's entry had been an intervention, an abrupt change of subject, a signal for the older man to calm down. This has happened before, Kingdom thought. Often.

Dave Gifford's body was sprawled in the armchair, his legs apart, the half-empty beer can dangling from one hand. He was humming to himself now, a Strauss piece, *The Radetsky March*, his eyes gazing sightlessly at some point on the ceiling.

Andy stood up. When he wiped his hands on his jeans they left brown marks from the peat. 'There's telly across the way,' he said, 'if you're interested.'

Kingdom had supper in one of the huts, sitting at the end of a long pine table laid for five. The room was cheerless and cold, pictures from the wall already stacked in one corner. Two of the fellow guests were sisters from Birmingham, big sturdy girls in their early twenties who ate in total silence, exchanging grimaces from time to time when one or other of them found a bone in the trout fillets. The fourth guest was slightly older, an American PhD student from Stanford, California. He was forceful and articulate, lecturing Kingdom on his choice of footwear. The fit of the boot around the heel, he said, was the real key to the mountains. Too loose, or too tight, and Kingdom would be a cripple by lunchtime.

'Where are you headed?' he asked, as Andy appeared from the darkness with a bowl of luke-warm rhubarb crumble. 'Which peak?'

'Sgurr something,' Kingdom said, watching Andy distribute the crumble amongst the waiting dessert plates.

'Fasach,' Andy murmured.

The American laughed, his spoon already poised. 'Holy shit,' he said, 'I wish you luck.'

After supper, Hughie the instructor appeared. He'd evidently been asleep and he looked surprised when the girls told him that the meal was over. One of them pulled a face and said he hadn't missed anything.

'I bet,' he said softly, unfolding a map and spreading it on the table.

He began to take them through next morning's programme, pointing out the landfall they'd be making on the island across the Sound. The crossing was about four miles, an hour's moderate paddling if the wind stayed in the north-west. Kingdom remained long enough to find Sgurr Fasach on the map. As far as he could judge, it lay due west. A straight line from the Adventure Centre would put it no more than five miles away, but the country in between was a whorl of brown contour lines and the real distance, he suspected, would be far longer.

The American was still sitting in front of the television in the corner. Kingdom joined him when he heard the opening bars of the *Nine O'Clock News*. The lead item featured the latest developments on the Willoughby Grant murder. *The Citizen*'s deputy editor spoke glumly about the loss of a great newspaperman. Staff on the paper, he said, had been deeply shocked by what he called 'this callous, clinical killing', and the paper's board of directors would shortly be announcing a substantial reward for information leading to the murderer's arrest. Listening, Kingdom couldn't suppress a grin. All mention of Mr Angry had gone. Real life had put a bullet in Willoughby Grant's head and the fairy tale that had served the paper so well was over. In a brief accompanying profile, the BBC reporter revealed that even Willoughby Grant himself had been a fiction. The dead editor's real name was evidently William Green.

The story cut to the North Yorkshire Moors and another reporter offered an update on the investigation. The hallmark of all

473

the recent killings, she said, was their sheer efficiency and police were now concentrating on exactly how the killer had been moving around. Grant had been shot at a remote moorland spot north of Swaledale. The nearest trunk roads serving the area were the M6 and the A1. Thereafter, from the south, the killer would have been forced onto a series of secondary roads, ending up on the B6720 as far as Muker. From then on, he'd have been travelling on foot and local police were now appealing for any witnesses who may have been in the area. The search, said the reporter, was for out-of-area cars and unfamiliar faces, but even the police had admitted that the moors were popular with tourists who would – by definition – fit both these categories.

Kingdom was staring at the screen, oblivious to the American sitting beside him. The student had been asking Kingdom about the other murders. He'd only flown in the previous week. What had been happening? Who'd been killed? Kingdom ignored the questions. The A1, he thought. The B627 something. And the name of the village, the little place they'd shown, the name stripped across the top of the general stores. Muker. He was sure of it. Muker.

Kingdom walked at least a mile before he stopped to use the mobile phone. He followed the track inland from the house, doing his best to skirt the deeper puddles. The wind was rising again, and thin cloud veiled a crescent moon, but as his eyes became used to the darkness he could make out the line of the track, winding up through the heather, and the blacker mass of the mountains on either side. From time to time, a lone sheep would emerge from the shadows, clattering away over the loose scree at the foot of the steeper slopes, and once he disturbed a bird of some kind, something big and awkward that flapped away into the night. At first it was cold, the wind eddying down the valley, but he was moving quickly, and by the time he stopped to make the phone call he was beginning to sweat.

He crouched in the lee of an outcrop of rock, punching in the numbers Allder had given him, hoping the phone would work.

Allder should be home by now. He'd been booked on the late afternoon flight from Inverness.

The number began to ring and then a faint voice, barely audible.

'Sir?'

'Kingdom? That you?'

Kingdom smiled, fighting the urge to whisper, hearing Allder bellowing into the phone. He had some news from Rob Scarman. He'd been monitoring calls from the phone box on Shanklin seafront. Ethne Feasey had been talking to *An Carraig* that very morning, and Gifford had arranged for her to travel up to Skye. According to Scarman, she was due to arrive some time Thursday.

Allder paused. 'Will you be through by then? Only she's seen you, hasn't she?'

'Yes.'

'So what do you think?'

Kingdom had settled on his haunches, his back against the rock. It was getting colder by the minute. 'What about the rest of those transcripts?' he asked, changing the subject.

'What transcripts?'

'The ones on the seafront number. The one Feasey's been using.' He paused. 'We need to know who ordered the tap. And what she's been saying.'

'I know. It's in hand.'

'Yeah, but when? When do we get to know?'

Allder grunted something about procedures. Gower Street, as ever, were being difficult. As were the supervisors at the BT intercept centre. Kingdom waited until he'd finished. High up to his right, away in the distance, was a light. He peered at it, trying to decide whether it was moving or not. After a while, he decided it wasn't. He bent to the phone. Allder had finished.

'There's a solicitor friend of mine,' Kingdom said.

'What?'

'A solicitor. Out Ilford way. His name's Charlie Truman.' Kingdom spelled the name and repeated the phone number twice. 'Give him a ring, sir. Tomorrow. First thing. He'll be expecting your call. I'll have been in touch.'

'Why?'

'He's got a cassette of mine, an audio tape. I sent it yesterday, first class, from London. Get the cassette off him and listen to it. Then give it to the bloke who used to be in charge of "T" Branch. The one they just elbowed. The one you mentioned.'

'Wren?' Six hundred miles away, Allder sounded lost.

Kingdom permitted himself a grim smile. 'That's him. Jenny Wren. He used to be Annie's boss. He liked her. At least, that's the impression I got.'

'So what?'

'Just listen to the tape. Then you'll understand.'

'Yes, but why Wren? Why send it to Wren?'

'Because he's now in charge of Five's intercepts people. It's a kind of Gulag. The place they send the has-beens.' He paused. 'If he listens to the tape, I'm sure he'll oblige.'

'With what?'

Kingdom frowned, wondering whether Allder had been at the Scotch again. Maybe he's taken a bottle or two home, he thought. One of those special malts. All the way from Inverness airport. 'The phone transcripts,' he said patiently, 'the Feasey transcripts. What she and Dave Gifford have been up to. How much she knew and how much the customer knew . . .' He paused again. 'Wren will be able to access all that. He'll know.'

There was silence on the line for a moment or two, then a new note in Allder's voice. He understands, thought Kingdom. At last he's beginning to put it together.

'This cassette,' Allder was saying, 'where did you get hold of it?'

'Three-one-eight Queen's Gate Gardens. Flat two. That's the other thing. You should organise a visit. Soon as you can.'

'You mean a warrant?'

'No, sir. A visit. A Black and Decker job. If you do the place tomorrow, what we're after might still be there. It'll save us a lot of grief on the Willoughby Grant hit, believe me.'

'What are we looking for?'

'Anything. Maps. Petrol receipts, A weapon, maybe. Who knows?'

Allder began to ask for a name, the person who owned the flat, but Kingdom cut across him, repeating the address, then changing the subject.

'Andy Gifford,' he said.

'What about him?'

'He's here.'

'Back already?'

'No, sir, he never left. He's been here all weekend. And so has his father.'

'*What?*'

Kingdom held the phone at arm's length a moment, hearing Allder demanding to know more. Then he switched the power off and slipped the mobile into his pocket. High above, suspended in the darkness, the light shone on.

EIGHTEEN

It was Andy Gifford who woke up Kingdom in the bunkhouse next morning. He stood by the bed, his face at the level of Kingdom's pillow. Kingdom could smell the tang of the peat on his clothes. Something was steaming in the mug he held up.

'Tea,' he grinned, 'two sugars. Breakfast in the house when you're ready.'

Kingdom drank the tea then struggled out of bed. When he tried the shower, nothing happened so he made do with a cold-water wash in one of the row of basins. The American student who'd been sleeping in the bunk below had already disappeared, his paisley pyjamas neatly folded on his pillow. Kingdom began to dress, pulling on the heavy socks he'd bought at Millets, remembering Andy Gifford standing beside the bunk. Five-foot seven, five-foot eight, he thought. Exactly the height Clare Baxter had described.

Breakfast was served in the Giffords' kitchen. The room ran the width of the house at the back and was obviously a recent extension. There was an enormous cooking range, fuelled by bottled gas, and a couple of tall fridge-freezers. On a pin board beside the back door was a sheaf of bills from a cash-and-carry in Portree and a washing-up rota dating back to the early summer. Kingdom sat at the long deal table while Andy Gifford served eggs and bacon and nuggets of fried potato from a sizzling pan. There was fresh mud on his boots and Gifford wondered how long he'd been up.

Kingdom was demolishing the last of the fried potatoes when Dave Gifford appeared. He was wearing a dressing-gown over his

T-shirt and there was a comma of shaving foam under his chin. He had an envelope in one hand and a sheet of paper in the other. He passed the paper across the table towards Andy, ignoring Kingdom.

'What d'you think?' he said.

Kingdom watched as Andy abandoned the coffee pot and picked up the paper. Under a colour photo of an ocean-going yacht, there was a list of specifications. He read them quickly and then returned the paper to his father.

'Not a lot,' he said, 'for ninety grand.'

Dave Gifford peered at the photo again and then shrugged. 'Looks alright to me,' he said, folding the details into the envelope and leaving the room.

Kingdom and Andy Gifford set off for Sgurr Fasach about an hour later. They both carried light day sacks with sandwiches, chocolate and flasks of hot soup, and as they made their way inland Kingdom tried to identify the rock where he'd sheltered to make the phone call the previous night. Twice he thought he'd found it and both times he looked up, trying to locate a source for the light he'd seen. On both occasions, though, there was nothing except the browns and purples of the mountainside, dimpled with grey rocks.

At first they walked in silence, Andy in the lead. It was a soft, moist day, not a whisper of wind, the ground soggy underfoot. After a couple of miles, the path divided and Andy paused while Kingdom caught him up. From here on, he said, the going got tougher. Soon, they'd begin to climb. The trick was to find a rhythm. There were no records to break, no prizes to claim. Just getting to the top and back would, he said, be ample reward.

Kingdom listened to him, aware of the warmth in the man, his obvious love of this bare, bleak wilderness, trying to reconcile it with the voice he'd heard in the book he'd read on the plane. *Enemy Territory* had been full of bewilderment, and pain, and anger, and he'd assumed at the time that the Falklands themselves had played a part in all this: the numbing cold he'd described, the endless slog over tussock and bog, the incessant wind and rain, the hints of malevolence in the terrain and the climate. That judgment, though, had been plainly wrong. The west coast of Scotland was almost identical to the Falklands: treeless, windswept, sub-Arctic. Yet here he was, pushing steadily uphill, pointing out the names of the surrounding peaks, giving each a character. One was 'a pain', another 'a kitten', a third 'needed watching', a fourth you'd 'lie down and die for'.

The latter phrase brought a smile to Kingdom's lips. They were halfway up the first serious ascent, the air appreciably colder, *An Carraig* a small white dot a thousand feet below.

'So why go?' Kingdom asked between breaths. 'Why leave all this?'

Andy glanced back over his shoulder. He was still in the lead but only by a yard or so. 'The old man,' he said, 'it's for him really.'

'Why?' Kingdom said again. 'What's gone wrong?'

'Everything, more or less. The business has been OK, that's held up, but everything else has . . . I dunno . . . gone.'

'Like what?'

Andy looked round again, not answering. Then he stopped and slipped off the day-bag. A thin, fine drizzle had begun to drift in from the sea, almost a mist, and droplets of moisture clung to his face. Andy wiped his nose, then unscrewed the top of the Thermos, and for the first time Kingdom saw the tiny blue eagle tattooed on the back of his right hand. Gloves, he thought. The man had always worn gloves.

'My mum died,' Andy was saying, 'that was the start of it. They'd been close, really close, as long as I can remember. She'd never liked it up here, in fact she hated it, but she never once let on and he loved her for that. That was loyalty, you see. And loyalty meant everything to Dave. He thought the world of her.'

'Because she was loyal?'

'Yeah. And because she didn't winge. Ever.'

He found a seat on a rock and poured a cupful of soup, offering it to Kingdom. Kingdom took it, thinking suddenly of Ernie and his own mother. Same relationship, he thought. Same unquestioning devotion. Andy was watching him now, openly curious about his interest, and Kingdom told him about his own father, what had happened to Ernie over the last few months, how much he'd changed. By the time he'd got to the end of the story, the soup was nearly cold.

'Shit,' Kingdom said, offering the cup back to Andy. 'I'm sorry.'

Andy took the cup and added more from the Thermos. Then he nodded down towards the beach and the tiny collection of huts. 'Same with Dave,' he said. 'He's a bit younger, I know, but it's like he's caught some disease or other. Building that place, the pair of them, he was happy as Larry. And that made mum happy, of course. That's the way it worked. What she really felt about the weather and all the stuff there was to do didn't matter. As long as Dave was Dave. That's why she'd married him. The spirit of the man. I used to come up here sometimes, seven, eight years back, and the place would be chaos. Huts half-built, timber everywhere, no proper sanitation, people shitting in holes in the ground, nothing to eat but porridge and toast, but Dave was in his element. There was nothing could stop him. Nothing. He'd been in the service, the Marines, you probably guessed that already, and that whole thing up here was like one long exercise, the toughest anyone could ever throw at you, positively the worst.'

'And Dave?'

'Like I say. Loved it.'

'And your mum?'

'Killed her. In the end.'

'You serious?'

'Yes.' He nodded, his eyes still on *An Carraig*, the little white house by the sea. 'I've been up and down here a lot the last couple of years. The place was humming, really busy. Dave had cracked it. They both had. But it was daft, too, and stupid. Because they ended up with the one thing that Dave couldn't handle.'

'What was that?'

'Success. You know the old story?' He glanced across at Kingdom. 'The day the goose lays the golden egg is the day you discover you can't stand omelettes. That's exactly how it was with Dave. The business just grew and grew. The place was bursting. People were arriving from all over and it just got on Dave's tits. It was like trespass. Sartre's line. Hell is other people. He used to call them aliens, the monsters from outer space. He couldn't stand it, any of it. Drove him nuts.'

Kingdom nodded, taking the cup again, swallowing another

mouthful of hot soup. The Planet Zilch, he thought. Like father, like son.

'But that's why he'd built the place to begin with,' he pointed out. 'To get people up here. To make money.'

'Yeah. I know. But he couldn't handle it. Not when it worked so well.' He paused, flaking dried mud off the tops of his boots. 'I suppose you'd call it irony. Isn't that the word?'

He looked up and Kingdom nodded, finishing the soup.

'And your mum?' he said at last. 'What happened to her?'

'She got sick. About this time last year. She always suffered when the winter set in, colds and flu and so on, so Dave just put her to bed, thought nothing of it. The place was a factory by then. We were turning over twenty, twenty-five people a week, like I said in the van. Dave was worked off his feet, just keeping it all on the road.'

'And your mum?' Kingdom said again.

'She got pneumonia. She had no reserves, no strength at all. She smoked like a chimney. Thin as a rake.' He paused, taking the empty cup from Kingdom. 'She died in Portree Hospital two days after Dave brought her in. He wasn't even with her when she went. Broke his heart. Believe me.'

Kingdom looked away, thinking of Ernie again. 'Yeah,' he said, getting to his feet, 'I can imagine.'

They climbed for another hour, skirting one peak then traversing the head of a valley before beginning another ascent towards the next summit. The blanket of cloud was thicker now and a steady rain had set in by the time they reached the top. Andy was fifty yards ahead, a shadow in the enveloping mist. He'd stopped beside a cairn of stones. Kingdom joined him, breathing hard. Every bone in his body ached. He'd never felt so tired in his life. He looked round. To his right, there was a sheer drop of scree and rock face and tendrils of straggling heather. The view, if you chose the right day, must have been sensational.

'This it?' Kingdom asked. 'Sgurr Fasach?'

Andy shot him a glance, at once proud and faintly shy. 'No,' he said, 'change of plan.'

Andy was looking at the cairn now, and for the first time Kingdom saw the flowers. They looked fresh, half a dozen roses in a hideous green vase. Andy was down on his knees, rearranging them.

Kingdom caught his eye as he looked up. 'Your mum?'

Andy nodded. 'She's buried down near the house,' he said, 'but Dave always wanted to build a memorial. This was perfect, his favourite run.'

'*Run?*'

'Yeah. Dave used to run a lot. Still does. He's got various circuits, various routes, but this one has always been tops.'

Kingdom gazed at the flowers, remembering the path up, how rough it was, how slippery, the endless climbs, the sudden descents, the way the mountains played tricks with you, teasing you, offering crest-line after crest-line, each one more definitely the summit, testing your will to breaking point. Today, at a steady plod, it had taken nearly three hours. So what fuelled Dave Gifford? What drove him on? He put the question to Andy.

'Mum,' he said simply, 'though he'd never admit it.'

They took a different path back, following a track that plunged towards the sea, turned inland again, then doubled back on itself, offering yet another view of the island of Soay. They were still hundreds of feet up and Kingdom could just make out the shapes of the three returning canoes, red matchsticks on the slate-grey water. Going down the mountain was hard on the knees but took much less physical effort and Kingdom was able to sustain a conversation for most of the way.

The last straw for Dave Gifford had evidently been the building of the new bridge from Skye to the mainland. Not only would the bridge bring tourists by the thousand but it was also privately built and owned, an affront – in Dave's eyes – to everything the island had represented. The tolls would go to some remote bunch of shareholders hundreds of miles south. They had no connection with the island. They belonged to a world of company boardrooms, and expense account lunches, and sleek women. Skye, with its silence and its peace and its bare, clean, windswept spaces was – quite literally – none of their business.

Dave had done his best to stop the bridge being built. He'd written letters to the press, lobbied his local MP, contacted the Department of Transport. When none of that had worked, when many of the locals had gone on swallowing all the yatter about boosts to tourism and a new dawn for the island's economy, he'd begun to brood about guerrilla action. In a way, thought Kingdom, the bridge was the same kind of issue as Twyford Down, a threat to something rare and irreplaceable, another victory for the remorseless onward march of the men with the money and the power and the influence. In his prime, said Andy, none of these things had mattered to Dave Gifford. He was far too busy building his own little idyll to worry about the real world. But when *An Carraig* was prospering, when he himself had become part of what he hated so much, then he'd turned abruptly against it with a passion that was all the fiercer for being so frustrated. No one had listened to him. The bridge was nearly complete. Skye, his Skye, would be an island no more.

They were halfway down the mountain, the track running parallel to the sea, the little cove of *An Carraig* clearly visible a couple of miles down the coast. Listening to Andy talking about Dave Gifford and the bridge, Kingdom had wondered how much of his father's passion he shared. They were walking slowly now, Kingdom trying to spare his blistered heels.

'So what will you do,' he said, 'the pair of you?'

'Sell up.'

'Is that easy?'

'We've had offers. Nothing wonderful, but offers. There's another guy flying up from London tomorrow. He's only just got in touch. Seems to know all about us, though. Which helps.'

'And once you've sold?'

Andy paused, stooping to tug at one of his socks. 'New Zealand,' he said. 'Dad's idea. He thinks it's a bigger version of here. Without the bridge, of course.'

'And is he right, do you think? Will it sort him out? Do the trick?'

'I've no idea.' Andy grinned. 'But getting there should be fun. We're after a yacht. Something half-decent.'

'Was that what this morning was all about? The one Dave showed you?'

'Yes.' Andy kicked each boot against a rock, loosening some of the mud caked underneath. 'He can't resist interfering. That's his problem. We've spent the last couple of months looking at yachts, you know, doing it the sensible way, going from marina to marina, doing the thing properly, coming up with a short list, all that. Yet still he writes off for all these bits and pieces, special offers, bargain boats, anything that catches his eye. Mr Impulse. Mr Fidget. Just can't leave it alone . . .'

Kingdom was watching the canoes again. He could see the two girls now, plump black dots paddling hard against the current.

'So you've been away a lot,' he said lightly, 'the pair of you?'

'Yeah, since the start of September.' Andy gave each foot one last stamp, nodding along the coast, back towards *An Carraig*. 'Closed everything down completely. First time for five years.'

Inexplicably, the path began to climb again. The rain had stopped now but they were off the rockier slopes of the mountain and the stands of heather on either side of the narrow track brushed wetly against their legs as they passed by. Up ahead, Andy had stopped again. He was standing on a grassy plateau overlooking the approaches to *An Carraig*. Away to the left, at the back of the tiny white house, Kingdom could just make out Dave Gifford hanging up a line of washing. Andy was watching him, too. Kingdom joined him on the edge of the sheer drop. The wind was picking up and there were seagulls below them, side-slipping lazily in towards the cliff-face.

Andy glanced across at Kingdom. '*Chez moi*,' he said.

Kingdom followed his pointing finger. Behind them, hidden from the path, was a simple wooden hut. It was a decent size, about eighteen feet square, with a pitched roof covered in bitumen felt. The clapboard walls had recently been painted with creosote and the windows on either side of the stable door were picked out in white. Wires stretched tight over the roof were secured to stakes driven deep into the rock, a testament – Kingdom assumed – to the strength of the wind.

Kingdom gazed at it a moment, trying to calculate its position relative to the path he had taken last night. The light, he thought, hanging in the darkness. 'You live here?'

Andy nodded. 'Yes. And I built it, too. Everything hand-carried up the hill. Took forever.'

'**And you sleep here at night?**'

'Of course.'

Andy led him to the front door. It opened without a key. Inside was a bed, a chest of drawers, and a table underneath one of the two front windows. On the table was a manual typewriter and a pile of manuscript. Around the manuscript was a litter of books and maps and sepia photos of the kind that Kingdom had already seen on the walls of *An Carraig*.

'What do you use for light?'

'This.'

A Tilley lamp hung on a hook on the back of the door. Andy took it off and shook it gently. Kingdom could hear the paraffin slurping in the reservoir beneath the wick.

'And heat?'

Andy nodded at the chest of drawers. 'Sweaters,' he said, 'and thermal underwear.'

'Water?'

'There's a spring up in the rocks. Behind the hut. You can drink it, wash in it, whatever. No problem.'

Kingdom smiled, fascinated. If you were after the simple life, this was as perfect a setting as you'd ever find. For the second time that day he began to wonder about the years that separated father and son. The gap, he thought, was infinitely smaller than Andy Gifford would probably admit.

Kingdom sat down at the desk, glad of the weight off his feet. The view was breathtaking, the clouds beginning to clear now, weak autumn sunshine puddling the water below, and in the distance he could just make out the still blue shadows of the mainland.

Andy had retrieved a pair of binoculars from the floor beside the chair. He gave them to Kingdom.

'Take a look at the island,' he said.

Kingdom racked the focus ring until a rocky beach across the Sound was pin-sharp. A pair of black heads broke the surface of the waters offshore and then disappeared again. Kingdom returned the glasses. 'By the beach,' he said, 'what are they?'

Andy looked. 'Seals,' he said at last. 'There's a colony over there. The salmon farmers hate them.'

Kingdom nodded, sitting back, absorbing the view. He'd never seen anything quite so beautiful. 'You're a lucky man,' he said. 'People would kill for this.'

Andy looked down at him, smiling, saying nothing.

Kingdom glanced at the pile of manuscript, neat lines of type. 'You writing a book, or something?'

'Yes.'

'About what?'

Andy turned away, opening the top half of the stable door, leaning out, suddenly diffident, not wanting to talk about it. When Kingdom asked again, he shrugged. The book was an experiment, he said. He'd based it on a true story. Back in the eighteenth century a ship called the *William* had arrived off Skye. Her master evidently had a contract to rid the island of various miscreants but instead of rounding up the thieves and vagabonds, he'd simply kidnapped a hundred or so locals, bound them hand and foot, and thrown them in the hold. On the plantations of North America, they'd fetch a high price.

Kingdom was looking hard at a line of typescript. 'As what?' he said.

'As slaves.'

'And they went?'

'No. First they escaped from the ship. Then they were recaptured and taken on board again. The captain's name was Davison. He ordered his men to teach them a lesson. Some of them were beaten unconscious. By this point he was ready to sail but the locals staged an insurrection and appealed to the clan chief. They wanted Davison and his employer arrested. The employer was the key to it, a man called Macleod. Without him, Davison would never have arrived in the first place.'

Kingdom was examining a second sheet now, no less attentive. 'So what happened,' he said, 'to Mr Macleod?'

'Nothing.'

'*Nothing?*'

'No.'

'Why not?'

'The magistrate had to answer to the clan chief.'

'And what was his name?'

'Macleod.'

Andy stepped back into the room, closing the stable door behind him. The smile on his face had gone. He looked, if anything, resigned, a man for whom life and history no longer held any surprises.

'I'm afraid you're on your own tomorrow,' he said softly. 'I'm over to Inverness to pick up our friend from London.'

Kingdom awoke in the bunkhouse next morning with the sun in his eyes. He turned over, sheltering beneath a corner of the sheet, wondering whether he could summon the strength to make it through to the lavatories next door. When he tried, easing his long frame over the edge of the bunk, it was an effort to make his legs even bend. Ten hours' sleep had turned the aches and pains into an enveloping stiffness. His legs felt armour-plated, almost alien, as if they belonged to someone else, and both heels were badly blistered.

Kingdom limped across the bare wooden floor. He had the bunkhouse to himself now. Both the girls and the American student had begged lifts from Andy, leaving at first light. By now, they should be almost in Inverness.

Shaved and dressed, Kingdom made his way to the house. One of the dogs met him at the door, jumping up and barking as he pushed past. In the kitchen, he found Dave Gifford. He was on his hands and knees on the tile-patterned lino, mopping away with a floor cloth. He barely glanced up as Kingdom appeared in the open doorway. He was wearing the tracksuit bottoms again with a sweatshirt on top, and his face had an unyielding, determined look, as if someone was trying to distract him. On the rack over the cooking range hung a newly-washed red singlet and a pair of khaki shorts.

'Been running?' Kingdom inquired cheerfully.

'Tomorrow.'

'Up in the mountains?'

'Yeah.'

Kingdom asked about breakfast. He felt, he said, incredibly hungry. The mountains again. Their fault.

'You went up with Andy?'

'That's right.'

'Productive?'

'Immensely.'

Dave Gifford looked up. Kingdom could see the ring at the base of his neck where the leathery windburn stopped and the paler flesh began.

'What about today?' he said. 'You want company? Only Hughie . . .'

Kingdom had found the frying pan now, and the cupboard where Andy kept the eggs. Self-help was clearly one of *An Carraig*'s charms.

'No,' he said quickly, 'I'm off out by myself. Andy was marvellous. Told me everything I needed to know.'

'He did?'

'Yes.' Kingdom poured oil into the frying pan. 'Give or take.'

It was nearly eleven before Kingdom left *An Carraig*. After breakfast, he'd returned to the bunkhouse, packing the day-sack again. Under the sandwiches and the flask of tea, he'd stowed his camera, the mobile telephone, and the address book where he'd stored all the key numbers. Beside it, wrapped in a T-shirt, was the Browning Hi-Power he'd brought over from the mainland. The automatic was fully loaded, and he had two spare clips of ammunition.

Whether he'd need the gun or not, he didn't know. He'd never enjoyed using a weapon, and preferred not to carry one, but just now he had little choice. He'd liked Andy Gifford, no question about it. Unlike his father, he had a patience and a gentle good humour that sat oddly with the lurid psychological profiles that had appeared in *The Citizen*. So how come this man could kill without compunction? What had driven him to stalk his victims with such singlemindedness and dispatch them with such brisk efficiency? How many other Andy Giffords lurked inside the man he thought he'd got to know the previous day?

Kingdom toiled up the path, away from *An Carraig*, easing the stiffness from his limbs, trying to ignore the pain from his blistered heels. For October it was warm and he was wet with sweat by the time he crossed the tiny stream and began the steepest part of the climb, zig-zagging up the mountainside towards the sheltered little pocket where Andy Gifford had made his home. The path here was narrow, steps crudely cut into the peaty earth, and every few yards Kingdom would pause, catching his breath before clambering over yet another outcrop of rock. Coming down, in near darkness, had been a nightmare. Going back up seemed just as hard.

Kingdom had nearly reached the top when it happened. He'd stopped again, half-turning to adjust his day-sack and look at the view. *An Carraig* had disappeared behind the shoulder of the mountain but a haze had settled in the valley and sunlight on the burn glittered through it, a gauzy, almost magical effect. Kingdom gazed at it, tasting the air, savouring the wet, heavy smells of the heather, storing the moment away.

He turned back to resume his push up the hill, bending forwards, all his weight on his back foot. His boot slipped on the wet earth. Instinctively, he leant sideways into the hill, losing his balance, then his other foot gave way and he yelped with pain as the ankle turned. He fell heavily, the injured ankle wedged between a rock and the side of the hill. He distinctly heard something rip, a tearing noise, and the pain shot up his leg, and then he was sitting in a heap, his back to the mountain, his left leg still bent beneath him.

He knew at once that it was serious. When he tried to move, he cried out in pain. For a minute or two he did nothing. Then, very carefully, he began to straighten himself out, first one leg, then – with infinite care – the other. He reached down, unlacing his boot, pulling off the sock. At first sight, it was difficult to judge but when he looked hard he could see the faintest purpling of the flesh beneath the skin. He looked upwards, trying to gauge the distance to the hut. It was in sight now, no more than a stone's throw away. Two zigs and a zag, he thought grimly. Nothing he couldn't handle.

He put the sock back on and tightened the laces on the boot. Soon, he knew, it would start to swell. By that time, with luck, he'd have made it to the hut. Behind the hut, according to Andy, there was a spring. Cold water would be good for it. Cold water would bring out the swelling. Cold water would help.

He began to limp up the track, an awkward hopping movement, his left leg bent at the knee, the toe pointing downwards, giving him enough balance to shuffle slowly upwards. Every step was agony, hot, sharp, scalding pains, and they got worse and worse until he had to stop and rest for a while, fighting the urge to vomit. He was oblivious now to the views. All that mattered was the hut. Getting there, finding the spring, sorting himself out.

It took him the best part of an hour to reach the top of the path. On his hands and knees, he crawled across the grassy plateau towards the hut. He reached up and tried the door. It was unlocked. He pushed it open. Inside, he could smell something sweet and oriental, a joss-like scent. He took off his day-sack and threw it towards the bed. Then he crawled back into the sunshine, skirting the hut. The hut was protected on three sides by the mountain. In the shadow of the rock overhang, Kingdom could hear the bubbling of the spring. It was tiny, the diameter of a bucket, trickling away down a rock gulley behind the hut. The water was clear and clean and icy-cold to the touch. Kingdom took the boot off again, and then the sock, gasping as the pain hit him anew. He lowered his foot ankle-deep in the spring and sat back against the damp moss, waiting for the numbness to take away the pain. After a while, the throbbing began to slow and then stopped altogether and after a while he could feel nothing.

Back in the hut, he made himself comfortable behind the table. The typeface on the small, portable Olympia he'd already recognised. He'd had the calligraphic report on *The Citizen*'s communiqués for weeks now and he was letter-perfect on the fingerprints that Sabbathman's machine had left behind. The tiny pitted indenture on the left-hand rise of the 'o'. The lack of pressure on the capital 'K'. The way the serif on the upper-case 'T' didn't quite stretch the distance. He listed the tell-tales in his head, looking for matching characters in the manuscript on the table. Five minutes' work, and the evidence was overwhelming: the Sabbathman communiqués had been typed on Andy Gifford's machine.

But that, Kingdom knew, was only part of the treasure he'd come to find. Behind the throwaway lines about 'disconnecting' the Chairman of the water company, and 'sticking the knife' in Marcus Wolfe, lay a good deal of thought. Chances were that Andy Gifford might have made a draft or two, trying out ideas, polishing phrases, looking for that exact balance between overt threat and cheerful derision he'd made his trademark. Kingdom went through everything on the table without success. Then he tried the drawers. One was empty. The other was full of photos, each set carefully filed in separate envelopes. Kingdom shook them out, one after the other, recognising the faces and the locations from the files he'd lived with for the past six weeks.

Sir Peter Blanche, snapped at Jersey airport, caught full-face as he sank into the back of his chauffeured Mercedes. The patio of his house on the clifftops at Les Perques, a telephoto shot, 130mm at least, the table in the sunshine set for a continental breakfast, the plump pink folds of *The Financial Times* lying beside the jug of fresh orange juice. Then Bairstow, the civil servant up in Newcastle, a shot through the window of his office, the man bending over a telephone, deep in conversation. Another shot, the turnstile entrance he used at St James' Park, the foreground a mass of black and white scarves. In the third envelope were studies of Clare Baxter's house, shots taken at the height of the summer, the trees in full leaf, flowers everywhere.

Kingdom paused, studying another photo from the same envelope, oblivious now to the pain beginning to seep back into his ankle. Sinah Lane again, but a different house, the one across the road, the one that had been for sale, the one Ethne Feasey had graced with a visit. Kingdom beamed, holding the shot at arm's length, knowing at last that he'd been right. Andy Gifford had holed up in the empty house. A photo taken through the upstairs bedroom window proved it. Line of sight. A perfect view of the shrubs under which Clare Baxter always buried her spare key.

Kingdom leaned back at the desk, pleased with himself. The other two envelopes he barely touched. One was full of shots of Lister. What he looked like. Where he kept his boat. The other contained no photos but a sheaf of press cuttings on the Marcus Wolfe trial. Lister still bothered him: what had victim number four done to earn Andy Gifford's wrath? But the real clincher was the lack of a sixth envelope. Or a seventh. Or an eighth. The attack in Ford Prison had evidently been the last of the Sabbathman killings. With Wolfe dead, the cull was over. Willoughby Grant had indeed fallen to another hand.

Kingdom reached for his day-sack, pulling out the mobile

telephone. He dialled Allder's New Scotland Yard number. His secretary announced that the Commander was in conference but when Kingdom gave his name she apologised at once and went to fetch him. Allder was on the phone in seconds. He sounded out of breath, excitement rather than exertion.

'Listen,' he said, 'you ready for this?' Kingdom had settled full-length on the bed now. His left ankle was twice its normal size. 'That cassette,' Allder was saying. 'The one you gave your lawyer friend.'

'Sir?'

'I did what you said. I gave it to Wren.'

'And?'

'I got the stuff back in four hours. Instant turnround. Gold star service.' He paused, gulping, and Kingdom suddenly had a vision of what he must have been like as a kid, small, pudgy, excitable, bursting with enthusiasm. He was talking about the transcripts now, how far back they went, how they mapped out the entire campaign, a blueprint for the Sabbathman killings.

'Spelling it out?' Kingdom was astonished. 'Names? Dates? Locations?'

'Not quite, no, but near enough.' Allder began to explain. Dave Gifford had evidently dressed it up a little, the names thinly camouflaged, the locations crudely disguised, but the subterfuge was infantile, a code that even Gower Street could break.

'The master plan,' Allder repeated, 'the whole fucking works.'

'But why Ethne Feasey? Why tell her?'

'God knows. He was flexing his muscles, poor man. Trying to impress her.'

'And did he?'

'No. If anything, she was embarrassed.'

'Embarrassed enough to come to us?'

'Obviously not.'

Kingdom nodded, knowing that it must be true. Dave Gifford had fallen in love with Ethne Feasey. She was what he needed, the new woman in his life, someone who knew the meaning of loss. He was nuts about her. Literally. And he'd prove it any way he could. That, though, wasn't the issue. Not as far as the transcripts were concerned.

Kingdom still had the phone to his ear. Allder was talking to someone in the background. He heard a door shut. Then he was back on the line. Now for the big one, Kingdom thought. The million dollar question.

'So who was the customer?' he said carefully. 'Where were these transcripts going? Did Wren tell you?'

'Of course he did.'

'And?'

He heard Allder starting to chuckle. Revenge is a dish best served cold, Kingdom thought. And Allder was clearly enjoying every mouthful.

'Cousins,' he said, 'Mr Hugh fucking Cousins.'

'He had the transcripts all along?'

'From the start.'

'So he knew everything? The whole deal?'

'Before it even started. The tap was part of the "T" Branch surveillance operation on Twyford Down. They were trawling for names. Dave Gifford just turned up in the net. Pure chance. Gave them the whole thing on a plate.'

'Shit.' Kingdom whistled softly. 'And Cousins let it run? Is that what you're saying?'

'Yes.'

'Why?'

'God knows. We're still working on that.' He paused, the old briskness creeping back. 'Thanks for the address, by the way. Queen's Gate Gardens. Shame you didn't tell us who lived there.'

'Why?'

'They destroyed the place. Took it apart.'

'Yeah?' Kingdom grinned, trying to imagine the artists from the A-T Squad with their sledge-hammers and their hydraulic jacks getting to work on the cool grey spaces of Cousins' flat. 'So what did they find? Any maps?'

'No.'

'Petrol receipts?'

'One. From a BP place. Near Leeming.'

'Where's that?'

'On the A1.'

'Anything else?'

'Yes,' Allder was chuckling again, 'a Lee Enfield Enforcer. SAS-issue. One shot expended from the magazine. He'd parked it in his airing cupboard. If that's not arrogance, I'd like to know what fucking is.'

Kingdom nodded, grunting in agreement. The day-sack was on the bed beside him and he could see the dull metal butt of his own weapon, still wrapped in yesterday's T-shirt.

'So where is he?' Kingdom inquired, 'our Mr Cousins?'

'No one knows.'

'Have you tried Gower Street?'

'Of course. They're saying he's away. Operationally involved is the phrase they're using.' He paused. 'How's it going, by the way? You OK up there?'

Ten minutes later, in agony again, Kingdom was crawling back to the spring behind the hut. Another immersion returned the numbness to his ankle and when he looked at it closely he began to wonder exactly how serious the damage was. Already, it was mid-afternoon. Getting back down the path to the valley floor was out of the question. In a couple of hours, it would be dark.

He returned to the hut on all fours, hauling himself into the chair at the table. From here he had a perfect view of *An Carraig*, although it was several minutes before he realised that the minibus was back on the hardstanding beside the huts. He reached for the binoculars, sweeping the area, coming to rest on the tiny white-washed house. The front door was open, one of the dogs backing out into the sunshine. Its tail was wagging and the loudest of the barks drifted up through the still air. Kingdom adjusted the focus a little. Seconds later, Dave Gifford emerged. He was wearing trousers and a blazer. He'd even run a comb through his hair. He turned, making a gesture with his left hand, and another figure stepped out of the house. He was taller, younger, blonder. He was wearing jeans and a suede jacket. He was laughing at some joke or other, looking round, enjoying himself.

Kingdom froze at the table, recognising the smile, the easy manner, the attentive nod. The pub, he thought. The pub round the corner from the Home Office. The pub where he'd spent half the evening watching Annie in conversation with a total stranger. This same man below him now. The way he'd played her. The way he'd let her blather on. The angler with the fish. The musician with the prize instrument. What he'd done to her. Where it had all ended. Allder had been right. His phrase. His description. Mr Hugh fucking Cousins.

Kingdom watched for a second or two longer, making quite sure, then he put the binoculars down and reached for the day-sack, pulling out the Browning, checking the magazine, working the slider backwards and forwards, knowing at last what he had to do.

NINETEEN

It was dark by the time Andy Gifford returned to the hut. Kingdom heard his footsteps outside and then a pause as he caught his breath after the long climb. Kingdom was still on the bed, lying full length, his left leg propped up on the day-sack. The only time he'd moved in the last two hours was to call Dave Gifford at the house below. He'd told him he'd walked as far as a village called Elgol. He'd got the name from a map on Andy's table. He said he'd be staying until next day. Then he'd be back.

Now, Kingdom reached for the Browning in the darkness. The door opened and he could see the outline of Andy Gifford's slight frame silhouetted against the starlight. The door closed again and Kingdom waited until Andy had found the matches for the Tilley lamp.

'It's me, Andy,' he said quietly, 'and I have a weapon.'

Andy paused for no more than a second. Then he put the lamp on the desk and lit it. Kingdom stirred, the heavy automatic steady in his right hand.

'On the table,' he said, 'on top of the typewriter.'

In the warm yellow light of the Tilley, he could see Andy examining the ID he'd left earlier. The photograph would put it beyond doubt. Alan Kingdom. Special Branch. New Scotland Yard. Andy looked round for the first time, ignoring the gun.

'What's wrong with your leg?'

'It's the ankle. I think it's broken.'

'How come?'

'I fell. This morning. On the way up.'

'You've been here since this morning?'

'Yes.'

Andy nodded, looking at the table again. Kingdom hadn't bothered returning the photos to the drawer. They were neatly arranged beside the typewriter, each set in their separate envelopes, chronological order, Blanche at the top, Marcus Wolfe at the bottom.

'You've been through all these?'

'Yes.'

'Been up in the roof at all?'

Andy indicated the trap door in the ceiling. Kingdom had made one attempt to lever himself up, using the chair for support, but had given up after the first fall.

'No,' he said, 'I thought you'd save me the trouble.'

'What do you want to know?'

'What's up there.'

'You know what's up there.' He paused. 'The guns are up there.'

'Thank you.'

Andy smiled, saying nothing. Finally he laughed, the softest of chuckles, and reached for the bag he'd brought up from *An Carraig*. Kingdom watched him carefully, levelling the automatic at his head, but Andy ignored the warning.

'Don't worry,' he said, 'even if I had a weapon, I wouldn't shoot a cripple.'

He produced a tin of tobacco and some Rizla papers. On the window-sill, beside the binoculars, was a small carved wooden box that Kingdom had noticed earlier. Andy opened it, removing a lump of something black. Then he began to roll two cigarettes, crumbling the black resin onto the tobacco.

'How bad's the ankle?' he asked, not looking up.

'Bad. Hurts like a bastard.'

'Pity.' He lifted the first of the roll-ups and moistened the edge of the paper with his tongue. 'I haven't got anything fancy but this might help.'

He stepped across the hut and dropped the cigarette beside Kingdom's hand. Kingdom left it where it lay, the gun still trained on Andy as he returned to the table and lit his own cigarette. The bitter-sweet smell of the cannabis drifted across the room.

Andy picked a shred of tobacco from his upper lip. 'Am I under arrest,' he said at last, 'or what?'

Kingdom didn't answer. He hadn't smoked dope since Belfast. Annie, he thought, and those mysterious little matchboxes she'd acquire from an unnamed source at Stormont Castle. The stuff had been sensational, Dutch origin, the softest cosh in the world.

Andy was still waiting for a reply. 'So why did you do it?' Kingdom asked him at last. 'That's what I really want to know.'

'Is this on the record? Are you making notes, or what?'

'No,' Kingdom shook his head, 'just asking, that's all.'

Andy nodded slowly, upending the lid from the tobacco tin to catch the falling ash, and Kingdom could see the disappointment in his face. He and Kingdom had been friends. They'd been in the mountains together. They'd walked and talked. They'd compared notes. And now this.

'Why do you want to know?' he said at last. 'What difference would it make?'

'Are you denying it?'

'The editor bloke, definitely. The rest, no.'

'You killed them?'

'Yes.'

'And sent the notes afterwards?'

'Obviously.'

'For Dave? For your dad? Was that it?'

Andy studied him a moment, amused. Then he shook his head. 'No,' he said, 'Dave had nothing to do with it.'

'But he knew what you were up to? He approved?'

Andy was watching him now, reluctant to go any further, refusing to taint his father with any confession of his own. Kingdom put the gun down, settling back against the pillow.

'Tell me about Dave,' he said softly, 'and the woman, Ethne.'

For the first time, Kingdom took Andy by surprise. He could see it in his face, the way he ducked his head.

'Ethne Feasey?' he said.

'Yes.' Kingdom paused. 'They met up here, didn't they? Wasn't that it?'

Andy studied him for a long time, toying with some private

505

decision. Finally, he nodded. 'Yes,' he said, 'he tried to get her into bed. Gave it his very best shot. Wouldn't take no for an answer.'

'And?'

Andy shrugged. 'He fell in love with the woman. He found out what had happened to her, all the stuff about her business, and the bank pulling out, and her husband killing himself, and that did it for him. Turned her into something really special.'

'And he meant it?'

'Absolutely. Dave can't lie. It's not in his make-up. What he does, he does body and soul. With Dave you get the works. Nothing held back. He's a puppy like that.' He smiled to himself. 'Daft old bugger.'

Kingdom said nothing for a moment, watching the shadows dancing across Andy's face. He could see the love the man had for his father, a fondness that was all the more complex for being so clear-eyed.

'So Dave must have known,' he pointed out.

'Known what?'

'About the killings. You and that list of yours. Blanche. Bairstow. The rest of them . . .'

Andy frowned, trying to avoid a straight answer. Finally, he gave up. 'Sure,' he admitted, 'Dave knew.'

'And did he approve?'

'No, I told you. He did nothing.'

'That wasn't my question. I asked you whether he approved.' He paused. 'Approval's not a crime, not in my book. I'm just curious, that's all. I want to know how he felt about it all. Whether he thought you were crazy. Whether he thought you were wrong.'

'Dave?' Andy shook his head. 'He was for it. Definitely.'

'Why?'

'Because . . .' He shrugged. 'The business over the bridge just finished him. He thinks the whole thing's a fix. He thinks they're all spivs, in it for the money. He says the only thing they'll ever understand is the bullet. If he had his way, I'd be doing seven a week. Starting with the cabinet.'

'That picture. The one in *The Citizen* —'

Andy nodded. 'Dave's idea. He'd been sounding off about the defence bloke for a while, the minister, something to do with getting rid of regimental bands. Dave was always big on music. It meant a lot to him. Apparently the guy was going to some festival or other. Down in Kent. He wanted me to sort him out.'

'Kill him? The Minister of Defence?'

'Yes. He didn't mean it, of course. And I wouldn't have done it, either.'

'Why not?'

'Too public. Too much security. I'm not that crazy . . .'

'But you're saying that Dave sent the picture? To *The Citizen*?'

'Yes,' he said, 'I did the words but the photo was Dave's idea. Made his day when they printed it. Bought six copies for his scrap book. Down at the shop by the ferry. Newsagent was amazed.'

Kingdom closed his eyes a moment. 'So Dave approved,' he mused aloud, 'but who planned it?'

'I did, the nuts and bolts. Leave it to Dave and we'd have been banged up in seconds. He's great with the blacks and whites but fucking useless with the rest.'

'So you did the recces?' The preparations? Everything else?'

'Yes.' He nodded at the photos on the table. 'You've seen the evidence. Must have. You weren't up here to watch the seals . . .' He paused. 'Were you?'

Kingdom was inspecting his ankle again. 'No,' he said drily, 'I wasn't.' He looked up. 'So Dave *did* approve. Is that what you're saying?'

'Yes.' Andy nodded. 'Approved, but that's all. He thought they were animals, scum. He thought they had it coming to them. Like I say, the rest was down to me. Planning, reconnaissance,' he smiled, 'execution.'

'And you enjoyed it?'

'I did it.'

'What does that mean?'

'It was a job. Where I come from, you just get on with it. You're trained that way. You pick up certain skills, and when the time comes . . .' He levelled two fingers at an imaginary spot in the darkness beyond the window. 'Whammo!'

Kingdom watched him for a moment. The book, he thought. The Falklands. Lots of whammo. And lots of other things that had nothing to do with this neat, orderly dispatch of five sitting targets.

Like slaughter, real slaughter, and shredded flesh, and the smoking remains of very close friends.

Kingdom reached for the cigarette and Andy smiled again, tossing him the matches. Kingdom lit the roll-up, lying back, taking down the first deep lungful of smoke, holding it there, wondering whether it would get as far as his ankle.

'What did Dave say when he read the book?' he asked at last.

'What book?'

'The Falklands book you wrote.'

Andy frowned. 'He hated it,' he said finally. 'That was a real problem. Serial killing was fine by him, as long as I slotted the right blokes. But Longdon, shit, he went ape.'

'Why?'

'He thought I'd been disloyal.'

'To the regiment?'

'To my mates.'

Kingdom took another long pull at the cigarette. Already, the cannabis was beginning to work, stealing through him, relaxing him, loosening his grip a little.

'Dave was wrong,' he said quietly.

'You've read it?' Andy was staring at him now. 'How come?'

'I thought it was important.'

'It is. Except no fucker will give it shelf space.'

'They can't. It's not on sale.'

'That's what I meant.'

There was something new in Andy's voice, a bitterness that Kingdom hadn't heard before. We're getting closer, he thought.

'So what did Dave object to,' he said at last, 'specifically?'

Andy was brooding now, his elbows on his knees, his head bent low. 'He thought I had no right to say what I said. The way I said it. That's what it boiled down to. That's what he really meant. He thought it was none of my business. He thought I should never have started the fucking thing, let alone get it into print.'

'Why?'

'Because war's supposed to be a secret, what really happens, what it's really like. People don't need that in their lives. They shouldn't know. They shouldn't be told. That's Dave's line.'

'Shouldn't be told what?'

'The truth.'

'About what?'

'About war.'

'You mean that war? The Falklands? Longdon?'

'I mean all war. Any war. War, period. Vietnam. Bosnia. Normandy. The Somme. Makes no difference. Dave knows that and so does anyone else who's ever been there.'

'Including the politicians?'

'You're joking. They want to lock us up. Can you believe that? For killing the enemy?'

Kingdom lifted the cigarette again, remembering the inquiry now under way, the team of detectives dispatched to the Falklands, the holes they were digging on Longdon, looking for dead Argentinians.

'It's murder,' Kingdom pointed out, 'killing men in cold blood.'

Andy stirred, the smile back on his face.

'And war?' he said, 'What's that?'

'That's different.'

'No, it's not. It's just the same. It's murder. That's the problem. That's Dave's problem. No one ever talks about it. No one ever admits it. Everyone insists on keeping this silly fucking secret. War's horrible. War's obscene. No one survives it. Not even Dave. You either end up dead or maimed inside. And you know what?'

'What?'

'Maimed inside's probably worse.'

Kingdom said nothing, letting the phrase sink in. For the first time he realised that Andy had probably been through some kind of post-traumatic stress counselling. Not that it seemed to have done him any good.

'So you killed for that?' he said at last. 'Blanche? Bairstow? The rest of them? You killed them because war is so horrible? Is that what you're saying?'

'I killed because no one listens. I killed to make a point.'

'About what?'

'The killing. Longdon. My mates. What we've all been through.'

'So why didn't you say so? In those notes of yours?'

'You're joking.' He looked up. 'I'd never have got off Jersey. Even your lot would have twigged. Crazed ex-Para in crusade for peace.' He paused. 'I thought I was close to the bone as it was. The line about Killing Zones.'

Kingdom returned the smile, remembering the phrase from the first of the communiques. '*Welcome to the KZ*', it had begun.

'So how come you chose those targets?' he said after a while. 'I understand Blanche. He'd have come from Dave, directly or indirectly. But what about the rest?'

Andy shrugged. 'We've had a lot of people through here the last couple of years. You do a lot of talking, really get to know people. It's almost part of the deal. The hills. The open air. People have a lot to get off their chests these days. Disappointment. Anger. Frustration. Believe me, there's a lot of pain around. You'd be amazed.'

'And you listened?'

'Sure.' He nodded. 'Bairstow came from a bloke over in Aberdeen. He ran a marine engineering company. Bairstow had screwed him on some tender bid or other. He was at it all the time.'

'And you decided to punish him?'

'Yes.'

'By killing him?'

'Yes.'

'Bit extreme, wasn't it?'

'Not really, not from where I sat. I wanted five decent deaths. Five headlines. Five bodies. Bairstow measured up nicely.'

'Was the bloke from Aberdeen in on it?'

'Fuck no, of course not.'

Kingdom eyed the remains of his cigarette. The pain in his ankle had definitely eased.

'The MP on Hayling Island, Carpenter . . .' He looked up. 'Was that from a doctor? Jo Hubbard? Did she talk about him? Put you onto him?'

'Yes. He was a pillock, too. Wonderful choice. Inspired.'

'And Marcus Wolfe?'

'Dave's idea. Though he was too pissed at the time to remember.'

510

'And what about Lister? The one you blew up? What had he done?'

Andy didn't answer for a moment. The wind was sighing through cracks in the window frame. Finally, Andy began to roll another cigarette.

'We've got an instructor up here, bloke called Hughie. Really nice guy. Genuine. You've met him. He used to work for Lister, down in Devon, replacing water mains up on Dartmoor. He had some experiences after they took the company private. It's quite a complicated story but I'm sure he'd tell you if you asked.' He paused. 'He hated the man, and everything he stood for. He thought it was evil, selling water for profit.'

'So you killed him? This Lister?'

'Sure.'

'And did that help?'

'Help what?'

'Help make the point you wanted to make.'

'Sort of . . .' He hesitated, his head down again, concentrating on the cigarette. Then he shrugged. 'OK, I suppose I could have done it the proper way, Dave's way, written a letter to the papers, got hold of my MP, all that shit, but it's pointless, no one ever listens.'

'How do you know?'

'Because I tried. I wrote a book. And what happened? They binned it.' He leaned back in the chair, the cigarette between his lips, gazing up at the trapdoor in the ceiling. 'See,' he said at last, 'see what they made me do?'

Later, past midnight, Kingdom outlined the deal. In the morning, Andy would talk to Dave Gifford and ask him to send Cousins up to the hut. En route to the hut, somewhere on the path, Cousins would be shot.

Andy blinked. 'Why?' he said.

Kingdom refused to explain. He said he'd do it with Andy's rifle. The one with the sniperscope. The one in the roof.

Andy was staring at him now. '*You'll* do it?'

'Yes.'

'Who is he? This bloke?'

'It doesn't matter.'

'Who says it doesn't matter?'

·Kingdom began to laugh. 'Why the conscience,' he said, 'all of a sudden?'

'It's not conscience. I'm just curious, that's all. My hut. My mountain. My gun.'

Kingdom shook his head. 'It doesn't matter,' he said again, 'but it's well-earned, believe me.'

'Sure,' Andy said, 'but what happens afterwards? To me?'

'Nothing.' Kingdom eyed the table. 'You'll give me the type-writer and the photos. And the rifle, of course.' He paused. 'Where's the weapon you used on Carpenter?'

'In the roof.'

'I'll need that, too.'

'Sure, but then what?'

'Nothing,' he repeated, 'I'll take the gear and that's the last you'll hear of it.'

'You'll just go?'

'Yes.'

'And all this?' Andy gestured at the space between them, the remains of the roll-ups, three hours of steady confession.

Kingdom shrugged, easing his long body on the bed. 'Never happened,' he said briefly.

Andy nodded, taking it in, trying to understand it. Finally, he gave up, voicing the obvious question. 'How do I know you're not lying?' he said.

Kingdom had his eyes closed now, the gun abandoned on the bed beside him. 'You don't,' he yawned, 'but don't insult me by asking.'

Next morning, early, Andy talked to Dave on the two-way radio he kept in the bag he'd brought up the previous evening. Because the hut formed part of the *An Carraig* estate, Cousins should make time to come up and look at it. He broke off, listening to his father on the radio. The conversation finally over, he sat at the table, staring glumly at the rain driving in from the sea.

'He'll be up around ten,' he said. 'He's talking serious money. Dave says he's definitely interested. Thinks we might tie the deal up by the weekend.'

'I doubt it,' Kingdom said drily.

'Why's that?'

'He works for MI5. And he's probably here to take you both out.'

Andy looked round, astonished, the expression of a man who's finally lost his place in the script. 'You kidding?'

'No,' Kingdom smiled grimly, peering at his ankle, 'far from it.'

They waited an hour for the rain to ease. Andy had listened to the forecast the previous afternoon and thought the front might be through by mid-morning. When nothing had happened by nine o'clock, Andy unlocked the trapdoor in the ceiling and clambered up into the roof space. Kingdom stayed below, supporting himself on the chair, reaching for the gun as Andy handed it down. It was a Steyr G69, an Austrian bolt-action rifle much favoured by snipers, one of three models the ballistics people at New Scotland Yard had identified as Sabbathman's likely weapon.

Andy levered himself down from the roofspace. He had an automatic pistol in his hand. It looked like a Walther. He offered it to Kingdom.

'You said you wanted it,' he pointed out, 'last night.'

'I did.' Kingdom nodded. 'Leave it in the day-sack.'

They went out into the rain. Visibility was appalling, no more than a couple of hundred yards, and *An Carraig* was lost in the grey murk below. Kingdom hobbled to the top of the path, looking down, wondering quite how to set the trap. Andy stood beside him, rain dripping off the peaked hood of his anorak.

'You know anything about these?' he said. 'Ever used one?' He was carrying the Steyr.

Kingdom shook his head. 'Never,' he said.

Andy disappeared. When he came back, he was carrying a tin of white paint and a small brush. He set off down the path and Kingdom watched him as he danced down through the dripping heather. For a moment he was lost from sight, then he reappeared again, much further down. Finally he stopped, looking back up the

513

hill. Beside him, invisible if you were climbing the path, was a low outcrop of rock. He put the tin on the ground and levered off the lid. Then he dabbed a splash of white paint on the rock and wiped the brush on the wet grass. Minutes later he was back beside Kingdom, picking up the rifle and spreadeagling himself on the sodden turf. He brought the Steyr to bear on the rock, making tiny adjustments to the notched ring on top of the sniperscope. When he was happy with the range, he told Kingdom to lie down beside him. Kingdom got down on all fours, then lay flat on his belly. The pain and stiffness in his ankle seemed to have spread upwards through his leg, making any movement an effort.

Andy handed him the rifle and told him to line up on the white paint. Kingdom did so, easing the gun through a blur of heather and rock until he found the sighting mark. The optics on the gun were astonishing, the splash of white paint filling the sniperscope. Kingdom held his breath a moment, trying to steady the gun.

'Here.' Andy took the gun and adjusted the support strap, lengthening it for Kingdom's long frame. Then he looped it around Kingdom's left arm, showing him how to use the strap to tension the gun into his shoulder. 'It's got to be part of you,' he muttered, 'it's got to feel like you've just grown the bloody thing.'

Kingdom practised with the weapon, listening to Andy at his side. How to breathe. What kind of pressure to put on the trigger. Why there was always more time than you thought. At the end of the lesson, Kingdom looked up. He'd come to find Sabbathman. He'd come to put an end to the killing. And now Sabbathman was teaching him how to kill.

'How many bullets?' he asked, patting the box magazine.

Andy grinned down at him. 'If you miss at this range,' he said, 'you're fucked anyway.'

They moved into cover. Andy found a hollow behind the ridge that overlooked the track, no more than five yards from the head of the path. He waded into the heather, returning with handfuls of the stuff, making Kingdom take up the prone position again. Then he dressed him with the heather, checking from the path time and again before he was happy with the camouflage. If Cousins came from the kind of background Kingdom had described, then he was leaving nothing to chance.

The rain began to ease a little, the wind shifting to the north-west, and Kingdom lay beneath the sodden heather, shivering with cold. At one point, Andy offered to make a brew. The camping stove in the hut had already given them a rudimentary breakfast and there were two tea-bags left, but Kingdom shook his head. He could think of nothing but Cousins. Cousins was there for the taking. Unlike Annie, it would be the cleanest of kills.

They waited for over an hour while the mist slowly lifted and by the time Andy spotted the figure climbing up from the valley floor, the rain had stopped.

'There,' he whispered, 'ten o'clock. About four hundred metres.'

Kingdom wiped his face and peered down the hill. At first he saw nothing. Then he recognised the figure striding up the path towards him. Cousins was wearing a long, green waterproof. There was a hood attached to the collar but as Kingdom watched he reached up and pushed it back off his face. On his head, beneath the hood, was an old green cap-comforter.

Kingdom heard Andy stifling a laugh. 'It's Dave's,' he muttered, 'Dave must have lent it to him. Put a hole through that and he'll go barmy.'

Kingdom ignored him, easing up the rifle, sliding his forearm through the sling. Tracking Cousins through the sniperscope wasn't as easy as it seemed. The optics were almost too powerful, the image too big. For the first time he began to wonder whether doing this himself was such a great idea.

Andy was aware at once of his uncertainty. 'You want me to do it?'

Kingdom peered over the sights. Cousins was moving fast. In a minute or so he'd reach the rock with the splash of white paint. Already it was too late for Andy to take the rifle. Any movement now would simply give them away.

Kingdom shook his head, settling behind the gun again. Another thirty yards, he thought. Then he'll pause by the rock, turn for the next stretch upwards. He tracked the big, loping stride through the sniperscope, tilting slowly upwards, trying to pin Cousins' head in his sights. For the briefest moment, he caught the expression on the man's face, eager, keen-eyed, his breath clouding on the cold air, his cheeks pinked with the climb.

The rock was closer now, only seconds away. First pressure, Andy had said, only the slightest touch, then the shallowest of breaths, nothing dramatic, no hurry, and finally, when the moment came, just a gentle squeeze on the trigger. Kingdom was sweating now, he could feel it, and the warmth of his breath clouded the glass in the sniperscope. He peered over the sights, wondering exactly how far Cousins had got, whether or not he had time to wipe the scope, then he saw the man below him, already there, already at the rock, already turning for that final stretch upward.

'Do it,' Andy hissed, 'just fucking do it.'

Kingdom bent to the scope again, seeing nothing, firing blindly. The plastic stock jumped backwards into his shoulder and the bark of the single bullet rolled away over the hills. He felt Andy getting up beside him, pulling the rifle out of his hands, and he looked up at him, rolling over on the wet peat, the unvoiced question answered.

'Missed,' Andy said, 'you missed him.'

Andy worked another bullet into the chamber, crouching low. Then he skirted the top of the plateau, past the hut, and disappeared into the rocks above. Kingdom watched, helpless. Cousins would have a weapon. In the SAS he'd have spent years at this kind of game, perfecting his fieldcraft, honing his concealment skills, preparing for the moment when his life might depend on them. In the shape of Andy Gifford, that moment had now arrived.

Kingdom stared down the mountainside, knowing that he had to do something, make a decision, join this small, vicious, intensely private war that had so suddenly erupted. He closed his eyes a moment, gritting his teeth, then he tried to stand up. As soon as he put weight on his ankle, the pain made him gasp out loud. He did his best to ignore it, limping up through the heather, his body at a half-crouch. In the hut, he retrieved the big Browning, checking the magazine and working the first round into the chamber. The click of the slider sounded deafening in the windless silence.

Outside again, Kingdom edged carefully round the hut. To the rear, beyond the spring, the mountain shouldered upwards, a

tumble of bracken and moss-covered boulders. Height, he thought.
I need height. I need to get above the action, to look down on
whatever is happening. He began to scramble upwards, knees and
elbows, moving as carefully as he could, trying not to dislodge
loose rocks. Now and again he'd pause, listening for some tiny
noise, some clue to what might be happening, but apart from the
bubble of the spring water and the more distant murmur of the sea
there was nothing.

Soon the hut had disappeared, veiled by the mist. To the left,
in a gulley amongst the rocks, there was a rough path scabbed with
sheep droppings. The path eased upwards, the shallowest of
gradients. At the end of the path, an outcrop of rock loomed black
in the enveloping greyness. Kingdom hesitated a moment. Taking
the path would put more distance between himself and where he
estimated Cousins and Andy Gifford might be, but that didn't
matter. Height, he told himself. More height.

Beside the rocky outcrop, sweating now, he stopped again.
Fronds of dripping heather still clung to his anorak and he
wondered vaguely about removing them. He leant against the rock,
taking the weight off his ankle, pulling at the heather, trying to
imagine how Andy was coping. He'd know the terrain, every inch
of it. He'd know the places to avoid, the hidden, shadowed foxholes
where Cousins might be waiting for him. He'd be like an animal,
patrolling his territory, scenting his prey. He'd doubtless take his
time, working his way upwind, waiting for Cousins to make a
mistake, show himself, and when that moment came then Annie's
real killer, the one who'd sent her to her death, would be history.

Kingdom looked down at the Browning, warmed by the
thought, and he was still smiling when he heard the gunshots.
There were two, same weapon, the flat, sharp bark of the Steyr.
The reports pinballed around the mountain, bouncing from rockface to rockface, making it difficult for Kingdom to judge where
they came from. Somewhere back towards the hut, he thought.
Somewhere down below. Two bullets. Cousins winged, wounded,
maybe even dead.

Beyond the rocky outcrop, the path disappeared into the mist,
hugging the mountainside, circling back towards the sea. Kingdom
set off again, moving as fast as his ankle would permit, oblivious of

the pain now, wanting only to see Andy, make his peace, apologise for fucking it all up. Five kills, he thought, and not a single mistake. Then, thanks to Kingdom, this. Andy had been right all along. Attend to every single detail yourself. Trust nobody.

Kingdom stumbled on. The path rose before him, bare earth, worn rocks. Disorientated, he was about to stop again when he found himself on the edge of a shallow drop. Below him was a hollow protected from the worst of the weather, a bowl scooped from the flank of the mountain. A wind from nowhere stirred the wet heather, parting the curtains of mist, revealing the shapes of two men. The larger stood astride the smaller. A small, neat automatic dangled from one hand and he had his back to the ridge where Kingdom crouched. From thirty feet, Kingdom could hear every word.

'Your father says you were here,' Cousins was saying, 'all weekend.'

Andy Gifford lay face down, one leg twisted at a strange angle, one cheek pressed to the black earth, and Kingdom knew at once that he was injured. Cousins mentioned the weekend again, turning the comment into a question, and when Andy didn't answer, he put his foot on the back of Andy's knee, leaning slightly forward as he did so. At the first real pressure, Andy's whole body convulsed, as if Cousins had applied some kind of electric shock. The kneecap, Kingdom thought. He's smashed the kneecap. One bullet at least. Probably two.

Cousins was bending down now, his voice more urgent, every word, every intonation clearly audible. 'So?' he queried. 'Am I right?'

Andy nodded. 'Yes,' he whispered.

'And who else? Who else was there?' Cousins paused. 'Those girls in the van? At Inverness? Were they there?'

'Yes.'

'And the American?'

'Yes.'

Cousins stood up again, nodding, and Kingdom withdrew a little, sinking onto his haunches, recognising the exchange for what it was, Cousins adding more names to his list. The two girls and the American would know that Andy couldn't possibly have killed

Willoughby Grant. Another little problem for the new Controller of 'T' Branch.

Cousins stooped a moment and picked something up, tossing it to one side, and it was several seconds before Kingdom recognised the Steyr. Crouching beside Andy, Cousins had put the muzzle of the automatic to the back of his other knee.

'Who else?'

'No one.'

'I said who else?'

'Nobody.'

'You're lying. I know you're lying.' He paused. 'Last time of asking, Gifford. Who else?'

Kingdom had the Browning up now, both hands, waiting for Cousins to move. Crouched beside Andy, the two men were in line. Up on his feet, Kingdom might manage a decent headshot with no risk of hitting Andy. That, he knew, was his only option.

Cousins shifted his weight, the automatic still nuzzling the back of Andy's knee.

'Travis?' he said. 'Man calling himself Travis?'

Andy shook his head. 'No.'

'Gordon Travis?'

'No.'

Kingdom saw the automatic jump in Cousins' hand, heard the crack of the gunshot, watched the frayed denim around the new wound darken. Andy hadn't made a sound. For the first time, there was a hint of impatience in Cousins' voice. 'You're telling me your father's making it up? There was no Gordon Travis? Tall guy? Short hair? Up from London?'

'No.'

'And you didn't take him up the mountain? This Travis? Day before yesterday?'

Andy shook his head, an almost imperceptible movement, his eyes closed now, and Kingdom marvelled at the man's obstinacy, expending his last few ounces of courage in an act of simple defiance. He'd taken Cousins on, and for whatever reason, he'd lost. Yet even now, both knees smashed, he was claiming a kind of victory.

Kingdom stood up. He had a rock in his left hand. He tossed

it as hard as he could, beyond Cousins, watching it clatter amongst the loose pebbles on the other side of the hollow. Cousins reacted at once, moving sideways, away from Andy. A second later Kingdom fired, then again, feeling the big automatic kicking upwards in his hands, knowing at once that he'd missed. Cousins was a blur, footsteps on the stony ground. Then he'd gone.

Kingdom gazed after him, imagining shapes in the mist, the sweat cold on his face. He called to Andy. There was no answer. He called again. Then he peered over the edge of the drop, wondering about the skirt of loose scree. Finally he sat down and pushed himself off, sliding down on a raft of moving stones, holding the big automatic away from his body. He came to rest at the foot of the slope and struggled to his feet, limping across to Andy. Andy hadn't moved. Blood had pooled around both knees, the flesh pulped beneath the shredded denim, and Kingdom shuddered at the implications. He'd seen injuries like this in Belfast. Short of a miracle, Andy's days in the mountains were over.

Andy began to stir, one eye opening. He groaned as Kingdom knelt beside him and muttered something that Kingdom didn't catch. Kingdom stood up, pulling off his anorak and draping it across Andy's legs. As he did so, Andy's hand found his. This time, Kingdom understood every word.

'Shoot the fucker,' Andy whispered. 'Kill him.'

Kingdom nodded, looking down. It had started to rain again and Andy's tongue was out, licking the moisture from his lips. His face had turned the colour of putty and he was beginning to shake with cold and shock. Kingdom squeezed his hand, searching the gloom for some sign of Cousins, finding nothing. The man had simply disappeared. Andy was peering up at him now, bewildered, but Kingdom was still watching the line of rocks beyond the edge of the hollow, waiting for Cousins to make a move. The rain, if anything, had got heavier.

He glanced down at Andy a moment. Andy was trying to tell him something, his lips moving, his eyes dulled with pain. Kingdom knelt quickly beside him.

'What is it?' He put a hand to Andy's cheek, comforting him.

Andy was trying to move, levering his body up on one elbow,

his breath coming in shallow gasps, a single word forming and re-
forming. 'There,' he managed at last, 'there.'

'Where?'

'There.'

He made a vague gesture, a limp movement of one arm before
collapsing and Kingdom suddenly understood what it was he was
trying to say. He heard the voice first, pleasant, cultured, matter-
of-fact.

'Put the gun down,' it said, 'and then stand up.'

Kingdom did what he was told, his ankle throbbing.

'Turn round.'

Kingdom executed a clumsy pirouette. Cousins was five yards
away. He must have circled the hollow, emerging from the rocks
behind them. He held the automatic in both hands, his arms out
straight in front of his body, the classic pose.

'Move to your left.'

'This guy needs—' Kingdom nodded at Andy.

'Just do it.'

The voice had hardened, Cousins making tiny leftward movements with the gun. Kingdom didn't move, watching Cousins,
oblivious now to Andy. The cassette, he thought. The things they'd
done to her. Her screams on the tape. The choking noise she'd
made at the end.

'Tell me about Annie Meredith,' he said thickly. 'Tell me how
she died. Tell me how you did it. And for fuck's sake tell me why.'

'I said move.'

'No.'

Cousins took half a step forward, dropping into a low crouch.

Kingdom stared down at him, not caring any more. 'Why?' he
said softly. 'What did she matter to you?'

Cousins didn't answer. The bullet took Kingdom in the leg
beneath his right knee, shattering the bone, and he folded onto the
wet bracken, hearing the sound of his own scream echoing away
into the mist. Kingdom's hand found the wound and he began to
curse, the blood already running down his calf. Cousins had
retrieved the big Browning. He was bending over Andy, the way
you might check whether someone was asleep. He paused a

moment, long enough to see his eyes flicker open, then he put two bullets into his head, high above his ear, before thumbing the safety catch forward and pushing the Browning into the waistband of his jeans. Kingdom lay on the ground, staring at Andy. The bullets must have impacted on the rocky ground, ricocheting upwards again, shattering his skull. Where his face had been, there was nothing but blood, and bone, and gobbets of grey brain tissue.

'Get up.'

Kingdom didn't move, aware of Cousins bending over him, hauling him upright. The man was immensely strong. Kingdom looked at him for a second or two, still in shock, then reached out, a gesture of supplication, asking for support, both hands finding a hold on the collar of Cousins' waterproof, and Cousins hesitated for a moment, long enough for Kingdom to pull as hard as he could, driving his forehead into Cousins' face. He heard the gristly sound of Cousins' nose breaking and a gasp of pain as the big man sprang backwards, out of range. Cousins' automatic lay between them on the black earth. Cousins kicked it away and then retrieved it, one hand to his face. When he spoke, the blood bubbled pinkly around his lips.

'Foolish,' he said, 'very foolish.'

There was another path back to the hut, winding down the side of the mountain beneath a rocky overhang dripping with rain. Kingdom moved slowly, one step at a time, trying to support his shattered leg as best he could, and Cousins followed behind him, pushing him forward when he paused to throw up. Only when they were back beside the hut did he call a halt, bending briefly to the spring and sluicing his own face with water. Kingdom collapsed on the wet peat, his leg folded beneath him, wiping the vomit from his sodden sweater. The last few minutes had numbed him. If he felt anything, it was a curious sense of detachment. What might happen next was irrelevant. All that mattered now was Annie. How she had died. And why.

'Just tell me,' he muttered, 'just tell me why you did it.'

Cousins was still mopping his face, examining the handkerchief as he did so. Hearing the question, he frowned. 'I didn't do it.'

'No. But you let it happen. You sent her. I know you did.'

Cousins gave his face a final wipe and pocketed the handkerchief. 'She was front-line. Operational. Her choice, not mine. Hard to keep someone like that behind a desk.'

'You're saying she volunteered? That afternoon?'

'Of course. She was desperate for . . .' He shrugged, wiping his hands on his jeans. 'Battle honours.'

'But it didn't work out. She was set up.'

'So it seems.'

'So someone must have known. Someone must have told them.'

'Told who?'

'The Provisionals. The scum that took her out.'

Cousins looked at Kingdom for the first time. Then he began to laugh. 'Christ,' he said, 'it's true about you lot. You really are thick.'

Kingdom hesitated a moment, the blood pumping again, all control gone. Then he tried to lunge at Cousins, going for the Browning still tucked in his belt, but Cousins simply stepped back, taking his time, planting the kick high on Kingdom's chest. The impact drove the breath from his body, doubling him up, and Cousins closed on him, a chokehold around his neck, hauling him upright and dragging him backwards around the side of the hut.

The edge of the cliff lay across the turf, a dozen paces, no more. Kingdom was fighting for breath now, his vision beginning to grey, the pain in his leg indescribable. Very faintly, close to unconsciousness, he could smell the wind off the sea and hear the cry of the gulls beneath the cliff edge. Cousins pulled him upright, supporting him. When he let go, Kingdom collapsed.

'Stand up.'

'I can't.'

'Kneel, then.'

Kingdom's sight began to return, greys first, then the soft green of the Isle of Soay across the sound. Seals, he thought vaguely, trying not to look down. For a moment or two he thought of saving Cousins the chore of having to kill him. He'd do it himself, tipping his body forward over the drop, bringing an end to all the pain. The fall would be blissful, a release. He'd tumble through the air, feeling the wind against his face, and then there'd be nothing but darkness. They'd probably leave him there, rotting flesh, of no value to anyone, flotsam nudged by the tide, the kind of end he'd somehow always expected.

A shot rang out, and another, and a third, and Kingdom stayed rigid for a moment or two, wondering why he hadn't felt the impact, wondering whether he wasn't dead already. Then he turned round, very slowly, his broken limbs folded beneath him, and saw the figure in the red singlet and the khaki shorts, bent over Cousins' body. Dave Gifford had the rifle in his hands, the Steyr, and he put it in Cousins' mouth before pulling the trigger for the last time.

TWENTY

A week later, Thursday 21 October, they buried Annie Meredith. Kingdom was still in hospital in London, occupying a private bed on the west side of St Thomas' Hospital. Across the river lay the Houses of Parliament, and during his two previous visits Allder had developed a fondness for the view.

Now he indicated the wheelchair beside the door. Behind it stood a uniformed policeman.

'My pleasure,' Allder said. 'Funeral starts at twelve.'

The policeman wheeled Kingdom to the lift. The nurses had already dressed him and Allder had brought an extra rug in case it turned cold. Outside the hospital, the policeman helped Kingdom into the back of the Daimler, collapsing the wheelchair and storing it in the boot.

They drove south, out through Peckham and Deptford. Since Kingdom had returned from Scotland, Allder had been almost fatherly, the soul of reassurance. Now he patted Kingdom gently on his good knee.

'Done,' he said.

'What, sir?'

'The typewriter. The photos. The rifle. The Walther. All those goodies of Gifford's you brought back.'

Kingdom nodded, gazing out at the boarded-up shops and abandoned supermarket trolleys. Dave Gifford had found his son in the hollow where Cousins had killed him. The Steyr had been nearby. Kingdom glanced across at Allder.

'And the SOCO's happy?' he said.

'As Larry. Loves the idea. Loves it.' The hand again, on Kingdom's knee. 'Very swift indeed.'

Kingdom smiled for the first time. He'd put the idea to Allder six days ago, the moment the medivac plane touched down at Northholt. The material he'd brought down from Skye, the keys to the Sabbathman puzzle, should join everything else they'd removed from Cousins' flat. At the time, Allder had been dubious, slow on the uptake, shaking his head when Kingdom had explained the logic. Cousins, he said, should be fingered as Sabbathman. He was genuinely down for the Willoughby Grant murder. Why shouldn't he have done the rest?

'Don't see it,' Allder had said. 'Why should he have done it? What's in it for us?'

'Everything. You told me we're in a war. Wasn't that the phrase? Us and Five?'

'Yes, but—'

'So if Cousins turned out to be Sabbathman? Renegade MI5 officer? Recently promoted? Totally out of control? Wouldn't that settle it?'

Allder had nodded, warmed by the proposition but ever-practical. 'Proof?' he'd inquired drily.

'Won't matter. Gifford's stuff is proof enough. Cousins is dead. The case'll never see the light of day.'

'But what's the objection to Dave Gifford? He's an accessory. We'll get a result. Bound to.'

'You're right,' Kingdom had nodded, 'but he saved my life, too.'

Kingdom hadn't taken the idea any further, letting the ambulancemen manhandle him onto the wet tarmac, knowing that the RUC boys had yet to deliver their report to New Scotland Yard. He'd spoken to them on the phone from hospital in Inverness. They were promising Wednesday lunchtime.

Now, the car swept south-east towards the crematorium at Chatham while Kingdom waited for a verdict. Allder would have seen the report by now. Bound to have. On the outskirts of Bexley, the Daimler swerved to avoid an old man crossing the road. Allder hung onto the strap over the window.

'They've found the bloke in the photo,' he said, 'the one you brought back from Dublin.'

'Who have?'

'Your friends from Knock. The RUC lads. They picked him up on Sunday. They've been at him ever since.'

'Who is he?'

'UFF fella. Not a name you'll know.'

'*UFF?*' Kingdom was staring at him now. The Ulster Freedom Fighters were one of the loyalist killer groups operating in Northern Ireland, a particularly vicious splinter from the Unionist block. Protestants, not Catholics, he thought. Loyalists, not Provos.

'And what did he tell them?'

'Everything. In the end.' Allder glanced across at him, a man settling down after the meal of his dreams. 'The Unionists have been trying to wreck the peace talks. The last thing they want is Sinn Fein at the negotiating table. As far as they're concerned, there's nothing to negotiate.'

'And Cousins?'

'Came up with a little plan to wreck the talks. To prove once and for all that the Provos would always be at it.'

Kingdom nodded, following the smoke upwind. 'Sabbathman,' he said quietly, 'just fell into his lap.'

'Exactly.'

'Way back.'

'Yes.'

'When Dave Gifford met his ladyfriend. And Andy obliged with the rest. And someone took a good look at those Twyford Down transcripts.'

'Exactly,' he said again. 'Cousins was running a two-track plan. He knew all about the Downing Street contacts with the Provos, the secret channels. It was his job to be part of all that. But it went against the grain. He saw it the way the Loyalists see it. He hated the Provos. He didn't want them legitimised. He wanted them to stay terrorists for ever. He wanted a war without end. Thus Sabbathman.'

'And Fishguard?'

'Yeah, that was the second track. Anything. Anything to preserve the Union. Anything to keep the war going.'

Kingdom nodded, saying nothing. They were negotiating a stretch of roadworks now, the driver trying to avoid the worst of the ruts. Kingdom's hand went to his knee. In a couple of months, they'd said, he'd be walking again. After that, Allder had promised a lengthy convalescence. Time enough to put some sense back into his life, pick up with his kids, even make friends with his wife again.

'And Annie?' Kingdom said.

'Killed by our UFF friend.'

'The voice on the tape?'

'His.'

'Did he' – Kingdom shrugged – 'say anything about her?'

'Like what?'

'I dunno . . .' Kingdom shook his head. 'Daft question, really.'

They got to the crematorium forty minutes later. They turned in at the gates and drove slowly towards the chapel of rest. Close by, there was a car park. Allder was sitting up beside the window, looking for someone.

'There,' he said to the driver, 'the blue Toyota.'

They parked beside it. Allder got out and joined a thin, greying man in his late fifties. He was wearing a dark suit with a raincoat folded over his arm. He was carrying a file. Kingdom watched the exchange of handshakes, then the older man gave Allder the file. His head turned towards the car, and Kingdom saw Allder nodding.

Allder opened Kingdom's door. 'Francis Wren,' he muttered, 'wants to say hallo.'

Kingdom reached forward. Wren had an awkward, slightly wooden handshake.

'I understand you and Annie . . .' he nodded towards the chapel of rest. 'I just wanted to say how sorry I was to hear the news. How sorry we all were.'

Kingdom began to thank him but he stepped back, turning away, pulling on the raincoat against the bitter wind blowing off the river. The policeman helped Kingdom into the wheelchair and Kingdom caught Allder's arm as he tossed the file into the back of the car and closed the door.

'What was all that about?'

Allder looked down at him. 'Cousins kept strange company,'

he said, 'Ulster Unionists and the odd cabinet minister. Tory Central Office too, the backroom boys, one or two of the blokes who really matter. He did them all a lot of favours. Ending with Willoughby Grant.' He smiled. 'I don't think there'll be a problem with Five any more.'

The service lasted barely half an hour, a couple of dozen mourners scattered amongst the rows of seats. The pallbearers from the undertakers shouldered the coffin and walked slowly down the aisle. The organist played a hymn and when it came to talk about Annie's life the priest did his best with what few facts he'd been able to gather. Annie had evidently been born in Dartford. Her father had disappeared early on and her mother had died when she was scarcely four but she'd stayed in the area, brought up by an aunt. The aunt, sadly, had recently died as well leaving, Kingdom concluded, absolutely no one. As the priest intoned the final committal and the curtains closed behind the coffin, he felt a chill steal over him. It shouldn't have been like this, so cold, so cheerless. Not if he'd been bolder, more assertive. Not if he'd thought a little harder and cared a little less. The organist reached up for a bank of audio switches on a panel above his keyboard, and Kingdom suddenly found himself listening to the song he'd lived with for the best part of a year.

I wanna see sunshine after the rain
I wanna see bluebirds flying over the mountain again

Kingdom peered round, wondering whose idea this was, Elkie Brooks' 'Sunshine After the Rain', Annie's all-time favourite, the song she always sang to him when she was really happy, the lyrics she always got wrong. Allder was studying his hands, looking faintly embarrassed. One or two others assumed it was a cue to leave. People began to file out.

Oh where is the silver lining
Shining at the rainbow's end?

Outside, in the tiny garden of remembrance where the wreaths were displayed, Kingdom recognised the face for the first time. He was taller than the photograph had suggested but he had the same smile, the same strong chin, the same neatly barbered hair.

Kingdom looked up at the policeman, back behind the wheel-chair. 'Over there,' he said, 'the blond bloke.'

The policeman pushed him over. The man in the photo was examining the cards on the wreaths. Kingdom touched him lightly on the leg. He looked up, surprised.

'Excuse me?' he said blankly.

Kingdom caught the intonation in the voice, unmistakably foreign. German, he thought. Just like the letter he'd found in Annie's bedroom the night they'd wrecked her flat.

'My name's Alan Kingdom,' he said, 'friend of Annie's.'

The man looked down at him a moment, the smile widening. He was older than Kingdom had first thought. Perhaps late thirties, even forty.

He knelt beside the wheelchair. 'Yes?' he said.

Confused now, Kingdom nodded back towards the chapel. 'I was just wondering about the music. The last bit. Elkie Brooks.' He paused. 'Whose idea was that?'

'Mine.'

Kingdom thought about the photo again, the pair of them by the rail, the smile on Annie's face, the mountains in the background.

'You knew her?' he asked.

'Sure,' the man nodded, 'she was my wife.'

They talked for twenty minutes, a light rain beginning to fall. His name was Bernd. He'd met Annie in Dusseldorf when she'd joined a big German travel company. They'd married within a month. Kingdom nodded, recognising the pattern, the headlong dash down the highway, the absolute refusal to consult a map.

'And what happened?' he said.

'We split up. After six months.'

'Divorced?'

'No. She just left. There was never time.'

'Yeah,' Kingdom grinned, 'I can believe it.' He paused. 'You see her again? Keep in touch?'

'I wrote to begin with. Years ago. But then I gave up. She never answered the letters. Never.' He lifted a gloved hand, wiping the rain from the end of his nose. 'But she phoned recently. Found my number.'

'Why?'

'She wanted a divorce.'

'Really?' Kingdom was frowning now. 'Why?'

'She said she'd met this man, this guy. A policeman, she said. A detective from Northern Ireland. She said she wanted to marry him.' He paused, apologetic. 'Would that be you?'

'Yes,' Kingdom felt himself blushing, 'I suppose it would.'

'And she never told you?'

'No.' He shook his head. 'But she never told me anything. Maybe that's why I loved her so much.'

Allder pushed Kingdom back to the car park. The rain had got heavier.

'I've been thinking about your dad,' he said. 'How is he?'

Kingdom looked up, still brooding about Annie and his conversation with her husband. On reflection he didn't know whether finding out about her plans was good news or bad. Maybe it would have been better not to have known.

'Dad?' he said vaguely. 'You mean Ernie?'

'Yes. Is he getting better. Or what?'

Kingdom shrugged. He'd tried to get through to his father twice but both times the staff nurse on the ward had been less than helpful. 'Still very poorly,' Kingdom said. 'That's the phrase they're using.'

'And what happens afterwards? Once he's better? Once he gets out?'

'God knows.'

Allder nodded. They were back in the car park now. The police driver was already at the wheel of the Daimler and there was someone else sitting in the back. Allder brought the wheelchair to a halt beside the rear window, gesturing for the stranger to lower it. He did so, leaning out. He was a youngish man with a mop of curly hair and a well-cut linen suit. Kingdom recognised the face from the news report he'd watched at *An Carraig*.

'This bloke's taken over from Willoughby Grant,' Allder was

saying, 'at *The Citizen*. They're offering a reward for the Sabbath-man jobs. Information leading to the killer. I've told him you're the one who cracked it. Singlehanded.'

Kingdom blinked. It sounded a bit strong but he could see where Allder was driving. 'Yes,' he said, 'I did.'

'So my feeling is,' Allder was looking pointedly at the new editor now, 'that my friend has some money coming to him. Quite a lot of money.'

The man in the back was frowning. He'd clearly been through this before with Allder. 'I told you we need information,' he said. 'Facts. Faces. Names. Colour. I can't just blow fifty grand on bugger all.' He paused, looking at Kingdom. 'So why don't we talk? Either here and now, or maybe later?'

Kingdom began to answer but Allder got in first.

'Because we can't, my friend. I've told you. Not now. Not ever.'

'So what am I supposed to do? Invent it?'

Allder looked at him for a long time. Then he bent to the car window. 'You're a journalist,' he said quietly. 'If I were you I'd be keeping my eyes open.'

He stood up again, gazing out across the car park at the last of the mourners drifting back from the garden of remembrance. His hand found Kingdom and rested lightly on his shoulder, and for the first time Kingdom remembered Wren's file, still lying on the Daimler's back seat. He peered into the car, watching the smile spread across the newspaperman's face. The file was already open on his lap and he was uncapping a fountain pen with his teeth.

The wheelchair began to move.

'I thought we might take another look at those flowers,' Allder was saying, 'just you and me.'